CHAIN OF COMMAND

ALSO BY CASPAR WEINBERGER
AND PETER SCHWEIZER

The Next War

BY CASPAR WEINBERGER

In the Arena: A Memoir of the 20th Century
Fighting for Peace: Seven Critical Years in the Pentagon

CHAIN OF COMMAND

CASPAR WEINBERGER

AND PETER SCHWEIZER

ATRIA BOOKS

NEW YORK LONDON TORONTO SYDNEY

ATRIA BOOKS
1230 Avenue of the Americas
New York, NY 10020

For information address Atria Books, 1230 Avenue
of the Americas, New York, NY 10020

ISBN: 0-7434-3773-X

First Atria Books hardcover edition June 2005

10 9 8 7 6 5 4 3 2 1

ATRIA BOOKS is a trademark of Simon & Schuster, Inc.

Manufactured in the United States of America

For information regarding special discounts for bulk purchases, please contact Simon & Schuster Special Sales at 1-800-456-6798 or business@simonandschuster.com.

CHAIN OF
COMMAND

DAY ONE

PROLOGUE

Reston, Virginia,
Friday, October 26, 9:08 AM

T HE PAYMASTER was opening his third pack of Marlboros when the phone rang. He dropped the cigarette pack on the desk. He'd been expecting the call, but still his fingers trembled nervously as he picked up the receiver.

"What!" he demanded.

The paymaster was sitting in a large, bare room in a slightly run-down industrial park outside Reston, Virginia. He was five feet six, bald, and soft looking. He wore a pale blue short-sleeved polyester shirt and a dark blue polyester necktie. The sign above the door of the office read GILLILAND PRODUCTS. What kind of products, the sign didn't say. The paymaster had written a check in the amount of $936 to a graphic designer who wore too much hair gel to design the sign and another check in the amount of $458 to a painter to produce the sign itself. The paymaster remembered things like that—numbers, figures, amounts. That's why he was good at his job. Gilliland Products had never had a customer or even a visitor during the entire year of its existence. In fact, when you got right down to it, there was no such thing as Gilliland Products at all. Just this seedy little office situated between a tae kwon do school and a nearly bankrupt caterer. The office contained one chair and one desk leased as a package from Staples ($27 a month), a low-end computer leased from Gateway ($48 a month), and one telephone equipped with the most sophisticated encryption available anywhere on the planet. The paymaster didn't know how much the phone cost and didn't care.

"It's done," the voice on the other end of the line said.

"And?"

"We've been over this before. Initiate the termination procedures and proceed to Location Alpha."

"Roger that, Roger," the paymaster said derisively, stealing a line from the movie *Airplane.*

"Look, you little weasel, how about I spell this out. You think you're gonna pull a fast one, walk off with that hard drive? Uh-uh. If you don't burn that hard drive along with everything else, I will bury you in a hole where they'll never find you."

Burn the hard drive. Yeah, right. The paymaster's mama didn't raise no fool. That hard drive was the paymaster's ticket.

"Excuse me," the paymaster said, "but I know the procedure. Okay? I *wrote* the procedure." Which was a lie, of course. But who cared?

The paymaster slammed down the phone, finished opening his cigarette pack, lit up his forty-first Marlboro since he had come into the office the previous night. Then he took a Leatherman multitool out of his pocket and unscrewed the casing of the computer. Wouldn't you know it: as usual, the hard drive was always buried in a completely inaccessible location. As a result the Leatherman was really not up to the job of getting the retaining screws out.

The paymaster was beginning to sweat, and the Marlboro had burned right down to his lip by the time he got the first two screws out of the mounting bracket. He tossed his cigarette butt on the floor, started working on the third screw. At which point, the Leatherman slipped, and he gashed his finger on the sheet metal. Blood started oozing from the wound. The paymaster didn't like blood, it made him queasy. Which made him rush. Which made him careless. He stripped the fourth screw.

The hard drive hadn't budged. He planted his foot against the side of the computer and yanked. The sheet metal mounting bracket gave way, and the hard drive popped right out in his hand.

He smiled, opened his briefcase, took the dummy hard drive out of its factory-sealed package, and slid it into the drive bay.

Only it didn't fit because he'd ruined the mounting bracket getting the other one out.

He stared angrily at the offending hard drive. What was he going to do now?

Oh, for goodness sake! he thought. He was being paranoid. It's not like they were going to check. He had been absurdly cautious as it was. He slid the dummy drive in as far as it would go, plugged in the wire harness, slid the case back onto the computer, tightened the screws, and walked out of the building with the hard drive bumping around in his otherwise empty briefcase.

He started the engine of his Lexus, dialed a number on his cell phone, punched in a code—his mother's birthday as it happened—then backed out of his parking space.

He was halfway out of the parking lot when the first wisp of smoke began creeping out of a small black box mounted along the baseboard next to the desk he'd rented from Staples. By the time the paymaster's Lexus reached I-66, the entire building was enveloped in flame.

1

MICHAEL DELANEY sometimes had his doubts about people. But a gun? No doubts there. A gun would never lie to you, would never tell you it loved you and then leave you for somebody else, would never take your kids away, would never flatter you and then stab you in the back. You treated a gun right and it would be your friend forever.

Back in his drinking days, Delaney used to riff on this particular subject after he'd gotten eight or ten fingers of single malt in him. It had been kind of a joke, but kind of not.

But not now. Right now it was not funny at all.

Once you made friends with a gun, you knew that gun better than you knew your own brother. And the gun in his hand was a stranger.

JUST MINUTES EARLIER Secret Service Special Agent Michael Delaney had awakened to the irritating pulse of his alarm clock. Usually the clock was just a safety. Normally he woke up precisely ten minutes before he had to get up, a skill he'd developed back in the Special Forces, when snatching the maximum amount of sleep from a mission was nearly as important as knowing how to shoot your weapon.

Today, though, he woke with a fuzzy, aching head and a mild case of nausea. There had been a time when that happened a lot. But he hadn't touched a drink in eighteen months. So there had to be another explanation.

Michael Delaney had been sleeping in Walnut, a small cottage in the staff area of the Camp David compound. The room looked like 1950—lots of dark wood, a brass lamp, twin bed, an ancient space heater humming under the frost-rimed window. Camp David had been hit with an unseasonably early snow the day before, and through the window he could see that more snow had hit the ground overnight. The tall black pines were heavy with white.

Delaney took a quick shower, started pulling on his clothes, and tried to replay the previous night's events in his mind. He had a vague recollection that his team had been notified just before he went to bed that VPOTUS would be arriving for an AM meeting with POTUS. As a member of the presidential security detail, that meant a frenzied morning of work for Michael Delaney. Since 9/11 the already pressed Secret Service had found itself in a pressure cooker. Threats running the gamut from the usual kooks, to domestic terrorist organizations, all the way up to Al-Qaeda had increased alarmingly. The pace of the work seemed to grow more intense by the day.

Why was his memory so vague?

Someone was banging on the door. "Delaney!" It was Mark Greene, head of the presidential detail.

"I'm coming, I'm coming," he called.

"WHMO just called. They're pushing up the meeting to seven AM. Get a move on."

Delaney grabbed his Uncle Mike holster, swung it over his shoulder, snapped the quick release buckles, then drew his Beretta 9 mm and pulled back the slide three-quarters of an inch. It was a mechanical routine that he went through every day of his life, checking to make sure a round was chambered.

Which is when the cold sweat hit him.

There was a round chambered, yes, the brass cartridge gleaming dully in the dim light of the cabin. But something wasn't right. When you'd pulled back her slide, what, a thousand times, when you'd put ten or fifteen thousand rounds down her pipe, when you'd personally filed and sanded her sear and her trigger so she broke smooth and pure as the stem of a champagne flute, when you'd eased untold numbers of patches down her bore, spoiled her with several gallons of Hoppe's #9, when she'd led you unerringly to the X ring more times than you could count . . . well, you knew her. You just did.

And the sticky, nasty, crunchy, grabby action of this gun's slide? No. Absolutely not. It was not his weapon. The action of the Beretta in his hand was strictly factory.

More banging on the door. "Delaney! Now!"

When Delaney tried to pierce the fuzz in the back of his mind in order to come up with an explanation of how this fresh-out-of-the-box hunk of steel had ended up in his holster, he drew an absolute and complete blank.

"Now!"

There was no good reason why somebody else's weapon was in his holster. But there was no time to think. It would come to him in a minute—there had to be a rational explanation, didn't there?—and then when things slowed down later in the shift, he would get the matter squared away.

He charged out the door, found Mark Greene standing in the snow. Greene, a smart, smooth-talking veteran of the Secret Service, stood in the snow outside the cabin.

For a moment Delaney considered telling him about the strange weapon switch, but Greene spoke first. "You're running late. I'll shadow POTUS. Take one of the guys from uniform and run the perimeter."

Ordinarily doing a perimeter check in calf-high snow would have been anything but welcome. But today Delaney was glad for the opportunity to try and get a handle on what had happened the previous night. The good news was that nothing ever happened at Camp David. Several years earlier, a couple of bored sentries had taken a potshot at an eight-point buck, setting off a mad scramble by the Secret Service—but that was about as exciting as it got.

The snow had stopped falling in the Catoctin Mountains sometime in the night, but the six-inch blanket of white deadened the sound of the forest around them. The Camp felt unnaturally still and silent. Delaney trudged quickly past the presidential lodge. The lights were on, and through the window he caught a brief glimpse of the man himself, peering out the window. Delaney was struck by the president's grim expression. President Fairbank was usually upbeat and cheerful—almost inhumanly so—and so the dour, apprehensive look on his face was surprising. The curtain fell back, and Fairbank disappeared.

Delaney proceeded another fifty yards along the path until he reached Elm, a small cabin that was serving as a temporary command post for the Secret Service. There he found two supervisors from the uniform division behind a security video console.

Despite its rustic appearance, Camp David was crammed with

state-of-the-art electronic security features. In addition to several hundred marines available for sentry duty and a phalanx of Secret Service agents, four squads of navy antiterrorism units were on standby, just a three-minute chopper ride from a nearby facility. Hidden in the trees and the rocky ground of the compound were motion detectors, cameras, and a host of other sensors. To protect from an air attack, a phased array radar system tracked flights in the vicinity, its signals linked to two batteries of Patriot surface-to-air missiles. Portable Stinger missiles were also kept at fingertip readiness.

Delaney informed the duty officer of his assignment.

"Take Harrison." The duty officer, a red-faced Texan, pointed his thumb at a burly African-American named Blip Harrison who was nursing a cup of coffee over in the corner of the room.

"Anything I should keep an eye out for?"

The duty officer shrugged. "Other than snow ninjas?"

"Meaning what?" Delaney said.

"This doggone snow," the duty officer said irritably. "It's weighing down the branches of all these pine trees, then the branches break and fall down, and the motion sensors go nuts. We've had nine false alarms since midnight."

"You're sure they're false alarms?" Delaney said. The appearance of the strange pistol in his holster had him on edge.

The operator gave him a hard look. "Of course we are. We sent a team out every time. No footprints, no nothing."

There was a certain amount of resentment toward Delaney on the presidential detail. Delaney had once been a rising star in the Service and leader of the vice presidential detail—before the incident which almost destroyed his career—and some of the middle rankers felt Delaney thought he was too big for his boots.

"Ready, Blip?" Delaney said.

Blip Harrison, the burly black Secret Service agent, rose and headed silently for the door. Built solid and straight, he was one of the best in the division. His friends called him Blip because he had spent time in the navy as a radar technician.

The two headed out of the cabin and walked east along a wide and rocky path, then made their way through a cluster of hardwood trees. They caught a glimpse of a whitetail running off into the trees, nostrils steaming in the frigid air. In the distance they heard the thump-thump of helicopter blades, signaling the arrival of the vice president.

For the next twenty minutes the two men trekked through the

woods of fir, poplar, and pine, following the route that George Bush Sr. used to jog. The trail took them along the perimeter of the 125-acre retreat near where Jimmy Carter used to ski and along the twenty-foot-high chain-link fence topped with razor wire that encircled the compound. They passed by the helicopter landing pad where the vice president's helicopter, Marine Corp Two, was now standing, then headed down the horse trail built during the 1980s to accommodate Ronald Reagan's love of riding.

Delaney made conversation with the genial Harrison, gently probing to see if the uniformed agent could shed any light on what, if anything, had happened to Delaney the night before. Delaney was concerned about the possibility—however distant—that he had drunk so much that he'd blacked out. He'd had more than a couple of blackout drunks in his life, though not for a long time. Harrison, however, didn't indicate that anything unusual had taken place the night before.

By seven-fifteen the sun was peeking over the eastern lip of the Catoctin Mountains, bathing the woods in a golden light, and Delaney still was no closer to figuring out the mystery of the strange gun under his coat than he had been half an hour earlier. It was a glorious morning, and everything along the southern perimeter appeared to be secure. As the duty officer had said, falling branches cracked and thumped occasionally in the woods. But other than that, the air was silent.

The two men looped back through a thicket of hedge growth and headed back toward Aspen Lodge.

Suddenly a loud crack echoed through the woods.

The two men froze.

"That wasn't a branch," Delaney said. The blood was hammering in his temples, and instinctively he had the Beretta out in his hand. The butt felt unfamiliar, crude.

Crack! Crack! Crack! Crack!

"Condition red!" Delaney screamed into his wrist mic. "Shots fired! Condition red! We're two hundred yards from the putting green."

Harrison, too, had a Beretta in his hand. The two men began running toward the putting green. Harrison—younger and faster—took the lead. The two men crashed pell-mell through the thick, snow-covered undergrowth. Delaney's lungs burned as he sucked in the frigid air. And then they were bursting into the clear.

When he reached the putting green he saw four men in the pure white snow. Three men were on the ground. Only one was moving. One, a tall gray-haired man, lay motionless, his head surrounded by a corona of melting crimson snow.

"POTUS is hit!" Delaney screamed into his microphone. In the heat of the moment he broke radio code. "My God, the president is down!"

2

Somewhere in Eastern North Carolina
9:06 AM

MARY HAD BEEN secured to the chair with duct tape for over an hour. Despite the fact that the cinder block room was cold and drafty, its windows shattered by gunfire, she was drenched in sweat. Two unkempt men wearing heavy beards were slouched on the far side of the room. Both wore Soviet-era Makarovs in low-slung black nylon holsters on their hips, and both carried AK-47 knockoffs—Chinese-made she guessed—and both smelled like they hadn't taken a bath in several months. They were virtually indistinguishable except for the color of their beards: one was brown, the other black. Lying on the floor on top of a dirty sleeping bag was a girl in her twenties. Her hair was tangled, and she had a tattoo of an eyeball on the back of her neck. During the time that Mary had been in the room, the girl had never moved.

Mary was a tall woman, with glossy black hair, strikingly high cheekbones, full lips, and brown eyes that were just a hair too far apart. Beneath her sober blue dress she had the slim body of a woman who trained regularly at the gym.

Her purse lay on the floor next to her feet, some of its contents spilling out onto the dusty concrete. The men in the room apparently did not know much about her. They had underestimated her drastically—so badly, in fact, they hadn't even checked her purse. What she knew, but the two terrorists didn't, was that her purse contained a titanium-framed Smith & Wesson .38 with a shrouded hammer.

"How long are we looking at here, guys?" Mary said. She had been coughing, talking, moving around in her chair the whole time she had been restrained. Anything she could think of to keep the two men from noticing that she'd spent the past hour slowly rubbing the duct tape around her wrists against a rough weld bead on the back of her metal chair. She was almost free now.

The two surly, stinking men ignored her.

"Seriously," she said. "I need to get back to the White House by this afternoon."

One of the men eyed her briefly and smirked. "Should I hit her in the head, Ray?" he said to the other man.

"Good gracious me!" the other said, with mock politeness. "It would be unchivalrous to hit a lady."

"What you're suggesting is, I should *shoot* her in the head."

"Precisely!" the other one said. They both had strong southern accents, and both seemed to find themselves very amusing. One of them wore a T-shirt that read WHITE POWER on the front. A soft scuffling noise outside the building, like a small rodent moving in the leaves outside, interrupted their conversation. The two men immediately stopped laughing and peered out the window.

"Anything?" the taller of the two said.

The other shook his head, but they kept their eyes glued to the window. On the floor the girl with the tattoo still hadn't moved. Mary flexed her wrists, and the last shred of duct tape came free. She felt a burst of excitement as she leaned forward and scooped up the Smith in her purse. Unfortunately, as she was pulling the pistol out of the purse, the front sight snagged on her keys, which jingled loudly.

The two men whipped around, pointing their weapons at her. She had managed to get her hands back behind her just in the nick.

"What was that?" one of them said.

"I just kicked my purse," she said.

The man with the black beard stared at her, eyes narrowed. "I don't think so, sweetie," he said. "Your feet are duct-taped to the chair."

He had taken one step toward her when the door blew in.

With blinding speed, four men—all wearing black Kevlar from head to toe—burst into the room. There was a sudden explosion of automatic weapons fire and shell casings pinged off the floor. Mary sized them up immediately. They all carried Heckler and Koch MP5SDs—the suppressed model—so the noise of the submachine guns inside the tiny room wasn't quite as ear-splitting as it otherwise would have been.

The two bearded men fell to the floor and didn't move again.

"Secure!" one of the men yelled.

"Are you all right, ma'am?" one of the black-clad men said, pulling up his ballistic mask so she could see his face. He was obviously the Delta team leader, a young man of about thirty, probably of Latin American extraction. "Sorry about all this . . ." He waved vaguely around the room.

The other men were pointing weapons at the girl on the floor.

"Guys!" Mary said, pointing at the girl. "Behind you!"

The team leader whirled. At which point Mary pulled the gun from behind her back and fired five quick shots through the broken window.

The Delta team members turned back toward her, eyes wide, ears ringing from the sound of the unsuppressed revolver.

"Never assume, fellows," she said. "Never assume. I'm a pretty fair shot. I'd have killed at least three of you. Maybe all four."

"But . . ." The team leader blinked, tried to find some words in response.

"Captain," she said. "You were told that an exercise would be conducted with some high-muckety-muck jerk from the White House posing as a hostage, correct? So you busted in the door, assumed the woman in the power suit was from the White House, and so you didn't bother checking me for weapons. Just like your two bad guys over there didn't bother to frisk me, because they assumed that this was a silly put-on and therefore I wouldn't be armed. Never assume."

The two "white supremacist terrorists," a pair of Special Forces men recently back from a tour in the Middle East sat up, shaking their heads sheepishly.

"I'm sorry, ma'am," the Delta team leader said. He looked like he'd been punched in the stomach.

"Sorry? Why do I care if you're sorry. Just do it right next time. Now would somebody cut this duct tape off my ankles?"

Just then the XO of First Special Forces Operational Detachment Alpha, Lieutenant Colonel Jimmy Barger, walked in the door with a cell phone in his hand. "It's for you," he said, holding out the phone to Mary. "Urgent. From the White House."

She took the phone and answered. Her ears were still ringing from the sound of the gunfire and she couldn't quite make out what the voice on the other end was saying.

"Come again?" she said. Then her eyes widened. "I'll be there in an hour, sir," she said.

"Exercise over, guys," she snapped. Then she pulled off her high-heeled shoes with one hand, hiked up her skirt a couple of inches with the other hand, and began sprinting barefoot down the hallway. The seven soldiers in the room stared after her like they had just witnessed an alien landing.

"Who *was* that chick?" one of two bearded men said.

"That 'chick' is the president's foremost expert on terrorism," Barger said. "Her name is Mary Campos. But next time you see her, I'd advise you to address her as 'Colonel.'"

"Aw, man!" one of the Delta Force operators said. "That's cheating. That's totally cheating."

3

Camp David
9:07 AM

"WE NEED NIGHTHAWK ONE! We need Nighthawk One!" screamed Blip Harrison into his wrist mic, calling for the Marine Corp One helicopter.

Delaney reached the four men in the center of the putting green. President Fairbank lay flat on the ground, two holes in his chest, one in the throat just below his jaw, weakly spurting arterial blood. Delaney had seen enough gunshot victims in his life to know the president wasn't going to make it, not with his carotid artery ripped in half.

Sitting on the ground five feet away was Vice President Boyd, clutching his side, grimacing with pain. Harrison tried to calm the vice president as more Secret Service agents poured onto the lawn, setting up a human shield around them. Two navy medics arrived. One was pressing a bandage against the unconscious president's neck while the other began ripping off the vice president's shirt.

"Where's the shooter?" Delaney yelled. "Where's the shooter?"

"The shooter's down!" Mark Greene screamed, clutching his pistol and pointing at the third body on the ground. "The SOB just appeared! How did he get here? How did he get the gun?"

The prone, lifeless shooter was a red-haired man who wore what appeared at first glance to be a Secret Service uniform, but as Delaney got closer it became obvious it was just a rented police costume from a costume shop, slightly modified to match the Secret Service uniform. The badge on his chest was plastic. The red-haired man on the ground had been shot three times in the face. There was not much left of the back of his head.

"Nice shooting," Delaney said.

The chief of the security detail shook his head. "A little late, though, huh?" he said disgustedly.

Suddenly Michael Delaney was aware of the thump of rotor blades above him. Marine Corps One touched down about twenty yards away. The navy medics picked up the president's body and carried it to the helicopter, then escorted the pain-wracked vice president after them.

"Delaney, Harrison, Becker!" Greene shouted. "In the chopper with me! Mendez, pull everybody the hell back, and secure the scene. Don't touch anything!"

"Where's the shooter's weapon?" Agent Mendez yelled over the deafening noise of the chopper.

"Right there!" Delaney pointed to a pistol in the snow near the body of the shooter. "Don't touch it. It's evidence. Leave it for the FBI!" Before he was able to drop his hand, the chopper began to lift off the ground. Only seconds into the air, a gust of wind hit them, and the chopper yawed left, driving them directly over the blood-spattered snow where the three men had been shot.

There in the snow lay the shooter's weapon, not eight feet from Michael Delaney's perch in the doorway of the chopper. This time he had a better look at it than he had from the ground. The weapon had an inch-wide silver gash in the dark metal of the receiver. Somebody had obviously filed off the serial number. Michael Delaney stared at the gun in horror. The worn bluing on the receiver, the distinctively shaped custom-made burgundy Micarta grips—he knew them like an old friend.

The file-marked gash on the side didn't hide the obvious: it was Delaney's own Beretta.

STANDARD OPERATING PROCEDURE said that if both the president and vice president were injured, the president went to Walter Reed Army Medical Center, and the vice president went to Bethesda Naval Medical Center. But the injured vice president, Morgan Boyd, had insisted on accompanying the president, and soon they were airborne, heading for the naval hospital in Bethesda.

Delaney couldn't raise much interest in this breach of protocol. He was feeling light-headed, sick with apprehension. It didn't take a genius to see where things were heading: it was no accident that somebody else's pistol was in his holster this morning. Somebody was trying to frame him. But there was nothing he could do about it now.

The chopper headed at maximum speed toward the hospital, landing on the roof. Delaney lost track of the vice president as, gun drawn, he followed the president's gurney down a long hallway toward a pair of double doors. No one spoke other than the doctor and the navy medic, who held a brief whispered conversation. The president hadn't moved in fifteen minutes.

The attendant wheeled the gurney through the final doorway into an operating room.

"That's as far as you go, gentlemen," the doctor said to the Secret Service agents.

Agent Mark Greene pushed into the operating room anyway. "You can forget that, Doctor," he snapped.

"This is a sterile environment," the doctor said. "Do you want to be responsible for giving the president of the United States a life-threatening infection?"

"You do your job, we'll do ours."

The doctor scowled. Eyeing the ring of armed men around him, he apparently decided that this was an argument he was not going to win. He took his stethoscope from around his neck, listened for a heartbeat, performed a few other rudimentary tests, then shook his head. The doctor looked around the room at the faces staring at him, then at his watch. In a matter-of-fact voice, he said, "Time of death, 9:37 AM."

4

Headquarters, XVIII Airborne Corps, Fort Bragg, North Carolina

9:41 AM

WHEN THE PHONE RANG, General Bill Fairbank, commander of the army corps that included the 82nd and 101st Airborne, was sitting behind his large mahogany desk reviewing the latest intelligence summary from the 313th Military Intelligence Battalion. A large American flag with battle streamers attached hung beside him next to a photo of Jumpin' Jim Gavin, the legendary commander of the 82nd during World War II.

General Fairbank frowned. The phone that had just rung was not the office phone, but the secure line. It was reserved for the use of the president or the secretary of defense. You didn't call on that phone to talk about your golf game. It was strictly for emergencies.

"Fairbank," the general growled. He was a big, hard-faced man whose harsh voice betrayed the signs of thirty years of cigar smoke.

"General Fairbank, this is Morgan Boyd."

"Yes, Mr. Vice President."

"General, I'm calling from Bethesda Naval Medical Center . . ."

A sudden sense of dread ran through Fairbank's brain. Fairbank was not a man given to ominous feelings—but there was only one reason the vice president could be calling from that particular hospital.

"General, your brother has been shot."

Anyone sitting in the room with him would have had no indication that he had just received even the most insignificant bad news. "What's the prognosis?"

There was a brief silence on the line. "I'm afraid he didn't make it, General."

Fairbank nodded. "I understand."

"You'll be getting the official word from SECDEF any moment, but I wanted this to come straight from me. This appears to have been a terrorist action. Recent intel suggests there's more to come. As a result I'm raising us to Defcon Three." Boyd paused. "General, I know this is a difficult time for you and your mind is likely to be on family rather than war making. But for the moment I'm asking you to put that aside for the good of your country. I'm ordering the immediate deployment of elements from the Eighty-second Airborne. This was an attempt to decapitate the American leadership, General."

Fairbank considered the matter for a moment. "Deployed where, sir?"

"Orders will follow. I was hit, myself. I've got to meet with the cabinet, and after that I'm going into surgery. By the time I come out of the OR, I expect you to be saddled up and ready to roll. Is that clear?" There was neither a hint of sympathy nor of self-pity in his voice. Like Fairbank, Morgan Boyd was known as a man of legendary self-control.

"I'll have two battalions ready within six hours."

"I know you will," Boyd said. Then the phone went dead.

Bill Fairbank set the phone down gently and stared at the wall for a while. He hadn't spoken to his brother for years without the conversation ending up in a fight. They didn't like each other much. But still . . . They were brothers. For a moment his mind drifted blankly. His older brother, Dean, had been a shadow under which he had stood all his life. It seemed impossible that in an instant that shadow had simply been snuffed out.

"Pull it together," he growled softly. Then he stood up and grabbed his holstered 1911 out of the bottom drawer of his desk, started strapping it around his waist. The familiar weight of the weapon made him feel better, like the world was coming back into his control again.

"Sergeant Finley!" he yelled. "Get your flabby tail in here! We got work to do!"

5

Bethesda Naval Medical Center
10:02 AM

W E'RE READY, Mr. Vice President," Delaney said calmly. "The building is secure."

The vice president of the United States was a small man with dark hair, a long thin blade of a nose, and intense black eyes. Though he never mentioned the fact in his biography, he had spent most of his life in pain, the result of being thrown from a horse when he was in his teens. Morgan Boyd had grown up on a hardscrabble ranch in Montana—but unlike many politicians similarly situated, he never appeared in public in a cowboy hat and boots, never made a show of his hardscrabble roots, didn't affect the aw-shucks homespun image of a rancher's son. Morgan Boyd had hated every minute of his childhood. He had hated the cold, had hated the wind, had hated the frozen toes and the barbed-wire cuts on his hands, had hated everything about cows, from their smell to the vapid expression of their eyes. He had gotten a scholarship to Harvard at age sixteen and never looked back, becoming a political science professor by the time he was twenty-five, returning in his thirties to his home state to head the Political Science department at the University of Montana. According to legend he had worn a suit and a bow tie every single day of his life since he joined the faculty of U of M. In the past twenty-five years—so it was claimed—he had not taken a single vacation, had not walked a golf course, gone for a dip in the pool, or showed up for a photo op wearing a ten-gallon hat. He'd put on the suit and bow tie and never looked back.

Tiring of the posturing and lack of practicality he saw around him in academia, he ran for office, where he could put his ideas into practice. His drive, his intellect, and above all his indomitable will had eventually led him to the Senate. By western standards he was relatively liberal, using a jerry-built coalition of hard-pressed ranchers and college-town environmentalists to bull his way into office. He had been chosen as Fairbank's running mate, not because of any personal warmth between the two men, but to add a more liberal face to the ticket of the more conservative Texan, Fairbank. The rumors, Delancy knew, were that Fairbank had quickly grown to detest the vice president and had done everything he could to keep him out of the White House loop.

"Sir?" Delaney repeated. "We're ready."

"I heard you, Agent Delaney," Boyd said. He stood slowly, his face taut with pain. He was still wearing the now-tattered white shirt he'd been wearing when he was shot. "I was just thinking."

Delaney didn't reply.

"We've been through a few things together, haven't we?" the vice president said.

They did, in fact, have a history. "Yes, Mr. Vice President."

"When is this insanity going to stop?"

Delaney shook his head. "I don't know, sir."

Boyd reached out and put his hand on Delaney's shoulder. "Men like you, throwing yourself in front of bullets for the greater good, that's an honorable and extraordinary thing."

"Thank you, Mr. Vice President, but it looks like you're the one who took the bullet this time."

"That may be. But I just want you to know that your sacrifice doesn't go unnoticed by me."

Delaney held up his left hand. On his wrist was an inscribed gold watch which had been presented to him by the vice president two years earlier. "You've made that very clear, sir."

Boyd's press secretary cleared his throat. "Mr. Vice President? Chief Justice Potter is downstairs with the press."

Boyd nodded, released his hold on Delaney's shoulder. They headed for the elevator at the end of the hallway. Delaney was struck once again by how small and twisted the man looked. On camera he seemed a commanding presence, but when he moved he looked like a man who barely had the strength to get out of bed. But he refused assistance. He may have been a hard man to like, but he was impossible not to admire.

"The cabinet is gathering in the Situation Room," the press secretary said. "We'll go from this press conference back to the White House."

"No, there's still a bullet in me. They've got to get it out."

The press secretary cleared his throat. He was obviously concerned about who would make presidential decisions should any be required. "Ah, how long before the anesthesia wears off?"

"I won't be using anesthetic," Boyd said. The doors to the elevator opened, and they walked out into the glare of cameras. Boyd straightened, buttoned the jacket of his suit, and strode forward into the lights of the waiting cameras. His chin was high, his jaw firm, his eyes clear.

Without waiting for an introduction, he walked to the clump of microphones. He stood motionless for close to thirty seconds, no doubt waiting for the New York anchors to stop their facile analyses of the situation and cut to the live feed from the hospital. It was impossible to miss the red stain on his collar.

Finally he spoke: "At thirty-two minutes past eight this morning, an act of supreme treachery and shocking brutality was committed against this nation. In a clear act of terrorism, the president of the United States, Dean Fairbank, was assassinated." He stared stoically into the camera. "I am here to assure every American that in keeping with the United States Constitution, I will now be assuming the duties of president. In order to assure that this threat against our nation and our way of life is met with maximum resistance, I have already initiated Continuity of Government procedures, which will assure the American people and the world that our way of life will be preserved. Chief Justice of the Supreme Court Jack Potter is here to swear me into office."

He turned to his left, and a distinguished-looking white-haired man in a judicial robe stepped forward and held out a worn black leather-covered Bible. Boyd faced him, placing one hand on the Bible, wincing almost imperceptibly.

Justice Potter began to speak. "Please repeat after me, 'I, Morgan Boyd, do solemnly swear that I will faithfully execute . . .'" Thirty-five words later, in a ceremony unchanged for two centuries, Morgan Boyd became the president of the United States.

Boyd turned back to the cameras as Justice Potter stepped aside. "President Fairbank was a great man, who served his country with intense dedication for more than two decades." He seemed to be keeping his emotions in check only with steely determination. "But now is not the time for eulogies. Now is the time for action. I have been advised by senior security officials that this assassination may have been part of a broader—and still unfolding—conspiracy designed to destabilize and perhaps even bring down our government."

Michael Delaney was not so busy scanning the room for additional assassins that he didn't frown in puzzlement at this last statement. Senior security officials? What senior security officials? He had been with Boyd during the entire past hour, and there hadn't been a senior security official in sight.

"Therefore, in keeping with my constitutional obligation to protect the integrity of this nation, I am declaring a temporary state of emergency to stabilize the situation. Under the implied powers of Article Two of the Constitution, I will be authorizing the temporary deployment of United States military forces to the nation's capital to deter any other attacks from occurring. Additional security, police, and judicial measures will be taken on an as-needed basis."

He paused, then glared at the camera. "This attack on Dean Fairbank is an attack on each and every American. So as an elected representative of every American, let me address these cowards directly. The man you sent to kill the president is lying in the snow in a pool of his own blood. The same fate awaits anyone who attacks the American people. Our government and our system is bigger than any one man. Bigger than me, bigger than Dean Fairbank. The continuity of our government *will* be preserved. But make no mistake, that doesn't get you off the hook. I will hunt you down and I will bring you to justice. If you think you can tear down the greatest nation in the world, I say to you this: *over my dead body!*"

With that he ripped open his suit coat, revealing to the world for the first time that he too had been shot. Even the hardened journalists gasped at the blood-soaked bandages around his waist.

"*Over my dead body!*" the president of the United States repeated. His black eyes stared into the camera for a ten count, then he whirled and headed back toward the elevator.

Once safely inside the elevator, Boyd turned to his press secretary. "Well?" the new president said.

"Over my dead body!" the press secretary said unctuously. "That was beyond presidential. That was a brilliant, brilliant touch."

"If you think I was grandstanding," Boyd said, "then you don't have the vaguest understanding of the kind of man you're working for."

The press secretary flushed. "I'm sorry, sir. I wasn't thinking."

Atlanta, Georgia
10:02 AM

A brown panel truck with the markings of a major shipping company pulled up in front of the concrete safety barrier outside the Richard B. Russell Federal Courthouse on Spring Street. A smiling young man in a brown jumpsuit hopped out of the driver's seat.

A security guard carrying an M-16 immediately rushed over to him. Word of the assassination having spread through the country, security at all federal facilities was running at peak readiness. "Sir, you can't park here."

The brown-clad young man smiled affably. "Hey, I just left my hand truck across the street. Lemme grab it, I'll be out of here."

The security guard shook his head. "No, sir. Get back in your vehicle right now."

"Oh, lighten up," the delivery man said. "Won't take me thirty seconds."

The security guard would have none of it. He raised his weapon at the man in the brown jumpsuit. "Now, sir. Remove your vehicle."

The man in brown backed up a step. "Hey, easy does it, cowboy! I'll move!" He turned slowly as though to get back in the truck, then with an unexpected flash of speed, he whirled back toward the guard. But now there was a suppressed SIG-Sauer 9 mm in his hand. He fired two shots in such quick succession that they were almost indistinguishable. The guard fell like a marionette with its strings cut, two small holes just above the bridge of his nose.

"Hey!" The brown-clad young man yelled, tossing his pistol in the truck. "Somebody help this man."

A crowd quickly gathered. The young man in the brown uniform slipped through them and began jogging quickly up the street, turning the corner and heading south. He had just made it up to Peachtree Street when the sound of the explosion hit him. He was surprised at the force. It nearly took the breath out of him.

He pulled off his brown uniform, which had been secured with

Velcro tabs, tossed it in a trash can. He was now wearing a suit from Brooks Brothers. In the confusion no one noticed as he climbed into a white Ford Econoline van that pulled up briefly at the curb and then sped off.

White Sands Missile Test Facility, White Sands, New Mexico
10:11 AM

The black Chevy 2500 dualie with the camper shell pulled over to the side of the road next to a large, rusting chain-link fence. Plastered to the fence were faded signs suggesting that scaling the fence would be unwise.

Two young men of military bearing climbed out of the truck, pulled the camper shell off the back, dumped it into the ditch. They both wore surgical gloves so as not to leave fingerprints. The thing that reared up out of the back of the truck with a soft, motorized hum looked like a couple of long black toolboxes. But to the trained eye, it was recognizable as a Soviet-era GP-64 rocket launcher. The two men then heaved a large piece of half-inch steel plate up from the rear of the pickup truck, propped it behind the two tubes, where it would act as a blast baffle. The two men then crouched behind the truck.

"Countdown. Ten, nine, eight—" the taller of the two men said.

"Screw that," the shorter man said. "Fire in the hole!" He then pressed a red button on a small black box clutched in his hand.

The rocket launcher let out one deafening howl, then a second. Two stubby rockets armed with four kilos of C-4 apiece went streaking into the sky toward a distant cluster of buildings shimmering on the horizon of the striking expanse of dead-flat desert. The launcher hummed as it lowered itself back onto the bed of the truck.

"Forty-eight seconds," the tall man said. "That's our best time yet."

They had been practicing the op for over a month, shaving second after second from the drill. Only this time it wasn't a drill.

The V-10 engine growled angrily as they tore off down the highway. By the time the two hollow booms marked the impact of the rockets, the heavily modified Chevy was doing 130 miles an hour.

"We hit it?" the tall man said.

The shorter man shrugged. "Who cares? We're just sending a message."

6

Bethesda Naval Medical Center
10:23 AM

A S THE DOORS of the elevators opened, Delaney was met by
the face of Mark Greene, head of the presidential detail.

"You can stand down, Delaney," he said. "You're needed back at
HQ for a debriefing. The FBI wants to talk to you."

"What about you?" Delaney said. "You heading back too?"

"That's not your concern," Greene snapped. "Go down to the
lobby. Agent Rankin is waiting. He'll drive you." He turned toward
Boyd. "This way, Mr. President."

Greene led the president down the hallway toward the operating
room where the bullet still lodged in his side was to be removed.

Delaney walked down the hallway toward the stairs. He could
have taken the elevator, but he needed time to think. Halfway down
the staircase to the ground floor his knees suddenly felt so weak that
he had to sit down. For the past hour he had been so busy he'd had no
time to think. But now the enormity of the situation was beginning
to sink it. His gun. His gun. It kept running through his mind, the vision of his Beretta lying there in the snow next to the dead men. How
soon would it take before they traced it back to him?

Records on every single weapon owned or carried by members of
the Secret Service were kept at headquarters. Filing off the serial
number was pointless. It was intended to make it look like he'd made
a crude attempt to hide the identity of his own weapon. But the FBI
would use X-ray crystallography to dope out the serial number from
the underlying steel. And if that didn't work, they'd use ballistic
printing. Every weapon used by the Secret Service had been entered
into a database of ballistic "prints" that stored the distinctive markings
imparted by the bore to the bullets the gun fired.

The filed-off serial number would buy him some time. But not much.

He felt a vibration from his secure pager.

000076587 EAGLE EN ROUTE TO GOLD DOME 10:25 AM
00076588 DELANEY CONTACT HQ ASAP

Gold Dome was the day code for the White House. If he was still getting pager updates about the president's whereabouts, that meant they had not drawn any connection yet.

He put the pager back on his belt, pulled out his Nokia cell phone, speed-dialed a number.

"Blip? Delaney. Where are you?"

"Back at HQ. Is this line secure?"

"No. What are you hearing down there?"

"It's crazy. They're starting to debrief."

"Any ID on the shooter?"

"No. FBI, Secret Service, and Justice are all down here right now. Everybody's tripping all over each other. This is going to be a jurisdictional nightmare. Anyway, they're still trying to piece together the timeline."

"How'd the guy get in?"

"Better yet, how'd the *gun* get in?" Harrison said. He cleared his throat. "Ah, I can't really say on this line what we know about the guy. But it looks like he got in using some very sophisticated MilSpec stuff. Have you heard of IR countermeasure suits?"

Delaney whistled. "Chill suits? The guy had a *chill suit?* That stuff's strictly SpecOps."

There was a long pause. "Look, ah, tread softly, Mike. I don't know why, but everybody's looking at me cross-eyed right now. Like I'm a suspect or something. They even took my duty weapon and my credentials."

"Hang tight," Delaney said. "You didn't do anything wrong."

Delaney slapped the phone shut and ran his fingers through his hair. The assassination was now receding slightly as he began to consider his own fate. He'd been set up, no question. Whoever had taken his gun was an inside operator—very likely a fellow Secret Service agent. It didn't make sense that an unidentified person—even one dressed in an imitation Secret Service uniform—had managed to get that close to the president. Greene should have challenged the shooter before he got that close. And once the shooter unholstered, Greene should, first, have unholstered faster; and, second, thrown himself between the shooter and his targets. Something wasn't right there.

And what about what President Boyd had said—that there was an unfolding conspiracy going on here? Boyd had made a number of phone calls on the flight to the hospital. Maybe that was when he'd been warned there were more attacks in the offing. Was this the work of Al-Qaeda? It seemed unlikely. The shooter had red hair: he was no Arab, that was for sure.

No, this had the earmarks of an inside job. And if that was the case, Delaney's missing gun was probably just the tip of the iceberg. Would there be strange deposits of cash into his account? Records of phone calls from his home that he'd never made? Cleverly forged photographs showing him talking to known enemies of the United States? Probably all that and more. Whoever was behind this was meticulous and well equipped. If they planned to turn Delaney into the goat here, they'd make sure he looked guilty as sin.

Moreover, if they were smart—and they seemed to be—they'd make sure he didn't survive past the end of the day.

So. He had a choice. Turn himself in, let the mills of justice grind away, rely on the machinery of the federal justice system, pray for the best. Or trust no one, go freelance, take the fight to whoever was behind this monstrosity.

Suddenly—inexplicably—Michael Delaney found himself smiling. All his life he'd been bored easily, found himself getting depressed when things got too routine. It was only when he was behind the eight ball, scrambling for his life, that he felt truly alive.

All right, that was it. It was decided. Michael Delaney was about to become public enemy number one. So be it. If these snakes had managed to get to Fairbank, they had to have left a trail. All he had to do was find it.

The truth will set you free, right?

He stood up again. The weakness in his knees was gone now. He felt full of vigor and purpose as he headed back up the stairs the way he had come. When he reached the third floor, he walked out into a long hallway, checking signs on the doors as he walked by. Eventually he found the door he was looking for. Serology.

A plump young woman wearing a white coat sat in a chair reading a romance novel. She hurriedly tucked the book in a drawer, a slightly guilty look on her face.

"I was on break," she said defensively.

Delaney showed her his badge, identified himself as a Secret Service officer. "I need you to do something for me," he said. He took off his coat and rolled up his sleeve.

"Huh?"

"Draw my blood," he said.

"Why?"

"The president of the United States was just shot and you're sitting around reading a romance novel," Delaney said. "That's fine, I'm not mad. But it doesn't really put you in a good position to be questioning what I'm up to."

She swallowed, grabbed a vial and rubber tourniquet hose. "I see your point," she said.

When she had finished filling a vial with Delaney's blood, he said, "Please seal the vial, put your signature across the seal, and take the vial directly to Dr. James Bannerman and instruct him to run a chem panel and a tox screen."

"Yes, sir," she said.

"Then I want you to come up here, take a piece of letterhead, write on that paper precisely what you did here, find a notary down in the business office, then sign and notarize the statement."

"What do you want me to do with it then?"

"Take the statement home with you, put it in a drawer, and don't tell a soul. Not unless I personally clear it with you. Understood?"

"Yes, sir."

IN A MATTER of minutes he was down in the lobby.

"Where were you?" demanded the fresh-faced young agent who was waiting for him. He was a young guy named Rankin who had emerged as a protégé of Mark Greene.

"Got held up," Delaney said airily. "Where's the car?"

Rankin walked toward the front door. A black Ford Crown Vic sat at the curb, engine idling. The two men slid into the car.

"Oh, shoot," Delaney said.

"What?" Rankin said irritably. He was obviously eager to get his charge back to HQ with a minimum of delay.

"I was on black bag duty today. With all the confusion, I left the bag by the elevator." Black bag duty meant he was carrying a bag containing two MP5 submachine guns and several hundred rounds of ammunition. "How about you run in there and get it for me?"

"You left the black bag in there?" Rankin said incredulously. "Hey, that's not my problem. How about *you* run in there and get it."

Rankin looked at the young agent with the steely gaze he had cultivated during his years as a sergeant in the Fifth Special Forces. "Son, while you were playing delivery boy this morning, I was busy laying my life on the line to protect the president of the United States. In so doing, I turned my ankle. Now start thinking like a Secret Service officer instead of an Egyptian cabdriver. Get your butt out there and get that bag before somebody makes off with it and kills another senior administration official."

Rankin, white-lipped, got out of the car and stalked into the lobby of the hospital. Delaney felt only slightly bad as he slid across the seat, dropped the car in gear, and pealed out of the parking loop. He'd never liked that little brownnoser anyway.

7

Situation Room, the White House
11:03 AM

ESTABLISHED BY President Kennedy after the Bay of Pigs disaster in 1961, the Situation Room had been used by every president since in times of crisis. It was the inner sanctum of the White House national security apparatus and provided the commander in chief with rapid and secure presidential communication channels for national security information. Physically it was a singularly unimpressive room, but even after two years in the White House, Mary Campos still felt a sense of awe as she entered the room.

"I'm sorry I'm late," she said. "I just flew up from Fort Bragg."

Everyone in the room looked at her. The members of the cabinet sitting in their red leather upholstered chairs around the large cherrywood table showed every emotion from grim-faced determination to grief to stunned disbelief. Some were reading wire service reports, while others stared blankly into nothingness. National Security Council staff members seated just behind them were preoccupied in knots of uneasy conversation. Young military officers, the so-called Watch Team Duty officers who monitored intel and news reports, were moving in and out of the room through the side door as new intelligence came across the transom.

"There's been another one," a young marine captain said, holding a printout in his hand. "Number four."

"Where?" It was the demanding voice of National Security Advisor Admiral Frank Boettke, Mary Campos's boss.

The young officer handed him the printout. "Jesus God," Boettke said.

"The fourth what?" Mary said.

"You didn't hear?" Boettke said. "There's been a truck bomb at the federal courthouse in Atlanta, a missile attack at White Sands, a mortar attack at the naval base in San Francisco, and now a train's been derailed at the Proving Grounds in Maryland."

"Casualties?" Campos said.

"They're still tallying. The truck bomb killed at least thirty people. It's a miracle more didn't die. The others have been pretty superficial at least in terms of casualties—though the White Sands attack has burned up half a billion dollars' worth of building and equipment, and some radiation may have leaked out."

"I'm sorry, sir, I haven't been briefed. Is this looking foreign or domestic?"

As Boettke prepared to answer she caught a glimpse of Morgan Boyd coming into the room with a phalanx of aides.

"That's a question they are probably going to want you to answer," Boettke said dryly.

Everyone rose as the new president walked into the room. The slow, painful gait brought on by his old back injury was more evident than ever. "Sit," Boyd said, dropping into his chair. "Folks, let's take thirty seconds to pray for Dean Fairbank."

Thirty seconds ticked by. Mary Campos bowed her head but let her eyes drift toward Dean Fairbank's successor. His dark hair, as always, seemed to need a trim, and his beard was so heavy that he looked in need of a shave the minute he walked out of his bathroom in the morning. The pallor of his complexion today only heightened the effect. His face was oddly asymmetrical, as though someone had squashed one side of it in a vise. His eyes were black and piercing, his nose long and thin. He looked exhausted, but undefeated, as though he were running on a mix of will and anger. His voice, however, was large, out of all proportion to his body, the deep rich baritone of a radio announcer.

"All right then," Boyd said. "I'm sure you've heard what happened in excruciating detail, so let's not waste time on gossip. I will say this, however. As Dean Fairbank's life was fading, his thoughts were not about himself, but about his family and his country. He grabbed me by the wrist as they put him on the gurney, and he made me swear that I would bring those who perpetrated this assault to justice. We owe it to him and we owe it to Marcia." Marcia was the assassinated president's immensely popular wife. "And, by God, we owe it to America."

The room was silent for a moment. Then everyone burst into applause. The danger in any transfer of authority is that at some moment of weakness, there will be a vacuum of power leaving the nation rudderless. It was clear that Morgan Boyd had no intention of allowing that to happen. An almost visible relief showed on the faces around the room. In times of crisis, nothing is more consoling than strong leadership.

"We'll be holding a funeral for President Fairbank the day after tomorrow at 2:00 PM at Arlington National Cemetery," the new president continued. "Our protocol folks will handle all the logistical arrangements."

Heads nodded around the table.

Boyd placed his fists on the table and leaned forward, his face suddenly businesslike. "Okay. We have clear reason to believe that we are in the midst of a grave national emergency. Therefore, this meeting will now go into COG session." The president looked around the room then pointed at the door. "Admiral Boettke, it's time for you to head to Highpoint. All non-cabinet officers, please step outside." Mary Campos rose to leave. "All non-cabinet officers except Colonel Campos. You stay."

The major COG provisions, Mary knew, had last been updated during the cold war era when surviving a nuclear attack was the prime objective of the plan. Many of the provisions still stood. Mary's boss, Admiral Frank Boettke, would be flying with an F-16 escort straight for a hardened facility buried deep under the mountains near Bluemont, Virginia, code-named Highpoint, where he would establish a sort of "shadow government" that could take over the reins of government in the event of some sort of catastrophic attack on Washington, DC. Additionally in Pennsylvania near Raven Rock at a base code-named Site-7, a number of senior Pentagon generals would establish a backup staff to take command of the military in the event that the Pentagon was severely attacked.

Boyd waited until the room had cleared. "As all of you know, it was determined early in the administration that the continuity of government protocols were outdated and needed revising. President Fairbank appointed me to revise and implement the new COG protocols. In fact the meeting I had with him this morning was on this very subject. We were just in the process of rolling out the new protocols. President Fairbank himself had approved them in general outline, but the executive order had not yet been signed. As my first act as president, I will now sign the new protocols." An aide placed a leather-bound volume in front of the president. He opened and signed the document inside.

When he was finished signing the document, President Boyd looked up at the cabinet officers. "I have recruited a small team to smooth the implementation process. This team, which will be known as the Protocols and Procedures Section—some have taken to calling it Unit P—is here to assist you. I trust you will give them your fullest support." He looked around the room. "In broad strokes the new COG protocols are intended to serve the same functions as they always did, to provide survivability and operational continuity of the core operations of our government. I think you will find most changes to be fairly minor. Unit P will be a Justice function on par with the FBI or Secret Service and as such under the authority of the attorney general. That said, however, there may be some resistance to following certain details of the plan. In the event you have questions about particular provisions or instructions, Unit P members will be final arbiters. Their word has the force of my office behind it. Is that clear?"

Heads nodded uncertainly around the table.

"You'll notice, ladies and gentlemen, that in addition to Colonel Campos, one other non-cabinet member has remained. I think you all know John Rancy, my legal advisor."

A tall, lean man with bright blue eyes looked around the room.

"I depend on John a great deal and will need his assistance," the new president continued. "He was, in fact, instrumental in drawing up the new COG procedures." Boyd turned and looked at the attorney general of the United States, Sheila Evans. "Attorney General Evans, this is in no way a reflection of your competence, but I am now relieving you of your position as attorney general. Mr. Rancy will be taking your place in an ex officio capacity, pending senatorial approval. Painful as it is to do this, I am going to have to be making some swift, sure legal decisions and as a result I will need the assistance of someone I've worked with for a long time and who understands me intuitively. The United States thanks you for your excellent service, Ms. Evans. I apologize to you and to your family for the abruptness of this move, but I feel it is unavoidable."

The room was silent.

"You mean . . . ," she said finally.

"Yes," Morgan Boyd said. "I'm afraid so."

All eyes watched as the stunned attorney general walked slowly across the room and out the door.

Secretary of State Solomon Fordyce raised his hand tentatively. "Mr. President, with all due respect, COG is all about maintenance of existing structures. Doesn't it seem a little early to be implementing major personnel changes?"

"The new COG protocols," Boyd said, "are all about chain of command. And the preservation thereof. As I'm sure we're all aware, there's always a shakeout period when a new president replaces an old one. In this adminstration I expect—no, I demand—your honest opinions prior to the making of presidential decisions. Once I make a decision, unproductive second-guessing and backward-looking chitchat will not be tolerated." He gazed around the room. "Sometimes members of the administration or the bureaucracy feel compelled to test the resolve and authority of the new guy. Well, folks, the shakeout period is officially over." He looked around the room, still smiling distantly. "Clear?"

"Yes, Mr. President," the abashed Fordyce said.

"Good. First order of business, Admiral Boettke, you'll be taking command of Bravo team, as per COG procedures. Please proceed immediately to your post at Highpoint."

Admiral Boettke rose and marched swiftly out of the room.

"All right, now to get down to business. The reason I'm taking such precipitous action is that we just lost the highest elected official in the country, and came inches away from losing the second highest. We are currently subject to an unfolding wave of attacks. Someone wished to decapitate the nation. I will not let that happen. In fact, I am deploying U.S. military forces around the country to forestall further attacks. Mr. Rancy, if you would, please brief the room."

Rancy stood. "The strike against the presidency was highly sophisticated." He had a high, clear Irish tenor and a peculiar halting quality to his speech, like someone who had almost—but not quite—mastered a childhood stutter. "Intel, obviously, is still coming in, but indications are that these terrorists have at their disposal a wide variety of weapons including precision-guided munitions and large quantities of highly explosive materials. They are coordinated and effective. Fortunately loss of life—thus far—has not been on the order of 9/11. But the scale of the attacks appears to be much larger and, frankly, a great deal more sophisticated. And their tentacles reach much deeper."

"Are you suggesting that there's some sort of . . . conspiracy?" asked the secretary of defense, Adam Robinson.

"Yes. Early evidence indicates that the attack at Camp David had inside assistance."

"What kind of inside assistance?"

"I'm afraid I can't reveal that at this moment."

The Sec Def was not used to hearing those words. "I trust we'll be briefed in more detail shortly," he said sharply.

"Of course." Rancy smiled smoothly. "Now, President Boyd and I have consulted and he has determined that we will need to set up an official inquiry to coordinate the investigation into these attacks. I will be heading that inquiry. Colonel Campos, since this is your area of expertise, I want you to find out everything you can about the shooter and whom he might be connected to. The FBI will get you up to speed."

Boyd rose. "Thank you, John. I will be outlining the details of my plans over the next several days. Using the new COG protocols, I plan to use broad executive powers until this situation is stabilized. If any of you, upon review of the plans, can't support my actions, I'll expect your immediate resignation."

The secretary of defense spoke again. "Mr. President, did I understand you to say that you intended to deploy military forces inside the borders of the United States?"

"Yes, you did."

The secretary of defense was a longtime politician who had served both in Congress and in a number of administrations. He had not moved up the political food chain by throwing himself on too many grenades. He cleared his throat. "I assume you've got John working on the Posse Commitatus issue?"

Boyd looked at his new attorney general. "John?"

"That's actually been a major part of the legal end of the new COG work. For those of you unfamiliar with the issue, the Posse Commitatus Act of 1878 prohibits the deployment of regular military troops within the borders of the United States. Notwithstanding the 1878 act, certain narrowly proscribed deployments have been made since that time. We believe that we've got ample precedent to allow deployment. Nevertheless we'll be conferring with Congress shortly in order to pass legislation to establish a nice bright statutory line within which the military may operate."

"I haven't seen these new COG protocols myself," said Larry Rhine, the labor secretary, who was generally considered to be the most liberal member of the cabinet. "What are we talking about here? I trust we're not talking star courts and suspension of habeas corpus."

Without blinking, Rancy said, "There are a number of fairly aggressive measures contained in the plan. And, yes, habeas corpus is one of them. But naturally that would be used only in the most extreme cases."

The labor secretary shook his head in wonderment. "Is this a matter for discussion, Mr. President? Or has the decision been made? I must be honest—this spooks me a little."

"Now is not the time for Nervous Nellies, Larry," the president snapped. He looked toward the door as an aide entered the room and tentatively handed him a note. Boyd read the note and looked up. "Another bomb just went off in Los Angeles—outside a major movie studio in Burbank, more specifically. Thirteen people were killed and a major movie studio flattened." The room was silent. "Larry, people are dying on the streets of our country as we speak. Now is the time for decisive action. If we do overreach a little, we'll pull back after we've stopped the bleeding."

John Rancy leaned forward. "Trust me, Larry, any of these more . . . extreme . . . tools will be used very surgically, very sparingly."

The labor secretary clamped his mouth shut. He was obviously not happy with the measures. But equally obviously, he was not prepared to fight a losing battle against the new president on the issue.

"Anyone else?" the president said.

No one answered. "Good. Then Colonel Campos and Mr. Rancy will move forward with the investigation. Defense Secretary Robinson, please stay and we'll start ironing out the mobilization issue. The rest of you, get back to your posts. Protocols and Procedures Section will be contacting your shortly with specifics on COG implementation."

As Mary Campos rose to leave, John Rancy approached her and said, "I'll need you to join me. We're taking the chopper back out to Camp David. The FBI is setting up a temporary command post to supervise the investigation. We'll get briefed on their progress, and inform them who's running the show."

Mary nodded vaguely. She was still feeling blindsided by the speed with which President Boyd was moving. Something about the whole business concerned her. She was a dyed-in-the-wool conservative who had spent her entire adult life in uniform. But the idea of American troops in the streets of America made her very uneasy— American troops who, if she had understood Rancy correctly, might well be empowered to pull people from their homes and hold them without charges and without access to a lawyer.

"Let me grab my things," she said. "I'll meet you at the chopper."

8

Staunton, Virginia
12:08 PM

THE PAYMASTER pulled into the small western Virginia city of Staunton around lunchtime. He was not a sentimental man and didn't notice the beauty of the white-peaked mountains in which the Shenandoah Valley was nestled. He pulled off of Interstate 77 and wound through the snowbound town until he reached Shutterlee Mill Road, where his mother lived. Her house was well outside of town, out where the commercial strip had petered out. It was a small wood-framed farmhouse with one small hayfield in back, a large neatly kept yard, and a fifteen-year-old Cadillac parked in the driveway. The vain old hag, driving a Caddy when she could barely afford a Kia. He'd been sending her checks since he was twenty years old, his mother too proud or too lazy to take a job after his old man kicked the bucket.

"Hi, Ma," he said, coming through the unlocked front door and tossing his briefcase on the threadbare couch in the living room. He hated coming home, hated the ancient furniture with the stained antimacassars on the backrests, hated the smell of lavender, which permeated the place, hated the black-and-white photographs of all the long-faced, sour people in his mother's family tree going back to before the Civil War. Too good for this world, all of them, noses in the air. Made him want to puke. He had fled Staunton a long time ago—in large part because of the harridan living in this very house. "Ma? Ma? Where you at?"

He found the answer to his question in the kitchen. His mother was sitting in a chair looking at him with a strange expression in her eyes. It took a moment for the whole thing to register: the duct tape across her lips; the plastic zip-clasp securing her neck to the lattice of the straight-backed wooden chair; the muscular hard-faced man with the gleaming knife pressed against her neck.

"What the—"

The muscular man said, "You didn't actually think we'd take your word for it, did you?"

"Huh?" the paymaster said. "Who are you? What are you doing to my mother?"

"The hard drive, you moron. We sent a guy over to Reston. You took the hard drive out, stuck a replacement in there. If you'd bothered to screw the new one in, we'd have never known. But you didn't bother, did you?"

The paymaster blinked.

"How it works is this. Tell us where the hard drive is, we don't kill your mom. If you're cheerful about it, we might not even kill you."

The paymaster felt a thin smile run across his lips. "Go ahead, stick that thing in her neck," he said. "You'd be doing me a favor."

Then he started to run.

He didn't see the other man, the huge guy with the pistol, until the sound of the gun was filling the room. He felt like he was being hit in the chest with a hammer. Then a strange floating sensation came over him, like a huge flower had blossomed inside his face. Lavender. Then the world went black.

BADGER LOOKED DOWN at the weasely-looking man lying still on the floor, blood pouring out of his face. There were two neat holes in the front of his white shirt, center mass, and the left side of his face was a bloody ruin. "You idiot," Badger said to his partner, Gustaphsen. This was the last time he was going to work with this cretin. "What were you *thinking?*"

"He was trying to run away!"

Badger pointed to the briefcase on the couch. "Open it."

Gustaphsen lumbered over to the couch, opened the case. It was empty.

"You idiot," Badger said again.

Gustaphsen looked at him. "What's the big deal? We got the guy, didn't we?"

Badger looked at his partner and shook his head. "You think they care about the *guy?*" He kicked the dead man in the ribs. "The *guy* is nothing. The hard drive is what we're after."

Gustaphsen looked sullen. "Oh. Well, why didn't somebody tell me?"

"Because, you ape, you didn't need to know. Now go waste the old lady—*quietly!*—and let's get out of here." Badger was eager to get out of the lavender stink of the house. What was it with old ladies and lavender?

Gustaphsen lumbered into the other room, muttering under his breath. He came back after a minute, wiping a bloodstained kitchen knife on his pants. His shirt was splattered with red.

"It's done?" Badger said.

"Jeez!" Gustaphsen said, waving the knife. "What do you think this is, ketchup?"

Badger walked out the door toward their waiting Chevy Suburban, pulled out his cell phone, hit the speed dial. This was not a call he was looking forward to.

"It's me," he said. "Yeah, well, we've had sort of a hitch in the op . . ."

9

Washington, DC
12:15 PM

MARY CAMPOS was silent as the marine helicopter lifted off the helo pad. As the Washington monument came into view, she turned to the soon-to-be attorney general. "So this protocols and procedures outfit. I was a little unclear on their role in COG."

"I would say their job is just to, oh, keep everyone rowing in the same direction."

"What does that mean? Are these guys lawyers, civil service, functional experts, what?"

"No, not by and large."

"Give me a clue here. What kind of background do they have?"

"I would term it . . . they're coming from a more DOD perspective."

She digested this for a moment. A Department of Defense perspective. That didn't help her much. "Soldiers? Is that what you're saying? These Unit P guys are soldiers?"

"Not . . . ah . . . not *all* of them."

"Come on, Mr. Rancy, why the vagueness? Whatever their role is, I'm going to know within days. If these people are on our team, I need to know what their charter is, what their skills are."

Rancy smiled. "The head of the Protocols and Procedures Section—I hate the term Unit P, by the way—will be joining us at Camp David. His name is Dirk Pardee. He'll answer all your questions."

"It sounds like you're talking about security. That's Secret Service's jurisdiction."

"It's not so much a question of jurisdiction as it is of practicality. Think of it this way. Secret Service, FBI, Border Patrol, postal inspectors, DEA, CIA—all these groups have gotten large, fat, and bureaucratic. Add the jurisdictional issues, and what you have is a recipe for a great deal of hand-wringing and not much action. Homeland Security is too big. I convinced President Boyd of the need for a small, focused, stripped-down, cross-functional, cross-jurisdictional team of professionals who work at the sole discretion of the president and whose charter is restricted to maintaining the continuity of the government of the United States."

"And they report to . . . who? Homeland Security?"

He shook his head. "No, to me. To Department of Justice, that is to say."

Mary Campos looked out the window of the chopper. In the streets of Washington, DC, below them, the tiny people were moving along, busy as ever, people from all walks of life going about their business. And yet somehow everything looked different than it had just twenty-four hours earlier, as though the sun had changed colors slightly, painting the whole world in a different, paler light. When she looked back at Morgan Boyd's lawyer, he was studying her face carefully.

"Look, Colonel Campos," John Rancy said. "You and I are not children. We're realists. Governments—even the most benign governments such as our own—cannot exist without instruments of coercion. Without the implicit threat which lies behind the gold leaves you wear on your uniform, there is no United States. The right to worship freely, the right to speak your mind on matters of politics, the right to paint yourself blue and stand in the middle of the Mall reciting scatological poetry—all of these rights we treasure—they exist only because men with guns are willing to defend them."

"Sure, but—"

"Please. Let me finish. You, above all, should know that the freedoms we treasure so deeply are under unparalleled assault right now. We have clear evidence that terrorists have penetrated the Secret Service, Mary! This is a *fact*. How high, how broad, how deep is the disease? Do these murderers have allies in the FBI? The Pentagon? We have no idea. So I won't insult you by sugarcoating this matter. If the president is to defend and maintain the continuity of the constitutionally legitimate authority of this nation, he may need to have at his disposal a handful of guys with the guns and the will and the training required to bust into FBI headquarters or Secret Service headquarters or even into the Pentagon and drag out the traitors who are trying to destroy us. That's what Unit P is for."

Mary frowned thoughtfully. "Have you ever walked into a room and the people were talking about something and you got the impression that they were already way deep into a conversation and you were about twenty steps behind?"

"Sure. What's your point?"

"I'm feeling that way right now about you and President Boyd. President Fairbank's corpse, if I may be indelicate, is still warm, and you seem to already have a twenty-point agenda in mind for this administration. I'm just trying to catch up with you, okay?"

Rancy nodded. "I understand. Let me give you a little background. It's no secret that there was no love lost between Dean Fairbank and Morgan Boyd, that Morgan was on the ticket exclusively for political rather than ideological reasons. President Fairbank treated Morgan Boyd like a redheaded stepchild from day one. I would go so far as to say that Fairbank was overtly contemptuous of him. Just to make the Boyd wing of the party feel wanted and loved, he gave Morgan Boyd two small jobs: He said, 'Here, Morgan, go off in a quiet corner and lead a nice blue-ribbon panel on terrorism, and while you're at it, go tinker with the COG protocols.' Well, instead of spending his time attending the funerals of retired third-world dictators, Morgan Boyd went to work. He recognized that the COG issues were intimately tied to everything that the terrorism panel was grappling with. To sum it up, he viewed the work he was doing on terrorism to be work that had the potential to make or break this nation. I don't like speaking ill of the dead. President Fairbank was a decent enough fellow. But as a strategic thinker? Let's face it, he wasn't in the same league as Morgan Boyd. He was, quite frankly, a much smaller man. So while President Fairbank was running around focus-grouping about tariffs on Brazilian steel and whether to increase Medicaid deductibles by four percent, Morgan Boyd was busy sketching out a plan to secure the future of our way of life."

Mary Campos didn't say anything. She had liked President Fairbank as a man, but there was some legitimacy to Rancy's critique: he was not a big-picture statesman, being more focused on small political gains than on larger historical challenges. The war on terrorism had sometimes been overshadowed by the domestic minutiae. It had occasionally made her job quite frustrating.

"Colonel Campos, let me tell you something that President Boyd said to me this morning on the way down to the Situation Room. He said to me, 'You and I, John, have a historic opportunity. We can either face this problem of terrorism and solve it, or we can tuck our fiddles under our chins as the world goes down in flames. Every millisecond that we squander is one millisecond that we move closer to the abyss.'" Rancy's cool blue eyes looked straight into hers. "That's why there's a lot of urgency here. That's why he's going to move quickly and aggressively and not worry a great deal about making friends. We are faced with a unique mission. If President Boyd succeeds, he will go down in the history books as the greatest president since Lincoln. If he fails, well, it won't matter what the historians think of him."

After spending the last fourteen years of her life watching terrorists edge closer and closer toward the acquisition of chemical, biological, and nuclear weapons, Mary Campos felt some sympathy toward Rancy's argument. In fact there was something heady about the notion that her own chosen field of expertise was going to be central to the administration's goals.

"May I call you Mary?" Rancy's voice had gone low and confiding.

"Of course, sir."

"Mary, the president has had his eye on you for a long time. He believes you have a very important role to play in this administration. Not only are you a preeminent expert on terrorism, but you're also a soldier and a very effective communicator. In this day and age, silly as it seems, the importance of being telegenic can't be underestimated. But obviously you're not just a pretty face. You're tough, you're courageous, and you're smart as a whip. You could be a terribly important asset to the president in his future plans. Quite frankly I believe—and the president is with me on this—that you're ready to move to a role that would give much fuller rein to your talents."

"What are you saying?"

"Preliminary indications are that there's a domestic terrorist network in operation here that's more extensive than anyone would have believed only a few months ago. It's very important that we shine a glaring light on these bastards, that we root them out, and that we destroy them. Quickly. The president wants you to be more than just a glorified White House liaison on this investigation. We want you to direct that effort. Under my supervision, of course. Let's say we want you to be the public face of that effort."

"I'm eager for the opportunity to do that, sir."

Rancy looked out the window. They were scudding over black trees now, and a light snow had begun to swirl around them. "Now is not the time for doubting Thomases. This is a critical, critical moment. Bold and decisive and gutsy action will be required here. I won't kid you. There will be criticism of our efforts. But if you prove yourself on this investigation, the sky's the limit for you."

Mary Campos was no politician, but she'd spent enough time in Washington to know this was code for something. Code for what, however, she wasn't sure. "I'm just a simple soldier," she said. "You're talking way over my head. I like to talk in the concrete."

"A simple soldier. Sure you are." John Rancy laughed loudly. "You want concrete, let's put it this way: President Boyd will undoubtedly be shaking up the cabinet once things are stabilized, looking to people he trusts. If you demonstrate the level of loyalty and efficiency that both President Boyd and I believe you are capable of, we'll find something in the cabinet for you. Homeland Security have any appeal to you?"

Mary blinked, astonished. She still thought of herself as a field-grade midranker who wrote obscure papers that were read by a couple of specialists at the Staff War College and not much of anyone else. Suddenly she was looking a cabinet level job in the eye. It was almost too much to comprehend.

John Rancy's cell phone rang. He listened briefly, then hung up.

"There's been another one," he said. "Chicago. A young man just walked into the Mercantile Exchange with a bomb wrapped around his chest. He was shot dead by an alert guard before he had a chance to detonate." The chopper descended through the swirl of snow, and suddenly they were bumping down on the helicopter pad at Camp David. As the whine of the turbines began to wind down, John Rancy turned to her. "This is a war, Colonel. Are you ready to do battle?"

"Yes, sir. Absolutely."

He smiled without showing his teeth. "Outstanding."

10

Western Maryland

12:21 PM

MIKE DELANEY had the pedal to the floor of Agent Rankin's black Crown Victoria. He had called HQ with a far-fetched story about why he had left the hospital without Rankin. He was counting on confusion to give him a brief operating window before he was declared a fugitive. He just hoped he could reach Camp David before somebody made a move to shut him down. A light snow was falling again, and the roads were getting a little dodgy for the kind of speed he was maintaining. He was drenched in perspiration. Twice already his wheels had lost purchase for a moment. Absent the advanced driving instruction he'd received in the Secret Service, he'd have probably ended up in a ditch.

As the adrenaline began wearing off, he started to question his current course of action. A day ago, he'd been a normal enough guy, respected, well on his way toward a decent government pension. Today he was on the verge of becoming a fugitive from the law. How had he gotten here?

Only two years ago, everything had been looking up for him. Born in the small South Carolina town of Central, son of two hardworking cotton mill hands, he had joined the army straight out of high school, desperate to leave the grinding poverty of his childhood behind. He had entered the U.S. Army an uncertain, angry young man—not quite a nerd, not comfortable with the jocks even though he lettered in three sports a year, too intellectually restless for the poor kids he grew up around, too rough around the edges to fit in with the more affluent kids—and he had thrived on the discipline and challenges of army life. After serving briefly as a rifleman in the Big Red One, he had gone through Airborne and Ranger training, passing through a billet in the Eighty-second Airborne, and eventually ending up a member of the "quiet professionals" in the Special Forces. Many people think of the Green Berets as rompin' stompin' light infantry—which to a degree they are—but the Special Forces also are the intellectual mavericks of the army.

After showing a talent for languages, he had been assigned to an A-Team in the famed Fifth Special Forces operating out of Fort Bragg, North Carolina. By the time he completed a bachelors degree in history at the University of North Carolina, he had begun to get restless again. At thirty-one he was close to maxing out his potential advancement as an enlisted man, and his back and knees didn't take to carrying hundred-pound packs full of entrenching tools the way they once had. Contacted by a former army buddy who had moved on to the Secret Service after retiring from the army, Delaney had jumped at the chance to stir things up a little.

Within a year he was serving in the Secret Service. His intelligence and decisiveness had helped him move quickly up the ranks. He had worked in the investigative division for several years, arresting some major counterfeiters, before transferring to the protection side of the Service. Two years ago he had reached a high point in his career by being appointed head of the security detail assigned to protect Vice President Boyd.

Which is when disaster had struck.

New Delhi, India.

The sun began rising out of the yellow smog of the city just after 6:00 PM, but Delaney had been up since four, preparing for Morgan Boyd's speech before the Indian Parliament. His head was pounding despite the four Excedrines he'd swallowed after brushing his teeth.

Mike Delaney had always liked a drink. Back in the army days, everybody drank like fish—just a bunch of young knock-around guys, they'd drink till two then be up at five doing PT. That's just how it was back then. It had never really been a problem—but over the years it had gotten harder to keep up the pace. After joining the Secret Service, he had decided that the drinking was slowing him down, and he'd given up alcohol cold turkey. But then one thing led to another, and he had started drinking socially again, and then before he knew it, he was back to the old patterns.

The pressure and long hours of the vice presidential detail kept him from drinking regularly—but when he did drink, he drank a lot. But it never affected his performance.

And as a rule, he never drank a drop during overseas assignments.

The night before Boyd's parliamentary speech in New Delhi, however, Delaney had met with the head of India's Special Detachment Seven (SD7) of the India Police Service, their Secret Service equivalent, and the affable Indian— one P. K. S. Gupta—had offered him a drink in honor of intraservice cooperation. Gupta had quite a collection of single malts, and by one o'clock the two men had sampled most of them.

Delaney had awoken fuzzy headed and wrung out.

But he dug into the work, and everything went well. Morgan Boyd's speech on the issue of Jammu and Kashmir had been well received, and the crowds lining the streets had been generally calm and enthusiastic. Then halfway back to the hotel, things had gone awry. The motorcade had included four Jeep Grand Cherokees stuffed to the gills with Secret Service agents, two armored Cadillac limousines containing the vice president and his wife, Joan, as well as several members of the Indian Parliament and fifteen Indian SD7 police riding big Honda Goldwings.

Delaney rode in the back of the lead Cherokee. As they turned a corner, he knew they were in trouble. During their entire trip, the street had been lined with uniformed Indian troops in their distinctive olive drab uniforms and cockaded berets, keeping back the crowds. But suddenly, there were no Indian soldiers, not for at least 150 meters. Was it intentional, an entire unit abandoning their posts? Or just typical Indian lackadaisical planning? Delaney didn't have time to sort it out. As the motorcade rounded the corner, the crowd surged forward, cutting off the lead Cherokee and the lead motorcycle escort from the rest of the motorcade.

"Back it up!" Delaney yelled into his wrist mic. "Get back to the Parliament. We'll close ranks as fast as we can!"

But by then the crowd had surrounded the lead Cadillac, where Vice President Boyd was seated. The crowd didn't look threatening at all, but the first rule of motorcade work was that mobility was everything. And these cars weren't moving. Delaney rolled down his window, climbed out, so his entire torso was sticking out of the Jeep. Trained to read facial expressions and body language in a crowd, Delaney immediately saw two men in the crowd who didn't look right. Where everyone around them was smiling and craning their necks excitedly, these two wore grim faces and were pushing through the crowd, shoving people left and right. Something gleamed in one man's hand.

"Shooters!" Delaney screamed into his microphones. "Shooters at three o'clock! Get that goddamn limo moving!"

But the limo was going nowhere.

"Intercept! Come out heavy!" Delaney yelled into the Jeep. That meant go to heavy weaponry. He and three other men bulled their way out of the car. He had his Beretta in his hand, and the three other men were coming right after them carrying MP5s at combat ready.

The crowd melted away in front of them.

But they were too late. The two men he had spotted had already reached the vice president's limousine. One of them slapped a peculiar square armature of wire against the window. Delaney didn't have to guess what was attached to the armature: it was a shaped charge ribbon.

The two men stepped back, covered their ears. A deafening blast showered the crowd with shrapnel, and the bullet-resistant glass window disappeared as though made from tissue paper. Delaney put the front site on the nearest man's face, fired twice. The man went down, a piece of his head splashing red against the Cadillac.

As Delaney threw himself in front of the gaping window, the second man aimed an AK-47 toward the interior of the limousine and fired. Delaney and the three other Secret Service agents unleashed a barrage of fire. The second man's head, for all intents and purposes, ceased to exist.

The entire city of New Delhi seemed, for a brief moment, to have gone still and quiet. Delaney didn't even notice until his feet got wobbly that he had been shot.

The disciplinary hearing cleared Delaney of what it delicately termed "specific negligence." But they had found out about the drinking the night before. A reprimand was added to Delaney's file, and he was demoted briefly to uniform duty. Because the retirement of a number of top agents had left the presidential detail undermanned, Mike had been able to return to protective detail work—this time as a low man on the totem pole of the presidential detail. It was only later Delaney found out that Morgan Boyd had personally intervened to smooth his return to the plainclothes detail.

The ever-efficient Indian security apparatus had taken a full eight months to announce that the attempted hit on the vice president had been engineered by a group of Hindu extremists. Six low-level members of the organization—including the lieutenant who had directed his men to abandon their posts—were immediately imprisoned. But no one of any consequence was ever arrested. The head of the Special Detachment Seven, P. K. S. Gupta, had been promoted to a cabinet-level internal security position later that year when a new (and virulently anti-Muslim) Hindu party government was elected.

Miraculously—other than Delaney—there had only been one casualty in the attack. Unfortunately, it was Joan Boyd, the vice president's wife.

Since that time Delaney's career had languished, and Morgan Boyd had become one of the world's leading spokesmen against international terrorism.

Before the attack, Morgan Boyd had been a tough, aggressive, and difficult man. Tough but fair, the kind of man who didn't suffer fools gladly. He was, however, one of the few politicians Delaney had protected whom he had deeply admired. He was a man of principle, a man who seemed uninterested in focus groups and pork barrel politics. He did what he thought was right, and the devil take the hindmost. After the attack Delaney had little contact with Boyd, but from what he had heard, he had become a changed man—harder, colder, obsessed with only one issue, the fight against global terrorism.

Delaney's last meeting with Boyd had been brief. He had been called into the vice president's office, and Boyd had said to him, "I know that the Secret Service investigation into your actions during the attack in India has not been entirely positive. But I believe you did your duty with distinction and that you saved my life when you took that bullet. I want you to know that I don't place the blame for my wife's death on you, but where it properly belongs—on the bastards who shot her."

Then he had handed Delaney a simple gold watch. Engraved on the back were the following words: "May we free the world from fear."

Once he reached Thurmont, Maryland, Delaney turned onto Route 77 heading toward Hagerstown. He could see why FDR had picked the area as the presidential retreat back in 1935: a world away from Washington, DC, it was still close enough to return to the White House if a crisis developed.

The clouds were low, and the snow was coming down heavier now.

He followed Hunting Creek, a winding stream where FDR had fished with Churchill during the war, until the road came to a secluded entrance next to which an unobtrusive wooden sign read CAMP #3. The security fences and towers were barely visible from the road. Standing in front of the large metal gate were half a dozen marines.

A young corporal, his uniform lightly dusted with snow, approached the car, cradling his M-16. He cautiously scanned the ID, which had a gold stripe on it as proof that Delaney was on the president's personal detail.

"I don't think you're on the admit list, Agent Delaney," the marine said.

Delaney snatched the badge from his hand, shifted into his master sergeant voice. "Son, wake up! This is a crisis. Everybody's improvising. You know who I am. I've been here with President Fairbank a dozen times. I'm conducting the investigation and I need to get in there *now*. You think the White House has nothing better to do today than fiddling around with admit lists?"

The marine looked nervous, indecisive.

"Forget it!" Delaney snapped. "Get Colonel Waring on the horn right now. I'll let *him* ream you out instead of wasting my own breath." Waring was the head of the marine detachment at Camp David.

"No need of that, sir." The marine walked over to consult with his sergeant. Delaney's heart was in his throat. Moments later the marine waved him through, and Delaney relaxed. The gates opened and Delaney began to climb up the steep hill to the main area of the compound.

It was snowing heavily now, and as he looked off to his left, he could see the helicopter pad where three helos were now resting. Men and women in suits—FBI agents he could tell—were swarming all over the place, pulling boxes of equipment off the choppers.

Delaney kept his head low as he drove past them, then down by the tennis courts and the waterworks, which provided fresh drinking water for the facility. When he reached the small parking lot near the cabins, he pulled in and shut off the engine.

Delaney stepped out of the car and started walking toward the cabins. He tried to fix his mind on the murky events of last night. Still nothing there, nothing past about nine o'clock. He took a trail heading east from the parking lot toward the president's lodge, Aspen. The carpet of snow which had so smoothly covered the ground earlier in the day was now dotted with the imprints of dozens of boots. FBI agents were busy photographing, fingerprinting, and otherwise tracking down physical evidence throughout the compound.

Despite all the activity, however, the retreat was profoundly quiet. Delaney intentionally made eye contact with everyone he saw, nodding to them as he walked confidently past Hickory, the large building with its two-lane bowling alley, bar, and dance floor, and then down to Walnut, the small cabin where he had slept the previous night. He peered in the window. Noticing no one inside, he stepped through the front door and closed it behind him.

The contents of the cabin were untouched—coffee cups in the sink, rumpled clothes still piled in the corner of his bedroom. Delaney was taking a monumental risk returning—but he knew that if anything could be found to vindicate him, it was likely to be here.

Unfortunately, he found nothing.

He looked out the bedroom window and caught a glimpse of Holly, a larger cabin, which was being used as a recreational area. He vaguely remembered having dinner the previous night, so he walked quickly out of Walnut and across a clearing into the larger building. Painted brown with a white border, Holly was dark and empty. President Carter had used the place as a conference room for the Camp David Accords between Egypt and Israel, but now it had been partitioned into cozy reading and billiard rooms.

In the dining area at the back of the cabin he found clean dishes draining on a rack next to the sink. He remembered eating off of them the night before. He began furiously searching the sink, the refrigerator, and the cupboards, trying to find something else that might jog his memory. Outside he heard a crunching sound, someone walking along the path. As he turned from the cupboard to get away from a nearby window, his elbow bumped a metal bucket that the cleaning crew had been using. The bucket fell to the floor with a hair-raising crash. The footsteps outside ceased then started again, moving rapidly toward the back door of the cabin.

He grabbed the bucket, set it back on the shelf, then threaded his way back through Holly and out the front door. Skulking around aimlessly—this was no way to operate. Someone was going to demand to know what he was doing there pretty soon. He had to find something. Quickly.

Which is when it struck him. The cleaning crew had cleaned the room. They shouldn't have done that. The entire camp was a crime scene; the cleaning crew should obviously have been instructed not to disturb anything. In fact, none of the other buildings had shown any signs of being cleaned.

The cups and plates in the draining rack! Whoever took his gun probably slipped something in his coffee the night before. Whoever cleaned up this morning would have cleaned the drug residue out of the cup.

He felt a wave of frustration rising in his chest. If they had sanitized the place already, the likelihood of his finding anything that would clear his name was slim to none. There were a couple of things he could check . . . but right now it was looking like this entire expedition had been a waste.

Camp David Helicopter Pad
1:50 PM

Mary Campos and the ex officio attorney general stepped off the chopper onto the helo pad. They were met by a coterie of FBI agents. One of them stepped forward and introduced himself as Assistant Special Agent-in-Charge Leonard Smith. Smith was a light-skinned black with peculiar, intense green eyes. He shook hands and welcomed them.

"This way." He led them swiftly to a nearby cabin where a temporary command post had been set up. Smith introduced some of the staff who would be assisting him.

John Rancy then explained to Smith what Mary's role would be in the investigation—to a less than enthusiastic reception by the FBI men—and then suggested they get straight to the briefing.

"Let's begin by saying that the investigation is still ongoing," Smith said. "Oh, I know that's obvious, but what I'm saying is that everything I tell you right now is provisional and subject to change. Anyway, I'll begin by telling you what we know about the shooting itself and then I'll spiral outward from the crime scene, as it were, and what we believe to be the, ah, context of the shooting. The deeper meaning, if you will."

"I'm sorry, can I interrupt?" Campos said. "What does that mean— 'deeper meaning'?"

"We believe the shooter did not act alone. But I'll get to that as I move forward if you don't mind."

Colonel Campos nodded. "Of course."

"All right. The shooting itself. At nine-oh-four this morning a white male walked out of the woods next to the putting green at Camp David. He was dressed in a uniform that approximated those worn by the Secret Service's uniformed agents. He hailed the head of the president's security detail, Agent Mark Greene, who was accompanying President Fairbank and Vice President Boyd. Approaching the three, he drew a Beretta semiautomatic pistol from his holster and fired one shot, which struck President Fairbank in the neck. The shooter got off three more rounds, hitting President Fairbank twice in the chest and President Boyd once in the abdomen.

"Agent Greene immediately unholstered his weapon and fired, hitting the shooter in the forehead, killing him immediately."

Mary Campos frowned. Something about the sequence of things

puzzled her. It seemed surprising that Greene had allowed an unidentified man—somebody he couldn't have recognized—to approach that close to his principal. It seemed sloppy at best.

The FBI agent bent over his stack of papers, flipped a few pages.

Leonard Smith continued. "A number of agents responded immediately—including Charles Harrison, Art Becker, and Michael Delaney, all members of the president's detail. Becker had been inside Marine One, while agents Harrison and Delaney had been patrolling the perimeter of the retreat and happened to be nearby."

Campos's eyebrows went up. She knew Michael Delaney. But for the time being, she saw no reason to mention this.

"President Fairbank and Vice President Boyd were tended briefly by navy medics who responded to the scene, then airlifted via Marine One to Bethesda Naval Hospital, where the president was pronounced dead."

SAC Smith clapped his hands together smartly. "So. Those are the facts of the shooting itself. Now. The identity of the shooter. Using AFIS we have matched the shooter's fingerprints to a thirty-two-year-old plumber from Anniston, Alabama, by the name of Doyle Edward Pilgrim. Military records indicate Doyle Pilgrim spent four years in the United States Army, where he served as a heavy equipment operator for the Fourth Mechanized Infantry. Other than basic training and infantry school, he received no specialized combat training in the military. We have recently learned that Mr. Pilgrim was a member of an organized militia group known as the Brotherhood."

The Brotherhood. Mary Campos sat back in her chair. That was interesting. The Brotherhood was probably the fastest-growing right-wing extremist group in the United States. As a professional student of terrorist groups, she had been keeping an eye on them. They hadn't struck her as particularly dangerous—but you could never be too sure. Organizations evolved quickly, and the intel never seemed to keep up.

"Let's talk about security at Camp David," Smith continued. "The retreat is a one-hundred-twenty-five-acre compound surrounded by woods. In those woods are a host of sensors, including motion detectors, metal detectors, chemical sniffers, and cameras—including Fourth Gen night vision and FLIR. Bottom line, it's possible to infiltrate anyplace, given enough information. But Secret Service feels confident that without inside information, the chances of someone successfully blundering through the woods without being detected are zero."

Campos interrupted again. "Wait a minute . . ."

"Yes, that's right," Smith said. "I'm saying that we believe this was an inside job. It snowed last night, allowing us to follow the footprints of the shooter. He followed a circuitous path, which led through a series of blind spots in the night-vision camera coverage. However, he walked right in front of several FLIR—forward-looking infrared—cameras. We were initially puzzled about that. However, we soon discovered something that answered our questions. Apparently, when he reached the edge of the putting green, he stripped off a very unusual suit. It resembled a gillie suit of the type used by snipers, but with a twist: underneath the cotton surface of the suit was a layer of thermal gel such as you might use to keep soft drinks cold in a cooler. Basically you throw a suit like this in the freezer overnight and it will make you completely invisible to infrared detection."

"I assume," John Rancy said, "that suits like that are not available down at Wal-Mart."

"That's correct, sir. In fact, there is only one known place where a suit like this can be obtained. That's from SOCOM."

SOCOM being the Special Operations Command, the military command based in McDill AFB in Florida, which oversaw the fourteen thousand men of the Special Forces, the Seventy-fifth Ranger Regiment, the navy's six SEAL teams, and the army's Delta Force antiterrorism squad.

"The design of the sensors in the area surrounding Camp David is what we call an interlaced field." An assistant placed a map on the easel. The map used color-coding to show the location and approximate fields of coverage of the various sensors. "The idea being that if somebody manages to outwit the motion sensors—say by crawling at an incredibly slow rate of speed—then their weapon will be picked up by metal detectors. If you use camouflage, your heat signature will show up on FLIR. And so on. It's redundant, in other words. In this case Doyle Pilgrim's tracks led directly through the line of sight of conventional cameras and FLIR, but completely avoided the night-vision cameras. Most significantly, however, the particular route that Mr. Pilgrim followed passed directly by two metal detectors." He looked around the room. "The metal detectors never made a peep last night."

"You're saying he didn't bring his own gun into Camp David," Mary Campos said.

The agent nodded. "The weapon he used is a Beretta model ninety-two, standard issue of the Secret Service."

The room was silent for a long time.

"It's nearly impossible to escape the conclusion that Mr. Pilgrim's route was prearranged by someone with inside knowledge of the sensors. We believe his weapon was planted by someone within the compound so that he could pick it up and use it after he'd made it through the security perimiter. Folks, I'll just say it plain out: we believe the Secret Service has been penetrated by a terrorist."

"Who?" John Rancy said. "Who's the traitor?"

"We're working on that. The serial number's been filed off. Right now they're trying to reconstruct it using x-ray crystallography. If that doesn't work, they'll use another technique. Each and every weapon used in the presidential detail has been ballistically printed—meaning that the ballistic markings made by the barrel on the bullet are recorded in digital form. The lab is doing a ballistic analysis of a bullet recovered from President Fairbank's body as well as one harvested from the weapon itself. Assuming the two match—and that's virtually guaranteed—then its just a matter of matching the weapon to the ballistic print on file." He smiled coolly. "That's assuming the barrel too hasn't been modified. If there's a match, that should lead us to our inside man. We're talking about a matter of hours here before we know."

"And in the meantime?"

"President Boyd is being guarded exclusively by people from his personal detail, not people from the previous team. Once we know who the bad apple is, we'll get the rest of the team back to work."

"Where are these people coming from?" Rancy said. "If there's one insider, who's to say there aren't more?"

"That's what we're concerned about. We've got a massive operation going right now to track the workings and membership of this Brotherhood outfit. But being honest with you, we're talking about a group that's organized in cells, that probably has several hundred members, and that's operating in several states. It's a huge, huge investigative undertaking."

"Colonel Campos," Rancy said, "I'm putting you on the spot, but what wisdom can you shed on this group, the Brotherhood?"

Campos squinted thoughtfully. "There's been a lot of activity out of them recently. Among right-wing groups of their general ilk, you can pretty much divide the spectrum in half. On one side are the so-called Christian Identity groups which are basically racists hiding behind the guise of religion. Anti-Jewish, antiblack, antiforeign. On the other side of the spectrum are the patriots. They tend to be militia-oriented, very pro–Second Amendment, virulently anti–federal government. The patriots, by and large, focus their anger against the federal government. They believe that the federal government has overstepped its constitutional bounds and that armed militias may be required to preserve the rights of individual citizens.

"The Brotherhood is on the patriot side of the field. Most patriot groups are composed of high school dropouts with beer guts who've been carrying a chip around on their shoulder since they failed the Postal Service entrance exam. They talk a lot and stomp around in the boonies with their AK-47s, but they tend to be pretty benign.

"The Brotherhood is a little different. More sophisticated—both operationally and ideologically. Their basic claim is that America has become weak, that we've abandoned our roots—God, country, discipline, responsibility, morality, whatever—and that the federal government needs to be taken down a peg. They're unusual among these kind of groups in that there's not even a hint of racism, anti-Jewish sentiment, anti-Catholicism—all the things that tend to make most right-wing crazies smell so bad.

"But that's not to say they aren't scary. In fact, what's most scary about them is their effectiveness in recruiting. The leader of the Brotherhood is a man from Alabama named Paul Miller. Very bright, charismatic, good-looking guy. He's about forty but has great rapport with Gen Xers. Knows how to snowboard, jumps out of planes, has a black belt in karate, plays a mean guitar. They've put on a big recruiting drive at a number of southern and midwestern universities, and they've been very successful picking up young supporters. They seem to appeal to disaffected kids with a taste for adventure who are looking for some identity, some meaning, some structure—the same kids who, under other circumstances, might just as easily join left-wing groups like PETA or Earth First or the antiglobalization crowd. He organizes the group on anarchist lines, just like Al-Qaeda, just like the Bolsheviks or the IRA—autonomous cells, information compartmentalization, everything's need-to-know."

"What are they trying to accomplish?" Rancy said.

Mary frowned. "Hard to say. Paul Miller's claim is that there will be a violent revolution that will result in the collapse of the federal government and a return to what he calls True America—which according to his teaching is a sort of Jeffersonian democracy. His public claim is that he's training his people to survive and channel this period of violence, not to cause the violence itself. But our latest intel—

which, by the way, is pretty darn sketchy—is that within the organization he may have been advocating more, ah, direct action."

Rancy waved his hand irritably. "Direct action. What does that mean?"

"Not clear. Bombings? Truck highjackings? Possibly even assassinations."

"I think we can safely add the last one to the list, don't you, Colonel?" Rancy said dryly.

Campos flushed. "I'm just telling you what we knew as of two days ago. What else have you got, Agent Smith?" she said.

"I could go over it in more detail, but that's the broad brush for right now. Like I say, that ballistics report is going to tell us a lot."

Rancy nodded. "Good. Tell you what, Colonel Campos. Why don't you stick around here, get acquainted. I need to get back to the White House."

"Yes, sir," she said.

She watched John Rancy walk out of the room. "If you feel like it wouldn't cause any problems," she said to SAC Smith, "I'd like to walk the property a little bit, get the lay of the land."

The FBI agent cleared his throat. He obviously would have preferred that she disappear into thin air. But given that she was the personal representative of the president, he was in no position to make that happen. "Fine, ma'am, but please stay on the path and be judicious about touching things. As far as we're concerned, this entire compound is a crime scene."

"Of course. I'll take the loop around the property." She paused at the door. "Send somebody after me when you get that ballistics report."

SAC Smith gave her what passed for a smile. "I'd be happy to."

DELANEY WALKED QUICKLY down the path toward the putting green, stopping when he got close enough for the bevy of FBI agents scurrying around the scene to see him.

The shooter had come out of the woods, that had been obvious from the tracks in the snow at the crime scene. But how had he gotten through the trees? The property was surrounded by an electric fence, and interlaced fields of sensors and cameras. Delaney had spent a week working up a Threat Prep—a standard Secret Service exercise in which agents tried to uncover weaknesses in their own defenses—trying to figure out a way to get into Camp David.

The theory he'd used was this: a shooter wearing a chill suit with gillie-type modifications would do a two-day sneak-in with a ceramic-barreled, polymer-framed pistol. It seemed like a workable plan. The electric fence was no kind of obstacle to a serious intruder. Once you got over that, moving at an infinitely slow pace in a heavily camouflaged gillie suit would minimize the risk of visual detection. The nonmetallic weapon would mask it from the metal detectors. The chill suit full of thermal gel, which would be incorporated in the gillie, would mask it from FLIR. The gillie suit would mask standard visual detection. The problem he found in his plan was that even in freezing temperatures, body heat warmed up the thermal gel in the chill suit within four to six hours. According to his projections, there was no way to make the stalk without risking infrared detection.

He stared at the putting green. Unless, of course, you knew where the sensors were.

Which this guy obviously did. Because he had inside help—help from the same person who had undoubtedly drugged Delaney and stolen his Beretta, then planted the weapon and given the shooter the layout of the sensors. Instead of going with a ceramic gun, they'd used Delaney's weapon—which served two purposes. First, it avoided the problem of using a failure-prone ceramic-barreled gun; and second, it turned Delaney into a fall guy, thus deflecting attention from whomever had really provided the insider knowledge of the security provisions. Armed with that knowledge of where the night-vision cameras and motion detectors were, the shooter had simply walked or crawled around them.

Delaney sighed. It was a beautiful setup, he had to admit. He shook his head. There was nothing here. He'd put himself at risk over nothing.

He was so lost in thought that he didn't notice the sound of footsteps approaching until they had almost reached him.

He turned and smiled confidently. It was a woman in a long dark coat. Their eyes met for a long, uncomfortable moment. The smile died on his lips.

"Mary?" he said finally.

Lieutenant Colonel Mary Campos continued to stare at him for several seconds. Then she slapped him hard in the face.

11

The Oval Office
3:19 PM

MORGAN BOYD stood behind the desk, looking out the window of the famous Oval Room, hands clasped behind his back. "How did it go with Campos?" he said.

"She's on board," Rancy said.

"Good."

There was a momentary silence.

"I took your recommendation to use her," Morgan Boyd said. "But I believe your explanation as to why she was a good fit for the job was a bit thin. She's basically an academic. I'm sure she's done a little knocking around in the military, but—it's not like she's a trained investigator. Or a seasoned Washington administrator either, for that matter."

"She's smart, she's tough, she's articulate—"

"That's crap, John, and you know it. Give me the real reason."

"Just look at her, Mr. President. There may be a better-looking woman in the United States Army, but if there is, I haven't met her. With a little sub rosa assistance from our press office, the media will turn her into a household name. We need her out there in a flak jacket with war paint on and a gun drawn. I mean that literally."

"Go on."

"This week the big story is the assassination. Next week I think we want the big story to be Mary Campos. Her picture on next week's cover of *Time* magazine with a submachine gun in her hand. Kevlar, combat boots, the whole bit. 'America's Avenging Angel Leads the Administration's War on Terror.' Like that. *60 Minutes, 20/20,* we want to see her face everywhere. Yesterday is not soon enough."

Boyd continued to look out the window. "I know you better than that, John. There's more to it."

Rancy laughed. "Do you remember the story in Machiavelli about Messer de Orca?"

"Refresh my memory."

"Here's the recap. During the late fifteenth century the Romagna section of Italy had become disunited and lawless. Duke Cesare Borgia, who had recently acquired control of the province, decided that it needed to be restored to peace and order. So Borgia brought in a fellow named Rimirro de Orca to act as his agent and restore peace to Romagna. Machiavelli described this fellow de Orca as a 'cruel and efficient man.' Anyway, de Orca did precisely what he was hired to do: he brutally repressed the dissenters in the area, imprisoned the thieves, hung the murderers, branded the drunkards, kicked in doors, banged heads, whatever it took. When he was done, the province was safe to live in again. But of course de Orca's methods were so brutal that everyone hated him by the time he was done. So Borgia then had this fellow de Orca arrested. He was taken to the town square in Cesena, where he was drawn and quartered. The people, according to Machiavelli, were left 'satisfied and stupefied.' Bottom line, the peace was restored through brutal means, but Borgia managed to walk away the hero."

Morgan Boyd blew a long breath out of his nose.

"We'll be forced to do some rather ugly things before our path smooths out, Mr. President. Someone will eventually have to pay."

"And you mean for it to be Campos."

"As opposed, say, to me? Yes."

Boyd turned away from the window. Rancy was smiling faintly. The president looked at Rancy for a long time without speaking.

Camp David
2:20 PM

Delaney rubbed his face, still feeling the sting of Mary Campos's slap against his cold skin.

"Gee, Mary," he said. "Great to see you too."

She looked at him sourly. "What are you doing here?" she said.

"I was detailed to pick up some equipment that got abandoned here in all the confusion." He frowned curiously. "What about you? Why are *you* here?"

"President Boyd asked me to ride herd on the investigation."

Delaney frowned. Curiouser and curiouser. It wasn't like she had any experience in law enforcement. "You? No offense, but why you?"

"It looks like a terrorist attack. That's my field, so he wants me on it."

"Oh." He stood awkwardly. He and Mary Campos had had a brief relationship. Which he had bailed out of in a somewhat abrupt and craven way. "Look, I'm sorry I didn't call you. I was—"

"Whatever," she said brusquely.

"The divorce was coming through and I just . . ." He shrugged. How was he supposed to explain to somebody that he'd just gotten scared—that losing his wife, losing custody of his daughter, struggling with his sobriety and everything else had just been too much.

"I don't *care*," she said. Then she looked at him through narrowed eyes.

Delaney realized that he had a prize opportunity here. "So what have you heard? I left HQ a couple hours ago and I haven't heard anything. We know who the shooter is yet?"

"I shouldn't be talking about it."

"Oh, come on, Mary. It's *me*. I'm in the Secret Service. There's nothing you can tell me now that I won't know in three hours anyway."

Mary Campos looked off toward the putting green. The cold air had rouged her cheeks. She looked more beautiful than ever. He had missed her, missed her a lot, thought about her constantly over the past few months. And yet he'd never made the call. Why not?

Mary finally spoke. "It's looking like it's a group called the Brotherhood. Militia types." She folded her arms across her chest. "I guess I shouldn't say this, but it was an inside job. Someone in the Secret Service planted the weapon for the shooter to find."

Delaney made a pretense of astonishment. "You're joking!"

"Have you noticed anything odd? Anybody who you might be suspicious of, who's been talking negatively about President Fairbank, anything like that?"

Delaney shook his head. Suddenly something struck him. "You know, I was over at Holly. All the rest of the cabins were left as they were, but somebody cleaned up there. Makes you wonder why, huh?"

Mary Campos nodded vaguely.

"You might ask the cleaning crew if they were specifically instructed to clean that cabin."

Suddenly Mary looked on her guard. "Why?"

Delaney shrugged. "Just a thought. If this was an inside job, then whoever provided the gun might have switched somebody else's weapon, not their own. They could have drugged the other agent—put some kind of narcotic or barbiturates in his coffee or something—then lifted his gun while he was sleeping. Next morning the cleaning crew comes in, washes all the drug evidence down the drain."

Mary shook her head. "No, that doesn't make sense. If their weapon had been missing, they would have reported the gun missing this morning."

"Maybe they didn't notice the switch. Or maybe in the confusion, they didn't have time."

From behind them he heard a voice calling. "Colonel Campos? Colonel Campos!" They turned to look and saw a young FBI agent racing down the path toward them. The young man stopped and breathlessly continued, "Ma'am, SAC Smith sent me to get you. They've run the ballistic print on the shooter's gun."

Delaney's heart jumped. The ballistic print would lead straight to him. "You know what?" he said. "I really need to get a move on. Great seeing you, Mary."

Mary Campos glared at him, then turned to the FBI agent. "Who is it? Who's the inside man?"

"I don't know. SAC Smith has the details," the young agent said.

Delaney began walking briskly down the path. He had been in combat before—once in Panama, and once in Grenada, once in Somalia—but he had never been this frightened. He concentrated on breathing slowly. Walk quickly, but not too quickly. You are a man of purpose, a respected federal agent, a man doing his job on his own turf. No one can hurt you.

An FBI agent was approaching him. Delaney smiled pleasantly. Pleasantly, but not too pleasantly. The president of the United States had just been shot. This was not a lovefest, not a Baptist church barbecue. The FBI agent returned his greeting.

As soon as the agent had disappeared around the bend, Delaney began to sprint. And as he ran he began doing calculations in his head. Two minutes for Mary to get to the command post, thirty seconds for her to alert the guards, thirty seconds before the alert teams were in the cars and heading down the road after him. Three minutes before the navy choppers were airborne.

No way he was going to make it.

Recalculate. Close off the avenues of attack. But how? First he had to stop the guys on the ground. He reached the black Crown Vic, jumped in, cranked it up, and started tearing down the road. One and a half minutes, tops, before the guards started shooting to kill.

He pulled up to the guard shed. The road was narrow here—and after 9/11 it had been further narrowed by concrete crash barriers to keep out truck bombers. They had intentionally created a bottle-neck—one vehicle in or out at a time. As he pulled up in front of the guard post, he stopped the Crown Vic so that it blocked the road completely. There were two vehicles outside the gate, both of them huge black FBI Chevy Suburbans. Probably armored, probably full of weapons and armed men, most likely HRT guys. Hostage Rescue Team agents were among the best trained tactical operators in the world. Forty-five seconds.

He hopped out of the Crown Vic, leaving it so that it blocked the gate perfectly.

"Sir," the marine guard called to him. "You need to move the ve-hicle. You can't park there."

Delaney smiled and waved. "No sweat, son, I just need to talk to these FBI guys for about two seconds."

"Sir!"

Delaney ignored the marine and flashed his Secret Service badge at the tinted passenger-side window of the closest Suburban. Two hulking guys in black climbed out of the rear seats, eyeing him with the blank-faced gaze of professional soldiers. The window slid down, and a grim-faced agent wearing black tactical gear looked out at him with a skeptical expression.

"Guys," Delaney said. "We've got suspicious movement on the motion sensors right down there." He pointed vaguely, then grabbed the handle of the door and yanked it open. "Slide over, let's go check it out."

The driver frowned. "How come they haven't radioed us?"

"It's probably just a deer or falling snow. Leave those two guys to guard the gate, we'll check it out, be back in thirty seconds."

The driver hesitated. Fifteen seconds? Ten? How soon before the alarm went off?

"Dammit, can't you FBI people do anything without getting pa-perwork sent down in triplicate from E Street?" He knew that would get their goat. The HRT people treasured their reputation as action-oriented mavericks within the staid culture of the FBI.

"Hold your position," the driver said to one of the other agents. "Let's go, just you and me."

The HRT man in the passenger seat climbed out, and Delaney jumped in.

"Sir!" The marine was yelling. "Wait!" The marine sergeant ran out of the guard box waving his hands frantically.

"Step on it," Delaney said.

The driver, who wasn't paying attention to the marine guards, punched the gas, and the Suburban fishtailed briefly then tore off down the road.

"You got an MP5 in here?" Delaney said. "All I've got is my Beretta."

"Whatever we got, it's back there." The driver thumbed the back-seat. Delaney looked over the seat. Nestled in a rack on the door he found an MP5 submachine gun and an M203 grenade launcher with a pistol grip converter. Delaney grabbed the MP5. When they had gotten about a hundred yards down the road, Delaney pointed the MP5 at the HRT man's neck.

"Stop!" he shouted.

The HRT man stamped on the brake, then looked over at De-laney, confused. Then he must have heard something in his ear mic, because he said, "Delaney? You're Delaney?"

"Tell your guys to get out of the other Suburban, that the threat is on foot."

"What?"

Delaney fired off a deafening three-round burst just inches from the man's neck. "Do it!"

The HRT man spoke into his wrist mic. "Team Two. Out of the unit. The threat is on foot."

"Now get out of the car!"

Another shot across the HRT man's face convinced him to bail. He was out of the Suburban with a gun in his hand, firing away be-fore Delaney had even managed to slide across the seat and put the truck back in gear. The flat pieces of lead were pancaking across the bullet-resistant glass with a series of ugly, hollow smacks.

Nice shooting, Delaney thought as he wheeled around, tires smoking, and tore back down toward the guard post. If that glass hadn't been bulletproof, they'd have been picking his brains off the sunroof. He grabbed the M203 grenade launcher, poked it out the window as he rolled up on the second Suburban. The four HRT men had just jumped out of the other Suburban. Delaney fired the grenade launcher into the grille of the big vehicle. There was a terrific explosion and engine parts came raining down into the snow.

The HRT operators caught on quick. He ducked his head below the bullet-resistant glass as they unleashed a hail of lead at him. Several bullets came through the open window and ricocheted around inside the truck. He stood on the gas, the big engine growled, and the huge truck took off like a jackrabbit. Nothing like a hopped-up V-10 engine, he thought.

So much for the guys on the ground. With the Crown Vic blocking the concrete barrier bottleneck and the other Suburban out of commission, he had about three minutes before the navy choppers got a bead on him.

Delaney found himself grinning as he tore off down the road. He hoped he hadn't hurt anybody in the Suburban. He was pretty sure they'd be all right. There was only shrapnel to worry about, and those guys were head-to-toe Kevlar.

Three minutes. They'd have the best people on those choppers—SEAL Team Six operators—each chopper containing a sniper and four other heavily armed men, plus a door gunner on an M60. They'd have infrared, night-vision goggles, the whole bit. On the snowy roads, he was doing ninety on the straightaways . . . but there weren't many straightaways. The choppers could top 140 knots. So he still had about three minutes. Maybe four, four and a half, tops. No way to outrun them, no way to outgun them.

His mind went back to E&E, escape and evasion training at Eglin Air Force Base, universally considered to be the most hated part of Ranger training, searching his mind for ideas. Unfortunately this was not a swamp like the Florida locale where he had done his E&E course. Back in E&E training, he and a buddy—Lou MacGregor—had managed to hide for six days in a gator hole, eating weeds, raw frogs, and finally the legs and backstraps of a bull alligator who had made an unsuccessful attempt to reoccupy his home. But this was a mountainous, snowbound area. Not a lot of gator holes up here, and not a lot to eat this time of year. Worst of all, every step he took would leave tracks in the snow.

The one advantage he did have was that the snow was still falling. The snow would cover tracks, obscure vision, slow down everybody's movement. But only if he could stay undetected until more snow had fallen.

Nine miles from Camp David he turned onto a narrow paved road that ran along a steep hillside. It was heavily wooded, and along the roadway was a 150-year-old stone church called Harriet Chapel. Farther down the road he found a small narrow dirt track that cut into the deep woods.

Overhanging tree branches obscured the view from the air. He drove for more than a mile, fighting to keep the big vehicle from sliding off the side of the road. Finally Delaney found what he was looking for: a small brushy ravine leading down into a stream forty feet below. He twisted the wheel, and the Suburban plunged over the side. He tried to brake, but it was pointless. The truck tore down the hill at a breakneck pace, smashing into the stream at the bottom. The airbag exploded in Delaney's face.

He climbed groggily out of the seat, his left arm aching from getting smashed against the door, then looked around. Good. A chopper would have to be dead overhead to see him. If they were going down the main road, they'd miss him.

That gave him about five minutes till they figured out that they'd overrun him. Then they'd backtrack, split up, and start fanning out down the secondary roads. He had to camouflage the truck. Fortunately the swirling snow would make him hard to see. But still there was the heat signature to deal with.

He scrambled up the steep snow-covered hillside, using ash trees to pull himself through the thick snow, which was almost up to his knees as he climbed the twenty-five-foot bluff. When he reached a small plateau, he braced himself against a tree and pressed down on the shelf of snow below him. Large pieces began sliding down the deep incline, piling up next to the big truck.

Delaney scrambled back down the hillside. Most of the truck was still covered with a thin layer of snow. But snow on the hood had melted. It would glow red on the FLIR screen of any chopper. He opened the hood, started frantically shoveling snow on top of the engine block. He could hear the thrum of chopper blades in the distance. He slammed the hood shut, pulled more snow off the bank, and began piling it on the hood and windshield. Then he splashed through the stream and stuffed the truck's twin tailpipes with snow.

The chopper was getting closer.

He jumped in the front seat, lay down, shivering in his suit jacket and sopping shoes, hoping the cocoon of snow would protect him from the eyes in the sky.

The Department of Justice
2:47 PM

The head of Unit P—the recently established Protocols and Procedures Section—marched into John Rancy's new office and saluted his new boss.

He was not wearing a uniform, but he might as well have been. His carefully pressed suit, every crease knife sharp, his military bearing, his sidewall flattop—they practically shouted military. "Sir," he said, saluting as he stood attention before Rancy's desk.

Rancy was seated, but he did not invite Colonel Pardee to sit. Men like Pardee had to be made to understand their place. "The salute is not necessary, Dirk," the ex officio attorney general said. "You're a civilian now."

Pardee had become a civilian not because he desired to be one, but because certain irregularities in the accounts of his Special Forces unit had been discovered when they returned from duty in Afghanistan. In lieu of pursuing an embarrassing legal case against him, the army had allowed him to retire.

"Yes, sir," Pardee snapped. Rancy liked people like Pardee. They were like hammers—simple and trustworthy tools . . . as long as you didn't put your thumb in their way. Pardee was tireless, tough, smart, and just the slightest bit crooked.

"I heard there was bad news," Rancy said.

"Yes, sir." Pardee did not elaborate.

"The FBI has figured out the identity of the man inside the Secret Service who appears to have supplied the shooter with the gun."

"I'm glad to hear it, sir."

"I don't mean that in the sense that we have him in custody, Dirk. He got away."

"I see, sir."

"I'm putting you in charge of tracking him down. I want you out there personally."

"What's his name?"

"Michael Delaney. The file's right there." He pointed to a manila folder on the edge of his large desk.

"I'll find him, sir." Pardee picked up the file, glanced at it, his face opaque. "I know this man. He was in my unit back when I was a captain commanding an A-Team in Kurdistan right before the first Gulf war."

"Tell me about him."

"He was my senior noncom. A very resourceful soldier."

"Training?"

"The usual. Speaks Farsi, Arabic, maybe something else, I don't recall. As a Special Forces operator, obviously, he's jump qualified, has his Ranger patch, expert in any weapon you can name. Small group tactics, insertion, land navigation—knows all that stuff like the back of his hand. Superb shooter, checked out on demolition, field medicine, sniper ops. Didn't mind a stiff drink . . . but otherwise kind of a Boy Scout as I recall."

"Mm," Rancy said.

"There are quite a few opportunities for creative accounting when you're involved in black ops overseas. Delaney was not one to avail himself of those opportunities. We had a little dustup over the issue as a matter of fact. Had to put another man on the paperwork. I'd characterize him as a stick-up-the-keister type."

John Rancy said nothing.

"I must admit I'm a little surprised to hear that a man like Delaney would be part of an assassination plot. Seems uncharacteristic."

Rancy just looked at him. "It is not your assignment to make that sort of determination."

Pardee's face showed nothing.

"Michael Delaney is a good man. I worked around him when he was head of the vice presidential detail, and I like him a lot." The ex officio attorney general of the United States paused. "Find him and kill him."

12

Camp David
3:21 PM

M ARY CAMPOS sat at a long table in the temporary command center, staring at the file in front of her. It contained virtually everything that had ever been committed to paper on the life of Michael O'Donnell Delaney. GS-12, salary of $57,421 a year, divorced a year ago from his wife of fourteen years. Daughter, Sarah, age seven, whom he hadn't seen but once since his ex-wife relocated to Charlotte, North Carolina, six months earlier. Excellent credit, but barely a nickel in the bank. Child support payments of $630 per month. Father and mother deceased. Graduated cum laude with a degree in history from UNC Chapel Hill after studying at night for six years. His honors paper was included—a 110-page study of the takeover of the U.S. embassy in Iran. She flipped to the back: footnotes referred to sources in Farsi, Arabic, and French.

She'd dated him for just over two months and he'd never even mentioned that he spoke a foreign language. But then their relationship had been a peculiar one. Romance between a Secret Service man and a White House functionary wasn't strictly off limits—but it could have created some potential problems, and so they had kept it a secret from their coworkers. Not that, in the grand scheme of things, it had been that huge of an affair—it only lasted a couple of months, after all—but she had really liked Mike Delaney. A lot. Maybe even loved him. It had hurt her deeply when he had walked out of the room in the middle of a minor fight and then never even called her again.

Mary sighed. Best not to think too much about it.

She looked back down at the file. The military records showed nothing but distinction. He had been trained in virtually every known way of killing other human beings.

The only spot on his blameless record was the thing in New Delhi two years ago, which had resulted in his being demoted. She had seen the pictures of Morgan Boyd, his face covered with blood and tears as he cradled his dying wife in his arms, surrounded by men with guns. She had never even made the connection to Michael Delaney. There was a copy of the cover of *U.S. News & World Report* in the file and there he was, Michael Delaney—grim-faced, a Beretta gripped in his hands, pointing down at the prone body of the dead Hindu extremist, blood on his shirt from the bullet he'd taken, oblivious to the heart-wrenching scene just a yard behind him. Another piece of news that she had never heard even a word about in their two-month relationship. What else had he held back? A lot, apparently.

At the back of the folder she found his Secret Service application form. She flipped through it, pausing on the seventh page. "Has any relative or friend advocated the violent overthrow of the United States government? If so, please specify."

He had checked the box that said YES. Underneath, Michael Delaney had written: "My wife has a cousin by the name of Paul Miller of Anniston, AL, who is a member of a crackpot Nazi-type organization called the Brotherhood. I don't know if they advocate the actual overthrow of the government. But if they do, I would not be surprised."

"Hey! Guys!" she called, waving toward Leonard Smith. "Take a gander at this."

SAC Smith peered over her shoulder. "Son of a gun," the FBI man said.

"I assume you've already sent people to Miller's address in Alabama," she said.

"Yes, ma'am," Smith said. "HRT went in this morning. There were eggs sitting in a frying pan on the stove. They figured he must have scooted the second he heard the news about the assassination."

"Huh. Odd. If he's behind the assassination, you'd think he wouldn't have been taken by surprise and had to leave in the middle of fixing his breakfast."

Smith shrugged. "If I had made a practice of figuring out the psychology of every criminal I arrested, I'd have quit on the second scumbag."

Mary nodded. "Still no word from the navy chopper teams about Delaney?"

Smith shook his head. "Everybody's coming up dry. They figure he must have gotten through in the snow. He's probably halfway to DC by now, heading cross-country. We're putting up roadblocks, watching his house, tapping his phones, tracing his credit cards . . . He'll come up for air pretty soon."

"No doubt," she said. "No doubt."

The phone rang, Smith's personal line. "Yeah," he said. Then his tone became more deferential. "Yes *sir*, Mr. Rancy." He frowned and hung up the phone.

"This bomber," he said. "The guy who got shot trying to blow up the Mercantile Exchange? Looks like he had a handler. Chicago PD just picked him up."

"A handler."

"The man they just arrested drove the drop-off car, had a radio tuned to the same frequency, that sort of thing. Apparently a security camera got a couple frames of him as he was dropping off the bomber. Chicago PD enhanced the video, got the plate number, pulled him over. There were bombs, guns, you name it in the car. Mr. Rancy said he was sending some kind of special unit out there to bring the handler back to DC and interrogate him. Protocols and Procedures or something? What's he talking about?"

"Unit P."

SAC Smith looked at her blankly. "Unit P? What the heck is that?"

Fort Bragg, North Carolina
3:05 PM

They were lined up single file in their maroon berets and battle-dress uniforms, more than three hundred members of the 505th Parachute Regiment, standing at attention in the dark. These were the Panthers, and they wore patches with a soaring black cat on their shoulders. Each man was weighed down with a heavy Alice pack and carried an M-16 or an M4 carbine on a tactical sling. Behind them, dozens of army trucks were waiting, their diesel engines rumbling in the still night air.

Standing in front of the men was General Fairbank, big and grim as death. Strapped to his side was an M1911A1 in .45 caliber. The U.S. Army had switched to 9 mm years ago, and army brass rarely carried sidearms. But no enlisted man ever referred to Bill Fairbank as "the brass." He was a soldier, a fighter. He was one of them—even if he did carry three stars on his collar. They called him Gunslinger.

They had all heard stories about him when they started jump school. About how the tough old bastard had participated in nighttime airborne helicopter assault in Panama as a full colonel. Fairbank's boots had been among the first to hit the pavement at Torrijos International Airport. The rule was that officers at his pay grade didn't jump—the Pentagon had too much money invested in them. But rules didn't apply to Gunslinger Fairbank. Fairbank led from the front.

Six years earlier he had jumped over Grenada. Fairbank had gotten cut off with a small detachment and ended up in a firefight. With some luck and the force of his unshakable self-confidence, he had stared down an entire squad of Cubans, convincing them to surrender to his empty pistol. The .45 on his hip was the same one he'd carried into battle that day.

During Desert Storm, Gunslinger led the deepest, fastest attack in world history, moving Airborne forces 770 kilometers in a hundred hours, capturing 5,000 enemy soldiers and enough equipment to outfit three 15,000-man divisions. "The road home is through Baghdad," he had told his men. As his forces advanced he told them that Saddam Hussein was like the king of Babylon in the Old Testament: "Thus shall Babylon sink, to rise no more," he read from the book of Joshua, "because of the disaster I am bringing upon her."

When his forces reached the Euphrates River and the advance to Baghdad was called off by Washington, Fairbank had been furious. In full view of armed Iraqi soldiers on the other side, he had unzipped his fly and relieved himself in the Euphrates to demonstrate his disgust.

Even now as the corps commander, he made regular parachute jumps, trained in the martial arts at the unconventional warfare school, and kept up his marksmanship on the range. For the young soldiers standing before him, he was a living, breathing, American hero, a throwback to the days of Patton and Bradley—when a general was a soldier first and a manager second.

Next to Fairbank stood Sergeant Major Tom McCarthy. A sternfaced, raw-boned man with a large scar on his right cheek, McCarthy was the highest ranking NCO in the Airborne Corps. And he had been put there by Fairbank.

Fairbank scanned his troops as he paced silently in front of their ranks.

"At ease," he growled. Then he walked up and down the line some more. The wind was grabbing at him, audibly snapping at the flag that flew behind them. "I guess you all heard, boys, that I lost my brother today. I didn't like Dean a great deal. He and I never got along, not for ten straight minutes in our lives. But I voted for him. Hell, he was my brother. What kind of worthless son of a bitch would vote against his own flesh and blood? He was the president of the United States. He was my commander in chief."

The general pointed at the flag behind the men. "Turn around. Look at the flag." The men turned and stared at the red, white, and blue cloth writhing in the air above them. "That's *our* flag, boys. From buck private to general officer, from street sweeper to president, black, white, brown, Christian, Muslim, Jew—we are all brothers beneath those stars. Today a bunch of sons of bitches are out there trying to tear that flag down and spit on it. You and I, we have been appointed to the greatest privilege in the world, to defend what that flag represents, against all enemies, foreign and domestic. That flag, boys, it's not like the flag of France or the flag of Spain or the flag of Japan. It doesn't represent a piece of ground or a bunch of people who just happen to speak the same language. It represents something eternal and pure. An idea. The rare and crazy notion that all men are created equal. That flag stands as a beacon to the world that says, 'We are all brothers.'

"Brotherhood has a special meaning to the men of our profession. We *know* what it means to trust another man with our lives. To carry a man on our back through gunfire. To bust into a room full of enemies, trusting that the man behind us will not shoot us in the back. To die even, sometimes, bleeding into the arms of a comrade-in-arms. That is our privilege, boys. That is our privilege and our sacred trust!"

The soldiers cheered and put their fists in the air. He raised one hand, and they went silent.

"I serve in a mighty Airborne Force—famed for deeds in war—renowned for readiness in peace," the general began, reciting the airborne creed in a stentorian voice. "It is my pledge in all that I am—in all that I do." The soldiers now joined in, their voices creating a deep rumble that echoed across the concrete. "I am an elite trooper—a sky trooper—a spearhead trooper . . ." The creed continued, line after line until its conclusion: "In peace or war I never fail. Anywhere, anytime, in anything—I AM AIRBORNE!"

The men roared until he quieted them with a raised hand.

"We have been called to get in those planes and fly up to our nation's capital and protect that flag. But remember, each of you, as you go to your posts today, that our ultimate duty is not to that flag, but to what that flag represents."

Some of the soldiers looked at him curiously, like they'd lost the thread of what he was talking about.

"I have lost a brother today. Well, so have you all. You are all my brothers, boys. You are all my brothers. Make me proud!"

Another cheer ran through the ranks.

Fairbank turned quickly away from his men, looked off into the distance. He felt something on his cheek, running down the side of his nose. "I'm not crying am I, Sergeant McCarthy?" he said quietly to the hard-bitten noncom standing next to him.

"Hell, no, sir!" Sergeant Major McCarthy said.

"You're a kind man, Sergeant," Fairbank said.

"I believe the general has misspoken, sir. No one has ever accused me of that before."

"You're right, Sergeant." The general surreptitiously wiped his eyes, then turned to watch his young soldiers as they filed onto the waiting C-130s. "What I meant to say is you're the meanest, saltiest, ugliest old bastard this side of hell."

"I'm undeserving of such munificent praise, sir." McCarthy didn't even crack a smile. "Fine-looking young men, General."

"The best, Tom. The best. And I want to protect our investment. Give me a back-channel line of communication with the men of the 505th."

McCarthy's brow furrowed. "A back channel, sir?"

"Yes. They'll be under the command of the National Command Center at the Pentagon using a SATCOM system. I want a way to communicate with them that NCC is not privy to. Give the boys some old TRQs, the high-freq radios, with Turkey-43 encryption. And set up a channel into my office."

"Isn't that a little unusual, General?"

"It's a little unusual seeing me crying like some six-year-old girl too, isn't it? Nothing that's happening right now is usual. That's why I'm asking you to take care of this personally. And keep it under your hat."

13

FBI Gulfstream IV,
33,000 Feet above Fort Wayne, Indiana
4:15 PM

THE HANDLER was not talking. When asked who he was, he just repeated the same thing over and over. "I am a patriotic American citizen. I love my country. I have nothing else to say."

The FBI agent accompanying the Chicago bomber's handler was a sincere-looking fellow named Davis who had gotten hired by the Bureau because of his expertise in tax accounting. "We have you on tape, sir," he told the handcuffed man in the chair. "You dropped Barry Dale Crooks off in front of the Mercantile Exchange with a bomb and a radio tuned to the same frequency as the radio in your car. Your car contained thirty sticks of dynamite, several Ruger Mini 14 semiautomatic rifles, and over two thousand rounds of ammunition."

"I am a patriotic American citizen. I have nothing to say."

The thin, dark man in the back corner of the aircraft lit a cheap cigar and rolled his eyes. Agent Davis wasn't really sure who the dark-skinned man was. He had been told that the man was with some supersecret unit—Something-or-other Section—which Davis had never heard of. Davis assumed he was CIA. But maybe not. In the confusion he had not been very well briefed before he left the Chicago field office. The dark-skinned man had two other men with them, young soldier-looking guys—one white and one African-American—who carried submachine guns. The stink of cheap cigar started wafting through the cabin.

Agent Davis went back and asked the dark-skinned man to put out the cigar. The FBI had strict regulations about smoking on government property. The dark-skinned man blew smoke through his long blade of a nose and said, "I've just gotten a call from Colonel Campos, who is in charge of this investigation. She has instructed me to interrogate the witness. For your protection, I'd advise you to go sit up in the cockpit."

"Excuse me?"

"Go sit up in the cockpit." The man had a hint of a South American accent, but he was obviously completely fluent in English.

"This is *my* prisoner," Davis said hotly.

"Not anymore." The man's black eyes glittered slightly. "You gave it the old college try, my dear friend, and you failed. People are dying, and results are required."

"I don't understand what you're saying."

"Do you want to talk to Colonel Campos?" The dark-skinned man held out his cell phone. "She is operating under the personal authority of Mr. Rancy, the acting AG."

"She really said that?" Agent Davis said finally. "That I'm supposed to go sit in the cockpit?"

"No, my friend. That's just my personal advice."

Agent Davis felt like he was in the middle of something that wasn't like anything he'd ever been involved in. Agent Davis liked a nice set of rules, liked everything laid out, what was right, what was wrong, what his responsibility was. But right now it was all a big frightening mess. He studied the face of the man from Whatever-it-was Section, but that only made things worse. It had something to do with the look in the dark-skinned man's eyes, a lack of concern, a lack of compassion, a lack of almost anything human at all. It was like looking into the eyes of a hawk or a crocodile.

The dark-skinned man walked over to the handler and said, "Agent Davis has asked me to extinguish my cigar. I'd sure hate to get in trouble with the FBI, huh?" Then he stuck the cigar in the handler's eye. It made a crackling sound, and the handcuffed man in the chair screamed in agony and then spat out a curse.

Agent Davis decided to go sit in the cockpit. With the door closed. The dark-skinned man was right. There were some things it was better not to know about.

It only took a minute before the screaming started.

Camp David
4:28 PM

SAC Leonard Smith called to his assistant, "Where are those phone records? I need those phone records on Delaney."

"They're just coming through, sir," the young woman said. She pulled a stack of paper out of her printer, then handed them to him.

Mary Campos came and looked over Smith's shoulder. "I don't see anything especially suspicious on his home phone or his cell records," Smith said. Smith was looking at the most recent month. She was relieved, knowing there would be no calls to her in the past few months.

"Wait, look here . . ." Smith flipped over to another sheet. "We've got a terminal-by-terminal breakdown of calls from the Secret Service. Let's see, this one is apparently his line at the White House. Son of a *gun*. There it is . . . eighteen calls to Anniston, Alabama." He snapped his finger at a nearby agent who was busy typing something into a laptop computer. "Pull up this number."

The agent took the paper, typed the number into his computer. "Comes up to Paul Miller, 212 Cherry Blossom Lane."

"Oh, yeah!" Smith said jubilantly. "I knew this guy was wrong. I *knew* it! There's our smoking gun."

Mary Campos felt much less happy about the discovery. She had thought she was really in love with Delaney. Then, boom, he had disappeared on her. Angry as she was at him for abandoning her, she couldn't quite believe that he would sell his government and his job and his president down the river.

But there was no time to think about it though. Too much work to be done. Right now they had to follow the evidence. If Delaney was guilty, the FBI would figure it out. If he wasn't, they'd find that out too.

Washington, DC
6:40 PM

About the time the plane transporting the Chicago Merc bomber's handler landed at Reagan National Airport, the dark-skinned man came in the door carrying a legal pad. There were a couple of spots of red liquid on the yellow paper.

"It's basically a matter of rapport," the dark-skinned man said. "I just had to cozy up to him a little and he turned into a real Chatty Cathy. His name is Ron Baker. He's the number-three man in the Brotherhood. Here's a list of sixteen cells in the organization, their leadership, and most of the locations where they train."

Agent Davis took the paper tentatively. "I'll take custody of my prisoner again."

"Oh, I forgot to mention," the dark-skinned man said. "That poor fellow was apparently in much worse health than you would have thought by looking at him. He suffered a heart attack during our Q&A session. Sadly, we were unable to resuscitate him."

Suddenly Agent Davis felt very afraid.

"Don't worry, my friend," the dark-skinned man said with a pleasant smile. "We'll take care of all the paperwork."

DAY TWO

14

Western Maryland
6:40 AM

EVENTUALLY the falling snow had entirely covered the Suburban, darkening the interior of the truck so that it was impossible to tell if it was day or night. Toward the end of the afternoon Delaney had begun shivering uncontrollably. He had curled up in a fetal position, but his thin clothes just weren't enough to warm him. He searched the interior of the FBI truck, but there were no warm clothes. Two shotguns, an MP5, high-explosive and fragmentation grenades, thousands of rounds of ammunition, a brace of 1911s, two rolls of duct tape. But nothing with any insulating qualities.

He knew that if he spent all night in this kind of cold, he would likely die of hypothermia. That was when he realized: seat cushions. The foam seat cushions would make excellent insulators. He had pulled out his handmade Emerson tactical folding knife and slit open the vinyl seats, ripped out the three-inch-thick foam and wrapped himself up like the Michelin man, looping duct tape to hold the whole mess together. Half an hour later he had stopped shivering. He had lain in the rear deck of the truck all night. He had not slept, not for one minute.

AT DAYBREAK he had decided it was time to move. It was a risk to move. But it was a risk to stay too. If they still had choppers in the air—and in all likelihood they did—he would expose himself as soon as he went in motion. But the longer he stayed in the area, the sooner a dog patrol or a sharp-eyed cop or a hunter might stumble across him.

He strapped the MP5 across his chest on a tactical sling, then climbed out of the door of the Suburban. The sun was just brightening the horizon. The snow had ceased falling sometime during the night, and the sky was completely clear. One hundred percent visibility. That was bad. He quickly cut several branches off a small pine tree near him, lashing them together with duct tape. Then he threw them over his shoulder, climbed up the hill, and began hiking down the side of the dirt road on the ridge above. His feet were wet and cold inside his thin Rockports. The going was slow. He had to hop from tree to tree in an attempt not to leave a trail of footprints that would be easily visible from the air. He'd been lucky yesterday: the falling snow and the haphazardness of the initial helicopter pursuit had masked his retreat. Today was clear and bright. He'd have to be careful and smart. By the time he'd made a klick or so, he was drenched in sweat from the exertion; but his toes were numb. Another kilometer and his fingers had started going too.

In the distance he heard the blades of a helicopter coming over the mountain to the northwest. He figured they'd be going slow, working a north-south grid. That gave him about a minute. He leaned the pine branches he'd gathered against a tree, covered them with snow, then crouched underneath them. The chopper thundered over about thirty seconds later. It seemed to pause—but maybe that was just his imagination. He held his breath so the cloud of warm air from his lungs wouldn't leave a red smear on the FLIR screen in the air above him. He could hear the beating of his heart even over the sound of the chopper.

But then it was gone.

He stepped out from beneath his shelter of pine branches and continued down the snow-covered track. Within a few hundred meters the forest cleared. In the distance—maybe another klick or so—he saw a farmhouse with smoke pouring out the chimney. To heck with it, he thought: time's a-wastin'. He gave up on trying to mask his tracks and began running at maximum speed toward the house, the MP5 cradled in his arms.

When he reached the house, several dogs began barking wildly inside. He approached the front door and knocked hard. An aging man, his hair squashed down like he'd been wearing a baseball cap on his head, answered the door. He carried a nice old Browning over-and-under in his hand and had a plug of tobacco in his cheek. Two yellow dogs poked their noses out the door at his knees, still barking.

Delaney showed his badge quickly without revealing his name. "Secret Service, sir. I assume you've been watching the news?" Delaney said. "I'm part of the dragnet here. I got separated from my team and my radio's on the fritz."

The old man eyed him suspiciously.

"You mind lowering that shotgun?" Delaney said. "I'd like to step inside for a moment."

The old man spit some tobacco out the door. "Don't see no need of your coming inside," he said.

Delaney had a moment of hesitation. When he'd fired at the HRT truck he felt moderately justified. Those were men paid to put their lives on the line. And he was pretty sure he hadn't hurt them anyway. But this old codger was just a civilian. Delaney didn't want to put a gun to this man's head.

"Sir, I'm cold, I'm separated from my people, I'm bushed, and my radio's not working. I just need to use your phone."

"Wouldn't do you no good. I stopped paying the bills after them fools kept overcharging me. Caller ID? I don't got no caller ID. Charged me a dollar-ten-a-month for caller ID, after I'd done told them three times in a row, I don't got no caller ID, don't want no caller ID, wouldn't know what to do with it if I had it." The man looked at Delaney's feet. "City shoes, huh? You ain't dressed real good for somebody that's supposedly out beating the bushes for an assassin."

Delaney smiled. "You're not kidding."

"Federal guvment," he said, disgustedly. "I was with the Marines at Chosin Reservoir. Uncle Sam didn't give us no decent boots there, neither. It ain't right, Uncle Sam putting a man out there in harm's way in the snow, don't give him a decent pair of boots." He sighed theatrically. "I s'pose if you want to come in and have a cup of coffee, I could spare you a change of socks or something. Keep you going till you find your buddies."

"Thank you, sir, I wouldn't mind. That's very kind."

They went inside, and Delaney sat in the kitchen at a round wooden table on which sat a salt shaker and a rusting coffee can with an inch of tobacco spit in the bottom. The house was fragrant with the odor of dog and Red Man tobacco. Delaney had never been so glad to be in a stuffy, smelly, overheated house in his life. The dogs stopped barking once they'd gotten a good smell of him and done a little slobbering on his hands. The old man clumped gimpily back into a hallway, came out with a pair of socks and some old work boots, then poured Delaney a cup of steaming coffee from an ancient blue enamel coffeepot on the stove.

"Looks like these here boots might fit you. My shiftless boy bought them to hunt in, didn't never even use them."

Delaney stripped off his shoes and socks. His toes were bluish white.

The old man squinted clinically at his feet. "Yep. Yep. Couple more hours out there, by God, they'd be sawing off your toes. You want to see mine? I lost three of them in *Ko*-rea. Turned black, plumb fell right off."

"Please, don't trouble yourself," Delaney said.

"Course, frostbite, hell, that was the least of our problems. Lost eighty percent of my company to the Chinese. Poorest country in the world, them Commies still had sense enough to spend money on a decent pair of boots."

Delaney nodded, pulled on the new socks and shoes. The boots were a little big, but they were better than his frozen Rockports. After a couple of minutes listening to the old man talk about his war experiences, pins and needles started shooting through his feet as warmth and circulation returned. The heat, the languid conversation, the coffee, the return of feeling in his feet—these all conspired to make him feel drowsy and complacent. Which was not good. You got comfortable, you got lazy and let down your guard.

"Don't get me wrong," the old man said. "I ain't no Commie lover. This here's the greatest nation in the world."

"Amen to that," Delaney said, draining the coffee. He set the cup down. "I guess I better get back out there."

The old man eyed him for a moment, dribbled some spit into an old coffee can, then said, "You really in kind of a fix, ain't you?"

"Yes, sir, I am."

He hesitated then said, "Wait here."

The old man came back out wearing a camouflaged hunting jacket and a stained wreck of a hat with the Massey Ferguson logo on the brim. "Let's go, son." He led Delaney out the front door and into the frozen yard. Delaney followed, the old man's two mangy yellow dogs in tow, as he crossed the yard toward an aging GMC truck.

"Might could loan it to you," he said. "Just to get you back to your buddies."

Delaney's heart soared. "Thank you, sir!"

"You'll have to push her," the old man said. "She ain't got no starter."

The old man got in the driver's side, turned the key, pressed on the clutch. "Okay, son, start a-pushing!" Delaney pushed the ancient truck. For a moment he was afraid he wouldn't be able to get the truck moving out of the frozen rut, but after a little rocking the truck started inching forward. "Push, boy, push!"

Finally the truck got up a little speed on the frozen ground and the old man dropped the clutch. The engine roared to life. The old man shifted into neutral, then got out. "There you go, son," he said. "She ain't got no heat but, by God, she'll take you 'bout where you want to go."

"You saved my life, sir," Delaney said. "I won't forget this."

"Just catch them dadgum fellows that killed the president."

"You better believe that's high on my list right now," Delaney said. "I'll get this truck back as soon as I can."

"Take your time. I ain't going nowhere till this snow melts."

Delaney put the truck in gear and drove off. In the rearview mirror the old man was stroking one of his dogs with one hand, waving with the other.

Norbert Justice went inside his house feeling warm and pleased with himself. It wasn't every day you got the opportunity to help out a real-life G-man. Or was he Secret Service? Norbert hadn't quite caught what the fellow said. Poor dumb city boy out tromping around in his Sunday-go-to-meeting clothes, looked half froze to death.

Norbert went in the kitchen, poured himself a cup of coffee, then went into the living room to look at the TV. Every channel was covering the assassination business nonstop. They kept showing the fellow that had done it. Then they talked about how it was some type of conspiracy, that some other fellow from the Secret Service had been in on it. There was something familiar looking about the face of the Secret Service fellow who'd helped kill President Fairbank.

Norbert didn't see too good no more, what with the cataracts and all. After a minute he got up and put on his glasses, squinted at the TV some more. What he saw gave him a funny feeling in the pit of his stomach. Uh-oh, he was thinking. Dadgum it, if that wasn't the fellow he'd just gave his truck to. He was so mad he could spit.

He got up and went to the phone, then remembered it was dead. Maybe he shouldn't have been in such a hurry to get in a fight with them morons at the phone company. He sighed. Well, he'd just have to take a ride in the Chevy, get himself down to the sheriff's office, let them know what a fool thing he'd just done.

Maybe he'd have to embroider the story a little so he didn't come off so gullible. Tell them he'd been held at gunpoint, something of that nature.

"Sophie! Albert!" The dogs came running. "Y'all want to take a little ride?"

Camp David
11:29 AM

SAC Leonard Smith set down the phone, then punched his fist into the palm of his hand.

"What?" Mary Campos called to him from the other side of the room.

"We've got contact!" Smith yelled. "A farmer spotted Delaney around seven-thirty this morning. He says Delaney stole his truck at gunpoint. The old man says he got off one round at him with a shotgun, but isn't sure if he hit him or not."

"Seven-thirty!" Mary Campos said. "How come we don't find out about this until three hours later?"

"The old man says he was tied up," Smith said. "Once he finally got free, the roads were so bad he ended up in a ditch. Took him a while to get out of the ditch."

"Oh for God's sake." Mary hadn't slept all night and was starting to get irritable. "Do you realize what this means?" She pulled out a map, pinned it on the wall, then drew a big red circle with a marker. Inside the circle were Washington, DC; Baltimore; Charlottesville; Wilmington; and the southern suburbs of Philadelphia. "That circle represents everything within three hours of here. He could be anywhere by now!"

Old Executive Office Building
11:33 AM

In a small room in the basement of the Old Executive Office Building, Dirk Pardee, head of Unit P, received a phone call from Smith at the FBI. And like Colonel Campos, he immediately drew a red circle on the map indicating how far Delaney could have traveled in the previous three hours. With Pardee was his best team—eight men he'd trained himself. A year ago, Badger had been associated with the CIA,

Runnels had been doing security for a Kurdish political faction, and the others had been working various dull industry jobs here in the States. They'd all jumped at the chance when he'd told them about Unit P.

Pardee was not a *what-do-you-think-guys?* kind of commander. He preferred to do the thinking and let the subordinates do what he told them to. "All right," he said. "Our boy grew up in South Carolina. He has no known connections with either Philadelphia or Baltimore. The roads are bad to the north. Let's rule this out." He drew a large red squiggle across the top of the map. "Only an idiot would attempt to hide in a small or medium-size town. Places like that, everybody went to high school with somebody or whatever, people talk, you'd be too conspicuous. He drew another squiggle across western and southern Virginia. "He wants to hide out, he's got two choices: head for the hills or go to a large metro area. A guy like Delaney, he could do either one comfortably. DC is home territory for him. So is this part of South Carolina." He drew a circle around the northwestern corner of South Carolina. "Also he's got kin in northern Alabama, this Paul Miller guy that runs the Brotherhood."

Pardee eyed the map. "Northern Alabama, and northern South Carolina, these are both the tag end of the Appalachians. Wooded, remote—he's probably hunted and fished these places all his life." He tapped the map thoughtfully. "According to the intel that Gonzalez got yesterday from the Chicago guy, the Brotherhood has a bunch of hide sites in Alabama. Delaney knows this. Therefore he knows those hills will be swarming with Feds. Therefore it's down to two places." He slashed at the map with the red pen. "Here and here."

There were two circles on the map now: Washington, DC, and a small area around the tiny town of Walhalla, South Carolina.

He eyed the map for a long time. "I know Delaney. Delaney's a proactive guy, not the kind of guy who likes to play defense. He's not gonna hide, not just yet. He's gonna come right at us." He marked an X through the South Carolina circle. "Men, he's within ten miles of this room."

The eight tough men in the room nodded in agreement. The analysis was flawless.

"The FBI is sitting on his house, his friends' houses, his ex-wife's former house, his bank, his grocery store, his former bank, his former banker's grocery store, the whole works. He knows this. So what's his next move? As we speak, he's ditching the old man's truck and stealing . . . let's see . . . a ten-year-old full-size van, probably with tinted windows and commercial markings on the side."

More nods all around.

"So what do we do?" Badger said. Badger was a stocky, muscular man from Wisconsin—hence the name.

"NSA is tracking every phone number the guy has ever called. He's going to call one of those numbers. The second he does, we know where he's calling from. We get a chopper in the air and we look for that van. Got it?"

The men nodded.

"All right then. Let's get over to the chopper. It's hurry up and wait time."

Beltsville, MD
11:31 AM

Heat. Michael Delaney had felt precious little in twenty-four hours. So after he parked the old man's truck in the parking lot at a Motel 6 in Beltsville, jimmied the lock on an aging Chevy van and climbed in and hotwired it. He cranked up the heat full blast, then started driving. The van was perfect. Well maintained, tinted windows, all kinds of plumbing tools in the back. You never knew when a propane torch or a right-angle drill might come in handy.

The heat flooded him with a feeling of goodwill, which in turn made him want to sleep. He almost ran off the road, bringing on a flood of adrenaline, which perked him up a little. Sleep was not an option—not yet.

He drove through Beltsville until he found a Wal-Mart at the intersection of five streets. The more escape routes you left yourself, the better. He sat for a few minutes letting the heat soak into his body, then got out into the cold again and walked into a store where he bought a pair of insulated boots, six pairs of wool socks, six pairs of underpants, an insulated brown jumpsuit, a bag of beef jerky, a pint of milk, and a cheap but well-insulated hunting jacket camouflaged with Mossy Oak Breakup, a camo pattern that was vastly superior to anything the United States Army ever used and perfectly suited to eastern forests. He paid cash, thankful he'd just taken a couple of hundred dollars out of the bank two days earlier. He left Wal-Mart with thirty-one dollars and change.

There was a pay phone outside the Wal-Mart. He dialed a number. "Jamie?"

The line was silent for a moment.

"Jamie, it's Delaney." James Bannerman was a doctor at the Bethesda Naval Medical Center. He'd been a corpsman in the army, then left and gone to medical school. They had been friends for nearly twenty years.

"Look . . . ," Bannerman said.

"Did you get the thing I sent you?"

"Yeah, but . . ."

"I didn't do what they said I did. Okay, Jamie? You know me, Jamie. I've been framed."

His friend sighed. "Okay, yeah, I had the lab run a chem panel on it."

"And?"

"It came up positive for barbiturates."

"Have you called the FBI yet?"

"No."

"Good. Don't. Write up a report, sign and date it, then lock it in a safe somewhere. Put the vial in a locked refrigerator and leave it there. Don't speak to anybody until I tell you to. I have to go."

He hung up and sprinted for the truck. One minute. If the FBI was doing their job, they'd have trap-and-traces on the phones of his close acquaintances, looking for suspicious calls. A call from a pay phone would definitely qualify as suspicious. Which meant there was a strong possibility they'd be scrambling a chopper by now. Probably HRT or Delta. It would take them ten minutes, minimum, to get there. The Beltsville police would be quicker, but they had too many entrances to cover and didn't know what he was driving. So he should be okay.

Not that that was reason to dawdle.

As he started to back out, a car pulled in behind him and stopped. Delaney waited a few seconds, then a few more, then a few more. A minute went by, and still the car behind him didn't budge. He didn't want to make a scene. But he couldn't wait much longer. He backed up a few feet and blew his horn. The woman in the car behind him, a Cadillac, studiously ignored him. He waited another ten seconds. She didn't move as she waited for a man to get in his car and open up a parking spot. Now Delaney was getting nervous. The man getting in the car she was waiting for was talking on his cell phone. They could be there for a while. He climbed out of the truck, ran over to the Cadillac.

"Ma'am," he called through the window, "would you mind backing up just a hair so I can get out?"

The driver of the car, an extremely large woman with a pile of dyed red hair and chins that lapped over the collar of her sweater, stared straight ahead. One of those people who'd sit for five minutes waiting for a parking space close to the store in order to save a thirty-yard walk.

"Ma'am," he said. "Ma'am! I'm in kind of an emergency."

The woman had her lips pursed, eyes straight ahead, knowing full well that she was in his way and not caring. He knocked hard on the window. Finally she turned, looked at him sourly. He smiled, pointed at his stolen truck, then made a sweeping motion with his hands, indicating the direction he wanted her to move. She sighed, as though she had been asked to perform some herculean task, then turned her head slowly to the front again and ignored him.

He weighed the advantages and disadvantages of putting his boot through her window. Probably not prudent. He knocked again. A tiny smile crept onto the woman's face. She was enjoying herself. He looked at his watch. Three and a half minutes since he made his call.

"Thanks a lot, lady!" Delaney called, smiling brightly at her. "You're too kind, really."

He climbed back in the van, backed up, and blew the horn. Still the woman in the Cadillac didn't move. Four minutes.

Finally the car she was waiting for backed out, and the woman edged forward into the now-vacant spot. He backed up, dropped the truck in gear, then pulled slowly out of the Wal-Mart parking lot. But by that time police cars were converging from all directions, lights flashing. They were too late though. He was onto Baltimore Avenue heading toward the Loop just as they started bailing out of their cars and holding up the traffic coming out of the shopping center.

Delaney permitted himself a small grin. It had been close—but he'd made it.

He'd made it about half a mile down the road when his grin faded.

A chopper was coming over the rise. Not an FBI chopper, not Maryland State Patrol—this was an Air Force helicopter, an MH-53M Pave Low, the kind run by the AFSOC, the Air Force Special Operations Command, the guys who supported SOCOM special ops guys. Men in black Kevlar were hanging on the skids. Delta maybe? Possibly HRT. Hard to know. But it was okay, he thought. They didn't know what he was driving.

The Pave Low thundered over his head. He kept driving, waiting for the chopper to appear in his rearview mirror. But it didn't. He pressed the accelerator a little harder, nudging his speed up to sixty. Suddenly the chopper descended in his rearview right into the path of the oncoming traffic. Cars skidded and slewed back and forth on the road.

He reached over for the MP5, pulled back the slide. But then he threw it on the floor. No, if they got him, they got him. First, a shoot-out with the FBI's Hostage Rescue Team or with the Delta Force hot-shots, would certainly result in his death. But aside from that, they were just honest guys, guys like him trying to do their jobs. No way was he going to widow the wife or orphan the kids of a decent cop or soldier just doing his job. No way.

He let his foot come off the accelerator. It was all over. He felt a curious sense of exhaustion coming over him as the van began to slow.

LIEUTENANT COLONEL DIRK PARDEE was the first man out of the chopper. He had a 1911 in one hand and a megaphone in the other.

"Turn off the engine!" he screamed into the megaphone. Behind him the other Unit P operators swarmed out of the Pave Low and fanned out around the vehicle, their MP5s trained on the tinted windshield of the big white van.

"Careful, guys," Pardee yelled. Then, into the megaphone, "Open the driver's-side window, Delaney, and put both your hands out the window, with the keys in your right hand."

The tinted window came down a crack. Two trembling hands slipped out through the two-inch crack.

"Badger, I want you to take the door," he yelled. "Benston, I want you to jam him back into the driver's side. Make it look like he's struggling."

"Yes, sir," Benston said. They'd already been over the takedown procedure in the chopper. But Pardee was a belt-and-suspender man.

"Then you shoot him in the head. I don't want him alive."

"Yes, sir."

Pardee pointed at Badger, then at the door. The short beefy operator grabbed the door and yanked it open. Immediately Benston was through the door and wrestling.

"Shoot!" Pardee screamed. "What are you waiting for! Shoot!"

But then he came around the door and saw what was going on. The man in the front seat of the car wasn't Delaney. It was some Hispanic guy in a painter's uniform.

"I ain't do nothing!" the man was yelling in heavily accented English. "I ain't do nothing!"

"Back in the bird!" Pardee yelled.

Unit P piled back into the Pave Low, and they thundered up off the highway, leaving the bewildered painter lying on the front seat of his truck. They reached the parking lot of the Wal-Mart thirty seconds later.

"Hate to tell you," Badger said as they flew over the lot. "This is a blue-collar area. Lots of regular, working-class folks. You know what every single one of those jokers drives?"

Pardee cursed. He didn't need the answer: it was right there below him. There were probably five hundred cars in the parking lot. And there must have been fifty full-size vans, ladders stacked on top, words stenciled on the side.

15

The Oval Office
2:15 PM

PRESIDENT MORGAN BOYD ushered General Bill Fairbank into his office and offered him a seat. There was only one other person in the room, the new attorney general nominee, John Rancy. Rancy didn't rise, didn't move, didn't speak. It was almost as though he were not in the room at all.

"Coffee, General?" Boyd said.

"Wouldn't mind a cup, Mr. President. Didn't get much sleep last night."

Morgan Boyd poured the coffee himself, then sat. The president didn't sit behind his desk but instead sat across from the general on another of the upholstered chairs that were gathered in the center of the room. Rancy sat on the other side of the room studying a thick, bound volume of some sort. He seemed to be ignoring them entirely—though Bill Fairbank knew that certainly would not be the case.

"First," Boyd said, "I wanted to say how sorry I am about your brother."

"Thank you, Mr. President."

Boyd sat silently, collecting himself. Fairbank watched him carefully. He'd never liked the man or agreed with his politics—but he admired Boyd's toughness. Toughness was a quality that meant something in Bill Fairbank's world.

Finally Boyd said, "I was born on a ranch. Didn't much like it. I'd rather read a book than fix fences in zero-degree weather. But there's one thing I'm grateful for about growing up where I did. The people I grew up around were practical, and they spoke their minds without beating around the bush. I kept that habit. So let me speak my mind.

I just got shot. Your brother just got shot too. A thing like that makes you mad and it colors your judgment. Sometimes you make rash decisions. But here's the thing, General, I'm paid to make the tough decisions. And I'm making one today."

"Yes, Mr. President."

"Intel that the FBI has developed today indicates that the people who shot your brother are affiliated with a group called the Brotherhood, which is centered in Alabama. We've got the locations of a number of their training centers and weapons caches. What we're looking at is more than just a couple of angry rednecks. These guys are smarter and better funded than any domestic terror group ever. What we're in the middle of is an insurrection, General."

Bill Fairbank had a hunch he knew where this was going. As far as he was concerned his paratroopers had been called to the nation's capital primarily as a confidence-building measure for the American public and not for any military purpose. They had deployed at various government buildings, set up checkpoints along the Mall—but they were not actually accomplishing anything of military significance. He was afraid that was about to change. And if it did, it was going to put him in a bind.

"General, the Posse Commitatus Act of 1878 prohibits the use of American military forces within the borders of the United States. There are sound historical reasons why this law was passed. But like all reasonable rules, there are invariably exceptions. There may be as many as five hundred members of this Brotherhood, scattered throughout several states. They have bombs, guns, training facilities, and they may have even developed chemical and/or biological weapons. I'm going to have to send in military units against these people. I don't have any choice."

Morgan Boyd stopped speaking, met the general's gaze. Fairbank didn't say anything.

"General, there's a disease abroad in this world. It's robbed you of your brother, and me of my wife. Every day terrorists blow up children in Israel, cut off people's arms in Africa, kidnap missionaries in the Philippines, shoot old women in Kashmir . . ." His face was hard. "The time for half measures came and went a long time ago. Foreign aid and soft words will destroy our world. It's time to get out the hammer and start knocking these people down. Not reactively, not in some limp-wristed, piecemeal way. But in a consistent, clear, rigorous way. Right up and down the line, General. Up and down the line, across the globe. I believe the world is balanced on the edge of a precipice. If the United States has the will, we can usher the globe into a period of prosperity and stability unmatched in history. But if we sit around wringing our hands, we will watch as the promise of democracy slips away, replaced by warlordism, religious mania, sectarian violence, ethnic and tribal conflict. There will be a reign of death and terror like nothing we've ever seen. It'll be Rwanda from one side of the map to the other."

Boyd stood and looked out the window.

"It's easy to sit here in this room and be complacent, to say, 'Oh, the world's always been a mess, these things will sort themselves out.'" The president shook his head. "Uh-uh, 9/11 was just the prelude, General. If we don't act now, if we don't act boldly, how long before somebody sets off a nuke in Times Square? How long before some angry scientist in Tajikistan decides to uncork that stash of smallbox he's been keeping back there with the strawberry Popsicles in his freezer? How long, General? How long? And if that happens, what kind of blood scourge will the people of the United States unleash on the world? Hm?"

"You're preaching that particular issue to the choir, Mr. President," Fairbank said.

"Good." Boyd looked at him with his black, canny eyes. "In the long run, I believe our real challenge will be from foreign rather than domestic terror. But we've still got to clean up our own backyard. You understand what that means, don't you?"

"You're asking if I'm willing to command my boys to shoot American citizens."

"If worst comes to worst, yes."

Bill Fairbank was not an indecisive man. If you'd asked him the question forty-eight hours earlier, he'd have said, absolutely not. But something in him had changed since Morgan Boyd had called to tell him that his brother had been murdered. Fairbank still didn't like the idea of troops on Main Street, but it didn't seem as unthinkable as it had before. "Mr. President, I'm opposed to using U.S. troops against American citizens."

"American citizens? I'm talking about people who are making war against the United States. I'd say they've pretty much renounced their citizenship."

He had a point.

"General," Boyd continued, "law enforcement will be overwhelmed by these people. There are too many of them, and they're too well armed. You command the forces most appropriate to move against the Brotherhood. I'm not asking a hypothetical question. I'm going to give you an order. What I want to know is, will you obey that order or not? Somebody is going to obey that order. If not you, somebody else. So, General, will you fight these murderers and terrorists, or will you stand on the sidelines waving pom-poms while other men do the work?"

Fairbank didn't answer.

"I need a hammer, General. Not just for the next few weeks, but for the historic task that lies before me. Will you be that hammer?"

The general leaned back in his chair and thought for a long time.

Bill Fairbank and his brother had fought all the time when they were kids. Dean had been the elder, the fair-haired boy, the mother's favorite. Bill Fairbank had always resented his brother's easy manner, his talents, the way things seemed to just come to him without effort. Whereas Bill had had to scratch and claw and fight for everything he'd ever gotten. But there was one thing that had united the two. Call it blood. Bill had been three years younger than his brother. Once, in elementary school, an older kid had taken a dislike to Bill and started tormenting him every day. Bill had fought back, but the bully was so much bigger, he couldn't really defend himself. In passing one day Dean had mentioned the bully to their father. Their father had given Dean a hard look and said, 'What kind of brother are you, letting a thing like that go on?' The next day before school when the bully punched Bill in the stomach and threw his books on the floor, Dean approached the bully and said one word: "Don't." The bully—who was older and larger than Dean—had laughed at Dean and said, 'Or else what?' Dean had departed from his usual pattern of smooth talk that day: he had proceeded to methodically beat the bully to the floor. That was the last time the bully had ever bothered Bill Fairbank. But it was also the last time Bill had ever let someone fight a fight for him. There were two messages he had taken to heart that day. First, sometimes the strong had to step up and do nasty things to defend the weak. And, second, that you never, never, *ever* let somebody mess with your brother.

"I want *you*, General," Boyd said. "Not somebody else. You're hands-down the man for this job. So I'll give you twenty-four hours to think it through. By noon tomorrow I either want your resignation or your enthusiastic support for our cause."

Fairbank rose from his chair and saluted. "Yes, Mr. President."

AFTER FAIRBANK LEFT, Morgan Boyd turned to John Rancy and said, "What do you think?"

Rancy looked off into the distance, eyes narrowed. "He'll say yes. The fallen prince's brother girds up his loins, climbs on his steed, and rides out seeking vengeance. Very Shakespearean. It'll make fabulous TV."

"That's not what I'm asking."

Rancy laughed. "Regardless what he decides, he'll need to be watched, Mr. President."

"That's what I think too."

16

Merryvale Apartments, Connecticut Avenue,
Washington, DC
6:21 PM

MARY CAMPOS had not slept in a day and a half, so she had decided it was time for a rest and a change of clothes. Once she got home, though, she was so wired she felt sure she wouldn't sleep, so she changed into a pair of sweats and took her customary run through Rock Creek Park, around past a row of Gulf State legations, and then back up to her apartment.

She opened the door to her apartment, her gray track suit stained with sweat, and flipped on the light. Only the bulb was burned out. She stood in the middle of her living room, breathing heavily, then moved toward the light switch on the far wall. Suddenly she felt cold. Something was wrong in the room. What was it? A smell—that was it, a smell that didn't belong there.

She moved catlike across the room, reached into her purse for her .38 Smith. Her heart jumped.

"It's not there," said a voice behind her. Then the light came on.

She whirled. Standing in the doorway of her bedroom, there he was: Michael Delaney.

"America's most wanted, huh?" he said. "Right here in your living room."

Her face hardened. "What do you want?"

"Morgan Boyd really picked you to run the investigation?"

She took a couple of slow steps to her right, feeling behind her with her hands. "Well, not run it exactly. I'm more the coordinator from the White House side. FBI's obviously doing the real work. A guy named Smith." She hooked one finger around the drawer handle on the sideboard behind her.

Delaney smiled, held up something small and black. "I have the little Glock too. Remember, you told me where it was once."

Mary didn't bother pretending she hadn't been after the gun in the drawer. Delaney was too smart for that. "I assume you're not here for the tearful reconciliation where you tell me how sorry you are about the spineless way you dumped me," she said.

Delaney's face was impassive. It had always been so hard figuring out what he was thinking. Maybe that was part of his appeal: he wasn't one of these dull sensitive academic types that her friends kept hooking her up with.

"I didn't do it," Delaney said.

"That's it? You came here to tell me you didn't do it?"

"Somebody drugged me, switched my weapon, and then left it where the shooter could find it."

Mary felt a nameless tug. She was still attracted to the man. He had that rugged, still quality that she had always found incredibly attractive. Washington was full of grinning fast-talkers, waving their hands and begging for attention. She couldn't stand men like that. "Okay, so turn yourself in," she said.

"You must be joking."

"Then we're at kind of an impasse here, aren't we?"

"Where was my pistol planted?"

"Why?"

"I'm trying to work through this thing. Just give me a little information, and I'll go away and leave you alone forever."

She laughed. "Oh, terrific!"

"Be angry, be sarcastic. Fine. But tell me where the shooter got my Beretta from. Where was it hidden?"

"You ought to know."

"For God's sake, just tell me."

"We found a plastic sandwich bag by a bush next to the putting green. There was gun oil in the bag and an impression of a gun in the snow. Obviously you left the bag next to the bush with the gun in it. The shooter picked it up there, then started firing."

"No prints on the bag, I assume?"

Mary smiled thinly. "Oh, there were prints on the bag."

"Whose?"

"Yours, of course."

He frowned. "Okay, so maybe they pressed my fingers on the bag while I was sleeping."

"If you accept this cockamamie poor-Mike-Delaney-got-framed scenario."

Delaney didn't seem bothered by her derision. "Whose footprints did they find in the snow?"

"Just yours and Blip Harrison's."

"I was with Blip the whole time. He didn't plant the gun."

"He's been suspended. We're looking hard at him too."

"He's completely blameless." They stood quietly for a moment. "I see you brought your briefcase home, Mary. You always bring work home with you. Are there photographs?"

Mary sighed loudly. "This is ridiculous. You need to go."

"Do you have crime scene photos?"

"Yes."

"Show me."

She figured he'd get them whether or not she wanted him to, so she opened her briefcase, tossed him a handful of eight-by-tens. Delaney flipped through them until he came to a photograph of the trail and the bush at the edge of the putting green. "There," he said. "There's a third set of footprints."

She frowned, looked at the picture, then shook her head. "No, those are Mark Greene's. While he was on the putting green with the president he said he heard a noise in the woods and went over to look. Then he came back."

Delaney looked at her steadily.

"Oh, come on!" she said. "You want me to believe Mark Greene did this? The head of the president's own security detail? That *he* planted the weapon?"

Delaney smiled a little. "You'd rather believe Mark Greene than me?"

She shook her head. "Your whole scenario is way too baroque."

"Look, Greene knew all the personnel there. He would have known immediately that some guy walking out of the woods in a rent-a-cop uniform was not Secret Service. No way he would have let somebody like that approach into point-blank range. No, Greene let him get off the killshots, then he executed him."

"I guess he was on the grassy knoll too?"

Delaney ignored her sarcasm. "Okay, forget Greene for a second. Look at this from my point of view. Let's assume I wanted the president dead. Would I plant my own gun?"

"The serial numbers were filed off."

"Give me a break. I'm a law enforcement professional. You think I haven't heard of X-ray crystallography? You think I don't know that every Secret Service weapon has been ballistically printed? You think I don't know they'll inventory everybody's weapon? Please! If I wanted him dead, I'd have paid cash for a Glock at a gun show and then smuggled the weapon into Camp David. I'd have to be an idiot to use my duty weapon!" He felt his voice rising.

"You want to calm down, Mike?" Mary said coolly.

"I had a vial of blood drawn from my arm yesterday morning by a phlebotomist at the Naval Hospital. She can testify that she took it straight out of my arm, sealed the bottle, and signed her name across the seal. The vial was then taken to Dr. Jamie Bannerman who took it to the lab and had it tested. It came up positive for barbiturates."

"Let's say that's true. Maybe you're addicted to pills and somebody used that fact to blackmail you."

"The whole time we knew each other, did you ever see any evidence of barbiturate abuse in my behavior?"

"So maybe you took them intentionally to bolster your goofy theory. Maybe you took a sleeping pill last night. It doesn't mean anything."

"At least get somebody you trust to go to this doctor and check out my story." He handed her a piece of paper with two names on it. "That's the doctor and the blood technician."

"Fine."

"Somebody you trust, okay. Don't send just any old flunky from the FBI. I don't want them in danger."

"Whatever, Mike."

"Okay, okay, okay, forget the evidence and the theories and all that." Delaney stared at her. "Look into your heart, Mary. Does any of this match the Mike Delaney you know?"

"Are you talking about the Mike Delaney I thought I loved? Or the Mike Delaney who blew me off without even bothering to make a phone call of explanation?"

Delaney looked at the floor. "Look, I . . ." Then his voice trailed off.

"No. Forget it, Mike. It just won't wash." It was all too crazy. Conspiracies didn't exist, not in the real world. It was impossible for a large group of people to keep their mouths shut. Somebody always talked. No, this was just what it looked like: an agent embittered by a demotion had let himself get sucked into some kind of nutty plot. It was sad, it was ugly, it was small and tawdry—but that's what it was.

"I saw your file," she said finally. "The head of the Brotherhood is your wife's cousin. The FBI says you used to go hunting with him every time you and your wife went to visit your in-laws down in Alabama."

"Paul Miller? You think that loser is behind this?"

"We know he is."

"That's a bunch of crap. Paul Miller is a half-decent hunter, lots of fun to spend a few hours with around a campfire. But he's completely and totally nuts. Plus, he's a BS artist who talks a big game and then never does anything."

"Then why did you call him eighteen times last month?"

"Me? I haven't talked to that idiot in years."

"It's right there in the briefcase. Your phone records. Seventeen calls from your station at the White House."

Delaney didn't pick up the briefcase looking for the evidence. He just looked at her skeptically. "If I were really involved in a conspiracy to kill the president, would I be sitting around the White House making phone calls about it?"

"He has several hundred members in his organization. He's well funded. This entire operation has been meticulously organized."

Delaney snorted. "Paul Miller couldn't organize a church picnic."

"Then who's behind the murder of the president? Who's blowing up all these buildings?"

"That's the sixty-four-thousand-dollar question, isn't it?"

"No, it's not. There is no sixty-four-thousand-dollar question. We know the answer. Paul Miller and the Brotherhood are behind this."

"I listened to the AM radio in the truck I borrowed this morning. They were dropping guided missiles on White Sands yesterday. Even crummy Soviet-era guided missiles would have cost a mint. Where did some hick like Paul Miller, a guy who can barely make a living selling insurance, get the money to buy guided missiles?"

"We don't know that yet."

"Qui bono," Delaney said.

"What?"

"Qui bono? It's Latin. Who benefits? Think outside the box for about ten seconds. Let's just say for the sake of argument that I've

been framed, and that Paul Miller is working for somebody else. Somebody smarter and richer and better organized than he is. Who benefits when the president gets murdered?"

Mary didn't especially want to pursue that line of thought. But even when she did, it didn't seem to lead anywhere. She shrugged.

"I'm going to find out who did this thing," Delaney said.

"The wheels are in motion, Mike," she said. "The Brotherhood is going down."

Delaney laughed. *"Qui bono.* I'll be in touch. *Qui bono."*

He walked over to her and kissed her on the lips. Then he was gone.

She stared at the door. The arrogance! The nerve of the guy! He didn't even tie her up. Like he was so confident, so full of himself, that he figured he could just give her a big smooch on the lips, and she'd get all weak in the knees and wouldn't call the cops.

Well, Mr. Smarty-pants didn't know her as well as he thought he did. She reached for the phone, dialed 911. The phone rang five times then clicked over to a recording. *Due to unexpected call volume, the Washington, DC, Police Department is unable to respond to your call. Please stay on the line and we will address your emergency at the first possible—*

She slammed down the phone. Good ol' Washington, DC: as usual it stood as a model of stupendous governmental efficiency. She dialed again, but then when the dispatcher answered—an actual person this time!—Mary Campos hesitated for a moment and then said, "You know what, never mind. I'm fine."

After she hung up, Mary was so mad at herself that for a moment she could hardly think. How could she let that jerk get under her skin like this? The guy had dumped her without even a phone call, then he'd helped kill the president, and now she was protecting him like she was some lovestruck high school girl. But then she sat down and looked at the photographs of the shoeprints in the snow. She had always prided herself on her ability to cut through all the self-interest and look the hard questions in the face. Did a bunch of Alabama rednecks have what it took to pull off this operation? Maybe. But supposing they didn't . . .

And say what you want about Michael Delaney, he was no idiot. Why would he have given his duty weapon to the assassin? An agent in his position could easily have smuggled an untraceable weapon into Camp David.

There was more to this than met the eye.

When the president dies, who benefits? Who benefits?

WHO BENEFITS? It was the same question that Michael Delaney was asking himself as he drove down Connecticut Avenue. And the problem was, he just didn't have enough data yet to answer the question.

One piece of data was troubling him, though.

It had been a close shave that morning. He had thought he was cooked when that chopper dropped onto the highway behind him. He had stopped dead in the street, waiting for the black-clad men to run out after him. Only, they'd jumped all over a vehicle behind him. He had been so stunned that for a moment he'd just sat there, staring into his rearview mirror.

The men had not been more than fifty meters behind him. Plenty close to make out the faces. And he recognized two of them. Badger Lewis and Dirk Pardee. Northern Iraq, 1991—Captain Dirk Pardee had been the leader of the ODA (Operational Detachment-Alpha, also sometimes called an A-Team) posted to assist a Kurdish faction in the hills outside Kirkuk. Delaney had served under quite an assortment of dislikable officers, but Pardee had been in a class by himself. He was tough and smart, but completely amoral. He had tried to get Delaney to help him cook the books so he could rake off money intended to buy uniforms and equipment for the Kurdish militia. Delaney had almost come to blows with the man over that. They had settled the matter by letting Badger Lewis, the team's demolition expert, take over the accounting. Delaney had always felt it had been a cowardly decision on his part. But when you were two hundred miles of donkey trails away from the nearest friendly border, sometimes you made field-expedient compromises.

Delaney had later heard through SpecWar good ol' boy network that Pardee had been kicked out of the army for similar shenanigans after he'd been promoted to Light Colonel.

So here was the question: what the hell was Pardee doing climbing out of a U.S. Air Force Pave Low in the middle of Maryland? He obviously wasn't in Delta, since Delta was part of the army. The FBI didn't admit anybody after the age of thirty-five, so it was impossible that Pardee had become part of their Hostage Rescue Unit. Which left . . . what? Some kind of goofy CIA black-op unit? The CIA had been in bunker mentality for years, it was CYA up the wazoo over at

Langley. Given that the CIA was statutorily prohibited from operating on U.S. soil, there was no way in the world that they'd let CIA operatives with machine guns in their hands land in a public place on United States soil.

Which left . . . what?

There had been whispers about some kind of strange outfit that had been cobbled together as part of the COG effort that Morgan Boyd was leading. Boyd was a clever man, and an experienced Washington hand; if anybody in this town could scrape together a few nickels of "black budget"—that is, hidden, off-books funding—for the purpose of assembling a small, focused antiterrorism unit, it was Morgan Boyd.

But supposing that to be the case, why would Boyd hire a guy like Pardee? Pardee was basically a thug, albeit a fairly polished one.

Not enough data, that's what it came down to. Where would he get the data? That was easy. It was time to take a ride. But first, he needed a new car.

DELANEY DIDN'T WANT to take pleasure in stealing cars. But the truth was, it was kind of exciting. He tried to think of it as aggressive borrowing. Everyone would get their cars back unscathed eventually, and they'd have a good story to tell the office Christmas party about how the crazed assassin Delaney had stolen their car.

It was obvious that Pardee had guessed he would steal a commercial van—and had therefore hit the first van he saw coming out of the Wal-Mart in Beltsville. Pardee had been right on the money in his general calculation . . . but he'd been off by about fifty feet in the specifics. So Delaney had ditched the van and picked up a car parked outside a restaurant on the next cross street, the door open and the keys in the ignition while a parking attendant went inside to talk to the maître d'. It was the perfect stolen ride: a five-year-old Saturn—unpretentious, American, virtually invisible, but with surprisingly good pickup.

Delaney had tossed his bag on the seat, hopped in the Saturn, and driven away, a soothing violin quartet playing on the exceedingly good after-market stereo.

At a little after nine he had headed east out of DC, stopping at the Wal-Mart in Centreville, where he shoplifted some camping supplies and some beef jerky. Delaney offered up a brief prayer of gratitude to

Sam Walton, then headed south, taking back roads only, winding his way out into farm country, on into the Shenandoah Valley, down US 11, heading toward Alabama.

He started nodding off around Lexington and finally pulled over outside the tiny town of Natural Bridge, where he parked his car on a side road and hiked up a heavily timbered hill, still ankle deep in snow. At the top of the hill he wearily erected the tent, set his alarm to go off in two hours, and fell asleep.

DAY THREE

17

Northern Alabama

12:21 AM

ASSISTANT SPECIAL AGENT-IN-CHARGE Wayne Goodall, day-to-day chief of the FBI's Hostage Rescue Unit, looked through his night-vision binoculars down on the cluster of buildings from the ridge on the opposite side of the valley. He was clad head-to-toe in black—Kevlar helmet, ballistic vest complete with ceramic inserts, dripping with flashbangs, ammo pouches, and various weapons.

"Firebird One?" he said into his radio. They were running in burst mode, fully encrypted.

"In position," said his first sniper team.

"Firebird Two?"

"In position."

"All right then. Let's move out." He pulled on his AN/PVS-14 monocular night-vision glasses, then gave a hand signal to the two squads of HRT operators. They began filing slowly down the hill, fanning out into two separate groups. Team Three would come from the north, Team Four from the south. It was just before midnight. If everything went right, they'd be ready for the assault just before daybreak.

THE APPALACHIAN MOUNTAIN range peters out in northeastern Alabama right about where Interstate 20 cuts into the state, coming over from Atlanta. Large parts of Cleburne and Calhoun counties consist primarily of mountainous woodland, most of which is part of the Talladega National Forest, but large swathes of it are still privately owned. According to the HUMINT the FBI had developed, there were anywhere between five and fifteen Brotherhood installations out here—depending on how you did the math. Most of them were simple cabins, but one of them was supposed to be a full-fledged training camp, and several others consisted of at least a couple of buildings, some of them heavily fortified.

ASAC Goodall was not happy. This was a rush job. And rush jobs were where people got hurt. He had been instructed in no uncertain terms that the United States government was not going to sit on its hands. That meant they were going to hit one of the fortified locations, a cluster of three buildings on a remote, unpaved logging road perched on the side of a small mountain near Oak Level, just a couple of miles from the Georgia border. He had sent a light plane over to take surveillance pictures, so they had a pretty clear knowledge of the physical layout. But other than that, they knew nothing. How many Brotherhood members were there? What was their level of training? What kind of defensive measures were built into the location? There were no answers to these questions. On an ordinary mission he would never go out himself. ASACs didn't bust in doors. But he felt obliged on this particular instance to lead the mission. He wasn't throwing his men to the wolves while he sat in a comfy chair back in DC.

The surrounding forest was mainly planted pine, meaning that the trees were all exactly the same height, the treetops growing densely together, blotting out so much light that there was virtually no underbrush—ergo, no cover for his men. Choppers would give away their approach. Cars would give away their approach. The lack of clear land made parachuting impossible. So it came down to a stalk on foot in the middle of the night on unfamiliar terrain.

And if these guys had night vision? Or motion sensors? Or booby traps? You could buy second-generation Soviet night-vision gear from Cabela's or Orvis for a couple hundred bucks. Motion sensors from the spy store went for next to nothing. And anybody could go to a gun show where six bucks would buy you army field manuals about how to make field-expedient booby traps. If these guys were halfway on the ball, this could end up being a costly mission. Not that HRT wouldn't prevail. They'd take these guys—that was a given. But Goodall was not interested in having to drive up to the home of some nice woman and tell her that her husband had just been shot to death in some cobbled-together mission in Alabama.

The good news, however, was that so far the two sniper teams, who were operating as their forward surveillance units, had only spotted a couple of men—both of them wearing civilian clothes and carrying hunting rifles.

BY FOUR O'CLOCK in the morning it was clear that the timetable was in trouble. Team Three—Goodall's team—had made decent time and was all set up at the rally point. But Team Four had run into underbrush and a steeper-than-expected climb onto the far side of the ridge. Sometimes it was hard to tell just from a topo map how hard the going would be. One operator had slid forty feet down the hill and sprained his ankle already. And they were still six hundred meters away from the target, fighting blackberry briars and rock, darkness, and unstable ground.

Six hundred meters didn't sound like much. But it wasn't like they were hiking down a city street: they had to move through the dark, across unfamiliar terrain, carrying equipment and weapons—all without making any noise. Plus, the men were exhausted; they'd been busy airlifting equipment last night, and so nobody had slept for over a day.

If Team Four didn't make it to its rally point within an hour, he was determined to scrub the mission. HRT was a never-say-die outfit. But there was a limit. A stalk was one thing: but if these Brotherhood guys were ready, this would turn into—well, into an infantry charge. HRT was not interested in refighting World War I, thank you very much.

Goodall hunkered down behind the group of boulders that would be their last scrap of decent cover before they made the final assault, looking at the cluster of buildings through his night-vision binoculars. They were 150 meters away. All three buildings were dark. He took a sip of water. This was bad. If he weren't under direct orders, he'd scrub the mission right now. What was the damn rush? Surround them, starve them out. Or send up a couple of nice armored vehicles the next day. He looked at his watch. 4:25 AM.

"Progress?" Goodall whispered into his radio.

Baron, head of Team Four, came back, sounding out of breath. "Four hundred yards to rally point. We'll make it by five."

"You sure?"

Long pause. "I *said* we'll make it."

Everybody was jumpy and irritable.

———

TEAM FOUR made it to the rally point twenty minutes late. The sun still wasn't up . . . but it would be soon.

"You know what to do, boys," Goodall whispered. "Fan out. Work from tree to tree. Nice and quiet and slow. Only one man at a time exposes himself. We'll surround the outbuildings; Team Four gets the main cabin. We breach on my signal."

Everyone nodded. He gave the command, and the black-clad figures crept up out of the boulders and began moving out, crouched low, MP5s and shotguns locked on the target buildings.

They worked from tree to tree, just like they'd practiced.

Finally they had gotten to within ten yards of the target, and there was still no sound or light coming from the cabins. Goodall held up his fist, waiting for Team Four to collect on the far side of the small clearing. Then he studied the three buildings. From the distance they had looked like ordinary wooden cabins. But now that he was closer, he decided there was something strange about them. What was it, exactly?

The wood, that's it. Protruding from a couple of places were thumb-size pieces of steel rebar. Then he saw it: the wood wasn't wood at all. It was concrete that had been poured into some kind of wooden form and painted to resemble wood. And the door, now that he looked at it more closely—hell it didn't even vaguely resemble wood. It was just a flat steel plate. Jesus God, these weren't cabins, they were freaking pillboxes. They were little fortresses.

It was just at the moment he was realizing they had underestimated their targets when suddenly he heard a metallic grinding noise. His brow furrowed. What the hell was that? Then he saw, through his NVGs, some kind of motion in the wall. A rectangular piece of the wall about six inches wide and three inches high was sliding open. It was a gun port.

He felt a sudden burst of emotion—not fear but anger. Somebody in Washington had decided that a grand gesture was required, so they'd rushed the op when they should have waited for better intel. And now he and his men would pay the price in blood, widows, and orphaned children.

"Fall back!" he screamed. "Trap! Trap!"

Then a green light blossomed in the middle of his NVGs, and whoever was inside the bunker of a cabin started shooting. The noise was deafening. To a man who had spent his life around weapons, the sound was impossible to mistake. It was a Browning .50 cal machine gun, one of the most fearsome antipersonnel devices ever made. The 750-grain bullets would chew right through half an inch of plate steel. An eight-inch pine tree trunk was no obstacle to them.

He saw the tracers sweeping toward him, and he stepped out from behind the tree and fired methodically into the six-inch hole. I can do this, he thought. This is what I've been trained for.

Then he heard the second machine gun. And the third. This was a lighter caliber, .223, probably a SAW Squad Automatic Weapon. And it was coming from his flank. They must have been underground, waiting.

Nice work, a detached part of his brain thought. A perfectly executed L-shaped ambush. If they were ready on the other side of the buildings too, it would be a total massacre.

Then the Browning hit him, twice, once in the arm and once in his gut.

He fell and lay there, looking at the sky, watching the tracers claw the darkness above him. In an odd sort of way, it was quite beautiful. He couldn't move, not really. The pain was on him so heavy, it was like a bull squatting on top of his chest. He felt broken, pulverized, a doll flung into a trash heap.

The firing didn't last all that long. There was a good deal of screaming, some of it possibly coming from his own mouth.

Then there was silence.

After a moment a man appeared, standing over him. For a moment he thought maybe everything was okay, because the man wore a Kevlar helmet and a ballistic vest, and an AN/PVS-14, just like all the men in HRT wore. But then he noticed the SAW the man was carrying. No Squad Automatic Weapons in HRT.

"This one's still alive," the man with the light machine gun said.

"Not anymore," said a second voice.

There was a shock, like someone had banged him in the head with a rock. Then Assistant Special Agent-in-Charge Wayne Goodall saw a brief vision in his mind—Jenna and the boys at the beach last summer, everyone laughing, the wind tousling their hair. And then it was all gone.

18

"WIPED OUT, COLONEL."

"What do you mean, wiped out?"

Now that the center of gravity of the investigation was shifting away from Camp David, the Bureau had moved their command post back to the FBI building. Mary Campos was talking to the director of the FBI, a red-faced, portly man of about fifty named Albert Brown. SAC Smith stood nearby, arms folded.

"HRT sent in two squads, Colonel Campos," Brown said. "Because of the terrain, the lack of roads, the concern about detection, etc., the backup units were out of visual range. Sometime after five o'clock this morning, the number two man in HRT, who was acting as assault leader, radioed that they were making the final approach to the location. We didn't hear anything after that."

"So how do you know they were wiped out?"

The director shrugged. "I don't. But it's a safe bet right now. The backup units are still making their way in."

"Has it not occurred to anybody to use a helicopter?"

Albert Brown looked at her irritably. "Yes, Colonel, that occurred to several people. They decided it wasn't such a brilliant idea after the first one got shot down by a guided missile."

She blinked. "Oh, my God!"

"No kidding."

"I need to get down there," Mary said.

"What for?"

"I want to see it with my own eyes."

"John Rancy is sending me down. The Gulfstream's leaving in twenty minutes—if you can be ready by then."

"I'm ready now," Mary said.

"We'll be meeting a General Fairbank. I guess he's Dean Fairbank's brother."

"*Bill* Fairbank?"

"You know him?"

"Yes. We go back a long way. My father retired as a two star; he was Fairbank's battalion commander back in Vietnam, then Bill was on Dad's staff when Dad rotated back to the Pentagon. What in the world is he doing down there?"

"I think President Boyd is talking about invading Alabama." He said this with a thin smile. Any other time, it might have provoked a laugh. But just then, it didn't seem very funny.

"Before I go," Mary said, "I have a quick question on the investigation front."

"Yes?" SAC Smith said.

"Have we looked at Mark Greene at all?"

Smith's eyebrows went up. "We debriefed him of course . . ."

She shook her head. "No, I mean, have we *looked* at him."

Smith crossed his arms, looked at the director. "You have anything in mind we ought to be looking for?" the director said.

"I don't want to lead us down a blind alley, but let's just look at the facts. Michael Delaney is a trained law enforcement professional. He knows firearms up one side and down the other. Anybody who's watched five episodes of *CSI* knows about x-ray crystallography and ballistic printing. Why would he plant his own gun, a gun he knows would be traceable straight back to him? Greene's the senior man there; he has access to everything; and his footprints are near the location of the bush where the gun was left for Pilgrim to pick up. I think we should look at the possibility—however remote—that Delaney was framed."

"Framed!" The director exchanged glances with SAC Smith.

"Why would he have run if he was innocent?" Smith said.

"We've got, what, a thousand agents working this case right now?" Mary said. "We can spare a couple to make sure we're not going after the wrong man."

The director hesitated, then finally nodded at SAC Smith.

Smith said, "Yes, ma'am, I'll put some people on it." But from his tone of voice, Mary didn't think he took her very seriously.

———

Just Outside Natural Bridge, VA
6:23 AM

Delaney woke up with a tiny shaft of sunlight coming through a gap in the tent door and hitting him right in the face. It felt like the blade of a knife had lodged in his eye.

He looked frantically at his watch, which was beeping anemically. He'd overslept by four hours! He climbed out of the tent and looked down the hill. His heart sank. There at the bottom of the hill was a Virginia State Patrol car parked smack in front of the car he'd stolen. The state trooper was standing in front of the car, writing something down in his notebook. Delaney had switched the plates, so if the trooper just ran the plate number for stolen vehicles, he'd be all right. But most likely it would come back with a make and model. Which wouldn't match the car. At which point things would get a little dicey.

Delaney considered hiking back down the other side of the hill. But that didn't seem like such a fabulous idea either. Where would he go? The trooper must have heard something, because he looked up the hill and spotted Delaney.

Delaney smiled and waved. "How you doing, trooper!" he called heartily. "I'll be right down."

What were the odds that the trooper would recognize him? Not that his face was exceptionally distinctive. But facial recognition was a tricky thing. There were plenty of studies in the criminology and psych literature about how difficult it was to recognize the faces of strangers. He'd been in the middle of crowds all day yesterday and nobody had given him a second look. But police were different. They were paid to look hard, to be suspicious, to study faces. Right now he could walk down the hill and bluff. Or he could run. If he ran, the game was over. There'd be dogs and choppers and the whole bit. And this time there was no falling snow to hide his tracks.

Delaney didn't bother to mess with the tent, he just grabbed the sleeping bag, tucked his MP5 inside it and started down the hillside, trying to look as blameless as he could.

"I know, I know," Delaney said as he approached the trooper. "I'm probably trespassing here or something. See, what happened, I'm heading down to my sister's funeral in Alabama and I started falling asleep on the highway, figured if I didn't get some sleep I'd run off the road and kill somebody. Better trespassing than traffic fatalities."

"Uh-huh," the trooper said, face impassive. He was a young guy, not exceptionally certain of himself. "You own this vehicle?"

"Sure." Delaney smiled and slapped the hood. "Hundred and forty-two thousand miles on this puppy, I've never even had to change so much as a water pump."

"Sir, would you put that sleeping bag down so I can see your hands."

Decision time. Should he try to talk his way out, or shoot his way out? The trooper might have already made him. If so, he could talk till he was blue in the face and it wouldn't matter. The trooper hadn't touched his gun yet, though. But shooting just wasn't a moral option here. He'd already decided that.

Delaney kept smiling, set the bag on the hood of the car—gently, so the MP-5 wouldn't clunk against the sheet metal.

"I need your license, registration, and proof of insurance, sir."

"Sure." Delaney slapped his back pocket. "Hm. I must have left my wallet in the car."

"Would you mind getting it, sir?"

"Not a problem." The Beretta was sitting in the glove compartment. Unless the cop was a fool, he'd keep a close eye on Delaney as he opened the glove box—at which point he'd spot the 9 mm. Then the cop would get nervous, draw his duty weapon, and Delaney would have no choice but to surrender.

Delaney made a show of digging around in the seats, looking on the floor.

"Gosh, trooper, I can't seem to find it."

"You try the glove box?"

Delaney sighed loudly. "Okay, okay," he said, backing out of the car and holding up his hands. "You got me. I admit, I got a little bit of recreational pharmaceuticals in there. I mean, you know, it's just one joint."

The trooper pulled his weapon. "All right, sir, if you would, assume the position."

Delaney didn't move. "Trooper, before you do that . . . look, I've just spent the past six months humping around the boonies in Kurdistan. I'm a major in the U.S. Army, Fifth Special Forces. I don't expect that to cut a lot of ice with you, but I got back from duty two days ago, a couple of old high school buddies and I got together, one thing led to another. I mean, before yesterday I hadn't even *seen* marijuana since we won the state football championship my senior year in high school."

The trooper had his 9 mm pointed in the general direction of Delaney's left lung.

"Am I asking for special treatment? Okay, maybe it's not right. But I really am on the way to my sister's funeral. And you bust me, not only will I miss her funeral, it'll be the end of my military career. I've served in Somalia, Iraq, Afghanistan, Panama, places you probably don't even remember the army went to. I'm about six months from retirement. You bust me and I'm out on my fanny with no pension, no job experience other than pointing guns at people, and a dishonorable discharge in my back pocket. Before you run me in, just consider all of that."

"Special Forces?"

Delaney nodded.

"What unit?"

"Like I said, right now I'm with the Fifth Special Forces. I started out with a rifle company in the Big Red One. Did a bit with the Seventy-fifth Rangers. Then I was with Tenth Special Forces. Officers rotate around a little. I was with the Fourth Mech for a while as XO of a company, then did two years at the Pentagon, two years at Fort Sill . . ."

The young trooper looked at him carefully, thinking. Delaney could see he was a good-natured kid, that if Delaney's spiel was true, he didn't want to ruin some military hero's career.

"Look, are you gonna run me in or not? If you are, let's just get it over with. If not, I've got till four o'clock to get to Birmingham, Alabama, for that funeral I was telling you about."

"Show me your military ID, I'll let you go," the trooper said.

Delaney pointed up at the tent on the hill. "It's up there. I left it in the tent."

The trooper blew out a long breath.

"Don't worry, trooper. I'll go get it."

The radio crackled in the trooper's car, something about an accident with fatalities on the interstate.

"Nah, nah, forget it." The trooper waved his hand, then holstered his duty weapon.

Delaney felt relief rushing into his veins like a shot of whiskey.

"Here," the trooper said, "let me get this sleeping bag for you."

Before Delaney could move, the young trooper had picked up the sleeping bag. It took a moment for the trooper to realize there was more inside the bag than polyester filling. He frowned, pulled back the cloth, and saw the muzzle of the submachine gun staring at him. The trooper's eyes went wide, and he dropped the load, started clawing for his pistol.

Just Outside the Talladega National Forest, Alabama
6:28 AM

It took the eight-man team an hour to jog quietly down the trail from the site of the ambush. They were all wearing head-to-toe hunting camo and carried hunting rifles at port arms. They had left their military weapons behind at the cabin where they'd ambushed the HRT operators. All of them carried false identification, including hunting licenses with all the appropriate stamps.

At the five-kilometer mark, the trail intersected with a slightly overgrown logging road. Sitting in the middle of the road, engine idling, was a Kenworth logging truck, its flatbed piled high with enormous oak timbers. The driver quickly jumped out at the approach of the men.

"Everything okay?"

The leader of the eight-man unit, a dark-skinned man with a long blade of a nose, nodded. "Stow this somewhere, would you," he said, tossing the rifle to the driver. His accent had a slight South American lilt.

The huge logs on the truck had been hollowed out, each log just big enough to fit one man. The driver helped the team leader and his men open the concealed doors into the logs and crawl inside. When the team was concealed, the driver closed the doors, lashed the hollowed-out logs shut, and got back into the cab of the truck. It took no more than five minutes.

It took the driver another half an hour to thread his way down the mountain and hit the main road. Within half a mile he had to slow his rig. In front of him were several state patrol cars, lights flashing, and a team of nervous-looking men wearing blue coats that said FBI on the back in yellow letters.

He pulled up at the checkpoint and stopped. "What's going on?" he said to the state patrolman who came up to his cab. "Sounded like something done blew up back there. I hope didn't nobody get hurt . . ."

"Driver's license and registration, sir," the state trooper said, obviously not in the mood for chitchat.

While he was talking, two FBI agents were walking slowly down the side of his truck, looking under it with mirrors.

"Who you work for, bud?" the trooper said.

"G&L Lumber. Picked up a load this morning, heading down to the mill in Anniston."

"See anybody unusual in the past couple hours? Hunters? Anything?"

The driver shrugged. "Seen a couple hunters in a red pickup truck back there. Had 'em a half-decent little buck. Four-pointer, it looked like."

"Is that your rifle?" The cop pointed at the rifle the team leader had handed him. How come he didn't take the dadgum thing back inside the hideaway like everybody else had?

"Sure."

The trooper pulled his pistol. "How about stepping out of the car, sir."

"Good golly!" the driver said. "What's got into *you?*"

"Just step out of the car, sir."

The driver shrugged amiably, climbed out. The trooper cuffed him and then the FBI men came over. One agent pulled out the rifle, sniffed the barrel, seeing if it had been fired recently.

"This is your weapon, sir?"

"That's what I just told Depuddy Dawg." The driver wanted to play this right. He had to seem mildly irritated—but not so much so that he drew any suspicion. "Why would I be carrying a rifle, wasn't mine?"

"Sir, we're just being cautious here," the FBI man said smoothly. "When did you last fire this weapon?"

The driver had no idea when it had last been fired, of course. He shrugged broadly. "Went hunting over the weekend. Had me a big old eight-point buck in plain sight, not seventy-five yards out, missed the dadgum thing two shots in a row." He smiled and tried to look shamefaced. "I got buck fever like you wouldn't believe, can't hardly hit the side of a barn door."

"So it's been several days?"

Another shrug. "I guess, yeah." If they didn't like that answer he was preparing another story about how, oh, that's right, he'd loaned it to his nephew just last night.

But the FBI agent said, "It hasn't been fired today." Then, to the trooper: "Paperwork look okay?" The trooper nodded. "You check his manifest?"

"Ain't no manifest on raw lumber," the driver said.

The trooper nodded a second time. "Yeah, they don't typically have a manifest, not coming straight out of the forest."

"Uncuff him," the FBI man said to the trooper. While the patrol-man was getting the cuffs off of his wrists, the FBI man said, "You have kids, sir?"

"Two little boys," the driver lied. "Leon and Henry."

The FBI man took something out of his pocket, handed them to the driver. "Something for your kids, just a little token for your trouble."

The driver looked at what the FBI man had handed him: two plastic badges that said I'M A JUNIOR G-MAN on them. "Why thank you, sir. My boys'll be tickled pink."

He climbed back into his rig, dropped it into gear. Before he popped the clutch, though, he put the badge on his shirt.

"I'm a junior G-Man!" he said loudly as he pulled away from the checkpoint. Damnation. He must have lost five pounds just standing there.

Then he pulled something that looked like a Nokia cell phone—but wasn't—off the seat. It was a Raytheon SATCOM phone switchable to either TDMA or DAMA modes. He pressed the star key and then, without a trace of the homespun Alabama accent he'd been using just minutes earlier, said, "Mission one hundred percent, no casualties, extraction on schedule."

Just Outside Lynchburg, Virginia
6:33 AM

Delaney grabbed his Beretta out of the glove box and pointed it at the trooper. The young state trooper was desperately trying to get his weapon out of the holster, but the gun just wasn't coming out.

In moments of extreme fear, Delaney knew, fine motor control disappears, sound gets blotted out, and vision narrows. It was standard combat psychology, the hardwiring of a million years of predator/prey relationships. Some people got it worse than others. And some people hardly got it at all, remaining calm and alert under the most desperate circumstances. The kid was obviously one of the former. While Delaney was one of the latter.

He walked swiftly toward the terrified young state patrolman, who was still jerking feebly on his holster. Delaney laid his hand gently on the young man's gun hand.

"It's okay," Delaney said softly. "If I'd meant to kill you, you'd already be dead."

The wind went out of the trooper's sails. More predator/prey instinct. Sometimes when an animal realizes its time is up—a wildebeest with a lion locked on its neck, a chicken in the grip of a fox—the prey simply relaxes into its destruction. Which was exactly what the young trooper did.

The patrolman stared at him through glazed eyes.

"What's your name, son?" Delaney had to repeat himself before the young man ever answered.

"Trooper Dale Stephens," the young man finally stuttered.

"Dale," Delaney said. "I'm going to take your weapon now. Okay?"

The young man nodded. Delaney pulled the 9 mm Glock 19 out of Trooper Stephens's holster then escorted the young man back to the police car. He put him in the backseat, then closed the door. Cop cars didn't have handles in the back. He wouldn't be able to get out. Delaney then climbed in the front. The young man had begun to weep in the backseat.

"Now come on, kid," he said. "I've been in a lot of dicey situations. Sometimes I did better than others. You ever had a gun pointed at you before?"

The young man shook his head.

"It's a learned response. Go home, practice. Think about how you felt when you saw that MP5, how you felt when I came out with that Beretta. Practice responding to the stimulus, overcoming the instinctual response to freeze or run away. Work through the fear, concentrate on your technique: draw, acquire target, shoot. Okay? Draw, acquire target, shoot."

"Yes, sir."

"The whole thing's a psychological game. You're lucky, kid. Now you know what you're up against. Lot of people don't get that second chance. Next time you'll be ready."

"Yes, sir." The patrolman was still weeping.

"Trooper Stephens, I just want you to know for your own peace of mind that I didn't do what they said I did. You're going to look back at this many years from now and realize that instead of getting taken advantage of by a criminal, you helped out an innocent man."

"Yes, sir." The trooper's voice was dull and lifeless.

Delaney thought for a minute. If he left the trooper there, somebody would pull over and help him and then they'd be on his trail in no time flat. The Shenandoah Valley was a narrow strip of land without a great deal of room to run or hide.

"How do you work the flashers on this thing?" Delaney said. "I feel like picking up the pace a little."

The young man pointed.

Delaney flipped on the lights and headed for the interstate.

19

Talladega National Forest, Northern Alabama
11:40 AM

THEY WALKED IN SILENCE through the little clearing around the three buildings—Mary Campos, General Bill Fairbank, and Albert Brown, the director of the FBI. The bodies still lay where they had fallen. Evidence technicians were moving all around them. There hadn't been a single survivor, not even the sniper teams.

"What do you think?" Mary said finally.

Fairbank had a plug of tobacco in his cheek. He spat then pointed at the buildings. "Reinforced concrete. These weren't houses, they were bunkers. You couldn't knock a hole in them with a grenade. Peepholes, machine gun mounts—they were purpose-built for defending against an infantry attack. Now you can see, given the way the land slopes off in the front and back of the property, that anybody who was planning to attack the place would have to come across here and here. Right along the ridge top. The tunnels came up here, here, here, and here on the slope, allowing them to flank their attackers. You got interlocking fields of fire from the buildings, plus flanking fire from the tunnel exits. It's an L-shaped ambush. This was professional work, straight out of the Ranger handbook."

"So they were well prepared?" the director said.

"It goes deeper than that. They took out both of the sniper teams too. That means they had night-vision-equipped countersnipers. Probably two of them, one to take out each sniper team. Then when the chopper headed over, they took that out too, with the missile. Then, boom, they're gone. Where'd they go? There were FBI roadblocks for miles around here, but they just melted into thin air. There was a prearranged retreat plan here, probably with vehicles waiting."

"I'm not sure I understand what you're getting at," Albert Brown said.

"These people didn't improvise this ambush. They had intelligence. Either they were intimately familiar with HRT tactics, or somebody tipped them as to the precise troop strength and disposition they would be facing. You can improvise a win. You can't improvise a hundred percent massacre. They were prepared. They were organized. They had intel. This was a cold-blooded execution organized by pros."

Mary Campos spoke for the first time, asking a question she already knew the answer to. "General, is there any SWAT team in America that could have breached this position?"

Fairbank shook his head. "SWAT teams, SEAL Teams, Delta, HRT—at the end of the day, these guys are all light infantry. You don't attack fortifications with light infantry—not when the guys in the fort know you're coming."

"What do you need then, sir?"

"There's no law enforcement agency in America that could deal with this. Knowing what I know now? I wouldn't have attacked this position with anything less than a full rifle platoon supported by artillery and/or helicopter gunships. You want to take these guys?" Fairbank spat on the ground in disgust. "I hate to admit it, but anything short of the army, you'll just be burying more good cops."

He looked sadly around the site of the massacre.

"This here's prime guerrilla fighting territory. All the trees make it hard to see from the air. The terrain's too broken up for tanks. This is yard-by-yard country. If there's any more of this"—he made a long sweep of his arm, taking in the fortified position, the trees, the rocks, the tunnels—"then the army's gonna have to take this whole neck of the woods, inch by inch, tree by tree."

"There's no other way?" Mary said.

The general spat some more tobacco on the dry leaves. "Nope."

Mary Campos's phone rang. She answered it then frowned. It was the president's secretary. "General? It's the president."

She handed her cell to Bill Fairbank.

"Yes, Mr. President," Fairbank said into the phone. "I've just surveyed the scene. No, sir. No, sir. Yes, Mr. President, I agree." Then there was a long pause. "Yes, Mr. President, you were right. It's the army or nothing. Yes sir, I'm ready. I'll personally supervise deployment of the Eighty-second Airborne. Absolutely, sir. I'll crush these bastards."

He handed the phone back to Mary. He had an odd, distant expression on his face.

"Well, General?" she said.

Fairbank didn't speak for a moment. Then he looked around the isolated battlefield, scattered with the broken bodies of young men, and said, "Did I just make a deal with the devil?"

Mary didn't answer for a moment. But she knew the feeling. She'd asked that same question herself. Finally she pointed at the ground, at a young man with clear blue eyes, staring placidly up at the sky.

"There's your answer, General."

20

The United States Senate
7:00 PM

S ENATOR CHARLES TUNNINGTON, the senior senator from South Carolina, stood and applauded as President Morgan Boyd ascended to the speaker's podium. Tunnington, at age eighty, had seen a great deal of the world and was not shocked by much. He had grown up poor in Aiken, South Carolina, gone to college on the GI Bill after serving as an enlisted man in virtually every European campaign, from North Africa to the Ruhr, practiced law for a few years, and then served in Congress—three terms in the House and five in the Senate. He'd seen men blown into unrecognizable piles of meat, and dirty deals done behind closed doors; he'd found the body of his fourth and favorite son hanging from a rope in the basement of his own home; he'd dragged soldiers out of French brothels and knelt prayerfully in wood-framed Baptist churches; he'd drunk bootleg whiskey in the worst Carolina honky-tonks and sipped champagne with poets and painters and presidents; and he'd spent fifty years of generally happy marriage with the same strong woman. A hard man to surprise, indeed.

Still, he was a little surprised at how quickly Morgan Boyd was moving. Charles Tunnington was the kind of man who expected to be consulted when a president made major policy moves, but today he had not heard a word from Morgan Boyd. For a president to make a major policy speech without at least sneaking an advance copy of the text to Charles Tunnington—well, it just wasn't done, was it? Nobody had a reputation in the Senate for greater probity or integrity or had exceeded his record of legislative accomplishment. Charles Tunnington had *earned* the privilege of consultation.

He beamed broadly at the president, as though he had fathered the man himself.

The Senate and the House were hurriedly gathered in joint session to hear what had been billed as a major speech. Not just a bunch of eyewash about the dearly departed, the White House press office had assured them, but a speech of historic moment.

Morgan Boyd stood, surveying the room—the senators, the VIPs in the gallery, the TV cameras and reporters. Boyd didn't look bad, Tunnington thought, for a man who'd just been shot. Finally the new president raised his arms and the assembled legislators quieted.

"Before turning to the substance of this address," Morgan Boyd said, "I would like to announce that I have spoken today to Brian Polaski, the governor of Kansas, and he has agreed to succeed me in the office of vice president of the United States. He will be sworn in as soon as he arrives in Washington tomorrow." There was loud, long applause. The governor of Kansas was generally agreed to be an excellent administrator.

Boyd scanned the room, let the applause die down.

"Tomorrow," he said, "we will lower the body of a great American hero into the soil of this land. It's a matter of record that I differed with him on some issues. But I always respected him for his dedication to principle." He eyed the room silently for a moment.

"Principle. It is that, alone, which separates this nation from every other. We are a nation founded on principle. Not on clan loyalty, not on common language, not on geographical accident, but on principle. Principle is a fine and noble thing. But principle without action is empty. Not just empty, but morally bankrupt. To *know* what is right and then to stand by passively as evil is committed—well, there is no sin greater. We do not remember the names of the soldiers who pierced the side of Christ. We remember Pilate, who washed his hands of the affair.

"An attempt has been made to destabilize this nation. I swore just two days ago to preserve and protect the Constitution of the United States. I shall do so!"

Charles Tunnington made a point of being the first man to rise from his chair to applaud the line.

"At the heart of all democratic discourse," the president said, "lies a tension between practicality and principle. Sacrifice one at the altar of the other, and this fragile thing we call democracy collapses into anarchy or fascism. Right now, we must be practical. An assault has been made on us, and we cannot wash our hands of the need to act. We simply cannot.

"Two days ago, I reluctantly declared a state of emergency. By executive authority I have today initiated a number of temporary measures intended to ensure that those who would tear us down cannot do so. Today, as we are well aware, an entire team of FBI agents was brutally ambushed and murdered down to the last man. Half measures against these lawless cowards will not be adequate. Tonight I shall enumerate those measures.

"First, elements of the United States Army have been deployed here in Washington, DC. If warranted, other units may be deployed in other major cities. Plans have been drawn up for the protection of major state, municipal, and federal locations, as well as certain particularly vulnerable infrastructural elements such as dams, airports, and nuclear power plants. Such deployments will be made when and if warranted.

"Second, a number of judicial steps have been taken to assure that criminals and terrorists cannot manipulate the generous and humane qualities of our system in order to destroy it. As of today, habeas corpus shall be suspended in cases involving insurrection, terrorist acts, assaults against federal officers, treason, and seditious agitation. The right of the accused to have access to a lawyer is a cherished American right. But if I let terrorists hide behind lawyers and plan further attacks on the nation while their accomplices busily roam the streets with guided missiles, bombs, and weapons of mass destruction, then I am committing a crime against the nation myself. Upon the signature authority of a federal judge, suspects in these crimes may be arrested and imprisoned on a temporary basis without evidentiary hearings for a period of sixty days.

"Additionally military courts have been empowered to dispense summary justice—including capital punishment—in cases where a tribunal of military judges shall determine that public order is in clear and present jeopardy.

"All aliens within the borders of the United States shall be required to register current addresses and place of employment with local authorities within the next seventy-two hours. Any aliens failing to comply shall be subject to immediate arrest. Illegal aliens within our borders shall be subject to immediate arrest and confinement.

"A number of other measures are enumerated in the temporary order which I am signing today.

"These are harsh but necessary measures. Because of the extraordinary nature of the measures, I do not believe they can—or should—long stand without legislative sanction. I have, therefore, set these measures to expire in seven days.

"Why such harsh measures? In the short run, because we face an insurrection. But we don't begin to know the full dimensions of this attack. Are there connections to foreign terrorist organizations? We don't know. Some kind of link to Al-Qaeda? We don't know. I will say this, however. Whoever is behind this despicable murder, they do not represent the only threat to our way of life. There are threats waiting in the wings as soon as we knock this one down. It's time for the United States to move with vigor, time to crush terrorism wherever it raises its head—here or abroad.

"I stand before you, the Congress of the United States, because in you is vested the ultimate constitutional authority to make law. It is my intention and hope that the measures I have enacted by executive authority shall shortly be given legislative sanction by this noble body. Even such legislation, however, should be limited in duration. I propose that Congress extend legislative sanction to the measures in my executive for an additional ninety days while the immediate threat to this nation is suppressed. If at the end of that time additional extension of these measures is required, then it shall be at your hands.

"I have drafted language for such a bill, which I am calling the Freedom from Fear Act. Naturally the final form of the bill shall be in your hands. With your help and your resolve, we shall triumph! And when we do, these distasteful measures will dissipate like smoke from the guns of Gettysburg or Yorktown or Iwo Jima . . . and the sweet air of freedom will again prevail!"

The room burst into applause.

Morgan Boyd paused, and his big baritone voice went low and hard. "But hear me now, and hear me clearly." He lifted his arms in front of him, fingers curled slightly, as though supporting a large, heavy bowl. "Unless we act boldly and swiftly and surely, then the blood of the American heros who have died in the past two days—it will stain not only the hands of our enemies. It will stain ours."

The room was silent as a tomb for at least five seconds. Then most of the legislators in the room rose and applauded thunderously.

Charles Tunnington, however, was not one of them.

The applause continued for a full five minutes. In all that time, Charles Tunnington did not move a muscle.

As the president exited the room, trailing his handlers, he paused in front of Charles Tunnington and grasped the senator's hand. "Hello, Charles," he said. "I apologize for not discussing these issues with you earlier. But I've been run ragged today." Tunnington could see makeup on the president's face, masking the pallor of his complexion. He was sweating slightly too. Tunnington had seen this before in combat, men operating well past the point when they should have been resting with their feet in the air on a hospital bed. "I'd like you to join me at the White House for a drink this evening. Could you make it over by nine-thirty?"

Tunnington smiled without much warmth. "I'll check my schedule, Mr. President."

The president winked. "You're a good man. See you in a few minutes."

The White House
9:20 PM

When they reached the White House, Morgan Boyd and John Rancy went to the Map Room and sat. The Map Room was a warm, if somewhat formal sitting room with an Old World feel. FDR had used the room during World War II for his fireside chats. There was an elegant and slightly faded 1755 map of colonial America on the east wall, and the furniture was Chippendale.

"The Pontius Pilate line was really good," Rancy said. "That'll focus groups well in the South and West."

Morgan Boyd grunted, apparently lost in thought.

"Who wrote the speech, by the way?"

Morgan looked at him sharply. "See, Rancy, that's the difference between you and me. That's why you'll always be a sword bearer and never a prince. Who do you think wrote the Gettysburg Address? Some political hack? Some reporter who got tired of the miserable pay at his newspaper in Cleveland? No. The reason it was a good speech is that it was a complete and honest representation of the man, Abraham Lincoln. I just stood out there and told the world what I believed. That kind of sincerity cannot be faked, it can't be ghostwritten, it can't be focus-grouped, it can't be scripted."

Rancy blinked. "I'm sorry, I didn't mean—"

Boyd waved his hand. "It doesn't matter, John."

"It's funny, John, but I always had a naive faith in the American people. But when those shots went off in New Delhi, and I was holding my wife in my arms, her blood all over me and all those Indians running away like rats, I had the strangest realization—like the scales had come away from my eyes. I realized that the American people are no different from anyone else. People are weak and fearful everywhere. Fire off a few shots in New York City, people will stampede just like they do in India. Only order can save us. Without order, our precious freedoms will dissolve like smoke in the wind."

The room was silent for a while.

"It's really within our grasp now," Boyd said finally. His voice had changed, sounding almost wistful. "This is an historic opportunity. If we do everything right over the next few weeks and months, we'll have the means at hand to do what we should have done over the past twenty years—to fight terrorism seriously. I know we've discussed this a million times, John, but it's worth saying it out loud again. Most presidents occupy this room without the first clue what they really mean to accomplish in the world. But not me. The world is full of people who have death on the brain. They see the power of this country, they see our freedoms, our might—and all they want to do is wreck us. Even if the wreckage falls right on their heads and kills their own people. It's got to be stopped, no matter what the cost. Because if we don't stop the Brotherhoods and the Al-Qaedas of the world, one of these days they'll start dumping poisons in our water supplies, vaporizing cities with nuclear weapons, setting viruses loose that could wipe out half the world . . . And they won't even care, because they're so fixated on death."

"I know, Mr. President. I know." John Rancy's role had been well honed over the years.

"If we don't seize this moment, the death worshipers and the haters and the fanatics will strangle all the progress that mankind has worked so hard for over the past four or five centuries. Now is our moment, John. Now is our moment."

Rancy waited a moment to see if the president had more to say. When it became evident he didn't, Rancy said, "One other thing, Mr. President. I got a call from Mary Campos. She thinks the FBI need to take—and I quote—'a closer look at Mark Greene.'"

"Greene?" The president's eyebrows went up. "Really? Based on what?"

"She didn't say. But I talked to Smith at the FBI—the special agent-in-charge who's handling the investigation?—and he said he's pursuing the leads she gave him, and he's found a couple of unsettling connections. Nothing conclusive. Some negative statements Greene made about President Fairbank, a couple of odd vacation travel patterns, that sort of thing. Anyway, Smith wants to take Greene off your detail and do another more thorough interrogation. He wants to dig deeper."

The president looked thoughtful. Finally he said, "Handle it appropriately."

There was a knock on the door.

Morgan Boyd rose as an attendant opened the door to admit the white-haired lion of the Senate, Charles Tunnington.

"Ah, Charley!" Morgan said enthusiastically. Like many politicians, he could switch on the warmth at a moment's notice. "Come in, come in. We were just talking about you, buddy."

Northern Alabama
9:25 PM

On a good day, taking the interstate and driving a few miles above the speed limit, you can make it from the Shenandoah Valley to the northeastern corner of Alabama in around eight hours. But when you're mostly driving secondary roads, when you periodically have to stop to steal a car or shoplift food so that you can conserve your remaining thirty dollars in cash for gas, when you're being hunted by every police agency in the United States—the trip takes a little longer.

Delaney had ditched the cop car at a rest stop near Fancy Gap—with the young state trooper locked in the trunk—then dipped into North Carolina, where he had meandered through the Smokies and the Blue Ridge into Tennessee. The freakishly cold weather of the previous days had broken, replaced by an equally freakish warm front coming up out of the Gulf, and suddenly the weather was springlike. Which would have been fine . . . except that it seemed to have drawn half the populations of Charlotte, Nashville, and Atlanta into the mountains. The two-lane roads were clogged with cars, crawling along at DC-rush-hour speeds.

A nine-hour drive had turned into twelve. Delaney had cut through Chattanooga, picked up U.S. 11 again, headed down past Lookout Mountain, through Rossville and Trenton, Georgia, then crossed the border, stopping at the public library in Piedmont, Alabama. They had a pretty good map room, where he made photocopies of a number of U.S. Geological Survey topographic maps until a young lady approached him and told him that the library was supposed to have closed fifteen minutes earlier.

"I'm sorry!" Delaney said, hurriedly erasing a penciled circle from one of the maps. "You should have said something. I didn't mean to hold you up."

"Oh, it's no problem." The librarian was a plain-looking girl with big hands and sallow skin. "Doing some hunting?" she said.

"Thinking about it," he said.

"Wouldn't if I were you," she said. "Not around here."

"Oh?"

"You didn't hear?" she said. "Those creeps that assassinated the president? They just wiped out an FBI SWAT team. The hills are going to be crawling with federal officers." She leaned toward him, raised her eyebrows. "I heard a rumor they're sending in the army."

"Really?"

"You're not from around here." Not a question or a challenge, but a statement of fact. In a town this size, you knew everybody.

"I'm from Washington, DC. My family owns a couple hundred acres over near Thunder Mountain."

She nodded. "Well, I don't mean to rush you . . ."

"Sure." Delaney gathered up the topo maps, folded them neatly, and stowed them in a jacket pocket.

He was preparing to put the maps back in their drawers, but the librarian said, "Don't worry about those. We'll refile them in the morning."

"Thanks a million," he said. "Actually I am in a little bit of a hurry. I have to meet a friend."

The White House
9:40 PM

Senator Charles Tunnington sat erectly in his chair, looked around the Map Room.

"The first time I sat in this room," the senator said, "you were probably in high school, Mr. President."

"No doubt," Morgan Boyd said. He turned to John Rancy. "How about giving the senator and me a couple of minutes alone."

The two men watched as John Rancy left the room.

"Mr. President, I feel there are a few things I must say . . ."

"It's just us, Charley," Morgan said. "I didn't ask you here to be Mister-Presidenting me."

"No, Mr. President, I'd prefer to keep it on a formal plane today, if you don't mind."

Boyd shrugged. "As you wish, Senator."

"Before you say anything, Mr. President, I know why you asked me here. So let me tell you that on a personal level I sympathize with your anguish and your pain. I know you've lost a wife to terrorism. I know you took a bullet in your side from these people. Believe me, I wish the world was composed of rational, calm, humane people. But I know that it's not, and I know that measures have to be taken. When we catch these sumbitches, I'm all for hanging them by the neck until dead."

"Good," the president said.

"But that's merely a personal note. The matter at hand is rather less personal. You want my support for this misbegotten bill of yours. Well, I've been in the Senate with you for some years, and I agreed with you on some matters and disagreed on others. On matters of personal style, I never particularly cottoned to you, but I always respected you as a thinker. So that's why I'm puzzled. This bill of yours seems antithetical to everything you ever stood for as a senator."

"Quite the contrary," Boyd said. "I've always maintained that Emerson got it right: a foolish consistency is the hobgoblin of little minds. If we stick rigidly to a collection of dry abstractions about freedom and constitutional democracy—then we will watch as those freedoms and that democracy are methodically destroyed."

Tunnington shook his head. "No, Mr. President, you are simply wrong. You underestimate the strength and resilience of our system. But I know that you have made up your mind, so I see no sense in debating the point. I am here merely to give you a message. I will not, cannot—support this awful bill. I will fight it with every ounce of my strength."

"We're proposing a wide variety of measures in this bill. Is there any particular one which you find particularly objectionable?"

"The authorization for deployment of troops on U.S. soil."

Boyd leaned back in his chair and squinted at the ceiling thoughtfully. "When a nation is threatened militarily, military means must be used to fight the threat. It's that simple. We sent the best men that the civilian world has to offer against these people this morning and they were wiped out."

"So call out the National Guard."

"No offense against the fine people of the National Guard, but they just aren't prepared to fight what are obviously highly trained guerrilla soldiers. We're talking about very surgical uses of force."

"That may be your *intent,* but the bill does not specify how you can deploy these troops. It's a terrible precedent, Mr. President. It throws the 1878 Posse Commitatus Act in the dustbin. Both in letter and in spirit."

"Troops have been deployed in the past. Cavalry was deployed in the Indian fighting in the West well after 1878. Eisenhower sent the 101st Airborne to desegregate Little Rock. Military troops were deployed to assist in border patrol operations beginning in the eighties. There's been no abuse of those deployments, no precedent established which led us down some slippery slope to military dictatorship. And there won't be abuses here. The American people wouldn't allow it."

Tunnington shook his head. "It's bad law, Mr. President. Bad law, bad precedent, bad idea. You don't need it."

"Without military muscle, this entire bill is toothless. The terrorists will thumb their noses at the U.S. government, and there will be nothing we can do about it. I can dicker around the edges of this bill with you, Senator. But on the military element of the bill, there will be no negotiation."

"Then we're at an impasse."

Boyd sucked some air through his teeth, studied Tunnington for a while. "Is there anything I can offer you?"

"Offer me!" Tunnington shook his head sadly. "Shame on you, Mr. President. If this was a farm tariff bill or a defense appropriations bill, I might be able to work with you. But we're talking about the fundamental rights of American citizens. Troops firing on American citizens? This is the sort of thing that moved us to push George III out of this country in the first place. This bill will pass over my dead body."

"I would hope it doesn't come to that," Morgan Boyd said, trying out a hollow little laugh.

The senator did not smile at this forced attempt at levity but instead rose stiffly from his chair. His aging joints prevented him from making the brisk exit he would have liked, but he got the point across just the same. He walked out, and the door closed behind him.

Piedmont, Alabama
9:47 PM

Delaney headed south on State Highway 9 into the Talladega National Forest. After about five miles, he drove the car off the side of the road and into a ditch where it would be invisible from the road. He loaded his pack with beef jerky, several energy bars, a sleeping bag, and just under a gallon of water in a camel-back-type water bag. He decided the MP5 and the grenade launcher would only weigh him down, so he left them in the truck. Then he began hiking into the woods.

He hadn't practiced his orienteering skills lately—but it all came back pretty quickly. Night navigation was never a picnic, but it was what he had to do, so he just did it. He kept his Ranger beads in his pocket, clicking off one bead for every 108 paces—108 of his strides representing 100 meters on level ground. When the ground started getting steeper, he had to adjust his calculations, dropping to 90, then 85, then 80, then 70 as the terrain got more and more vertical.

He'd made about three kilometers when he heard the first chopper. Probably whoever it was would have night vision, but not FLIR. But it was impossible to know for sure. He had to assume that any IR signature he put out could get him killed. There was a creek just a hundred meters or so in front of him. He jogged quickly to the creek, found a pool just over a foot deep, pulled the drinking hose off his water bag, and stuck it in his mouth. Then he submerged himself faceup in the frigid water, raking rocks and mud over his body with his arms and breathing shallow breaths through the hose, which poked up out of the water. The blood vessels constricted in his head, giving him an instant ice cream headache, and his chest cramped up so that he could barely breathe. But he didn't move at all. The spotlight from the chopper appeared through the water, passed over, moved on.

If there was a spotlight, there probably wasn't even night vision. But you couldn't assume.

The water was horribly cold, but Delaney didn't move until he got so cold that he began to shiver. Finally he sat up, water and mud streaming from his clothes. The night was beginning to cool now. Unpleasant as it was, he was just going to have to take a chance with hypothermia. There was no time to waste, not tonight. Once he got moving again, the exertion of the hike would probably warm him up.

As it turned out, the hiking did warm him. There were no more choppers that night, and by daybreak he had made good progress. But he was exhausted. Three days with precious little sleep had left him without much in the way of physical reserves. He'd done this sort of thing back in his army days, of course, but he'd been a hell of a lot younger and in better shape. He still ran and worked out regularly— but the only way to practice marching is marching. He consoled himself by thinking about Stonewall Jackson's "foot cavalry" who had routinely marched with rifles and full packs twenty-five miles a day on crummy rations during the Shenandoah Valley campaign, or the Long March in 1935—six thousand miles under combat conditions—by General Chu Teh, perhaps the fastest combat march in history. What was this, he tried to tell himself—a day or two hiking around in the boonies?—it was nothing.

It was nothing, except that his feet were blistered and swollen and bleeding, his hip joints ached, his left ACL was inflamed, his lower back cramped up so bad every half a klick or so that he had to lie down and put his feet in the air, and he could barely keep his eyes open. But other than that? A walk in the park.

He checked the map with his flashlight; he'd made fourteen miles in the dark. Not bad for a broken-down has-been soldier. But he'd only made it about halfway to his destination. And daytime would be more dangerous than night. He'd be more exposed, easier to see, more tired, more irritable, more prone to mistakes.

As the white-hot disk of the sun cleared the far ridge, he stopped for a moment and took a deep breath. He knew from experience that the first appearance of the sun always brought a lift, a restoration of hope, and was therefore to be treasured. He looked out across the beautiful valley and for a moment felt a flash of wild enthusiasm that bordered on joy.

Then as quickly as it had come, the feeling died, replaced only by pain and grim resolve. He began plodding down the hill.

DAY FOUR

21

Washington, DC
7:20 AM

LIEUTENANT COLONEL DIRK PARDEE, U.S. Army (Ret.),
head of Unit P, was pacing the room when the phone rang.
"Pardee," he said.

"It's Rancy," the voice on the other end said. "We've had a sighting."

Pardee listened for another three minutes, then hung up the
phone. "Saddle up, girls!" he shouted.

TWO AND A HALF HOURS LATER, Pardee was standing in the
public library of Piedmont, Alabama. The sheriff of the county was
standing there next to him, along with a couple of FBI men.

"May I ask, dear," he said to the odd-looking, pale girl who worked
at the library, "how come it is that you waited an entire night to call us?"

The sheriff cleared his throat. "Ah, I guess you could say that's my
fault, actually."

Pardee turned and stared at the gangly, foolish-looking old man in
the gray Stetson. "I don't recall speaking to you, Sheriff," he said.

The sheriff didn't seem to notice his antagonism. "See, what it is,
ever' dadgum law enforcement office in northern Alabama been
swamped with calls how there's crazed gunmen wandering around
doing this, that, and the other and so Miz Poe here called our office
last night and it was fixing to be shift change and I had to get home for
supper and, well, what it done, it just slipped through the cracks."

Pardee continued to give him a hard stare. The old man didn't get
the hint.

"Then this morning, see, this here state trooper seen a car down in
the weeds off Shelburne Road. Over by Thunder Mountain? Turnt

out this car got stole from outside Rena's Café last night. Now I put two and two together and I said to myself—"

Pardee looked at the FBI men and said, "Could you gentlemen do me a favor, escort this clown out of here before I dope-slap him into the middle of next week?"

The sheriff retreated swiftly. Pardee turned back to the ugly librarian. "You were saying . . ."

"I knew it was him the minute I saw him. I have a good recollection for faces. Anyway, I saw that he was photocopying maps, so I left him to it. I figured that whichever maps he pulled out, that might assist the FBI in locating him."

"That was excellent tactical thinking, dear. You ever thought about running for sheriff?"

The ugly girl flushed. "He took out three map sections. Right here, here, and here." She pointed at several U.S. Geological Survey topographical maps. "And when I came up to him as he was finishing up, I saw him erase something off the map." She pointed to a ghostly circle on the map. "He said his family owned property near Thunder Mountain. But I think he was just trying to throw me off. This circle, as you can see, is not on Thunder Mountain, it's on Little Bear Mountain."

Pardee looked at the map, then spoke into his satellite phone. "Check on this. I'm looking at USGS map number TAL1276. I want the owner of a property located at latitude 34 75 81, longitude 76 55 29. I want NSA to vector a satellite on it right this very second, maximum resolution. We need to know the precise layout, every building, every stone, every tree. Clear? And if NSA gives you any crap, get Rancy to breathe down their necks."

He asked the girl a few more questions, then his cell rang. "Yeah?"

The voice on the other end said, "The property is owned by a Lisa Miller Delaney. Uh-huh, that's right, it's his ex-wife."

Pardee clapped his hands, grabbed the map, and started walking out of the library.

"Sir?" called the librarian. "Sir, those aren't available for checkout."

"Bill the FBI," he said.

As he was climbing into the FBI Ford outside, he made another call. "Pardee here. I think we have our first target for the Eighty-second."

22

Northern Alabama
11:51 AM

THERE WAS NO MOVEMENT around the cabin.

First Lieutenant John Gordon Davis, a twenty-eight-year-old platoon leader in the Eighty-second Airborne, wanted to be anywhere but on this ridge, looking out through his field glasses at the cabin situated halfway up the next hill. They called it a mountain, but to his mind it was a hill. Major Davis did not like his assignment, nor the lack of preparations that had gone into it. Nor the fact that the commander of the entire XVIII Airborne Corps was pretty much looking over his shoulder. Nor, especially, the fact that he was about to commit an entire rifle platoon against American citizens.

But Davis was a soldier. He took orders. Not like Captain Travis Scaggs, his predecessor in the command, who had been led off the tarmac by MPs that morning at Hunter AAF when he refused what he claimed were "unlawful orders" to command the attack in Alabama.

The cabin on the far ridge was just one step up from being a shack: rusty metal roof, two rooms and a porch, slat construction, a couple of grimy windows with no light showing. It looked more like something out of a Walker Evans photo than a hardened position requiring the use of an entire company of paratroopers. There was still nobody moving around the cabin. Then again, from what he'd been briefed, the HRT hadn't seen much movement out of their target either. He was taking it slow. First squad on the north side of the ridge, second on the left, third in reserve.

Captain Davis decided to hump on over with second squad to direct the final assault. He called out to the assembled men, "Let's play it safe. Take it slow. There may be unfriendlies patrolling the area. *Do not let yourselves be surprised!"* He made a circle around his head with his hand and the men began filing down into the woods.

THEY HAD BEEN moving through the heavy timber for about forty-five minutes, just approaching the far ridge, when two loud rifle shots ran out in quick succession. He knew from the heavy smack of the discharge that they weren't M-16s. Some kind of sniper caliber—.308 maybe?

"Hostiles! Hostiles!" came the voice of the platoon's point.

Davis reached for his AN/PNC-119 tactical radio, tapped the PTT button, and asked his squad sergeants if there were any casualties.

"I'm hit!" came the reply from Sergeant Ortiz.

"How bad?"

"My arm. It hurts like crazy."

Another loud smack from the sniper rifle—then a flash of something moving—Day-Glo orange—at the top of the ridge about a hundred meters away. Orange? Were they posing as hunters?

The entire platoon began firing, and the orange disappeared over the ridge.

"Cease fire!" Davis yelled. He could feel his heart pounding.

The M-16s went quiet. Davis signaled one of the squad leaders to circle around the hill and another to move up. "Go easy. They could be sucking us into an ambush."

IT TOOK ANOTHER fifteen minutes for the two squads to crest the hill. They found two men crouching over a third figure. All of them were dressed in head-to-toe camouflage, except for the orange hunting vests on their chests.

One of them turned, hearing the stealthy approach of the first squad. "Who the hell are you people?" the man screamed. "What's wrong with you? You just shot a thirteen-year-old boy!"

Davis signaled the squad to approach.

"Down on the ground," the troopers were screaming. "Everybody on the ground."

The two men complied, still yelling frantically.

Once it became clear there was no one waiting in the far trees to ambush them, Davis approached. The two men had now been restrained at the wrists with plastic zip cords. Davis looked at the prone figure. He was a blond-haired kid, not even old enough to shave, his green eyes looking up in the air with terror. Bubbles were coming out of his chest.

"Medic!" Davis yelled. Then, as a medic began putting a chest compress on the boy, he asked the two men who they were.

One of the men was sobbing. "You shot my boy," he kept saying. "You shot my boy."

The other man was calmer. He told Davis his name.

"Why did you fire on us?" Davis said.

"Fire on you?" The older man shook his head. "Junior there, he seen a buck moving down the ridge, took a couple shots at it."

"Oh?" Davis said skeptically.

The older man pointed at something forty or fifty meters away, a gray pile of fur. "It's right there, you stupid fool!" he said.

And sure enough, it was a spike buck, lying on its side, blood on its muzzle. "Oh, no," said Davis. "Oh, no, no, no."

The boy on the ground had stopped moving.

"Get on the radio, get a medevac in here, get the kid to the hospital," he snapped at his radioman. Then he left the medic and a couple of paratroopers with the boy and they moved on up the ridge. Davis had his orders. But he knew they had messed up. Shooting a thirteen-year-old boy? He stopped and lowered his head, feeling like he was going to throw up. But then nothing happened.

"You okay, Captain?" his platoon sergeant said.

"I'm fine. Let's just get up there and get this over with."

Half an hour later, the were inside the cabin. It was empty, dusty, abandoned.

"Any resistance?" came the voice of Davis's commander, Major Sanderson.

"No, sir. This was a fool's errand, a ruse. I don't think Delaney was ever even here."

Northern Alabama
12:40 PM

Michael Delaney, in fact, was several mountain ridges away, still working his way across country. His feet were now so swollen that he had a hard time getting them back in his boots after he had stopped to rest. Both of his big toenails had blood under them and his heels were chafed raw. But it was the only way. He was sure it was the only way.

He consulted the map again. Ten more klicks and he'd be there.

Northern Alabama, Just Outside the Talladega National Forest
3:15 PM

First Lieutenant Kevin Dettrick didn't care about the Constitution. It was nice and all, the Constitution, but you had a job to do, you let other people think about stuff like that. A couple of the other lieutenants in his company had asked him about whether what they were doing was legal or constitutional, whatever, and his response was, "Our job is to get these scumbag redneck terrorists out of this farm and bring our boys back home safely to Bragg. I'll leave the big picture to the brass at the Pentagon."

Dettrick studied the farm through his glasses.

In the briefing, the intel officer had kept calling the place a "training camp." Well, there was a firing range, a jungle gym, and a sort of dog track that maybe you could go jogging on. But otherwise it was just a farm. And a pretty miserable one at that. There was a one-story brick house in the center of a couple of hay fields, a broken-down chicken coop off to the side, a barn covered in peeling red paint, some goats wandering around.

Through his field glasses Dettrick watched as a young hippie-looking kid came out of the back door of the house, unzipped his fly, and did his business right there against the wall. "What?" Dettrick said to Sergeant Willets, his senior noncom, "these morons don't have flush toilets?"

Willets grunted. He wasn't much of a talker. Standing next to Willets was a smooth-talking Latin guy named Gonzalez. Gonzalez was attached to some kind of spook outfit that Dettrick had never heard of. Unit Z, Unit P, something like that, supposedly run out of the White House.

"What do you think?" Dettrick said to Willets.

Willets didn't reply. But the spook, who obviously liked the sound of his own voice, said, "Pop him with a sniper."

Dettrick snorted. "They already screwed up, killed a civilian already today. I'm not just blowing the guy's head off, find out he's just some innocent guy visiting his mother-in-law."

The kid slouched back into the building, one hand under his shirt, rubbing his belly.

"Hey, I'm just an observer." Gonzalez shrugged. "But I bet those HRT guys wished they'd been a little more, ah, proactive, huh?"

Dettrick ignored the spook. This was an Airborne op. Gonzalez was strictly an observer, that's what he'd been told. He took his radio handset, thumbed the PTT. "Go," he said softly.

From all around the farm paratroopers began coming out of the trees, as though they had materialized out of thin air. Dettrick grinned. This was sweet.

TEN MINUTES LATER the farm was secured. Dettrick felt a little let down. There had been no resistance, no nothing. Here he'd been told how these guys were a bunch of pros, watch for claymores and .50 cal Brownings and all this, and what did they have?—nothing but six scared college boys, a cute girl in a peasant skirt, some rickety-looking old M1 Garands, and an ancient rusty .45 caliber M3 grease gun. The grease gun was probably some kind of federal violation or whatever—not that it was Dettrick's problem.

Gonzalez, the Unit P guy, followed Lieutenant Dettrick into the farmhouse. The seven young prisoners were lined up on the floor with their arms secured behind them. They all looked like they were about to pee their pants.

"Good afternoon, children," Gonzalez said, "my name is Mr. Gonzalez. This is Lieutenant Dettrick, U.S. Army. You have been captured pursuant to Executive Order Two. You know how in the movies they always say you have the right to remain silent, the right to an attorney, all that wonderful verbiage?"

The seven kids nodded dutifully.

"Well, boys and girls, you do not have those rights." Gonzalez turned to Dettrick. "This is where I take over."

"Excuse me?" Dettrick said. "I don't have any orders with regard to you. They just told me to let you come and observe."

Gonzalez smiled broadly. "Sure, of course not. There are certain kinds of orders which one never commits to writing—do you understand what I'm saying?"

Dettrick suddenly was feeling a little bit in over his head. "No, I damn well don't, Mr. Gonzalez. You hold on right there, don't say another word."

Dettrick took his radioman in the other room and radioed his company commander, who was in a chopper somewhere, coordinating a number of simultaneous raids on other Brotherhood locations.

"Sir, I have this Gonzalez guy here and now that we've secured the location, he's telling me the prisoners are 'his.' Quote unquote. Please advise."

Major Jordan's voice came back, "We are under instructions direct from CINCUSA to offer all possible support to Unit P personnel."

CINCUSA? That was the commander in chief of the United States, the president himself! "Confirm that? CINCUSA?"

"Confirmed. CINCUSA."

Dettrick knew when to hold 'em and when to fold 'em. "Roger."

He ended the transmission, then went back in the other room. Gonzalez now had the seven prisoners seated in a row on the cheap folding chairs kept in the makeshift mess room—if that's what you want to call it. Their legs were all taped to the chairs with green duct tape.

"What's going on here?" Dettrick said softly to Gonzalez. "I was told to chopper the prisoners out ASAP."

"Just a little field-expedient interrogation," Gonzalez said. Then he turned to the now-secured kids. "Okay, children, Q&A time. You know what that means?"

The kids shrugged.

"What it means is, I ask questions, and you give me the right answers. Okay. That's how you and I become friends. Right answers, yes? Give me the wrong answers, suddenly Mr. Gonzalez is not your friend anymore."

One of the boys took this as his cue to say, "Sir, I'm an American citizen. I assert my rights under the Constitution not to speak. So you might as well stop wasting your breath."

"Ah!" Gonzalez smiled. "Courage. I like a courageous man, as a general rule." He then pulled a .45 caliber 1911 out of a tactical holster Velcroed low on his thigh. "Sadly, courage does not yield right answers in the context of the particularly knotty historical moment in which we find ourselves." Gonzalez shot the boy in the head, splattering the wall behind him in red.

Dettrick suddenly went cold. It was one of those moments where a thing happened, but it was so improbable, so wrong, that for a little while it seemed as though it had been a trick or an illusion rather than an actual event. "Holy Mother of God!" Dettrick said, when his mind finally caught up with what had happened. "What are you *doing?*"

Gonzalez ignored him. "Okay, children, let's all gird up our loins for some right answers. Who would like to be my friend? Show of hands, please?"

One of the boys started crying like a baby. The girl started hyperventilating. But they all managed to raise their hands.

Dettrick retreated to the corner of the room. What was he going to do? He'd been given orders. But if the White House was sanctioning what this spook was doing, so be it. There was nothing he could do.

"Question one," Gonzalez said. "Where are your weapons?"

They all pointed at the pile of junky old guns on the other side of the room.

Gonzalez laughed and clicked his tongue. "No, no, my friends. Where's the good stuff?"

Gonzalez approached one of the boys, stroked his face with the barrel of his .45.

"Okay, okay, *okay!*" The kid was literally screaming. "There's a trapdoor in the back bedroom. Goes down to a little storm cellar. There's a bunch of stuff in there."

Gonzalez smiled. *"Con su permiso,* Lieutenant Dettrick," he said with an ironic smile, "might I humbly request that you send one of your fine troopers back there to see what he can find?"

"Do it," Dettrick said. His mouth had gone dry, and the words didn't come out very clearly.

"Sir?" the young soldier said, not understanding him.

"Do it!" Dettrick yelled. "Go find the cache!"

The trooper trotted down the hallway. Gonzalez hummed to himself while he waited. Several of the kids were now weeping openly.

The young soldier returned. "It's there, sir," he said to Dettrick. "Two dozen M-4s, some M-203 grenade launchers, two SAWs, an M-60, a Stoner. Must be forty, fifty pounds of C-4 in there too."

"Plastic explosives!" Gonzalez said brightly. "My goodness. How scary! I do believe we have just prevented a bloodbath."

"Plus some books. Antigovernment-type propaganda, it looks like."

Gonzalez's eyes widened in mock horror. "Are you young people keeping seditious literature in your basement? It is very possible the possession of such literature constitutes grounds for turning each and every one of you over to a military tribunal, where you could potentially be lawfully tried and executed on the spot. Did you know we can do that, children?"

They looked dumbly at him.

"Isn't it amazing how quickly the veil of your Constitutional protections can be stripped away?"

Dettrick could hear a chopper coming over the ridge into the little valley where the farm lay.

"Ah, there's my ride!" Gonzalez said. "Lieutenant Dettrick, carry on. I'm sure you have orders as to the disposition of my young friends here."

Dettrick grabbed him by the arm and dragged him into the other room. "What am I supposed to do about *that?*" he shouted, pointing at the dead kid.

Gonzalez blinked. "Do?"

"I have to make a report! I radioed my superiors and told them the objective had been taken without casualties."

"Where did you attend university, Lieutenant?"

"West Point. Not that that has anything to do with anything." Dettrick was so mad he could hardly see straight.

"West Point! Wow! I myself am a graduate of the Chilean Military Academy in Santiago. We call it the West Point of Chile. But how pretentious that seems when I stand before an *actual graduate* of West Point. May I congratulate you! You—my goodness!—are the best of the best. Every soldier in the world stands humbled before you."

"Goddammit, look—"

"I'm sorry, we Latins beat around the bush, I know. What I'm saying is, you're a very bright and resourceful young officer. Perhaps the poor fellow in there was shot while assaulting one of your soldiers. Perhaps a radio problem kept you from hearing that, in fact, there had been a brief exchange of fire and—well, listen to me going on at the mouth!—who am *I* to try to instruct you, a West Point graduate? You'll think of something."

"For godsake this isn't Bolivia! The FBI will come in here and dig the slug out of the wall and send it to the FBI lab and do all kinds of tests and then they'll say, 'Okay, who has a forty-five caliber weapon in this unit, because that's not regulation.' And then I'm screwed."

Gonzalez shrugged indifferently. "There's a three-hundred-gallon propane tank behind this house. Were someone to hit it with an errant grenade, the resulting explosion would certainly get rid of any inconvenient evidence."

"And what about you? What do I say about *you* in the report?"

"Me!" Gonzalez laughed. "Lieutenant, I was never here."

The Unit P man then jogged confidently out the front door, disappearing into a chopper with civilian markings that was now sitting in the front yard near the sagging old barn.

Dettrick put his face in his hands. What in the name of God was he going to do? When he looked up, Sergeant Willets was standing in front of him. Willets was a tough guy, well into his thirties, had been around the block a few times.

"He's right," Willets said. "We need to get rid of the evidence. I presume you want me to get the prisoners outside, then pop the propane tank?"

Dettrick nodded mutely, then walked outside. A young paratrooper—one of the three men who had watched Gonzalez shoot the prisoner—stood on the lawn with his M-16 at his shoulder. He sighted on a tethered goat and fired. The goat bleated then collapsed. Dettrick watched as the young soldier shot all the goats in a matter of seconds.

"What are you doing, trooper?" Dettrick demanded when the soldier was done.

The young man turned, tears running down his face. "I don't know, sir," he said. "I don't know."

The White House

4:19 PM

Lieutenant Colonel Mary Campos entered the Oval Office. She wore green BDUs and boots, like she was about to go into the field. It had been strongly suggested to her by John Rancy that she dress this way to "show that the president was taking matters in hand." She had strongly resisted the idea, but he had finally more or less ordered her to do it.

Morgan Boyd rose from his desk, indicated she should sit.

"Well?" he said.

"The Eighty-second Airborne has rolled up nine locations today. I was down there this morning monitoring their progress. Three locations were abandoned, six were occupied. There has been virtually no resistance. None of the locations were hardened like the one the HRT hit. Several locations were staffed—if that's the word—by rag-tag groups of college kids. Another couple were older cells, which had some of the more established Brotherhood members—the usual collection of mill hands, dirt farmers, angry postal workers, and general kooks. Virtually every one of them was taken flat-footed. There's been enough intel generated from initial interrogations to give us nine more locations to hit overnight. One civilian, a young boy hunting in the woods, was shot and killed by accident. The paratroopers took him for a hostile, when he took a crack at a deer."

Morgan Boyd nodded, his black eyes misting over for a moment. "I'm sorry to hear about the boy. What was his name?"

"Allen Gerard Kindle."

The president sighed. "All right. Look, I've got the press office waiting for you downstairs. The media is slavering for information. I want you to go brief them. Tell them about this kid, be completely up-front about it. Tell them that the president is grievously saddened—as, in fact, I am—and that the FBI will be looking into this tragedy. If someone is at fault, they'll be held responsible."

"Why me? We've only got a few minutes to get ready before the nightly news crews have to file their reports and I'm not experienced at this." She motioned with her hand, indicating her green BDUs. "I'm not even dressed."

Boyd looked irritated. "You're dressed perfectly. I told you before, I want to put a face on our effort to root these people out. You're that face."

Mary Campos felt something stirring inside her, a seed of disquiet. "Yes, Mr. President."

"What about Delaney?" the president called to her as she approached the door.

"He's somewhere in Alabama. But we don't know where. He's an elusive guy."

"I want you riding herd on Unit P. Right now, that's their top priority. Rancy tells me that Dirk Pardee is a good soldier, but that he's also a bit of a slippery character. Sometimes you have to stand on his neck to get results."

"Yes, Mr. President."

"Thank you, Colonel."

She rose and walked toward the door.

"Oh, one last thing, Colonel. Mark Greene has been removed from duty. I understand that's your doing—at least indirectly."

"That's SOP in cases like this. But, yes, I do want the FBI to look at every possible scenario."

"Sure. But remember, Colonel, in the pressure of situations like this it's easy to lose focus. This hole in my side came from Delaney's gun. He came back to Camp David against express orders from his superiors, then shot it out with federal agents in order to effect an escape. Now's not the time to start chasing shadows."

The seed of disquiet continued to grow. "Are you instructing me to discontinue that avenue of investigation, Mr. President?"

Boyd's face was impassive. "Of course not. I trust your instincts. I'm just suggesting that the more you dig, the more spurious lines of investigation you'll be tempted to follow. Be vigilant, keep focused, and shepherd your resources."

"I will, Mr. President."

23

Northern Alabama
7:41 PM

MICHAEL DELANEY reached Red Mountain a little before sundown. He had hiked twenty-eight miles across country in a little over a day. He had just enough time to scout the area and make sure it was clear by the time the sun went down. You never really knew for sure—but he felt pretty good that there were no federal agents in the area. There were no choppers, no roadblocks visible, no strange lights or reflections or sounds in the woods. His ruse at the library appeared to have worked.

He rested, dozing wearily against a tree with the sleeping bag over his legs for around an hour, then began the trek to the top of the hill. When he reached the summit, he paused again, squatting in the dark, listening for a full half hour, not moving a muscle. Nothing out of the ordinary. Nothing to indicate an ambush might be in the offing.

Just a hundred yards away was a small hunting cabin. It had been used by his wife's family for three generations. The property was actually owned by a big international timber company, but the Miller family had sold the property back in the 1970s with the proviso that they would retain hunting rights on four hundred acres of the land for fifty years, and that the cabin would be allowed to stand as long as they had hunting rights. Over the years most members of the Miller family had lost interest in hunting, until only a couple of people in the family even remembered that the cabin existed.

Delaney got on his belly, piled a couple of pine branches on his back to break up his silhouette, and began crawling across the ground toward the cabin. The stalk took him two hours and twenty minutes. The windows of the cabin had been spray-painted black. But when he reached the front door of the cabin, he could hear somebody moving around inside.

He stood slowly, his Beretta in his hand, and kicked in the door. A white male, forty-ish, with hair that had been dyed blond at the tips, was sitting in a chair picking at his toenails with a small Case folding knife.

The man fell backward, lay there on the floor staring up at Delaney without speaking. Suddenly he began to smile.

"Mike Delaney," he said. "Boy howdy, brother, you about scared the wits out of me!"

Delaney shut the door, set his pistol on the rough kitchen table. "Hello, Paul," he said.

The White House, Washington, DC
8:15 PM

Lieutenant Colonel Mary Campos crossed her arms. She was seated behind her desk in the office she had been given at the White House just that morning, as Dirk Pardee came into the room. He immediately sat in one of the red leather chairs across from her.

"I didn't ask you to sit," Mary Campos said.

Pardee eyed her for a moment. "You and I have the same rank," he said. "If I'd stayed in, I'd be a bird colonel by now. Maybe a brigadier."

"I was not aware of that. And even if I had been, I wouldn't care. You're not an active duty officer, and you work for me. Now stand up."

Pardee stood. "Yes, ma'am!" He may have been a lieutenant colonel—this was news to Mary—but he had mastered the enlisted man's trick of responding snappily to commands while maintaining a hard gleam of disdain in his eye.

"What's our progress on Delaney?"

"We've lost him. He ditched a car near Thunder Mountain, used a subterfuge to convince us he was on the mountain, then while the Eighty-second was storming an empty cabin, he hiked across country. We suspect he stole another vehicle and moved on."

"Moved on where?"

"We don't know."

"He didn't drive all the way to Alabama, surely, for nothing."

"I agree. I imagine he's trying to hook up with Paul Miller, the head of the Brotherhood."

"Whom you have not found yet either."

"You could fit most of Rhode Island into the Talladega National Forest, ma'am. My team will be on him like white on rice when we find him. But until then we don't have much to work with. The FBI's got dogs, they've got choppers, they've got all kinds of guys stomping around through the woods. But you just can't rush this thing. Look at Eric Rudolph. Took the FBI five years to find him."

"Colonel Pardee, you worked with him. You're in his shoes, what would you do?"

"Me?" Pardee laughed. "I'd be down in a tropical paradise with no extradition treaty, drinking some kind of colorful beverage that contained a great deal of rum. But that's not Delaney's style."

"Oh? You say that as though you know him."

"I do. He was in an A-Team I commanded back in the eighties."

"You say running for the border's not his style. What is?"

Pardee looked as though he were choosing his words carefully. "He's the type of guy, always wants to wear a white hat. I think he's trying to dig up some kind of information which will justify what he did or muddy the waters. Somehow or other, he'll try to find something to make him look like a hero."

"What would that be?"

"I don't know. But I guarantee you this, he's looking for Paul Miller, just like we are."

"Find one, we find them both."

"Right. Problem is, we have no idea where Miller is."

"A safe house."

"That's my thinking."

"Find the safe house, you win the trifecta—decapitate the Brotherhood, nail Delaney and Miller both."

"Sure. But there's a reason they call them safe houses. If we knew where it was, we'd have them already."

"What do these men have in common—Miller and Delaney?"

Pardee looked thoughtful. After a long time he said, "The intel we have right now says they didn't think much of each other. But there's one thing they always used to do together: they're hunters."

"Where did they hunt?"

"Generally? The FBI says they used the little hunting cabin that the Eighty-second hit this morning."

"Are you sure? Was there someplace else? Reinterview the family. Think about hunters and fishermen—every serious outdoorsman I've met has kept some secret little area where the fish bite like nobody's business, where nobody else goes to hunt . . . you know what I mean? Their own little secret preserve. Find out that secret place, you find them both."

Pardee grinned, his eyes narrow as dimes. "You should have been a man," he said. "You'd have made a heck of a soldier."

"I *am* a soldier, Colonel," Mary said tartly.

Pardee saluted laconically, that look of disdain creeping into his eyes again. "Of course you are, ma'am."

PARDEE GOT ON the cell as soon as he walked out of Colonel Campos's office. "Gonzalez," he said, "I want you and your guys to do some reinterviews. Delaney's ex-wife, anybody who ever hunted with Miller, family members, whatever. We're looking for a secret hunting spot—something off the beaten path, something from a long time back, something so far off the radar that everybody has almost forgotten about it." Pardee listened for a moment. "Yeah. And Gonzalez? No rough stuff. I don't want a report coming back about some nice old church lady getting her hand smashed in a door."

Before he had a chance to clip the phone back on his belt, it rang again. "It's Rancy," said the voice on the other end.

"Yes, sir?"

"I've got a job for you. High priority."

"Sir, we're stretched to the limit."

"Like I said, high priority. I want you to handle this yourself."

Northern Alabama
9:39 PM

"So Paul," Delaney said, "assassinating the *president?*"

Paul Miller—the so-called supreme commander of the Brotherhood and Delaney's ex-wife's cousin—was still lying on the floor where he'd fallen when Delaney burst in the door. The room was small, bare, dimly lit by a pair of propane camping lamps. "You want to help me up, Mike?"

"Not really."

Miller looked resentfully at Delaney, then rolled over, stood up, dusted himself off. He was about forty, but looked younger—handsome, fit, with hair that was dyed blond at the tips. He wore hunting camo. The 1911 pistol in his hand was a dude's weapon—gold inlay on the receiver, green paua shell grips. Probably six or eight grand worth of pistol. Delaney wondered where he'd gotten the money for something like that. "I think I may have fractured a rib," the head of the Brotherhood said.

"Tough. Now talk to me. They're saying I assisted somebody who assassinated the president. You set me up."

Paul Miller laughed bitterly. "Set *you* up? What about me? I'm the one sitting here in the middle of the freaking woods eating freeze-dried soup and waiting for some SWAT team of federal storm troopers to bust in here and blow my head off."

"Yeah, the difference is, you're involved. Whereas I was framed."

Miller pointed over at a table against the wall. A single sideband short-wave radio sat silently, a green light winking on its front. "We were both screwed, cuz. Both of us."

"Explain that."

"I've spent ten years building up this organization. I've just listened on that radio to the whole thing go down in flames over the past eight hours. Six of my cells have reported in. They were hit by *federal troops,* Mike! You don't believe me, it's on the news. Not FBI, not Alabama Bureau of Investigation, not ATF. I'm talking Eighty-second Airborne! Mike, the United States Army is wandering around Alabama smashing in doors and blowing up buildings with mortars! And nobody in America is saying boo about it. It makes me want to throw up."

"You should have thought of that before you conspired to kill the president of the United States."

Miller looked at Delaney as though he were appalled at Delaney's stupidity. "You're not listening, Mike. I had *nothing to do* with killing Dean Fairbank. Zero. Nada. Nothing!"

"The assassin was a member of your organization."

"Oh, and that proves I was behind it, huh? I heard on the radio that they have phone records of telephone calls between you and me. I never got any phone calls from you. Did you ever call me? Because I sure don't recollect any seventeen phone calls from you last month."

Delaney didn't say anything.

"We're patsies, cuz."

"The difference is, you asked for it, Paul. You preached violence against the government. You preached that the federal government is trying to take away all our liberties and therefore deserved to be torn apart."

The room was silent for a while. Finally Miller sighed. "You want to know the truth?" he said.

"Lay it on me," Delaney said sarcastically. He knew from experience that Paul Miller's version of the truth was always guaranteed to be self-serving at best, and a pile of lies at worst.

"Look, yeah, I do happen to believe the federal government is out of control. I do happen to resent paying money to the IRS so that some fourteen-year-old crackhead in Atlanta can keep pumping out babies. I do happen to think Ruby Ridge and Waco were grotesque crimes. But hey . . . violent overthrow of the government?" He shrugged. "I'm a lover not a fighter, you know what I mean?"

"You're saying, if I'm correctly reading between the usual lines of patented Paul Miller horsecrap, that the Brotherhood is a big scam. You set the whole thing up because it was an easier way of making a living than holding down a real job."

Miller drummed his fingers on the table for a while. Finally, in a wistful voice he said, "Kids out there are so discontented, so lost. They're looking for a mission. I go on college campuses and I talk about the way the federal storm troopers are marching across America, and I tell them how they can come out in the woods and stomp around and shoot guns and be real Americans, real men—dadgum, Mike, you should see these kids, the way their faces light up!"

"You're a regular saint."

Miller avoided Delaney's eyes.

"But there's something you're still not telling me, Paul."

"It was a good little racket for a while. I'd get my kids to charge things on their parents' credit cards—dues, training sessions, whatever. They'd have to pay me for the official uniform, the handbook, literature, posters. And then there were fees for rank promotions, speaking fees . . . It is astonishing, Mike, the amount of discretionary income that college kids have today. So I was making a tidy little living . . ." His voice petered out.

"And then?"

Miller put down his fancy .45 and rubbed his hands together. It was getting a little cold in the cabin. "There was this guy . . ."

Delaney shook his head sadly. There was this guy. There was always this guy. Con men were always the easiest people to con.

"A guy comes to me. He's this nerdy little accountant guy. He says that he works for a powerful man who believes in our mission. Says this guy wants to underwrite our cause."

"How much did he offer you?"

Miller laughed bitterly again. "Man, this boy had *deep* pockets."

"How deep?"

"In the past twelve months I've received $3.73 million from him. And some change."

Delaney's eyes widened. "To do *what?*"

"Ah . . . well, you know, a certain amount of it kind of vanished into my lifestyle you might say." He sighed wistfully. "All my life I wanted a Cadillac. That new one? You know the one with the big engine? You ought to see the way the women look at you when you climb out of that car."

"Stick to the story. What happened to the money you didn't spend on Cadillacs and credulous college girls?"

"To some degree it paid for stepped-up recruiting efforts. Better collateral materials, posters, recruitment videos, stuff like that. But mostly it paid for weapons and property."

"Weapons and property. Did this person specify what he wanted you to buy? Or did you do it yourself?"

"He pretty much specified it. We started out buying M-16s and M-4s. Usually stolen military stuff. Then we moved up to grenade launchers, C-4, Berettas, SAWs, .50 cal Brownings, blasting caps." Miller hesitated. "Past couple months, though, he had me working on real heavy stuff."

"Meaning what?"

Miller cleared his throat. "Look, Mike, you're a federal agent . . ."

"Oh, give me a break! You and I are in this together. If we share information, maybe we have a chance. If not, we'll spend the rest of our lives in Leavenworth. Or worse."

Miller's eyes darted around the cabin. "Let's just say I spent a lot of time on the Afghani-Pakistan border."

"You're gonna have to do better than that."

"Stingers. LAWs. Soviet ground-to-ground missiles."

"I can see from that shifty look on your face that there's more."

"Ricin, VX, mustard gas, anthrax . . ." He shrugged, looked off into the distance.

"Oh, Paul, Paul, Paul . . . how could you be so stupid. And how much of this stuff did you actually buy?"

"That's the thing. Nothing. None of the deals ever went through."

"Did you talk to anybody in this country?"

"Sure. Some Syrian guys up in Jersey City. An Iranian who lives in Miami. A guy from Kazakhstan, some Belorussians . . . There were some others."

"You've been busy. How did you find out about these people?"

"This guy I was telling you about. He put me in touch."

"What was this man's name?"

"He never told me. I called him the paymaster. After the first time we met, I only talked to him by phone. The area code was in northern Virginia."

Suddenly Delaney heard something outside, the distant thump of helicopter rotors. It got louder and louder.

The two men froze. Delaney wondered if he should make a break for it. No. What was the point? If it was an assault team, they'd have night vision and they'd see him running. If it was a recon chopper scanning the woods, a man dodging through the woods would only call attention to the area. Better to sit tight and wait.

Delaney reached over and turned off the camping lamps. In the darkness he could hear Miller breathing. Then the sound of Miller's breath was overwhelmed by the thudding of the chopper's rotors as it came closer and closer and closer.

Anniston, Alabama
9:58 PM

Badger knocked on the door of the small brick ranch house on the end of a street that had houses on one side and a view of Lloyd Maines Chevrolet and I-20 on the other.

Badger had to knock three times before the door finally opened. He smiled.

"Mrs. Miller?"

The woman behind the door was thin and sour looking. "Ain't got nothing to say."

Badger kept smiling. He showed her a fake ID. "Adolph Kuhn,

ma'am, FBI. I apologize for barging in so late, but there's an urgent lead we need to follow up on."

The woman in the house was Paul Miller's aunt, Rosetta Jean Miller. Badger eased the door open and walked in, not letting the old lady stop him. The place smelled like a washroom at a truckstop. There was a television going with the sound turned up so loud he could hardly hear himself think. The old gal was watching reruns of *Touched by an Angel* on cable. Mrs. Miller wore a housecoat and fuzzy slippers, and her makeup was laid on thickly, but without skill. On the couch across the room, an ancient man with a few wisps of hair and a slack mouth stared at the television, apparently oblivious to Badger's presence.

"I don't have nothing to do with that boy!" the old woman said. "Plus which, I already said everything I have to say to that other man that come here yesterday."

Badger seated himself on the couch, still smiling. "Of course, ma'am. Sometimes little details will come back to you, though."

The old lady seated herself primly on an overstuffed chair with a lace antimacassar on it and said, "Well? Like what? Let's get it over so Mr. Miller, my poor father-in-law here, can get back to his show."

Father-in-law? Mrs. Miller had to be pushing eighty, so God only knew how old the man was. "You mind if we turn it down?"

The old lady grudgingly turned the television down to a level that was merely deafening. The old man continued to stare at the TV.

"What we're looking for," Badger said, "we're concerned your nephew, Mr. Paul Miller, may have taken a young girl hostage."

"He's a worthless boy, but he wouldn't do nothing like that."

"Like I say, we're not certain. We're just trying to make sure that a very nice young girl doesn't get hurt." He showed her a picture of a smiling model that he had cut out of *Cosmopolitan* magazine in a drugstore about five minutes earlier. "Isn't she a lovely young gal?"

The old woman squinted at the picture. "Hmph!" she said.

"She was a close associate of Mr. Paul Miller and now we're very concerned about her safety. What we believe is that Mr. Miller has transported her, possibly against her will, to a location somewhere in the woods—probably up near Talladega National Forest. But frankly we're not sure."

"I don't know why you're asking me."

"What we're wondering—I know you were very close to Mr. Miller's father and mother. We believe that Mr. Miller has a hunting spot, a place maybe that he didn't share with a lot of people, a secret hunting spot . . ."

The woman looked at him blankly.

"You wouldn't know anything about that, would you?"

"Hunting? What would I know about hunting? All I know about hunting is Mr. Miller, my husband, used to go off in a truck with his buddies from the war and they'd come home smelling of liquor and then I'd be up all night cleaning miserable little birds that you break your teeth on bird shot eating them, or either butchering some stringy, mangy old deer that wouldn't do nothing but set out there all year in the deep freeze, 'cause it ain't fit to eat."

"So you don't know anything about—"

"Hunting! What's wrong with eating a nice piece of beef from the Winn Dixie store? Where is it wrote down that blasting some poor little scared deer makes you into a big old man? Huh? Huh? Where is it wrote down?"

"Just think back a little bit. There's not some special place he might have told your husband about? Something he might have mentioned to you once?"

"Oh, that'd be the day! That'd be the day, when my husband confided in *me*. No, sir, all those little creatures wearing their little short skirts down at the furniture store, I'm sure they knew all his deepest secrets, all them secretaries and salesgirls, no doubt he told them all about his deepest hopes and fears and the rest, but not his wife of fifty years, no sir, not Mr. Miller, no he was too busy—"

Badger rose. He'd had enough. "Thank you, ma'am," he said. "Pardon the intrusion. I can see you won't be able to help us much."

He walked over to the door. *Touched by an Angel* started blasting again.

He had his hand on the knob when a second voice spoke. "Hey! Boy!"

Badger turned. It was the old man talking. Sly old goat, acting senile, probably so he didn't have to engage in conversation with his awful daughter-in-law.

The ancient man had a high, harsh voice that carried easily above the treacly strains of music thundering out of the television. "Set down, boy! I got a hunch what it is you want."

Arlington, Virginia
10:21 PM

Pardee palmed his cell. "What!"

"It's Badger," the voice on the other end said. "I think we got it. What happened, we're looking for a four-hundred-acre plot of land sold by the Miller family to Georgia Pacific about thirty years ago. The old man who told me about it was a little hazy on exactly where it was. He knew the name of the county, but not much more than that. We'll have to wait until morning when the courthouse opens and look through some plat books."

"The morning!" Pardee shouted. "Are you nuts? Get up there, drag the clerk of court out of bed, do whatever you got to do, but you *find* that property. Tonight. I'll be on the G-IV in the next hour or so. Tell Gonzalez to get the whole team saddled up. Screw the Eighty-second Airborne. We'll hit the place at daybreak, do it ourselves."

"I don't know squat about real estate. What if it takes longer than that to find this property?"

"Then I'll stick your head on a pole, how's that sound?"

"I'll get right on it, sir." Badger, expressionless, the perfect sergeant. Pardee loved him, loved him the way you'd love a pit bull or a fighting rooster that you'd trained with your own hands.

"Oh, Badger. Have a car waiting for me at the nearest general aviation airport."

PARDEE PULLED UP in front of a modest brick house on a modest street, parked, then walked four doors down, up the front walk to a blue-painted wood-frame house, pressed the button, then stepped behind a bush.

Special Agent Mark Greene opened the door and looked out the front door of his house with an irritable expression on his face. He was wearing blue seersucker pajamas and had a cocked Beretta in his hand.

Pardee stepped out from behind the bush.

"Pardee, I'm trying to get some goddamn sleep!" Greene said. "What are you doing over here?"

"Do me a favor, take that gunsight off my chest."

Greene let down the hammer of the Beretta, put the safety on, and said, "Come on in. It's too cold to talk out here."

They went inside, and Greene led Pardee into the living room.

Greene sat on the couch, still holding the Beretta in his hand, and said, "I thought we were supposed to stay away from each other."

"Why you think I was standing behind that bush?" Pardee said, sitting down in a chair opposite him. "I don't want every nosy old lady in the neighborhood staring at me."

Greene set the Beretta on the coffee table between them. There was a bottle of Jack Daniel's on the table with an empty glass next to it. Good. Perfect. Couldn't have asked for a better scenario.

"How you holding up under the strain?" Pardee said.

"What—you think because I had a couple slugs of bourbon before I went to bed that I'm wigging out on you?" Greene glared at him. "Give me a break."

Pardee grinned. "Hey, easy, bud, I'm not making a federal case here. Frankly, I'm a little on edgy myself. You mind if I have a slug?"

"Help yourself." Greene continued to stare suspiciously at him.

Pardee kept up his smile. "You gonna offer me a glass?"

Greene sighed loudly, stood, went into the kitchen, came back after about thirty seconds with a heavy glass. He dropped it roughly on the table next to the bottle. He still had the Beretta in his hand.

"Why all the hostility, ace? You gonna make me pour it myself?"

Greene folded his arms but didn't move. "What do you want, Pardee?"

"Couple things came up. We didn't want to discuss them over the phone, so we—" He broke off and gave Greene a hard look. "Could you set the weapon down, bud? You're making me nervous."

Greene set the Beretta next to the Jack Daniel's. It was too beautiful for words.

"You want a snort too?" Pardee said, reaching toward the bottle.

"Nah."

At the last second, Pardee's hand moved toward the Beretta. He lifted it, slipped off the safety, aimed it at Greene's head, and pulled the trigger.

Nothing happened.

"I had a hunch that's why you were here," Greene said. "Use my weapon? Make it look like a suicide? I'm all distraught over failing to do my duty? You asshole, I unloaded it in the kitchen while I was getting your glass." Greene pulled a second pistol out of his pocket, a .38 snub nose, and pointed it at Pardee. "Get out of my house."

Pardee took a moment to study the situation. It had been a little too easy, hadn't it. "Hey, look Mark, you think this'll all go away if I walk out that door? You're living in a dream world. If not me, somebody else'll take you out."

"I don't think so," Greene said. He still had the gun pointed at Pardee's forehead.

Pardee crossed his legs, gave him a smug look, leaned back, tried to look relaxed.

"I didn't get to be head of the presidential protection detail by being stupid or being slack or by leaving details unattended," Greene said. "I've documented everything that's happened so far. Named names, kept recordings, dates, the works. If I die for any reason within the next three years, my lawyer will release the whole thing to the media."

"Your lawyer?"

Now it was Greene's turn to look smug. "My lawyer."

"That would be Cheryl Billings, attorney-at-law, of Kretchmer, Billings, Wainright and Lee? Down on K Street, fourth floor, end of the hall?"

Greene's smug look faded a little.

"Yeah, we were a little nervous about that too. So I sent my guys in. Her safe was not very good. I mean, really, it was the kind of thing you can buy at Kmart. Took Badger about thirty seconds to get in. He replaced the material you had in there with a will and some crazy rantings. Kind of sordid, but no big deal. Just enough so that if you were found dead and the stuff came out, you'd look like a real loser to your kids, your mother, everyone."

Greene blinked.

"You don't believe me? The envelope you gave to your lawyer was addressed to Gail Parsons at the *Washington Post*. Inside there were six microcassettes, a typescript that ran thirty-one pages, a CD-ROM, and a few assorted papers. We burned them all, Mark."

Greene seemed to sag and deflate.

Pardee sighed loudly. "Hey, you're dead either way. If you die here tonight, we'll go in and replace the papers we put in there with a will and some kind of patriotic little statement about how hard you tried and how sad you are that you failed in your duty. Nobody will ever pay attention to it. If we have to wait, we go with the stuff that's in there now and you go down in history as the gay porn guy."

Greene swallowed, the gun still pointing at Pardee's face.

Pardee spread his hands helplessly. "I'm sorry as hell about this, Mark."

Greene just sat there. Finally he lowered the gun.

"Go out with some dignity," Pardee said. "If you want, I'll let you do it yourself."

Greene looked like a little boy who'd just watched his puppy get run over by a truck.

"We wrote you a suicide note. I was going to leave it here. But, look, why don't you just write it yourself. You're a good soldier, Mark. I didn't like this anymore than you would have if you'd been in my shoes. So why don't you write your own note, do it from the heart. Think of it this way, you're protecting the president, you're going out like a man."

Greene still didn't move. Finally he took a long breath and a pair of tears began to trail down his face.

Pardee took the Beretta, set it on the table. "Here's your duty piece. Do it with that. It'll be a nice touch."

Greene shook his head sharply. Suddenly he straightened up, wiped the tears off his face, and his mouth went firm. "No." He stood, walked briskly out of the room. Pardee's pulse was thrumming. What the hell was he doing? He had a pistol in his pocket that had been bought a month earlier under Mark Greene's name. Maybe he should have just shot Greene with the pistol, left the note, and hit the bricks. This was a delicate thing. If he did it wrong, though, the forensics would be screwed up and it would be obvious that Greene hadn't killed himself. Be patient. Be patient.

After a minute or so, Greene came back. In his hand, he had a knife, eight-inch blade, silk-wrapped handle.

"Seventeenth-century *tanto,*" Greene said. "It was commissioned by a personal retainer of the shogun Tokugawa Ieyasu."

Pardee's eyebrows went up. This was taking an interesting turn.

"I've always admired the samurai," Greene said. "They had a code of honor based on personal loyalty. You know when they got in a situation where duty and principle conflicted, they'd commit seppuku. Ritual belly cutting. I always wondered if I had the stones to do a thing like that." He shook his head disconsolately. "I should have done it six months ago. This whole business is a disgrace."

Wow. Pardee couldn't believe it.

Greene set the tanto on the table, poured himself about three fingers of scotch, stared at the beautiful old blade for a while. "There was a whole ritual. You purified yourself, washed yourself, put on your best robe. Then you wrote your death poem, stripped off your shirt, put the knife in your belly right here, cut across to here, then up, to here." Greene finger-traced a C-shaped line from the top of his groin around the margins of his belly.

There was something in Greene's eyes that Pardee had seen a few times before, when a man knew he was going to die, and he'd already crossed over. Greene probably hadn't admitted it, but on some level he'd known this was coming for a long time. And he'd been preparing, building up his courage.

"I don't know if we've got time for the ritual purification, Mark," Pardee said. "Just get some paper, write your death poem."

AFTER IT WAS over, Pardee drove to the airport. It was a real high. Being able to talk a man into killing himself, without even laying a glove on him? Amazing! He could still barely believe it. The poem Greene had written had been all about duty and failure. It was really pretty nicely written for a guy who was about to stick a knife in his own belly. Pardee wadded up the fake suicide note that he'd intended to use and threw it out the window. It disappeared into the blackness.

Pardee didn't get a guy like Greene. If their roles had been reversed? Pardee would have put a bullet in Greene's head the second he had a clear shot, then he'd have hit the road for Mexico.

Well. One man's meat, huh?

Paul Miller's Hunting Cabin, Northern Alabama
10:49 PM

The chopper seemed to hover forever over the cabin. But then it slowly moved away, and the rotor noise faded and finally disappeared.

Delaney felt his heart pounding.

"What were we talking about?" Miller said.

"You were telling me about this paymaster guy in Virginia who was paying you to buy weapons. Did it ever occur to you that you were being used as a front for Al-Qaeda or somebody like that?"

Miller frowned. "No! I know for a fact I wasn't working for Al-Qaeda. Among other things, I was just stockpiling the arms. We never used any of them."

"That doesn't make sense."

"It does if you believe that there's a revolution coming. It does if you believe in the mission of the Brotherhood. What I claimed was that civil order would fall apart. There would be some kind of catastrophic event—like a nuke going off in DC or on Wall Street, or a chemical attack, whatever—and then civil order would collapse and then the Brotherhood would be ready to help us restore America to its ancient and original purpose and purity."

Delaney rolled his eyes.

"Screw you, Mike! It's easy to see now, you know, in retrospect that I was being used. But at the time it seemed reasonable. Of course, sure, yeah, now that these people are busy calling me the ringleader of a presidential assassination, now that these people are busy rolling up my whole organization and killing off my kids and stuff—yeah, sure, *now* I can see it was all just a big setup. They wanted a fall guy. They wanted it to look like there was this big scary network of domestic terrorists."

"Which, of course, you are not."

"Go ahead, Mike. Rub it in, Mr. Pure-as-the-driven-snow. So it was a scam. At least I'm not some federal storm trooper out there burning up children in Waco or blowing away women at Ruby Ridge."

"Spare me that, would you?"

Paul Miller put his face in his hands and began to sob.

"You got yourself into this," Delaney said. "Act like a man for once."

Miller looked up, his blue eyes gone wet and red. "He's going to kill me," he said.

"Who is? The paymaster?"

"Of course not. He's just a pawn like me. Come on, Mike! It's right in front of you. Who stands to gain here? Whose agenda is promoted by what just happened?"

"*Qui bono,*" Delaney said softly.

"This is America. Do me a favor, don't talk Spanish. It's offensive to me."

"That would be Latin, Paul."

"Whatever. The point is, who wins when you and I get put down? That's what I'm saying."

Delaney didn't answer.

"Who wins when the FBI digs up this bunch of ragheads and Russians that I talked to about buying missiles and weapons of mass destruction? Huh? Who, Mike?"

"No riddles. Who did this paymaster tell you he was working for?"

"I may be dumb, Mike, but I'm not *that* dumb. You think I would have gotten involved in this solely on the word of some sleazy little guy on the other end of a phone line?"

"You're telling me you spoke with the top dog?"

"Spoke with him? I met with him in room 517 of the Hay-Adams Hotel. He told me there would be this big event, this precipitating event, which would set off a chain reaction that would set America back on course." Paul Miller shook his head, his eyes narrowed in disgust. "And when it happened, he would reach out his hand and lift me up. The Brotherhood would be the engine of a new American renaissance." Another bitter laugh. "The minute I heard about that assassination? I knew. I knew that was the event he was talking about. So I got right on the phone to the paymaster to find out what the next step of the game was. And guess what? Phone disconnected. He *betrayed* me, Mike. He hung me out to dry."

"Who, Paul? Speak his name. Was it John Rancy?"

"Rancy!" Miller laughed. "Rancy's just an attack dog. The man I talked to? The man who betrayed me? Mike, come on! It was Morgan Boyd."

DAY FIVE

24

Northern Alabama
5:25 AM

UNIT P wore a number of faces. They could be investigators, they could be interrogators, they could be cops. But the face that came most naturally was the one they were wearing as the two blacked-out MH-53M Pave Low IV helicopters crested the trees of Red Mountain, flying so low that they seemed to be constantly in danger of smashing into the undulating blackness below them. When you took off the mask, they were soldiers.

Inside the Pave Low, Pardee stood over the shoulder of the pilot, watching the two color screens, which showed where they were flying. The Pave Low IV, with its Interactive Defense Avionics System/Multi-Mission Advanced Tactical Terminal (IDAS/MATT) system was basically an old Vietnam-era UH-53 that had been given an electronic warfare face-lift, making it the most advanced night-fighting chopper on the planet. Their pilots, members of the Sixteenth Special Operations Wing (SOW) from Hurlburt Field in Florida, were the elite of the elite: paint the windows of the aircraft black and they could still fly it fifty feet above the ground through a twisting mountain pass at a hundred knots.

In the bay of each Pave Low were six Unit P operatives. All were veterans of the elite military units—the Seventy-fifth Rangers, the Special Forces, the SAS, or the GSG-9. They all wore BDUs featuring the Mossy Oak Breakup camouflage pattern—a pattern used by hunters, not by the military, Kevlar helmets, and AN/PVS-14 monocular NVGs. There were no tags in their clothes, no ID in their pockets, no serial numbers on their weapons. Most were armed with MP5SDs—the sound-suppressed models—but one carried a 12-gauge autoloader Benelli M1 Entry Gun, while another had a night-vision-equipped M24 sniper rifle—a weapon based on a Remington 700 bolt-action rifle in .300 Winchester Magnum with an HS Precision composite stock and a Harris bipod.

The op was fly-by-the-seat-of-the-pants all the way. Because of a glitch at NSA, there were no satellites online to provide surveillance, so they had nothing to prepare them for what they would find other than a 1:250,000 USGS topo map and a USGS aerial map that had been shot in 1974. Still, based on the story Badger had gotten from the old man, the cabin they were heading for was at least fifty years old, so it should be exactly where it had been when the photograph was taken.

"There!" Pardee said. He felt a flash of excitement, the thrill of the hunt. On the FLIR screen he saw a small rectangular smear of red, growing rapidly larger as they plowed toward it. He had been right. The red windows and plume of orange-white coming out of the chimney meant the cabin was occupied.

"I see it," the pilot said irritably.

"Hit it from each side," Pardee said. "Wherever you can find a hole in the tree canopy."

"There are no holes," the pilot said.

"Find one."

The pilot flared the aircraft suddenly, switching to the hover coupler so that he now controlled the chopper with the hover trim control stick next to his leg instead of using the collective and the cyclic stick, which were normally used to pilot the Pave Low. "This is as good as it's gonna get, sir," the pilot said.

Pardee scrambled back into the bay. "Ropes down!" he yelled. "Go!"

He pulled his NVG over his eye, grabbed the two-inch-thick braided rope with his Kevlar-lined gloves, and dove out of the bay into the swirling leaves below, fast roping to the ground in under two seconds.

A quick check showed they'd been lucky: nobody had been smashed to bits on a limb coming down through the trees. Instinctively the two teams fanned out into lines, which—as they charged the twenty-five meters toward the cabin in front of them—would close together forming a V, lessening the likelihood of friendly-fire accidents. Pardee motioned to Badger—who carried the Benelli—to blast the lock. The door didn't look very stout, and there was no point wasting time trying to breach the door with explosives.

Badger fired, and the 800-grain deer slug tore a ragged divot out of the door where the latch had been. Gonzalez tossed a flashbang into the room. There was a sharp thud as the explosive detonated, and a bright bloom of green-white on the lens of Pardee's NVGs.

The men of Unit P poured into the relative brightness of the lamp-lit room. The shooting was fierce but lasted no more than half a second.

"Secure!" came Badger's voice through the door. "Both targets down!"

25

Northern Alabama
7:10 AM

MARY CAMPOS arrived at the scene of the takedown with two cameramen—a still photographer from *Time* and a video cameraman from Fox. The sun was just coming up, and she'd had two hours of sleep that night. She wore black BDUs, a sidearm, and a Kevlar helmet—only because the White House had insisted. The cameramen were there for the same reason. Maybe that's how the game was played at this level, but the whole thing made her feel queasy. Turning the shooting of two men into a photo op was more than just bad taste—it was wrong. But what could she do? If that's what the president wanted, she had no real choice.

She felt sick, too, because Michael Delaney would be here, lying in the pool of blood where Unit P had left him. Michael Delaney, whose skin she had touched, whose lips she had kissed, whose . . . She shook her head sharply. This was not the time to dwell on that.

As soon as the FBI had arrived, the Unit P men had all disappeared, wafted into the sky by their Pave Lows—all except Pardee, that is, who had stayed on the scene.

"This way, ma'am." The ASAC from the Atlanta office of the FBI had met her at a clearing at the bottom of the small mountain—it was really nothing but a big hill—where Delaney had been killed, and now they were hiking up to the cabin.

"You're sure it's both of them?" Mary Campos said. "Miller and Delaney both?"

"Yes, ma'am."

Her heart sank. Up until she arrived, the reports coming in had been a little sketchy. There had been a brief firefight, two men killed,

Delaney and Miller *believed* to be the casualties—that's how it had been put to her.

They reached the top of the hill and approached a small cabin. As she walked toward the door, she could hear the *Time* magazine cameraman snapping away behind her.

"Get them out of here," she snapped, waving her hand at the two journalists.

Then she walked into the room. Seated in a chair facing the room was a man with blond-tipped hair, head thrown back, a swath of red on the wall behind him.

"That's Miller." Mary turned and saw Dirk Pardee leaning against the wall. "He got off one shot before we nailed him."

"And Delaney?"

Pardee pointed to a figure lying on a cot by the wall. Other than his head, he was completely encased in a green sleeping bag. There were tufts of polyester filling sticking out of the bag where the bullets had entered. Delaney's face was so shot up and bloodied that he was unrecognizable.

"You shot him like that?" she said. "He was just lying there sleeping and you shot him?"

"He made an aggressive movement. My operatives believed he had a weapon under the sleeping bag." Pardee's eyes were full of that disdain he loved directing at her.

"An *aggressive movement?* What does that mean? If somebody threw a flashbang into a room where you were sleeping, you'd make some aggressive movements too. That doesn't mean you should have blown him away."

Pardee let his eyes widen, full of mock surprise. "Gosh, ma'am! You want to second-guess my highly trained operatives? That's what this is?"

"I'm just saying. How do you know there was a weapon under there?"

"I don't."

"Have you touched anything?"

Pardee made a pretense of offense. "Ma'am, we were under very clear instructions not to touch anything once the premises and its occupants were secure."

"Asleep in his bed," she said. She was angrier, maybe, than she should have been, but Pardee rubbed her the wrong way.

She crossed the room, grabbed the zipper of the sleeping bag, yanked it open. A pale, empty hand slipped out. "There's your weapon, Colonel Pardee."

Pardee shrugged, crossed the room, stood over the corpse, stared down in silence. "Oops," he said finally. "Gee, I guess we made a little mistake, huh?"

Then he reached out and pulled the rest of the sleeping bag away from Delaney's bloody chest. An MP5 with a homemade suppressor on the barrel slipped out of the bag and clattered to the floor.

"Then again," Pardee said lightly, "maybe we didn't."

Mary Campos stared at the dead man. There was something about the figure that was disconcerting to her, something that was not right. She couldn't quite make sense of it. Maybe it was just the way that death transforms the living into meat: something essential disappears and what's left seems alien, no longer connected to the living breathing person it once had been.

"His wallet was sitting on the table," the FBI man from Atlanta said. He picked it up with gloved hands, showed it to her. There was Michael Delaney's Virginia driver's license, his Secret Service badge. He set the wallet down again.

Mary Campos continued to stare at the dead man. Suddenly she reached out and ripped back his shirt, popping the buttons off the cloth. Delaney had a long scar down the center of his belly from the surgery required to repair his spleen after he'd taken the bullet meant for Morgan Boyd in New Delhi.

But the dead man's belly—though bloody—clearly had no scar.

Unexpected relief flooded through her. She gasped and her knees nearly buckled.

"Ma'am, I really have to request you to stop touching things," the ASAC from Atlanta said gingerly. "This is a crime scene."

She let go of the dead man's shirt. She considered telling them it wasn't Delaney, but then rejected the idea. They'd know soon enough.

She looked up and noticed Pardee scrutinizing her face.

"What?" he said sharply. "What are you looking for?"

She shook her head. "I don't know." Then she walked slowly out the door, into the cool air.

She heard Pardee barking commands behind her, though she couldn't make out exactly what he was saying.

A minute later, Pardee came out and said, "It's not Delaney."

"How can you tell?" she said.

"I remembered that he had a tattoo on his arm. Picked it up in the army. The dead guy in there didn't have one."

She didn't say anything.

"But you knew that, didn't you, Colonel Campos." It wasn't a question, it was a statement.

"What are you standing here for, Colonel?" Mary snapped. "Delaney's not here. Go find him. He's got to be close."

Pardee shook his head. "I have to disagree. Whatever he wanted, he already got it. He's long gone."

"Where do you think he is?"

"I think he's heading back to DC."

Mary Campos felt her eyes narrow. "Are you working off some kind of information I'm not privy to?"

Pardee didn't answer for a moment. "I just have a strong hunch," he said finally.

It was an awfully specific hunch. Maybe a little too specific. Something here didn't smell right. But damned if she could figure out what it was.

FORTY-FIVE MINUTES LATER, Pardee and Campos were back on the FBI's Gulfstream IV, heading back to DC. While Campos slept, Pardee made a call on his encrypted SAT phone.

"Hello, Mr. Rancy," he said. "Is this a secure line?"

Rancy said that it was.

"We have a problem. Well, two problems. First—the man we shot? It wasn't Delaney. Delaney had been there, but he was gone by the time we arrived. He's still in the wind."

He nodded through the predictable howling from Rancy.

"Yes, sir. Yes, sir. But that's not all. I found a phone number written on a piece of paper on the table right where Delaney must have been sitting. It was the phone number for that guy. *The* guy. You know who I'm talking about. The guy in Reston. The money man, the paymaster. Delaney knows where the money came from."

More howling and threatening from Rancy.

"Yes, sir. Yes, sir. What I'm saying is, the guy from Reston took the disk drive with all the accounts, all the money flow, the whole nine. And we don't know what he did with it. If Delaney gets his hands on that disk drive, you're burned. And if you're burned, we're all burned. Yes, sir. I agree it's unlikely. I *will* get him. I promise you that. I'm close. I'm very close. And I think I know how I'll get him."

26

Northern Alabama
6:08 AM

SOMETIMES YOU'RE GOOD, thought Delaney, *and sometimes you're lucky. But it's always better to be lucky than good*.

Miller had told Delaney he'd take the first watch and let Delaney sleep. Which Delaney had done until about four-thirty. At which point someone banged on the door, and Delaney woke with his heart pounding and his gun in his hand.

It had turned out the man knocking on the door was a friend of Miller's, a close associate in the Brotherhood, who was bringing drinking water and ammunition up to the cabin. The burst of adrenaline had been so strong that Delaney didn't feel like sleeping anymore. So he had decided to get moving: he'd said good-bye to Miller and started walking down the mountain, making it to the far ridge, maybe a klick away, when he heard the choppers. And then the gunfire.

He had begun running then, finding an old logging trail and making another three or four klicks in pretty good time. At the bottom of the trail he saw a couple of hunters getting out of a twenty-year-old Jeep Wagoneer and heading into the woods with self-climbing tree stands on their backs. He had edged down to the road, waited for the crunching of their footsteps to disappear, then slid into the Jeep. The old machine was easily hot-wired. He felt a stab of guilt as he slid the big truck into gear and headed north toward Tennessee.

He'd gone about an hour when his hands suddenly began to tremble and sweat broke out across his entire body. The assault on the mountain cabin had been way too close. He felt like a cat who was running out of lives.

Finally the trembling got so strong that he had to pull over to keep from losing control of the Jeep. Off to the right, down a small incline, he saw a meandering stream, glinting brightly in the early morning sun. He took a couple of deep breaths, climbed out, staggered down the hill on legs that barely had the strength to hold him, knelt on a flat rock by the stream, and splashed water on his face.

Under the water a crawdad leapt up out of the mud and skittered away a foot or two, causing a couple of silver-backed minnows to dart upstream. Instinctively, Delaney plunged his hand into the water, pulled out the crayfish. Where had that instinctive reaction come from? It had been thirty years since he and Jerry Riggins used to goof around in the creek that ran down by the old mill—catching crawdads, making dams, throwing dirt clods at each other. Where had all that innocence gone? He stared into the tiny black beads of the crawdad's eyes. Its hooked claws waved fiercely at him, and its sectioned tail arched against his hand.

Then the crawdad twisted in his fingers, grabbed hold of his thumb with one of its claws. It hurt like the dickens, nearly drawing blood.

Suddenly, despite the pain, he began to laugh, watching the way the little creature battled against him. "Fight on, little brother!" Delaney said. Then he slung the crawdad back into the water. It scooted off into the current and disappeared.

When he reached the truck again, Delaney felt restored, all the tremors and weakness in his limbs passing like a tropical storm.

White House Situation Room, Washington, DC
10:49 AM

Lieutenant General Bill Fairbank entered the room with his battle face on, every crease in his uniform sharp as a knife, gold sparkling. He looked at the faces surrounding him. At the far end of the table was the president, studying Fairbank with his black, unreadable eyes. Next to him was General Slade, chairman of the joint chiefs, along with Admiral Chuck Levering, Air Force General Doyle Pierce, and the commandant of the Marine Corps, General Ivan Drugovitz. On the other side of the table was the secretary of defense, Adam Robinson, as well as Lieutenant General James Macy, commander of the Joint Special Operations Command.

"Please, General," President Boyd said. "Sit. I believe we're all acquainted."

Everyone nodded.

"General Fairbank," Morgan Boyd said, "I am about to make what has been a rather informal command into a more formal—if temporary—one."

Fairbank's brow furrowed.

"As of twelve hundred hours today, I am appointing you commander in chief, Domestic Operations Command. Knowing the predilection that you fellows have for acronyms, I'm sure they'll be calling you the CINCDOP by this time tomorrow. This command will be a temporary intraservice command. Because this is a temporary assignment, you will continue your direct command of XVIII Airborne Corps. Additionally, the entire apparatus of JSOC will also be temporarily under your direct command." JSOC, the Joint Special Operations Command, included the Seventy-fifth Ranger regiment, the roughly ten thousand soldiers of the Special Forces, the Air Force Special Operations Command, Delta Force, and SEAL Team Six. "Moreover, you will also have discretionary command authority over any unit in any branch within the fifty states and Puerto Rico that you deem necessary to perform your mission, irrespective of what command structure they are under right now."

Fairbank didn't like the sound of this. It violated nearly every notion he had about the way the United States military was supposed to be organized and deployed. "And what is that mission, Mr. President?"

"To secure domestic tranquillity."

Fairbank's face reddened. Had he not been sitting in front of the president of the United States, he would have exploded in anger. But he controlled himself. "Mr. President, if I may say so, that is a somewhat indistinct mission."

"I know you're concerned about statutory authority, General. But let me fill you in on some things. The mission of your command, as we speak, is being woven into the temporary state of emergency bill—we're calling it the Freedom from Fear Act—which I have introduced to Congress this week. I anticipate the bill coming to a vote within a matter of days. In the meantime you will continue to act under executive order."

"Sir, I'm sure you've been briefed by Colonel Campos already on the latest results of our efforts against the Brotherhood. Six more cells were taken down by the Eighty-second this morning, and Paul Miller was killed in a gunfight with this Unit P outfit. These SOBs will be history inside of a week. What more needs to be done?"

"I have received intelligence indicating that the domestic threat is not yet quelled. Other cells exist. Certain allied groups may be moving into action. It's even possible that foreign terrorists have been emboldened by our weakness. At any rate, a bomb went off in San Francisco today. A truck containing chlorine gas was hijacked in Houston and has not yet surfaced. I don't have to tell you what a truck full of chlorine gas could do if exploded in an urban area. It's a weapon of mass destruction. The television networks have been busy fear-mongering all morning . . . with the result that rioting and looting has broken out both in Houston and Dallas. I also don't have to tell you how delicate the balance is in our inner cities, General. We're going to need a military presence in many—if not all—of our major cities."

"So why not call out the National Guard?"

"I need professionals." He handed a piece of paper to an aide, who brought it down and put it in front of the general.

Fairbank scanned the deployment list. It specified units from twelve divisions including the Third and Fourth Mech, the 82nd, the 101st Airborne, the 75th Ranger regiment, the 10th Mountain, and several armored divisions. "Tanks!" Fairbank could feel himself growing angrier by the minute. "You want me to command tanks to roll in the streets of American cities!"

"These are temporary measures." Boyd's voice was soothing. "The bill in Congress has a ninety-day sunset period. We're talking about putting a lid on a burning cookpot. As soon as the fire cools, the lid comes off and we're back to business as usual."

Fairbank had been following the news and knew about the ninety-day sunset period on the legislation. But he also had sources throughout Washington—including several highly placed members of Congress. They were telling him that as it was currently written, the "sunset" provision of the bill provided for an infinite number of ninety-day extensions that could be invoked by the president without further congressional consultation if certain triggering events occurred. The thresholds for the triggers, according to Fairbank's sources, were not terribly high. The most important trigger provision stated that the president could extend the Freedom from Fear Act if there had been a "major act of terrorism" in the previous thirty days "within the borders of the United States or against any target representing an extension of vital American national interest." What did "major" mean? What was a "target representing an extension of vital

American national interest"? You could drive a truck through that kind of language.

"I can see you have reservations about this command," Morgan Boyd said. "But ultimately it comes down to this. You and I, General, are men of goodwill. It's a matter of record that both you and I fervently believe in restraining the unnecessary exercise of federal power. Two years from now, people will barely remember that we drove a couple of Bradleys down a highway here or there."

Fairbank couldn't even speak.

"Look at our history," Boyd continued. "Lincoln suspended habeas corpus, ordered troops against American citizens, imprisoned dissenters, did a host of other things that seem unpalatable when taken out of the context of the threat he faced. But he saved the Union, Bill. He saved our nation and extended the protection of the Bill of Rights to five million Americans who, up until that moment, had enjoyed the same legal status as milk cows. And I don't think any reasonable person today would argue that the United States was ever in danger of turning into some kind of fascist dictatorship as a result of Lincoln's actions."

Fairbank looked around the room. The joint chiefs were clearly not any happier than he was with this turn of events. But none of them looked like they were on the verge of quitting over it.

"Your country is calling you," the president said. "Are you going to join the pipe smokers and hand wringers who sit around up in Harvard Yard carping about Yankee Imperialism? Or are you going to stand up and be counted? Are you going to fight?"

Give him credit, the dark little president knew which buttons to press.

"Ninety days, Mr. President?"

"Ninety days. You have my word."

"Then I have my orders, Mr. President," Fairbank said.

"Good. I'll leave you gentlemen to work out the operational details." He stood and then said, "Oh, one last thing. The head of my protection detail, Mark Greene, didn't report to work this morning. An agent was dispatched to his home, where he was found dead by his own hand. Apparently he was disconsolate over his failure to protect President Fairbank. If you would, gentlemen, bow your heads. Let's have a moment of silence."

27

Western North Carolina
11:30 AM

DELANEY DECIDED to take a fresh route back to DC. The state trooper he'd "borrowed" up in Virginia would have been discovered and reported him by now, and they'd probably have checkpoints along both I-81 and U.S. 11 in case he came back the same way. This time he drove east out of Chattanooga, through western North Carolina on the beautifully scenic but infuriatingly winding U.S. 64. It didn't look that far on the map, but the mountainous driving set him back hours. Once he hit Hendersonville, he headed north, taking a chance on Interstate 64 for an hour or so, then on to the more lightly policed back roads into Boone, the small mountain city which was home to Appalachian State University.

He bought a map at a quick mart, gassing up the car with the last of his cash, then drove over to the campus. He found the electrical engineering technology department in a low-slung brick building. The office of Dr. Lou MacGregor was on the third floor. According to the sign on the door, MacGregor's office hours ran from noon until three. The door wasn't locked, so Delaney let himself in and sat down in a chair facing the desk—one that would not be visible to anyone entering the room until they were well inside the office. The room was bare of any pictures or trophies, other than the guts of a great number of electronic devices.

MacGregor had been a commo specialist back in Delaney's early days with the Special Forces and was probably the most complete soldier Delaney had ever met. MacGregor had left the service to earn a Ph.D. not long after Delaney had saved his life in a Panama firefight. He hoped MacGregor would still remember that night.

He let himself drift off, trying to catch up on badly needed sleep.

Within twenty minutes his sleep was arrested by the sound of the door clicking open. A tall, thin man, his red hair streaked with gray, stepped into the room, humming to himself. He paused for a moment, then picked up an electronic device, still apparently oblivious to Delaney's presence. He frowned at the device, punched and prodded on some buttons, then set it down.

"I had a hunch you might show up here," MacGregor said finally.

"How'd you know it was me?" Delaney said. "You never even looked at me."

"My students take baths," he said. "You smell like you just marched forty miles through a jungle."

"That sounds about right," Delaney said.

MacGregor turned around, seated himself, picked up a hand-carved wooden pipe, stuffed it with tobacco from a leather pouch, then lit the pipe.

"Still smoking that lizard dung, huh? That pipe smells almost as bad as I do," Delaney said. "How long's it been since Panama?"

"Nothing personal," MacGregor said, "but under the circumstances, let's skip the Old Home Week crap." His green eyes weren't unfriendly—but he didn't seem overjoyed to see Delaney either.

"I didn't do what they said," Delaney said.

"I didn't figure you did. Still, I'm not wild about getting charged with aiding and abetting a felon. I have a nice comfortable life here." He paused. "But I owe you, and I'm not a welsher. Tell me what you need and let's get it over with."

"I need to make a phone call so that it's not traceable. Can you help me do that?"

"That sort of thing is all a matter of degree. Anything can be traced, given enough time."

"Also I need some cash. I'm broke, I can't use my ATM, my checkbook, or my credit cards, and I'm tired of shoplifting. It makes me feel dirty."

"I assume you're armed?"

Delaney nodded.

"Let's go get the money first. You'll need to stand next to me with the gun so that when the FBI reviews the film I look like a hostage."

"Agreed."

MacGregor picked up a small piece of paper, scribbled a note on it. "I need to leave a note," he said, "let my students know I can't make office hours today."

As they were leaving the office, a muscular young man with spiked hair and baggy pants that hung down so low you could see the tops of his underwear approached and said, "Dr. MacGregor, hey, I need to talk to you about that test."

"The one you made a fifty-seven on?"

"Yeah. Look, I have some issues with that. See, you told us that we were supposed to—"

"Issues? What does that mean? I told you that you needed to know chapter nine. You obviously didn't know the chapter."

The muscular student looked at MacGregor like he couldn't believe the effrontery of the man. "Dude, I *studied!*"

"Sadly," MacGregor said, "some people work hard and still do poorly. Remember what I told you at the beginning of the semester?"

The student stared sullenly.

"You've got to flat know it," Delaney said to the kid. "Am I right? Is that what he said? That's what the old bastard always told me back when he was teaching me."

The student ignored Delaney. "I need some extra credit."

"Didn't you hear what my friend just said?" MacGregor said. "There is no such thing as extra credit in my class. You've got to flat *know* it."

"My old man's on the board of directors," the kid said, waving his finger in MacGregor's face. "This is *not* the last you've heard about this."

MacGregor took hold of the boy's finger and bent it around in a circle. Suddenly the muscular boy was on his knees, gasping with pain. "Pointing is rude," MacGregor said, patting the boy on the shoulder. "Next Friday is chapter ten. Study harder."

They left the boy there, gasping and holding his hand, walked down a flight of stairs and out the front door of the electrical engineering building.

"Whiners make me irritable," MacGregor said.

"I don't know for sure," Delaney said, "but I'm guessing that's not in the university's sensitivity training manual."

"I know his father. The old man's gonna tell me I should have broken his kid's finger."

THEY PICKED UP the maximum allowable withdrawal from MacGregor's ATM then drove through town, Delaney telling his story as they went. He was just explaining about the strange unit led by Dirk Pardee.

"Dirk Pardee?" MacGregor said. "Come on, Mike, they wouldn't put that crank in charge of an important outfit. You remember when he almost got Alvin Roundtree killed smuggling all that whiskey into northern Afghanistan?"

"That's what I'm saying. They shouldn't put a guy like him out there, but they have."

MacGregor was looking at him skeptically as they pulled up to a one-story brick home on the side of a mountain a couple of miles outside Boone.

As they entered the house, an attractive woman with gray hair walked out of the kitchen wearing a cooking apron over a track suit. She had a quizzical expression on her face. "I thought you were going to be at the office," she said.

"I ran into an old friend. Rachel, this is Mike. Mike, my wife Rachel."

Rachel MacGregor glanced at Delaney and smiled. Then her eyes widened. It was clear she recognized him.

"It's okay," MacGregor said. "He's explained everything to me. It's all a misunderstanding."

She seemed rooted to the spot.

"I promise," MacGregor said easily. "Why don't you stick with us while he's here, though. Just to make him feel comfortable that you're not calling the police."

"Sure, honey," she said, grudgingly. "If you're sure."

He smiled. "I promise. I trust Michael with my life."

"Let's get going with this phone call I need to make," Delaney said. "The sooner we're done, the sooner I'm gone, and the happier we all are."

MacGregor nodded. "Okay, here's the deal, Mike," he said. "I can go high-tech and buy you a couple of minutes completely free and clear. But if you go long, they'll nail you immediately. Or I can go low-tech and they'll eventually trace it, but it'll take longer."

"Sounds like low-tech is the way to go."

"Okay then. All I'm going to do is call a friend, have him patch me through the PBX where he works. That'll act as an absolute firewall on a trace. But once the FBI shows up at that location, they'll trace the original leg of the call and they'll have people at my doorstep as quick as they can scramble them."

MacGregor dialed a long-distance number, then said, "Reggie, hi, it's Lou MacGregor. Need to ask a favor of you. I'm testing a new device and I need a routing firewall. Do you guys still have an old-fashioned analogue PBX? Yeah? Excellent. What I need you to do is patch this call through to an outside line, so when I dial out, my call will appear to originate from your system. Yeah, Reggie. Yeah, of course it'll be long-distance. Yes, you cheapskate, of course I'll charge it to my account." He put his hand over the receiver and spoke to Delaney. "God forbid the Department of Energy waste a nickel on unauthorized long-distance calls." Then back into the receiver. "Thanks, Reggie. I owe you."

He handed the phone to Delaney.

"You've got a virgin line now. When you hear the tone, just start dialing."

Delaney nodded and dialed the number for Mary Campos's cell phone.

"Mary?" he said.

There was a long silence.

"Feel free to trace the call," he said. "It won't lead to me."

More silence. "What do you want, Mr. Delaney?" she said finally.

"I assume this call is being monitored?"

No answer. The fact that she called him "Mr. Delaney" made it pretty obvious that, one, the call was being monitored, and, two, she hadn't told the FBI that she and Delaney had had a relationship. If she hadn't told the FBI about their romantic connection, that suggested she was still keeping an open mind on the question of his innocence.

"I'll take that as a yes. Look, I know who's behind the murder. There is a very wide-ranging conspiracy here. But I don't have proof."

"Who is it?" Her voice sounded skeptical.

"I can't tell you now. It would put you in danger. But I'll have the proof soon. And when I do, I'll turn it over to you."

"That's good, Mr. Delaney. But you need to turn yourself in."

"I assume Paul Miller is dead."

"Why do you assume that?"

"Let me guess. There's some kind of special team. Maybe CIA, maybe even more black budget than that. They're under instructions to make sure he didn't survive that assault."

There was another pause. "That's ridiculous, Mr. Delaney. He resisted arrest and—" Mary broke off in the middle of the sentence.

"So he is dead."

No answer.

"Who led the team, Colonel? Dirk Pardee? That guy didn't leave the army by accident. He was pushed out. Look at the file on Pardee. Then ask yourself why a guy like him would ever be hired by the United States government."

"Why are you calling me Mr. Delaney?"

"Paul Miller received a lot of money over the past year or two. Several million dollars. You'll find that money didn't come in the form of twenty-five-dollar checks. There was one big donor, and that one big donor paid exclusively in cash. Find that donor, you'll know who killed President Fairbank. Put the FBI on it. Good-bye, Colonel."

As he hung up the phone, he heard someone knocking loudly on the door.

Delaney looked at MacGregor. "Expecting someone?"

MacGregor shook his head no.

"Ignore it."

The banging continued. "I know you're in there, Dr. MacGregor! I see your car!"

MacGregor scowled. "It's that whiner."

"Get rid of him, Lou."

MacGregor nodded, and Delaney followed his old friend into the other room, where he peeped through the curtain. A police car was parked at the curb. The lout whose finger MacGregor had bent was standing on the front porch, jaw thrust forward. Next to him was a police officer. The officer was banging on the door with his PR-24 riot baton.

"Uh-oh," Delaney said.

"What do you want me to do?" MacGregor whispered. "If I let them in, I'll get nailed for harboring a felon once the FBI does the phone trace and looks at the timeline. Nothing personal, but I'm not really excited about that prospect."

The banging continued. "I saw you look through the curtains, sir!" The cop's voice now. "We just need to talk, sir. I'm sure we can get this all straightened out."

More banging.

"I don't want to enter your home forcibly, sir!"

"You stand behind me," MacGregor said. "I'll just talk to them."

"All right," Delaney said. As MacGregor was reaching for the door, he saw a flash of black out of the corner of his eye. It looked like a man in a long black coat, crouching behind the hedge over by the garage. But that wasn't possible. How could the cops have gotten here that quickly? Even if they'd somehow traced the call, he'd been on the phone for less than a minute. Unless . . . He looked at Mac-Gregor.

MacGregor's face was expressionless.

The kid! Son of a . . . MacGregor had written a note, saying he was going to put it on his door so that his students would know he was going to miss office hours today. But then he hadn't put the note up. It must have said, *Help, I'm being held hostage by Michael Delaney* or something to that effect. The kid had been annoying, sure, but it had seemed like twisting the kid's finger was a little excessive, even for a hard-core guy like MacGregor. But he'd done it so he could get close enough to the kid to slip him the note without Delaney noticing.

"What have you done, MacGregor?" Delaney said softly.

MacGregor didn't even bother trying to look innocent, just scowled and looked off into the distance.

"I saved your life, Lou."

MacGregor sighed. "Mike, you killed the president," he said sadly. "I'm a patriot. You ought to know that."

Delaney shook his head. "I told you I didn't do it!"

"Just open the door, sir." The cop with the riot baton, still playing his role. Delaney saw another shadow behind the hedge, another plainclothes cop creeping toward the front of the house. "We'll straighten everything out!"

MARY CAMPOS GOT the news about Mark Greene from SAC Smith at the FBI.

"I don't like this one bit," she said. "I saw him just yesterday, and he didn't look the least bit suicidal."

"We're not handling the investigation. That's being done by local law enforcement. But they've been very forthcoming with what they've got. And right now it looks pretty self-inflicted."

"How can you be sure?"

"He wrote a poem about how he'd failed at his duty, then committed hara-kiri with a samurai knife. Handwriting analysis is ongoing, but the initial read was that it looked like his own writing. There was a loaded gun on the table in front of him. A guy like that, a tough man, trained in hand-to-hand combat and everything? The likelihood that somebody could make him write a poem then cut his guts out without there being any sign of struggle—I'd put that at about zero percent, wouldn't you?"

"I guess you're right," she said. Then she hung up the phone. Hara-kiri. Weird. It was hard to see how that could be anything but self-inflicted. Still, it was just another sign that something wasn't right. The problem was, now that she had started to suspect that maybe Delaney was right, she didn't know who she could trust.

DELANEY DREW HIS Beretta and grabbed MacGregor's wife by the arm. "If you believe I'd kill the president," Delaney said, "then I'd have no qualms about killing Rachel. You let them in, do what you have to do. But if you don't convince them that you were engaged in a prank or something similar, your lovely wife will die before I ever give up."

MacGregor's shoulders sagged.

"Ten seconds," Delaney said. "Then open the door."

"Just a minute!" MacGregor called through the door. "I'm getting my pants on!"

Delaney yanked MacGregor's wife down the hallway. "They'll search the house. Where can we hide that they won't find us?"

"We put in a wine cellar last year," she said. "There's a crawl space behind it."

They dashed down the stairs, turned left. At the back of a finished rec room was a small wine cellar. "Here," she said, pulling back a panel on the wall revealing a three-foot-high door.

"In," Delaney said.

She bent over and crawled through the hatch. Delaney followed, pulling the panel behind him, then closing the door. In the far corner of the low, dirt-floored space was a grimy furnace. "Over there," he said.

They scuttled over to the furnace. "Lie down," he said.

They lay down behind the furnace. Delaney could hear MacGregor's wife's breath, rapid and shallow.

"Easy," he said softly. "Breathe nice and slow and deep. Everything will be fine."

Coming from somewhere upstairs Delaney could hear the muted sound of a conversation. Then footsteps began moving rapidly throughout the house. Delaney's heart was beating hard, and there was a rushing sound in his ears. The seconds stretched by. Footsteps thumped down the basement stairs.

For a minute Delaney thought that they were gone, but then something creaked—the panel in the wine cellar being pulled back. The door opened, and light spilled into the room.

"Delaney!" a voice called. "Don't do anything stupid. I'm just going to talk!"

Houston, Texas
1:58 PM, CST

Edgardo Ruiz had been blessed. His landscaping business was finally taking off, with a couple of brand-new commercial contracts that were bringing in money like he'd never seen in his life. He was about to close on a house, and his wife had just had a third child yesterday, this time a son. Who'd have thought it? The son of an illiterate farmer from Chiapas about to become a prosperous American, sending his kids to parochial school, living in a nice suburb?

Truly, his luck was nothing short of miraculous.

Ruiz was ordinarily not a patient man. But sometimes you had to put things in perspective. The point being: okay, a big truck was stopping in front of him right in the middle of the ramp from I-610 to I-57 for apparently no good reason, blocking off all the traffic—okay, take a breath, it was no big deal. He and his crew would be a couple of minutes late to the job site. It wasn't the worst thing in the world.

But then the truck put on its flashers and stopped dead. Right in the middle of the road, not even bothering to pull over. In fact, the truck was angled like he was intentionally trying to make it impossible for anyone to get around it. It was a stainless steel tanker truck, the kind that carried milk.

Or chemicals.

Two young men, both big gringos who had obviously spent a lot of time at the gym, climbed out of the cab of the truck, walked back, and set a bag made of green canvas on a tube underneath the big tanker.

Ruiz honked the horn of his Mitsubishi landscaping truck. Okay, okay, what were these *pendejos* doing? It was fine to be patient and grateful and all—but there was a limit. One of the big gringos turned, gave Ruiz a big toothy grin, then extended his middle finger at him. The two gringos turned then and walked over to a black Jeep with darkly tinted windows that he hadn't noticed before. The Jeep drove off down the ramp.

Suddenly Ruiz remembered something. He kept the radio droning all the time, didn't pay much attention, but the host had said something about terrorists hijacking a truck full of some kind of chemical, how you could blow it up and then there'd be all this poison gas floating around.

Ruiz hadn't gotten where he'd gotten in life because he dillydallied or was slow to make decisions. He licked his finger, stuck it out the window. There was a stiff wind coming up from the south.

He climbed out of the cab. There were three young guys in white cowboy hats, right off the donkey cart from southern Mexico, sitting in the back looking at him with blank expressions. Everything here was so new to these boys that nothing seemed out of the ordinary to them.

"Corre!" he yelled. *"Corre! Vayance!"*

The boys in the truck didn't have to be told twice. You came to another country and somebody tells you to run, you run. They started pounding down the pavement against the traffic. As he ran, Ruiz saw other people jumping out of their cars and running too.

When the explosion came, it knocked him on his face. He jumped up again immediately, looked back. The plume of green gas was spilling through the air off in the other direction.

A Weedwhacker came flying through the air, smashing down on top of the car next to him. Okay, that was a little too close. He started running again. *Dios mio!*—it was a good day! His luck was holding.

Boone, North Carolina
12:59 PM

"Delaney! Easy, pardner!" the voice said. "I just want to talk!"

"Please . . ." MacGregor's wife whimpered. He could smell the strawberry scent of her shampoo and the musty smell of dirt that hadn't seen sunlight in years. "Don't kill me. I haven't done anything to you."

Delaney felt sick. It was all over. His heart was rushing.

"Delaney, my name is Special Agent Walter Gibson," the voice said. "Some things have changed."

Delaney didn't move. MacGregor's wife was weeping now.

Delaney looked around, trying to think of something. But there was just nothing left. He didn't even feel afraid now, just a huge weight of shame and sadness pressing down on him. What a way to go. A rat in a hole, holding a friend's wife as hostage. It was miserable, miserable, miserable.

He took a deep breath.

"All right, Agent Gibson," Delaney said. "I'll come out. I'm going to put my weapon on the top of the furnace, then I'm going to let Mrs. MacGregor go. When she's clear, call to me and I'll come out."

"Sounds like a plan," the FBI agent said.

Delaney reluctantly set the Beretta on top of the furnace. "Go," he said to MacGregor's wife. She sat up and scuttled in a crouch across the dirt floor.

"Okay, sir, Mrs. MacGregor's out. Put your hands up and come out."

Delaney showed his hands, stood slowly and walked awkwardly across the room, his head threatening to bang against the low ceiling.

When he reached the exit, he crawled out. Two men, one black and one white, wearing long dark coats and sober suits, stood above him, pointing Berettas at his head.

"I'll need you to turn around, Agent Delaney," the black agent said.

They cuffed him quickly, grabbed his elbows, and hustled him up the stairs.

MacGregor was staring at Delaney as he was pushed through the living room. "It's okay, Lou. You did what you thought was right."

Lou MacGregor just stared at him, a puzzled expression on his face.

Then Delaney was sitting in the back of a rented Ford Taurus. They were about to go when MacGregor came out of the house with Delaney's backpack, handed it to the white agent. The agent threw the backpack in the trunk of the car, and they were barreling down the road. Delaney looked back, saw a second Taurus pulling out to follow him. Agent Gibson sat next to him while the white agent drove.

They wound through Boone, then out the other side of the city, pulled up at the front door of a Hampton Inn. Why were they stopping here? A dark-skinned FBI agent got out of the trailing car, walked into the hotel. Delaney was puzzled. There was something familiar-looking about the FBI man, but Delaney couldn't place him.

Maybe they'd worked together on a case back when he did investigations.

After a few minutes the dark-skinned agent from the other car came out, and the two Fords pulled around and parked in front of a room. The dark-skinned agent got out of the other car, unlocked the door of room 138, then drew his pistol and stood by the door.

"Let's go, Mr. Delaney," Agent Gibson said.

"Why are we stopping here?"

"The FBI doesn't have an office in Boone. We're holding you here for security purposes until transport can be arranged to take you up to DC."

Delaney's eyes narrowed. "If there's no office in Boone," Delaney said, "then how did you get here so fast?"

Gibson shrugged. "Lucky coincidence, basically," the FBI agent said. "A team of us was flying over Boone from Alabama to DC in the FBI's Gulfstream when we got notified by local authorities that you had been spotted here. We landed and scrambled."

Delaney's eyes narrowed. "But if you have the Gulfstream at the airport, then why do you need to wait on transport?"

The white agent turned around and said to Gibson, "I told you we should of just shot him in the basement."

Then Gibson had a flat leather sap in his hand. It flashed through the air. Delaney tried to duck, but he was too late. There was a sharp, smacking noise, a flash of light, and then everything went black.

WHEN DELANEY AWOKE, he was strapped to a chair with duct tape. Several loops of tape ran around his face covering his mouth and nose, making it very difficult to breathe.

Standing in front of him were the two FBI agents, who flanked a third man, a tall, thin, dark-skinned man with a prominent nose and black shining eyes. The agent from the other car. Looking into those eyes was enough to let Delaney know that he had not been captured by the FBI. And that the likelihood of his walking out of the room alive was minimal.

"I have to tell you, Delaney, you have been going like a jackrabbit. I'm running on fumes." He had a South American accent. The man picked up a glass of water, popped a small blue pill in his mouth, and chased it with water. "I don't really approve of taking amphetamines as a general rule—I'm a just-say-no man generally—but sometimes you have no choice." He smiled. "They make me really jumpy, though. Unpredictable."

"MMMmmmph mmm," Delaney said. His head was throbbing, and his left eye wouldn't quite come into focus.

"I'm sure that wasn't polite, whatever you just said," the dark-skinned man said. "I suppose it goes without saying that if you yell when we take the tape off your mouth, Agent Gibson—or whatever he's calling himself today—will shoot you in the head."

The dark-skinned man carefully folded a white hotel towel, set it on the table next to the glass of water, then opened a black doctor's bag, took out a scalpel, a syringe, an ampule of clear liquid, and a pair of pliers, lined them up neatly on top of the white towel. Then he nodded at Gibson.

Gibson stepped forward and ripped the tape off Delaney's face.

"So I guess the rumors weren't true, huh, Gonzalez?" Delaney said.

Gonzalez grinned, looked around at his two henchmen. "Listen to this guy! *So I guess the rumors weren't true!* You are terrific, Delaney! So wholesome and courageous. If I were making a movie about you, I would go with Clint Eastwood in a heartbeat. No, never mind, he's getting a bit long in the tooth. Isn't that the phrase? Long in the tooth?" He shrugged. "Well. You get my point, no?"

Special Ops was a small world, almost like a village within the military. After you'd served there a few years, you'd met a pretty fair portion of the players. Delaney had run into Martin Gonzalez in Central America back in the 1980s when Delaney had been in the Special Forces. A buddy of Dirk Pardee. Gonzalez was a Chilean—supposedly he had been thrown out of the Chilean army—who had run guns during the Nicaraguan conflict, playing both sides of the political fence. Delaney had heard rumors that he had finally been executed—either by the Sandinista regime or by the Salvadoran government, depending on who was telling the story.

"You think this thing won't unravel eventually?" Delaney said. "And when it does, they'll send you away for a long time."

Gonzalez sighed theatrically. "The story of my life, Delaney. One day I'm up, the next I'm down." He smiled brightly. "But enough about me. Let's talk about you, my old friend."

"There's nothing to talk about."

Gonzalez turned to Gibson. "What do you think, Agent Gibson? Pliers first? Drugs?"

"I was looking at the TV the other day," Gibson said, "and I saw an interview with this retired French general. He'd been head of intelligence in, what, Algeria I believe it was? Back in the fifties? Recently accusations had surfaced that he'd tortured all these poor Algerians during their big revolutionary struggle. Give the man credit, he says, 'Yes, absolutely we tortured people right and left, and by golly I'd do it again.' And you know what he said was the most effective thing? Drugs? Electricity? Pliers? No, sir, none of that."

Delaney could see they were playing a little game with him. They already knew what they were going to do, but they were going to string it out, try and make him afraid. And it was working. He'd seen Gonzalez's handiwork one time, three dead Indians in the jungle, who'd taken a long, long time to die. Delaney knew enough to be afraid.

Gibson—if that was actually his name—picked up Gonzalez's glass of water, poured it over the white towel on which the scalpel, the pliers, and the syringe lay. "What this French fellow and his minions did, they'd wrap a wet towel around your face, squeeze it down over your nose and mouth until you passed out. It's like being drowned. They'd just keep doing that until your will broke."

"How terribly interesting!" Gonzalez said. "And it would leave no marks, so that when the autopsy occurred there would be no evidence of—what?—hinky-pinky?"

"Hanky-panky, I think is the word you're looking for," Gibson said.

"Thank you for that, Agent Gibson. I delight in the richness of expression which your language affords even me, a poor stuttering foreigner."

"Look," Delaney said, "whatever it is you want, I might as well tell you now. You'll get it eventually anyway."

Gonzalez made a comical face of mock irritation. "Oh, Delaney! Don't tell me you are a party pooper! And here I thought we would get a nice Clint Eastwood performance. You know, steely resolve, heroic battle of good and evil, so on and so on and so on."

"Just tell me what you want."

The white agent grabbed Delaney firmly by the head. Delaney tried to struggle as Gibson wrapped the towel around his head—but the other agent was extremely strong and there was nothing he could do. He sucked hard for air. A tiny, tiny, tantalizing stream of air came into his mouth, but it was so minuscule and cost him so much energy that he could see that it wasn't worth the effort. Only he couldn't tell that to his lungs. He felt panic rising, but he tamped it down. He met Gonzalez's eyes and stared as coolly as he could, willing himself not to fight for breath. After what seemed an interminable amount of time, his vision began closing into a black tunnel until all he could see was Gonzalez's face. Just as he was about to pass out, Gonzalez nodded slightly, and Gibson let go.

Delaney sucked raggedly for air.

"Bravo," Gonzalez said. "I knew we'd get that steely resolve eventually. Surrender just isn't in your DNA." He turned to Gibson, a humorous light in his black eyes. "Did you see the way he stared at me? It chilled me right to the bone, I must be frank with you, Agent Gibson."

Delaney had managed one breath when Gibson clamped down with the towel again. This time his vision began to close in after only ten or fifteen seconds.

Again Gibson let go. As soon as he had filled his lungs, Delaney screamed as loud as he could. "Help! Somebody help me!"

The towel clamped down again and this time Gibson didn't let go until everything went black.

When he came to, there was tape around his mouth.

"Next time you yell," Gonzalez said, "I will remove one of your testicles with my scalpel. It's quite sharp and quite clean, but I suspect the process will be fairly painful nonetheless."

Gibson ripped the tape off again.

"What do you want?" Delaney gasped.

Gonzalez nodded at Gibson, and the towel closed over his mouth and nose again. He willed himself not to fight, to simply hold his breath until he passed out, maintaining his stare at Gonzalez. It took every ounce of will he could muster. And snaking around in the back of his head was the thought of the pointlessness of it all.

After five or ten seconds, Gonzalez said, "Where's the disk drive, Delaney?"

Delaney held on until the cone of darkness closed down again and Gonzalez disappeared.

When he came to, he felt as though every cell in his body were screaming for oxygen, even though he was able to breathe normally. He sucked at the air. Then the towel went on again.

"The disk drive. Where is it?"

The cone of darkness narrowed and narrowed, then Gibson released the towel. Delaney felt his head slip over sideways. He was too oxygen-deprived to hold up his head. After panting for a few moments, his strength returned. "What disk drive?"

Gonzalez clicked his tongue sadly. "Oh, dear. Very disappointing. I was hoping to get some lunch before it gets too much later."

Gibson closed off his air again while the three men had an amiable conversation about whether to get pizza or fried chicken. The issue faded and disappeared, along with all sound, all light, all motion.

When he woke, Delaney felt nauseated. Gonzalez was very close to him, looking slightly worried. "Oopsie-daisey!" Gonzalez said. "You threw us a scare, my friend. Your heart stopped beating very briefly. For a moment I thought we had lost you for good."

"Screw you," Delaney said.

"You know, Delaney, I was going to give you a moment to let your body reoxygenate. But now I'm changing my mind. Where's the disk drive?"

The towel clamped over him again.

How long? Delaney thought. *How long can I keep this up?*

As the darkness came on again, he heard a thumping noise. It sounded like someone knocking on the door. The sound fading, fading, fading.

WHEN HE AWOKE the world had turned sideways. Or that's how it seemed. Each time he revived, the crawl up to consciousness had seemed longer, darker, harder. And when he finally came back, the world seemed more remote, more strange, more disconcerting. But —*sideways?*

The door was a long swath of white that ran laterally across his vision. Several people's feet seemed to sprout from the right side of his view and grow to his left. Something soft and vaguely scratchy rested on his cheek. No, wait, it was the other way around. His cheek rested on the soft, scratchy thing. There were loud noises around him too. Loud smacking sounds that he felt certain he was supposed to feel afraid of—and yet fear was among the things from which he seemed temporarily alienated.

And then he was fully conscious and everything became clear. He had fallen over in his chair, and Gonzalez and his crew were shooting out the door. It didn't seem to make any sense at all.

He realized that in the fall the duct tape around his chest had burst. His hands were still cuffed behind him and his ankles taped to the chair, however. He quickly wedged the back of the chair he was in against the bed, swiveled around so that his back and seat separated from the chair by several feet, and mule kicked the chair. It shattered, leaving the two wooden legs taped to his ankles.

Gonzalez and his men were still firing through the door. Who was shooting? It hardly mattered. Anybody who wants to kill Martin Gonzalez, he thought, is a friend of mine.

The gunfire had suddenly ceased, but still nobody seemed to be paying attention to Delaney. Self-preservation had taken first priority. He slipped the cuffs under his rear, pulling his knees up to his chest and working his hands underneath his shoes. Fortunately he had fairly long arms. If your arms were too short, the maneuver was impossible.

Outside the room he heard someone say, "Okay, I give up."

Then two men were hustling a third man in the door. It was MacGregor. What the hell was he doing here? It appeared he had just tried to single-handedly storm the room.

And failed.

But why? Delaney figured now was not the time to ask questions. Agent Gibson—or whatever the man's name was—stood with his back to Delaney, legs spread slightly in a shooter's crouch. Delaney kicked him between the legs as though he were trying to punt Gibson sixty yards downfield. Gibson let out an agonized grunt. Delaney hammered him on the side of the neck with his still-manacled fists, grabbed his Glock 19 as he went down, fired twice, instantly killing the two men who flanked MacGregor.

The suite they were in had two rooms connected by a door. Gonzalez, hearing the gun behind him, immediately ducked behind the door and began shooting methodically through the wall. Delaney flattened himself to the floor as a 9 mm round stitched the air just inches above his head.

Delaney charged for the door, the two chair legs flopping awkwardly, still duct taped to his legs.

"There's my car," MacGregor shouted, pointing.

On the other side of the parking lot was a five-year-old black Chevy Impala—the car that looked like a stodgy old Caprice but hid a Corvette LT1 engine with well over three hundred horsepower under the hood. They ran across the lot, dove into the Caprice, and fishtailed out of the lot. Gonzalez was behind them, firing, his bullets thunking into the metalwork of the car.

Then they were on the road, tearing back toward Boone.

"I didn't need your help," MacGregor said, after they'd gone about half a mile. "I had the whole thing under control."

"Yeah, right," Delaney said.

Then the two men began laughing maniacally.

When the postbattle adrenaline rush had worn down a little, Delaney said, "You want to tell me what happened back there?"

MacGregor took a moment to answer. "I guess you figured out, I gave a note to that snot-nosed kid when I twisted his finger. He went to the police. Obviously I hadn't heard your story at that point. So as we drove home, you told me about this black ops unit led by Dirk Pardee, a conspiracy that went all the way up the line to the president of the United States, and so on." He shrugged. "You and I have been through some things. But it was a long time ago. I figured you'd changed, gotten bitter, I don't know—the older I get, the stranger people seem to me."

Delaney laughed.

"Anyway, when those supposed FBI guys came in the house, they didn't show me their IDs. That seemed strange. You know how FBI people are. They're sticklers for procedure. I asked the white guy flat out for ID, and you know what he said? 'You'll see my ID when I decide you need to see it.' Got my Scottish up, if you know what I mean."

MacGregor was piloting the big car confidently down the city road at well over ninety miles an hour.

"Anyway, that made me suspicious. I asked the black fellow what FBI office they were from, and he said they were from the Boone field office. I happen to know there is no FBI field office in Boone. I asked him for his ID. He said he'd show it to me after they got you in the car. Then, as they were putting you in the car, I saw one of the other supposed FBI agents get out of the other car. And I recognized him."

"Gonzalez."

"Yep. Every once in a blue moon in some distant part of the world, a homicidal creep like Gonzalez has his uses. But in the FBI? Absolutely one hundred percent no way. Say what you want about the FBI, they don't hire thugs like Gonzalez."

"Don't tell me . . . ," Delaney said.

MacGregor grinned. "I may not have ever mentioned to you, but with my background and contacts, plus my expertise in RF microcircuitry, well, I don't think I'm speaking out of school here to tell you that I do a certain amount of consulting for various governmental agencies who don't like being discussed loudly in public. Bugs, RF beacons, transmitters . . ."

Delaney laughed silently.

"So I tossed a couple of little toys in your bag. A bug, a tracer beacon. Then I sat there in my kitchen and watched those guys drive away with you and tried to convince myself I'd done the right thing turning you in."

"Evidently you didn't succeed."

MacGregor took the next turn at forty miles an hour, tires shrieking. "Anybody behind us?"

"I think you can slow down," Delaney said.

"You know how boring it is to be a college professor," MacGregor said. "I mean I guess it beats being a galley slave, but—good Lord, it's dull."

"So you didn't really care if I was guilty or innocent. You just wanted a little action."

"Right. I never liked you much anyway." They laughed. "So anyway, after a few minutes I threw my receivers in the car, followed the tracer beacon to the hotel, and then listened in on the conversation in the room. It was obvious you were being tortured. So I drove back to the house, put on my flak jacket, strapped on a couple of weapons, and headed over."

"You didn't have much of a plan though, huh?"

MacGregor shook his head sadly. "You underestimate me." He opened his coat. Inside, strapped to one of the ceramic inserts in his bulletproof vest, was what looked like a block of C-4 with a det cap sticking out of it. "So the plan was to neutralize the guards outside the door, then surrender to the guys in the security car, let them bring me in the room. Then I'd open the vest and say, 'Okay, boys. Delaney and I leave right this minute or I pull a Hammas and we all die.'"

Delaney looked at MacGregor in disbelief. "That's the dumbest plan I ever heard in my life."

"Well, jeez, Delaney, I only had about five minutes to think it up. There were six of them and one of me. I had to do *something*." They threaded their way through the Ap State campus in silence for a few minutes.

"Where'd you get the C-4?"

MacGregor smiled impishly. "My wife took an art class a couple years ago. It's modeling clay."

All Delaney could do was shake his head. "I'm going to need a car," Delaney said after a moment. "Not this one."

"Would your old war buddy MacGregor forget about a detail like that?"

MacGregor pulled up in front of a dormitory. The irritating kid whose finger MacGregor had twisted was leaning against the hood of a bright yellow Honda Civic parked by the curb.

"Not *him* again," Delaney said.

"Wait here," MacGregor said. He went over to the young man, had a brief conversation, then came back and sat next to Delaney.

They watched the young man walk back into the dormitory.

"That's his car." MacGregor pointed at the yellow Honda. It was tricked out with an air dam, ground effects kit, and fat tires. "He tells me it's been very heavily modified. It's his pride and joy." He tossed Delaney a set of keys. "So don't break it."

Delaney looked at MacGregor quizzically. "How'd you manage that? Wouldn't think that kid would be your biggest fan."

MacGregor gave him a sly smile. "What do you think? I gave him ten points extra credit. Suddenly I'm his best friend."

Delaney gave him a skeptical look. "He'd loan his pride and joy to a wanted man for ten points?"

"Bud, you obviously don't have a clear sense of the level of desperation that bad grades raises in a kid like that. He flunks out of Double E, his old man'll nail his scalp to the wall."

28

White House Situation Room
2:40 PM

I KNOW YOU HAVE work to do, General," the president of the
United States said, "but before I give you your marching orders, I
want you to see this situation through my eyes."

As Morgan Boyd spoke, John Rancy picked up a remote control
and switched on CNN. The banner at the bottom of the screen read
HOUSTON, TX. On the screen was a confused mass of people stum-
bling and running through a street. The camera was bumping up and
down as though the cameraman were running just as frantically as
everyone else in the picture. There was no sound.

"I assume you heard about the truck full of chlorine gas that was
blown up in the middle of the 610/57 interchange a couple of hours
ago. Chlorine gas, as I'm sure you know, was actually the first poison
gas used in World War I. Luckily the truck was blown up in a stiff
wind on top of an overpass that was seventy-five feet in the air. The
smoke plume passed over the heads of everyone on the interstate, and
only a few people sustained serious injury. But close to hundred
thousand people were evacuated from the area, there was a general
panic, and several people sustained life-threatening injuries after
jumping from the overpass, getting hit by other cars as they bailed out
in the middle of the road, and so on. People are now panicking in
other cities. There's a protest in Houston right this minute where
concerned folks are appealing for a stronger response from yours
truly. The protest seems to be getting out of control. Some cars have
been burned, and a couple of shops have been looted."

Bill Fairbank watched the screen. The video cut to someplace else
in Houston, people screaming and waving signs that he couldn't

read. Then another cut, this time to Sacramento, California. A bunch of well-dressed people were yelling as a man in a suit stood on the steps of some sort of government building and tried to make a speech. He kept waving his hands to quiet them, but it didn't seem to be working.

"The governor of California," Boyd said. "CNN has been showing this clip over and over. They'll start throwing food at him in about five seconds." Boyd switched off the television as the governor was hit in the face with what appeared to be a half-eaten McDonald's hamburger.

Fairbank sat stone-faced.

"It's time to act, Bill. The American people are crying out to me. They want to feel secure."

"Yes, sir."

"I want you to implement the full deployment list I gave you this morning. I'll have rules of engagement drawn up for you by the time your men hit the streets."

"Yes, sir." Rules of engagement. Rules of engagement against American citizens. Fairbank had never felt so unenthusiastic about an order in his life.

"New York, LA, Chicago, Houston, Sacramento, Atlanta, Seattle, Philadelphia, Cleveland, Cincinnati . . . You've got the list. Lock these places down if you have to. If you have to block the tunnels into Manhattan, so be it. If you have to close down O'Hare, Hartsfield, LAX, Reagan, Kennedy, La Guardia, so be it. If you have to detain a cameraman or two, so be it. If you need to throw a couple of protesters in a paddy wagon, so be it. I'm giving you broad discretion. We need to stop the bleeding and we need to do it *yesterday*."

"You'll put that in writing, of course," Fairbank said.

Morgan Boyd ignored him. "I'll be announcing the deployment from the Oval Office at sixteen hundred hours. Then we'll segue to the Pentagon briefing room and you'll speak briefly. My press people have written a speech for you. You can pick it up on the way out." He paused, his black eyes studying Fairbank. "I can't emphasize how important it is to strike the right tone. Forceful, defiant, we shall not be moved. The people of America will be looking to you for strength."

"Yes, sir."

"That's all, General."

AFTER THE GENERAL had left the room, an aide entered and pointed at the phone. John Rancy had a brief, whispered conversation, then hung up. He looked up at the president, white-faced.

"What?" Boyd demanded.

"Delaney escaped. Killed three Unit P operatives at some hotel in Boone, North Carolina."

Morgan Boyd digested the news for a moment. "Bury it," he snapped. "I don't want a whiff of this reaching the press."

"That goes without saying, Mr. President."

"Send Pardee. Federalize the scene, sanitize it, get the bodies out, don't let local law enforcement anywhere near this. Whatever happened there it needs to go away completely."

"Pardee says the man on the scene is very experienced. He knows what to do."

Morgan Boyd nodded, then said, "What's happening in the Senate?"

"It's moving through committee a little slower than we'd hoped. But it's getting there. The big problem is Tunnington. He's threatening a filibuster."

The president looked thoughtful. "I can't keep up the momentum of this push under executive order. I need that Freedom from Fear Act, John."

"I understand, sir. Senator Gray has been working around the clock on it."

"I don't care how pretty his wife is or how well he plays the piano. And I for darn sure don't care how hard he works. A trained monkey can work hard, John. This is about results. Tell him I need that act by the end of the week, or I will personally drive him out of office when he comes up for reelection."

"But if Tunnington filibusters—"

"A man his age? His health could go south at any minute."

"Ah." Rancy's eyebrows went up slightly. "There is that."

29

Washington, DC
10:21 PM

AFTER A GRUELING six-hour drive through the back roads of North Carolina and Virginia, Delaney found the small row house in Columbia Heights without much trouble. It was just a block off Sixteenth Street. The last time he had been here, this had been a fairly run-down Salvadoran neighborhood, but gentrification was changing the character of the area. Many of the houses were spruced up now, with expensive front doors, extensive yard work, and other signs of rising property values.

Except for the house where Delaney was knocking. The roof still sagged and the paint was still peeling and there were still bars over the windows, everything the same as it had been eight years earlier.

The door opened, and a small, balding man looked at Delaney through a permanent, skeptical squint. He had one hand in his pocket, probably holding a small, cheap pistol.

"What the—"

Delaney reached out, clamped his hand over the small man's gun hand, pushed him back into his apartment. "Good to see you, Winston," Delaney said. "Been a while, huh?"

"Aw, man . . ." Winston Rogers had a whining voice. He was the kind of guy who believed that every bad thing that happened to him was somebody else's fault. Before entering the protection side of the Secret Service, Delaney had briefly been on the law enforcement side. He had busted Winston Rogers for forgery. The intaglio plates Rogers had produced, according to an expert from the mint, were the most beautiful work he'd ever seen. The case had been kicked on a technicality, and Winston had gone right back to business as usual.

Delaney yanked the little revolver out of Winston's pocket,

dumped the .22 Long Rifle cartridges into his hand, tossed the cheap little pistol on the couch, then looked around the squalid room. There were pizza boxes on the floor, beer bottles on the coffee table, and the carpet probably had not been cleaned since the Nixon administration. A pile containing hundreds of blank credit cards competed with the beer bottles on the table and spilled off onto the floor.

"I see you're still in business," Delaney said.

"Where's your warrant?" The small man fingered the fringe of long graying hair that encircled his bald spot.

"So I guess you haven't been watching the news much lately?" Delaney said.

"News? Only suckers watch the news. It's all a bunch of lies designed to keep the little man pacified and whistling in tune with the big rich folks." Winston's political philosophy, such as it was, had been developed during his freshman year at UC Berkeley in 1968 and had not changed since. It was a philosophy that allowed Winston to claim the moral high ground for himself while he kept up a busy career counterfeiting money and credit cards, stealing people's identities, and producing false documents for illegal residents of the United States. "What do you want, Gruppenführer Delaney?"

"I want a couple of false IDs, I want a passport, I want credit cards, and I want some government ID badges."

Winston Rogers looked at Delaney like he was an idiot. He obviously thought Delaney was trying to entrap him so he could arrest him for forgery.

"You really haven't watched the news?" Delaney said.

"I've been working on a project. I haven't even left my house in a week."

"Well, just to fill you in, right now I'm wanted for murdering the president."

Winston's eyes widened. "You whacked Fairbank? Fairbank's *dead?*"

Delaney shrugged. "It's all a government conspiracy."

Winston seemed transfixed.

"Turn on CNN."

Winston cleared some pizza boxes from in front of a huge widescreen TV, flipped the station to Fox. He stared in disbelief as they replayed a clip of Morgan Boyd's speech announcing his mobilization of the army.

Then the announcer said, "Meanwhile, fugitive Secret Service

Agent Michael Delaney was reportedly spotted earlier today in Boone, North Carolina, where a gun battle broke out at a Hampton Inn hotel under cloudy circumstances. The FBI is now saying they believe the gun battle to have been between rival drug gangs . . ."

Winston Rogers switched off the TV, a slightly dazed look on his face.

"See?" Winston said finally. "It's just like I predicted. The fascists are finally showing their faces." He stared at Delaney, like a starstruck kid looking at a famous actor. "But who am I preaching to, man? You're my hero! All this time, man, Gruppenführer Delaney, the ultimate fascist tool, is actually a mole for the revolution. You are *beautiful,* man!"

"Well, that's kind of you to say," Delaney said. "But time is of the essence."

Winston Rogers nodded vigorously. "Yeah, yeah, absolutely! Come on downstairs, let's get you equipped, huh?"

The two men went through a heavily secured door lined with a half-inch steel plate and guarded by an electronic lock, then down a staircase into a small, brightly lit room. The room was the polar opposite of the squalid upstairs: it contained two immaculate workbenches, a couple of neatly labeled file cabinets, various pieces of printing and embossing equipment, and a variety of artistic tools, all of them perfectly clean and meticulously organized.

"You heading for South America?" Winston said. "Or, what, someplace in the South Pacific maybe?"

"That remains to be seen."

Winston grinned, winked. "Right, I know, I know—need-to-know basis, huh?"

He pulled open a cabinet and retrieved a box of passports. "You want U.S.? France? I got beaucoup New Zealand. I like New Zealand because it's friendly, English-speaking, but a little off the beaten path. I got Belize here. Belize is real nice, I'm told. Great climate, great-looking women . . ."

"How about one of each?"

Winston looked at him blankly for a moment. "Look, I'm a revolutionary, man, right there in the trenches with you. But I got to make a living. You know how much investment I got in each one of these?"

Delaney set five one-hundred-dollar bills on the workbench.

"For the revolution?" Winston said. "I could give you a Belize, maybe."

"And a U.S."

"Man, come on!"

Delaney didn't pause to argue. "I also need a Virginia driver's license."

"How about Maryland? Virginia, I'm out of stock. Or Idaho, some reason I got a deal on Idaho, got maybe fifty blanks. All these puppies are factory original blanks, with the holograms and mag stripes and everything."

"Maryland would be fine."

"What about credit cards?"

"What would be nice is if I could credit everything to a real account. Not somebody else's, but an account I could actually be responsible for and pay off myself. Is that possible?"

Winston looked horrified. "Why on earth would you actually want to *pay* off a credit card? Don't tell me you're still hung up on all that bourgeois morality stuff?"

"Call me crazy . . . ," Delaney said.

Winston scratched his head. "I mean, sure, we could do it . . . I'll have to do some computer hacking, but, man, it just seems *wrong.*"

"Set aside your scruples."

He pointed to a tripod-mounted camera on the other side of the room. "Okay, okay, step over here, let me get a couple mug shots and we'll get this train rolling."

WINSTON ROGERS WORKED happily all night, without a complaint or a moment of irritation, humming to himself as he worked, discoursing on his two favorite subjects, the "fascist-money conspiracy" and the laziness of the current generation of forgers.

"It's all computers now," he was saying as he finished up a fake credit card. "Nobody understands about ink or photography. And engraving? *Engraving!* Forget it. You think any of these Nigerian guys know how to engrave an intaglio plate? Hah! All they know how to do is scan stuff into a computer. Nah, Delaney, the only people still engraving plates are in Russia now. I've seen some beautiful work from there, of course. Real artistry. Those guys still have a reverence for the craft, see?"

"That's very nice to know," Delaney said. "You about through?"

Rogers blew some dust off the credit card he had just completed, set it on the pristine workbench in front of him, and smiled proudly.

"Voilà! I'm so good, sometimes I scare myself." He gathered up his handiwork, put it in a small, cheap valise, handed it to Delaney. "Congratulations. You are now Jay Fiedler, a financial writer for *Business Week Online.* You have gilt-edged credit and a modest house in Greenbelt, Maryland."

"Thank you, Winston," Delaney said. "I won't forget this."

"You're also Jay Fiedler, Senate aide, if you need to be. Plus you've got plenty of credit cards, a pharmacy discount card, a few other odds and ends, just for the sake of credibility."

"You do fine work."

Winston looked around the room thoughtfully. "Hold on, hold on. You also need a cell phone." He started rummaging through a box, pulled out a large, crude-looking cell phone with a small port in the bottom into which a computer chip could obviously be mated. "I got this phone, it's got a little plug—see right here?—you plug in these ROM chips with pirate numbers on them, you can make one call, then dump the chip, plug in another one. Each time it will be as though you were using a totally different phone. That way they never get a fix on you, can't start triangulating on that number every time you use the phone, right? Ah! Here we go. I've got about ten chips in this little plastic bag."

Delaney put the phone in a shopping bag along with the passports and cards, and Winston escorted him to the front door. Delaney walked out into the early morning light, bone tired.

"Viva the revolution, man!" Winston said, grinning and making a fist.

"Yeah," Delaney said. "You too."

DAY SIX

30

Washington, DC

7:21 AM

DELANEY DROVE NORTH on Connecticut Avenue toward Maryland in his souped-up yellow Honda, trying out Winston's trick cell phone as he drove.

He reached Mary Campos on the first ring. "Hi, Colonel. Mike Delaney here."

"Yes?" she said guardedly.

"Did you ever check out the blood sample I told you about?"

"Yes. It verifies that you had barbiturates in your blood. Which proves nothing."

"It's just one more piece of evidence. I give you enough evidence, you'll start to see your whole theory start to crumble."

"What do you want, Mr. Delaney?"

"You're aware of some kind of weird little paramilitary unit run by Dirk Pardee, yes?"

There was a long pause as Mary tried to decide whether or not to admit to the unit's existence. "You're talking about Protocols and Procedures Section," she said finally. "Some people call it Unit P."

"Look up the personnel files on Dirk Pardee and Martin Gonzalez. Then ask yourself why anybody in their right mind would hire people like them."

"Mr. Delaney—"

Delaney hit the Off button, tossed the ROM chip out the window, then hung a U-turn and headed back south. They'd be able to track the cells his phone was activating and deduce that he was moving north on Connecticut toward Maryland. He turned quickly off of Connecticut onto Rock Creek Parkway, then headed over toward Virginia, crossing the Roosevelt Bridge. As he was crossing the bridge, he saw a column of Bradley armored vehicles pulling up on the far end of the bridge and stopping traffic, dozens of armed men hopping out and setting up a checkpoint in the middle of the highway.

His heart started pounding. Yet again, too close a call. He wondered how the five days' growth of beard and the bogus driver's license would hold up at a military checkpoint.

He swung past the Pentagon—which was surrounded by Eighty-second Airborne troopers, though none of them were stopping traffic—then cut over to the Columbia Pike, arriving fifteen minutes later at the campus of Northern Virginia Community College. He parked, walked inside the library to the reference section. There he found a crisscross phone directory, a directory that listed phone numbers in numerical sequence, followed by the name and address of the person using that phone. He scanned the listing for the number of the paymaster Paul Miller had given him. There was the name and address: Gilliland Products, 1295 Reston Industrial Way in Reston.

He located the address on a map, then walked to the back of the library's basement, where he found a row of study carrels. He found one unoccupied, went in, closed the door, set the alarm on his digital watch for noon, and promptly fell asleep on the floor.

Detroit, Michigan
11:40 AM

"Say the word *logistics* and people's eyes glaze over," Brigadier General Alonzo Treadway said to the reporter from the *New Yorker* magazine. "But people just don't realize how important it is."

They were standing on the tarmac, watching soldiers from the Fourth Mechanized Infantry Division trooping out from the row of C-130s parked along the side of Detroit Metropolitan Wayne County Airport. General Treadway was a tall black man with a shaved head, thick glasses, and a slightly studious look. He wore forest pattern BDUs and a sidearm. The reporter was a woman of about thirty-five, prematurely gray, who looked sorry she hadn't dressed a little warmer. A press liaison officer hovered nearby.

"You can talk about smart bombs and wireless communications and all that high-tech equipment, but the old adage holds true: the fellow who gets there firstest with the mostest generally wins the day. Even as recently as Desert Storm, the notion that significant portions of a mechanized infantry unit could be moved anywhere in twenty-four hours would have seemed laughable. But today?" He waved his hand at the flurry of activity. "These men will be at their posts less than twenty-four hours after receiving their orders."

A C5A Galaxy landed with a deafening roar and began taxiing toward the general and the reporter.

"That'll be our light armor and our transport—Humvees, M113A3s, and Bradley Fighting Vehicles. The United States Army's experience with low-intensity conflicts has forced a wide range of innovations in warehousing, IS systems integration, transport—"

The reporter interrupted: "Low-intensity conflict? Is that what this is?"

"This?" The general gave her a wan smile. "I don't know what this is."

The press liaison officer, a major wearing a pressed uniform instead of the BDUs that the general wore, stepped in and said, "Of course, the general is speaking on background, Ms. Sturdevant. That's not a quote for attribution."

"I'll let the general speak for himself as to what is or is not for attribution," the reporter said, smiling.

"It's not for attribution," the major said firmly.

"I'd best defer to the experts on that," General Treadway said, half-apologetically.

"I'd like to ride with one of your units, if I could," the reporter said.

"Put her in the first Humvee out of here," the general said.

"Yes, sir," the press liaison said.

AN HOUR LATER a column of Humvees was rolling down Michigan Avenue toward downtown Detroit. The driver sitting next to Eileen Sturdevant, the reporter from the *New Yorker,* was a talkative Detroit native who gave his name only as Sergeant Dickens.

"This here's a suburb called Dearborn," he said as they rolled through a prosperous-looking suburb of the city. "Over there that's your Ford Motor Company. Got a real nice museum down there a couple blocks. Mr. Ford—Henry Ford, I mean—he collected all kind of crazy stuff. Trains, cars, power generation systems, washing machines, you name it. He bought Edison's entire laboratory, rebuilt it over there, lock, stock, and barrel. Real interesting if you like machinery. Personally, I like dogs. My brother, he's an engineer, he goes ape over that place. Takes his kids out twice a year, showing them seventy-five-year-old washing machines and whatnot. You ought to see them kids rolling their eyeballs."

The soldiers all seemed cheerful and relaxed, not expecting much of anything. The only person who seemed nervous was the press liaison from the Pentagon. The cheerful travelogue continued as they moved toward the city center. Passing out of Dearborn, the area became a little seedier, a little more worn down.

"Have you read the rules of engagement that have been promulgated for this mission?" Eileen Sturdevant asked.

"Yes, ma'am," Sergeant Dickens said. "Had to read them to my platoon this morning. The gist of it is, if there's a significant and potentially lethal breach of public order, we're allowed to use restrained deadly force."

"Well, yes, that's what it *says,*" Eileen Sturdevant said. "But what does that mean to you?"

"Uh . . ." The young sergeant cleared his throat. "I guess, you know if there's people looking like they might kill somebody we can, uh . . ."

"Shoot them?"

"Yes, ma'am, I guess so. I mean, to save somebody's life . . ." He seemed eager to change the subject. "You might be interested to know this here area that we're passing into, it's the largest group of Arab folks living anywhere outside the Middle East. Got about eight dozen mosques around here." He pointed at what appeared to be a small minaret poking up above the tired-looking shop fronts around them. Eileen Sturdevant noticed that almost all of the signs around them were in Arabic or contained transliterated Arab names. Women in shawls and men in kaffiyehs were everywhere. And nearly all of them stared nervously—if not with outright hostility—at the column as it drove by.

The radio crackled, somebody saying something that Eileen didn't catch.

"Huh," Sergeant Dickens said, frowning. "Something's going on. Captain wants us to run a quick patrol down here." He turned off on a side street. They steered around, turned right again, then left.

"Don't know this area so good." Dickens suddenly sounded slightly nervous.

The radio crackled, issuing instructions on where to go. The column wound around for a while. Dickens was looking increasingly agitated. "Captain's using that stupid GPS map. Half the time those things send you the wrong way."

And as soon as he said that, the road they were on came to an abrupt end. A knot of dark-haired boys were playing soccer in front of them. Seeing the column of Humvees, the boys immediately quit their game and ran over, yelling, excited. "Look! The army!" They cheered and ran around the Humvees. Dickens blew his horn, waved the boys away to get back.

"Don't want to run over one of these kids," he said good-naturedly.

The boys continued to run around them. "Let me see your guns!" one laughing boy yelled.

Dickens blew his horn again.

Two soldiers emerged from the Humvee behind them, M16s in their hands. "Get back, kids!" one of them yelled. The boys backed off nervously, and the column began reversing slowly down the road. Several more soldiers emerged with weapons, walking beside the Humvees. A woman in a long black robe and traditional head scarf ran out of a nearby house, grabbed her son, and yanked him away from the soldiers, yelling something angrily at the nearest soldier and shaking her fist.

"Back up, please, ma'am," the soldier called. He pointed his weapon at her, and she ran back into the building, pulling her son by the hand.

"Did he just point a gun at that woman?" Eileen Sturdevant said.

"That wasn't intended as any sort of threat," the major from the Pentagon said quickly. "They use these ballistic slings now that keep the weapon in a ready posture. He wasn't actually *pointing* the rifle. It's a ready posture, that's all."

"I see," the reporter said. "Sergeant Dickens, what sort of training in crowd control do you and your men have?"

"Sergeant Dickens," the press liaison said, "I don't know that you need to address that issue at this juncture. I'm sure someone at a higher level can give Ms. Sturdevant a more comprehensive and accurate answer to that question shortly."

They started winding around again, and Sergeant Dickens began grumbling that they didn't know where they were going. In his apparent frustration, he began driving faster, braking harder, screeching his tires a little on the corners.

Suddenly they came around a corner and were confronted with a large crowd. Dickens had to slam on his brakes, and several members of the crowd jumped out of the way to avoid being hit. The Humvee behind him didn't have time to stop and slammed into them with a bone-jarring impact.

Angry soldiers emerged from the trailing vehicle.

The crowd had been listening to a man standing on a podium at the far end of a small urban park. But the approach of the column of Humvees silenced the speaker, and the entire focus of the crowd turned toward the infantrymen. They were obviously Muslims, most of the women wearing head scarves, the men dark-skinned, with Middle Eastern features. Many of them held up placards, some written in Arabic, others in English. WE'RE GOD-FEARING AMERICANS, TOO one said. Another read: STOP FBI HARASSMENT. Another: I'M AN AMERICAN CITIZEN. WHY CAN'T MY SON HAVE A LAWYER?

"Hey!" one of the nearby crowd yelled at Dickens. "What are you trying to do, kill me?"

Several others in the crowd yelled insults at the soldiers. Sturdevant had seen a piece on CNN this morning reporting that the recent crackdown on domestic terrorists had brought arrests and detentions of a number of Muslims, and that several Muslim communities had staged protests. She was excited to be witnessing one herself. This couldn't be better, she thought gleefully.

Dickens jumped out of the Humvee to check the damage to his vehicle, as did the driver of the Hummer behind him. The crowd seemed to view their emergence as a hostile act.

"We are Americans!" The man on the podium, a square-faced man in a blue suit, yelled through his megaphone. "We are Americans!"

Someone threw a wadded piece of paper at the lead Humvee, and the crowd cheered.

"We are Americans! We are Americans!" The crowd began to take up the cry, and it built into a roar.

The captain in the second Humvee emerged next to his machine-gun mount, one arm resting on the .50-caliber weapon. "Folks, y'all need to calm down!" he shouted.

The crowd began to close around the Humvees. More soldiers emerged, weapons at the ready.

"What are you going to do, shoot us?" yelled one man, pulling his coat open as though to make a target of his own chest. People were shaking their fists. Another wad of paper flew through the air. Then more paper. Then a sign sailed toward them like a Frisbee, banging off of Sergeant Dickens's face. Blood immediately began pouring from his nose.

"Back in the vehicles!" the captain in the second Humvee yelled.

The crowd only surged in tighter.

"Man your weapons!" the captain yelled. Of the ten vehicles in the column, four mounted machine guns. Soldiers sprang onto the tops of the Humvees and began rapidly feeding belts into the previously unloaded weapons.

"Stand back!" the captain yelled. But he was barely audible over the roar of the crowd.

"We are Americans! We are Americans! We are Americans!"

"Move out," the captain yelled. The Humvees began crawling forward.

"They ought to send these people back where they came from," Dickens said, wiping blood off his face as he dropped the Humvee in gear. He stomped on the gas, and the Humvee bucked forward, nearly hitting several angry crowd members.

"Easy does it, soldier!" the major yelled from the backseat.

Eileen Sturdevant couldn't believe her luck. This was going to make a fabulous story.

Something struck the front of the Humvee with a loud bang. A shoe. Something else hit the windshield, making a starburst crack. A rock? A brick? A piece of wood?

The crowd was still surrounding the truck, faces twisted with anger. They began rocking the vehicle from side to side. For the first time Eileen Sturdevant began to feel scared. She was a member of the ACLU, a proud liberal. In her mind the people in this crowd were the good guys, the underdogs. But they looked ready to drag her out of the Humvee and beat her to a pulp. Suddenly she was glad the other three occupants of her vehicle were heavily armed.

Sergeant Dickens continued to press forward in the Humvee.

"Slow down! Slow down!" the press liaison screamed. "You're going to kill someone, Sergeant!"

And indeed the crowd had gotten very tight around the Humvee. Finally even the wounded and enraged Dickens realized if he kept bulling forward, someone was liable to get crushed. He slowly brought the vehicle to a halt. The crowd was still banging on the sides of the Humvee, rocking it from side to side.

Behind them the captain was yelling something. Eileen Sturdevant couldn't make it out.

Then the machine guns opened up, and the screaming started. Eyes widened and the crowd fell back. People began running.

The press major emerged from the lead vehicle. "Cease fire!" he screamed. "Cease fire, goddammit!"

In about four seconds he had reverted from a smooth-talking rear-echelon major to a seasoned troop commander. He jumped up on the front bumper of the second vehicle and began screaming and jabbing his finger in the captain's face.

Meanwhile the members of the crowd continued their frantic flight.

Eileen Sturdevant scanned the ugly little park for casualties, but there were none. Inside of half a minute the entire park had emptied. A frigid wind whipped across the area, stirring the barren branches of a scarred old apple tree and sending abandoned placards tumbling silently, lazily, across the black dirt.

The major returned, looking much composed. "These men did *not* fire on civilians," he said to her. "Those were warning shots, that's all. Warning shots."

"I understand that," Eileen said. But she was already composing sentences in her head. *American citizens fled from the park like frightened deer, bullets paid for with their own tax dollars carving the air over their heads.* Maybe that was a little over the top . . . but something along those lines.

31

Reston, Virginia
1:40 PM

DELANEY DROVE the yellow Honda—now sporting Maryland plates—through the Wood Valley Industrial Park. It consisted of seven low-slung buildings, most of which seemed to have some sort of warehousing function. Several were occupied by only one company—one by a Japanese camera manufacturer, another by some sort of commercial lab. But Building C had a number of businesses in it. That is, it *had* had a number of businesses in it. It was now, however, a blackened wreck with a huge divot in the middle where Gilliland Products had once stood.

Delaney kept his recently purchased red Chicago Bulls hat low over his face as he scanned the area. He had left the telephone number and his wallet up in the cabin with Paul Miller on purpose. He wanted them to know where he was heading. And they'd taken the bait. There were two cars parked in the lot that didn't look right. The green van with the pizza delivery sign on it probably held a four-man team. Why would a pizza delivery truck be parked way over in the corner of the lot? And the Taurus with the two guys wearing sunglasses and earpieces may as well have had a sign on it saying UNDER-COVER OPERATIVES INSIDE. That probably left two more men—a takedown crew—inside the building itself. Big guys with plenty of CQC—close quarters combat—experience.

Delaney put on his blinker and drove slowly out of the parking lot.

THE MAN SITTING next to Delaney in the stolen van said his name was Ray. He was a white male with a week's growth of beard who stood just over six feet. From a distance he looked a little like

Delaney. Delaney had found him standing outside a homeless shelter with an empty wine bottle in his hand. The man had been eager to earn the hundred dollars Delaney offered him.

He was now wearing the same red Chicago Bulls hat, the same wraparound Oakley sunglasses, and the same bright yellow jacket that Delaney had worn when he did his reconnaissance patrol earlier in the afternoon.

"Here's how it's going to work," Delaney said. "You'll pull into the handicapped parking space in front of Building B. You'll get out and walk into the door of the burned-out building. Don't deviate from that path. Handicapped space, up the path, in the door."

"Then what?" the man named Ray said. "You're making me nervous."

"That's all you have to do."

Ray stared at him for a while then shrugged. "There's got to be a catch."

"Yes, there is. But it's nothing too serious, I promise. Some guys will come out and talk to you. Then they'll realize they made a mistake and they'll tell you to beat it."

He handed the man the keys to the Honda. As Ray started to get out of the car, Delaney said, "Oh, here." Tossing the man a black leather wallet the size of a pocket prayer book.

"What's this?"

"Just put it in your back pocket," Delaney said.

DELANEY PULLED HIS van around the side of Building F, the building that stood on the opposite side of the parking lot from the burned-out office where the paymaster had once worked. Using the van as a makeshift stepladder, Delaney clambered up onto the roof of the building and worked his way over to an air-conditioning unit where he could observe the far building.

Two minutes later, the yellow Honda rolled up and pulled into the handicapped parking slot. Ray got out, still wearing the red hat and the yellow jacket, walked up the pathway and disappeared into the building. Five seconds later, he was being hustled down the path toward the waiting green van by two men who could easily have had careers as pro linebackers. Another man emerged from the green van. One of the two big guys reached into Ray's jacket pocket and pulled out the leather wallet, which contained Delaney's Secret Service ID.

The man looked at it briefly, nodded curtly. The two big guys dragged Ray into the van. Tires squealed, and the green van pealed out of the parking lot followed by the red Taurus. The takedown had taken no more than twenty seconds.

Delaney jumped off the roof and began sprinting across the parking lot. He didn't have much time.

He ran through the steel frame that had once been a door and into the space that had once been the office of Gilliland Products. The space had been about a hundred feet deep and no more than thirty feet wide. It looked like the front had been finished as an office and the back had been a warehouse. Other than the collapsed steel roof members, there was little left. No indication that there had been anything stored in the warehouse area at all. And there had been precious little in the front either. A couple of steel wheels and a steel tube where a cheap office chair had been. A filing cabinet. It was locked, but he was able to pry open the lock with the Emerson folding tactical knife loaned to him by MacGregor. The filing cabinet was completely empty.

A burned-out desk lay in the corner of the room. The top had burned off, but the steel frame remained. A computer—which must have been sitting on top of the desk before the fire—was now lying on the floor inside the steel frame. He pulled it out and looked at it. It was clear from the scorching that the computer would never work again. But his mind went back to the question that Gonzalez kept asking him during the torture session in the Boone hotel room: *where's the disk drive?*

Interestingly, he noticed a gleam of bright metal on the screws that held the case to the frame: somebody had unscrewed the case after the fire. He pulled open the computer casing, looked inside. The motherboard was warped, and some of the chips seemed to have boiled from the intense heat. And there was a hard drive. So—given that the Unit P guys had been staking out the location for a while—this was obviously not the hard drive that Gonzalez was looking for.

He squinted, looked closer. Something was strange here. Then he realized: the metal rails on which the hard drive was supposed to be mounted were twisted, and there were no retaining screws attaching the hard drive to the rails. Moreover, the plug wire going from the hard drive should have been connected to the motherboard somewhere. Instead, the plug simply lay unconnected to anything on the bottom of the case.

He was puzzled at first. Why would a disconnected hard drive be in here? Then the answer came to him. Whoever had done this must have wanted to make it look as though they had left the hard drive to burn up in the fire, so that if anybody ever came back and checked they would see the drive and think that the computer had been burned intact . . . when, in fact, whoever had taken it, had switched the original drive for a dummy.

The flaw in that theory was that, if they were going to the trouble of putting the drive in there at all, why not do it right?

Maybe because they'd been in a hurry. They'd planned to do a neat job, but they had had trouble getting it in or perhaps didn't really know what they were doing, and so under pressure of time they just jammed it in as best they could, torched the place, and fled.

Gonzalez hadn't asked where the paymaster was. He'd just asked about the drive. Had someone broken in and stolen it before torching the place?

No telling. He surveyed the room. There simply wasn't any more evidence here to draw from—that's what it came down to.

He looked at his watch. He'd been there for seven minutes. That was probably two or three minutes too long. He trotted outside. There was a sign near the building that said, FOR LEASE, CALL RHONDA WHITELAW with the phone number and real estate agency name underneath.

Delaney sprinted back across the parking lot, climbed into the stolen van, and drove slowly away.

After he'd driven about five miles, he dialed Mary Campos again.

"Hi, Colonel, it's Delaney," he said. "I'll make this quick. Unit P seized a man they believed to be me. He is not me. He is an unwitting decoy, a homeless guy. I have his name, his Social Security number, and a videotape of his seizure by Unit P. I trust you'll contact Unit P and make certain that nothing nasty happens to him."

"Why would they do anything bad to him?"

"I'm just being cautious. Gonzalez tortured me when he captured me in Boone. He's not the sort of person to restrain himself from violence. Neither is Pardee for that matter. Did you check out their personnel files yet?"

"I have better things to do than run around doing your bidding. But, yes, I did. There's nothing unusual there."

"Then there's something that's been removed from his file. Let me represent to you the following: Dirk Pardee was forced into retirement due to persistent accounting irregularities in the various units he commanded. Martin Gonzalez is a former gun runner and worked as a torturer for, among others, a Communist regime in Central America. Don't take my word for it. Ask General Fairbank. Bill Fairbank will be able to tell you all kinds of things about Dirk Pardee. And when you verify what I'm saying, then ask yourself, why was this unsavory stuff removed from their records? And by whom? Bye-bye."

He hung up, pulled the chip out of the cell phone, and tossed it out the window. He drove another few miles, pulled into a strip mall in Tyson's Corner, and made another call.

"Good afternoon, Rhonda," he said, putting on a mildly officious manner. "My name's Pierre Davis with Gilliland Products. Yes . . . yes . . . exactly. I'm calling to straighten some things out about our lease at the Wood Valley Industrial Park. I know it's odd you didn't hear from us after the fire. It's a complicated situation. You may not be aware of this, but our office there is actually a distributorship, not a company-owned office. Gilliland's national headquarters are in Seattle. Frankly, we just found out that there had been a fire, and now we're kind of scrambling to get our ducks in a row vis-à-vis the insurance."

The leasing agent for the project was a chatty woman who sounded like she might have gone to college someplace like Sweet Briar. She was just so *shocked* at the tragedy and so *surprised* she hadn't heard from Mr. Rectinwald and so *worried* that something was *not right* and . . .

Rectinwald. Was that the paymaster's name? He assumed so.

The leasing agent would have gone on for a great long while if Delaney hadn't interrupted her. "Well, I sure appreciate your concern, Rhonda. Have you got that leasing agreement in front of you? Mr. Rectinwald—well, I'm embarrassed to say this—but it appears that he has absconded with funds from the company along with several very expensive pieces of inventory. Did he ever tell you what line of products we handle?"

"I don't believe he ever did."

"Well, trust me, our equipment is not cheap. He's got well over a quarter-million dollars' worth of demonstrator models, and by golly we'd like to know what he's done with them."

"My gosh!"

"So you haven't heard from him since the fire?"

"No, gosh, no, that's why I was so *concerned!*"

"Well, as I say, an insurance claim is in the offing. Could you give me the exact spelling of his name on the contract there?"

"*R-O-B-E-R-T A*-Period. *R-E-C-T-I-N-W-A-L-D.*"

"Home address listed on there?"

"Two-one-four-six Allenwood. Tyson's Corner. Do you want me to spell that too?"

"No, ma'am, I believe that'll do."

"And I've got a couple of phone numbers."

Delaney copied them down, then rang off. He tried the two numbers she gave him, but they had both been disconnected.

He threw out the chip, switched to another one from his dwindling supply, then drove across 495, stopped at yet another strip mall, and called the Reston Fire Department—this time from a pay phone—asking for the head of Arson Investigation.

"Johnny Purvis, Arson," a gravelly voice said.

Delaney gave him the same story he'd given the leasing agent, but this time saying that he was an investigator for Gilliland Products' home office in Seattle.

"Well, I'm tickled pink to hear from you," the arson investigator said. "Because I got to admit I had hit the wall on this case."

Delaney decided to take a chance. "There are a couple of puzzling aspects to this case. You think I could swing by your office sometime today, sit down with you for a couple minutes?"

"If you can do it right now. I need to get out of here to pick up my little girl from soccer practice at four."

"I'll be there in fifteen minutes."

32

Washington, DC
3:05 PM

MARY CAMPOS sat silently in the back of her chauffeured Ford. Was Delaney off his rocker? Was he lying? He had said that General Bill Fairbank had some negative information about Pardee. Was he blowing smoke? She was due for a briefing from the general in ten minutes. She decided to find out what, if anything, he knew.

The car rolled up to the White House, and she walked past the marine guards into the building and down to the Situation Room. The secretary of defense, the secretary of homeland security, the chairman of the joint chiefs, and General Bill Fairbank were already there.

As she was unpacking her briefcase, Morgan Boyd arrived.

"Let's not waste time," he said. "General, I'd like briefing on the deployment."

Bill Fairbank rose. "As we speak, units of the First Mechanized Infantry are rolling into New York City. We have already deployed advance parties in Atlanta, San Francisco, Chicago . . ." The list went on as he enumerated the units and their missions. Thus far, almost every unit was on or even slightly ahead of schedule.

The president interrupted. "Okay, what about this thing in Detroit? The liberal press is screaming about how we fired on innocent civilians. The fact that they were Muslims only further complicates things. Al-Jazeera is howling about it; people are making speeches at the UN . . . What exactly happened?"

"A ten-vehicle column from the Fourth Mech was instructed to check on a rowdy demonstration in a predominantly Middle Eastern section of Detroit. They apparently spooked some people in the crowd, the crowd got ugly, closed in around the vehicles, started throwing things, wounding one of the soldiers. The men manned their weapons, fired a brief salvo over the heads of the crowd, and the crowd dispersed peacefully. Other than one sergeant from the Fourth, no one was injured."

"That sounds reasonable, General, but there was a reporter there from the *New Yorker*, as well as some cameramen. It's plastered all over the TV right now. Women in head scarves running for their lives with babies in their hands while American troops fired on them."

"Yes, sir." Fairbank's face displayed no emotion at all.

"Are you happy with this?"

"Sir, the men showed great restraint I think. We are all well aware that line infantry units are not trained for this sort of work."

Morgan Boyd studied Fairbank's face for a while. "And?" he said finally.

"Sir?"

"Clearly you have something else you'd like to say. Go ahead and say it."

"Sir, I'm following orders. But I was not consulted on the rules of engagement. I believe them to be ambiguous and overly broad. Irrespective of that—if my men are tasked to do this sort of mission repeatedly, I think only the grace of God will keep American citizens from being shot by members of the U.S. Army."

Morgan Boyd nodded. "I am not going to disagree with you. So let us pray that God cleaves to us as we move forward. My response to you is simply that this course of action is the lesser of two evils. More Americans will be killed if we fail to act."

"Yes, sir." Fairbank continued to maintain his stone-faced expression.

The meeting continued for another thirty minutes, then the president dismissed them. After it was over, Mary Campos approached General Fairbank. "I wonder if I could have a word with you, sir."

Fairbank nodded curtly. "I'm on my way to the Pentagon. Want a ride?"

TWO MINUTES LATER, they were in the back of the general's car, steering toward the checkpoint on the Roosevelt Bridge.

"General," Mary Campos said, after they had engaged in some small talk, "you and I have worked together several times and I have great respect for you."

Fairbank didn't reply. Instead he looked out the window. The general had known Mary for a long time. Not only had they worked on several terrorism-related projects a few years back when both were posted at the Pentagon, but Fairbank also had served under her father—who was then a brigadier general—during Vietnam.

"Sir, could I speak candidly with you?"

Fairbank pointed his finger at the knot of M113A3 armored personnel carriers they were approaching. "Military checkpoints on the Potomac. Never thought I'd see that."

"Sir, do you mind my asking how you feel about what we're doing?"

"I'm doing my job," he growled. There was a long pause. Then he added, "But let's just say I have mixed emotions."

She nodded. "Have you ever heard of a Lieutenant Colonel Dirk Pardee?"

Fairbank looked at her sharply, his thick eyebrows lowering over his clear blue eyes. "Why do you mention that sneaky little sumbitch?"

"Could you tell me a little about him?"

"Why?"

"Because I need to know," she said.

Fairbank understood the game. Despite the fact that she was a much lower rank than Fairbank, she was also a direct representative of the commander in chief. If she asked, it wasn't for idle reasons.

He looked at her sharply, then said, "As you know, I'm a rarity in the higher levels of the army in that I came up mostly through Special Forces. Most of the top brass come from infantry, tank corps, or artillery. A SpecWar background tends to be a career killer once you hit brigadier, but for some reason I slipped through the net. Anyway, Pardee was a SpecWar operator too. I think he graduated from the Academy in '72, so he just caught the tag end of Vietnam. At that point I was XO of the Fifth Special Forces, which of course carried most of the army's SpecOps freight in Vietnam. Pardee was a captain back then. A very talented soldier in his way. By the midseventies we didn't have troops on the ground, but Special Forces operators got sheep-dipped up into some of those CIA-backed units in the mountains of certain nations whose names we still do not speak. Naturally I was aware of these ops because I handled the paperwork. Pardee led a group of training specialists, quote unquote. They did a lot of good work from a military perspective, but there were reports of some things that . . . smelled bad." Fairbank shrugged.

"After that, he rotated back to the States and into a line infantry unit, and I lost track of him. The next time I ran into him was about ten years later. I was a brigadier by then back at USASOC at Fort Bragg. Once again I was involved in staffing some black ops, this time out of Kurdish portions of Iraq. Once again, I got reports of some bad things happening on his watch. Things of a financial nature."

"Where did the reports come from?"

He looked at her with a strange expression. "I had been running the Ranger jump school at Benning in the late eighties. My top instructor was a sergeant named . . ." He hesitated, his face went hard. "This is where the story takes an odd turn. My top instructor was Michael Delaney. We were both SpecWar pros, and as you know, the laws of fraternization are a bit looser in SpecWar than they are elsewhere in the military. I kept up with him. He got word to me through back channels—in a very soldierly way, after exhausting the chain of command in his own command structure—that he was unhappy with the unit he was in and wanted out. I got him out. Later he told me some stories about Pardee."

"What kind of stories?"

"Pardee was supposed to be supplying uniforms, food staples, medical supplies, ammunition, and weapons to the Kurds. Which he did. But according to Delaney, he siphoned off a lot of money for himself. A *lot* of money."

"Do you know if he was forced out of the army because of that?"

"Not at that time, no. But later he was. I think it was something that happened in Afghanistan."

"Did Delaney have anything to do with his being removed?"

"Not so far as I know. Delaney had left the army by then."

The car was silent for a while.

"So how well do you know Michael Delaney?" she said.

"Apparently not as well as I thought," the general said.

"Does this thing he supposedly did . . . does it seem consistent with the man you knew?"

"Delaney reminded me of myself in some respects. He seemed like the kind of man who is more likely to be too honest than too, ah, circumspect. My experience, he's not the kind of guy to shoot somebody in the back. So to speak. And I never heard him say a word against the federal government."

"That sounds like a no, General."

"It seemed inconsistent with his character to me, yes." He scowled. "But how well do we know anybody?"

Mary didn't answer. It was the question that had been dogging her almost all week.

"General, have you ever heard of a man named Martin Gonzalez?"

"I've never met him, no. He was with the Sandinistas for a while, then switched sides and helped us out briefly. We had to cut him loose, though."

"Why?"

The general shook his head. "Let's just say, he's not the kind of guy you want on your team."

"I assume you've heard of Unit P by now."

"The black ops outfit that hit Paul Miller? Yes. They seem to have come out of nowhere. I'm a little vague as to who's authority they operate under. Are they under Homeland Security?"

"No. Justice. Rancy seems to be calling the shots. He keeps telling me that I'm in charge of them, but I get the impression Pardee snickers every time I leave the room."

Fairbank looked thoughtful. "So . . ."

Mary Campos nodded. "What if I told you Pardee and Gonzalez were both in Unit P?"

Bill Fairbank turned and stared at her. "I'd tell you whoever hired them had rocks in his head."

"General, I think Morgan Boyd hired them."

"Then he's gotten some very, very poor advice."

Mary Campos didn't add anything to the general's observation. He watched her face.

"I believe that's what we call a 'pregnant pause,'" the general said finally. "If you have something to say, say it."

"Let's just suppose," she said, "for the sake of argument, that Morgan Boyd didn't hire them in spite of who they were. What if he hired them *because* of who they were?"

The general's face hardened. "Colonel, are you telling me something you know? Or are you just guessing?"

She shook her head.

The general's face stiffened. "Morgan Boyd is our commander in chief. If you want to make accusations about the president of the United States, you'd better damn well have your facts straight."

Mary felt her face go hot. "Yes, sir!"

They drove the rest of the way in silence.

When they finally reached the Pentagon, Fairbank spoke to her in a softer voice. "I don't believe in whisper campaigns or talking behind people's backs. But if you find out there's some meat to the things you just implied—I want to know."

"Yes, sir!"

He fixed her with his hard gaze. "And, Colonel?"

"Sir?"

"Watch your back."

He about-faced with parade ground crispness and marched away.

Washington, DC

Dirk Pardee had nothing practical to do until Delaney surfaced again, so he was going over all the information the FBI had turned up on Delaney. He had spread out Delaney's phone records, bank accounts, personnel files—everything he could find—on a large folding table in the middle of Unit P's small offices.

Suddenly he noticed something odd. His cell phone records showed a number popping up a bunch of times back during the summer, a number that rang a bell in his mind. He frowned, stared at the number for a while. Then he looked at Delaney's home phone number. The number showed up there too. Then toward the end of the summer, the number stopped appearing in his phone records. Why did that number seem so familiar to him?

He picked up his own phone, dialed the number. It rang twice, then a voice said, "Hello, you've reached Colonel Mary Campos. I'm not available right now—"

He hung up the phone, frowning. No wonder! That's why she'd ripped open the dead guy's shirt in Miller's hunting cabin. She was looking for the bullet scar he'd gotten when he'd been tagged by the Indian terrorist. Why would she have thought to do that? The only way she'd know about the scar was if . . .

He snapped his fingers at the stocky young man working a computer on the other side of the room. "Badger, come here a second. I want you to check on something . . ."

"Yes, sir?"

"I know delicacy is not your strong suit, Badger, but I want you to poke around a little—quietly and unobtrusively and not making a big deal about it, okay, because I don't want to come off looking like an idiot here—and see if there's any possibility that Delaney's been boning Mary Campos."

The usually stone-faced Badger's eyes widened slightly. "You're kidding me."

Pardee gave him a cold stare.

"Yes, sir!" Badger snapped to. "I'll get right on it, Colonel!"

Reston, Virginia
3:20 PM

Criminologists and psychologists, Delaney knew, have done a host of studies on facial recognition in recent years, and the verdict was pretty well in: people are miserable at recognizing, remembering, or identifying the faces of strangers. Much of facial recognition is contextual: if a police officer hands you six mug shots and says, "Is the man who shot you among these six faces?"—chances are almost even that you'll point to one of the faces and say, "Yes, that looks like him"—Whether the real shooter's face is among the pictures or not.

On the other hand, if the shooter showed up in your office smiling and dressed in a nice suit, you might never even notice him.

Delaney was counting on context to play in his favor. What law enforcement official would expect the most wanted man in America to walk into their office and pleasantly chat about something entirely unconnected to the crime for which that man was being sought? It was a risk, yes—but right now doing nothing was the most risky strategy of all.

He pushed open the door of the Reston Fire Department's administrative office wearing a pair of sunglasses and a baseball cap, walked up to the counter, and told the clerk that Johnny Purvis was expecting him.

The arson investigator came out in less than a minute and led him back to a small, cluttered office. He was a large man with a gut that was just held in check by a starched blue shirt. As he sat down, he looked at Delaney curiously.

"Have we met before, hoss?" Purvis said.

Delaney felt a spurt of adrenaline. "Don't believe so."

Purvis narrowed his eyes. "I got a good memory for faces. I know I've seen you."

"You ever watch *America's Most Wanted?*" Delaney said.

"Now and then."

"I have several celebrity clients. I represented Harrison Ford when he had that crazy stalker who eventually showed up in his house. You might have seen me on the show."

Purvis grinned, waggled his finger at Delaney. "See? I told you I remembered you."

Delaney laughed, feeling the sweat oozing out of every pore. He was beginning to have a lot of respect for actors. It was hard pretending to laugh when you really didn't think something was all that horrendously funny.

"Anyway," Purvis said, "I'm relieved you came by. I hope you can fill me in a little on this fire."

"Well, maybe I can, maybe I can't. Here's what we know. My client, Gilliland Products, manufactures medical devices. A little camera on a stick that they shove up your nether regions, if you know what I mean. The thing runs about a quarter million dollars. Now they awarded this fellow Robert Rectinwald a distributorship. Meaning, that office over there at the industrial park, it's his lease, his office, his business. Just for the record, the headquarters company maintains they bear no liability for any harm he may have caused, should he turn out to be responsible in some way for the fire. Anyway, the point is, he leased the building personally. Gilliland Products loaned him a demonstrator model, which he was supposed to take around to proctologists and gastrointestinal specialists and so on, and demo the product.

"Well, he sold a few machines real quick. But then his numbers fell off, and the national sales manager back in Aspen got worried. Okay, then starting a few months back, he suddenly got real hard to reach. Didn't return phone calls, sat on some checks and some invoices, so on, so forth. Headquarters sends me out to take a peek at him, see what he's up to. And all of a sudden he gets real cagey acting. So I go back and start taking a hard look at his credentials." Delaney sighed, spread his hands. "Well, this character Rectinwald, he claimed he had a masters degree from Rutgers, turns out they never heard of the guy. Claimed he'd been a top sales performer for a competitor. Well, no, actually he'd been fired for punching holes in his sales manager's tires after the guy threatened to cut his per diem by three dollars a day. So I run his credit bureau? I don't know what kind of due diligence these cats in the home office did before they signed this agreement with him, but . . ." Delaney let his voice trail off. What he was trying to do was get Purvis to reveal what he'd found out about the paymaster.

Purvis laughed. "I ran him too. Imagine my surprise. No D and B, no credit bureau, no nothing."

"You ran him through the crime computer, I assume?"

"Yeah. No wants, no warrants, no judgments. But that wasn't the strange part . . ."

"What?"

"Well, you know in the grand scheme of things, this ain't the biggest case on the planet. Nobody got hurt, the property owner's carrier is gonna pay to rebuild . . ." He shrugged. "But, you know what it come down to? This fellow just teed me off." He scrabbled around in his desk. "The leasing agent had a photo of him, some kind of security thing in case they had to unlock in the middle of the night, they'd know who to let in or not." He came out with a Polaroid photo, pushed it across his desk. "Look at that boy. You ever seen a nastier-looking little rat in your life?"

Delaney squinted at the picture. Rectinwald was indeed one shifty-looking character—narrow-faced with a pathetic little mustache, thinning hair, and suspicious, protuberant eyes.

"So normally I wouldn't even bother looking for fingerprints in a place like that. But this time I did. I ran the prints through AFIS, got nothing. So just for grins, I got permission, ran them through the DOD database. Out comes a name."

"Let me guess," Delaney said. "It wasn't Robert Rectinwald."

Purvis laughed. "Guy's real name is Nolan Ferris Jr."

Delaney wrote the name down.

"But here's where it gets strange. When I asked for his service record, I got nothing. Brick wall. Sorry, can't help you."

"They tell you why?"

Purvis shook his head. "You know the Pentagon. They make their mind up, you're wasting your time."

"As it happens," Delaney said, "I've got a back-channel source in Records over at DOD. Maybe she can come up with something."

"She?" Purvis gave him a randy smile. "You *dog* . . ."

"Nah, nah, it's nothing like that."

"Now I been pretty generous, opening my kimono here," Purvis said. "I trust you'll reciprocate?"

"Absolutely."

Purvis stood, put out his hand, and they shook. "Well, I hate to run, but if I don't get moving, my little girl's gonna call me on her cell phone, start bugging me about how I'm late again. Twelve years old, she's already nagging me like a professional. I feel like I got two wives. You hear about those fellows over in Saudi Arabia, they got three, four wives?—boy, I don't know how they do it."

33

Washington, DC

10:35 PM

COLONEL MARY CAMPOS was a woman who ran her life according to iron routine. The last week had played havoc with her schedule, but after the first two days she had forced herself to return to her apartment every evening and go for her regular four-mile run in Rock Creek Park, no matter how crazy the events around her. Running in that isolated location at a late hour was not, perhaps, the safest activity in the world. Her position with the White House, however, gave her the right to apply for that extremely rare and highly prized item: a DC concealed-carry permit. She availed herself of the opportunity. Mary had found an interesting rig some years back that strapped on over both shoulders, allowing her to mount her small-framed Glock 26 in a Kydex holster—barrel-up—between her breasts. A more heavily endowed woman wouldn't have been able to do it, but with her trim build, the Glock rode easily and unobtrusively under her sweatshirt but over her jogging bra.

It was almost ten-thirty by the time she got into her running gear. She had been up since five and didn't feel even vaguely like running. But she hadn't gotten where she was by punting every time she felt a little worn out.

She ran down Connecticut onto the access road and down into the park. She was finally shaking off the fatigue, hitting her stride, her mind clearing a little, as she came under the first of the great barrel-vaulted bridges over Rock Creek Parkway. There was no traffic now, and her footsteps echoed in the high brick vault. Then the echo seemed to develop an echo. She had never noticed the odd acoustical effect when she ran there in the past. But then she put it out of her mind, attributing it to the lack of competing noises due to the lateness of the hour.

But after she came out of the vault, she realized it wasn't an echo, but a second set of footsteps, someone trailing her. Why hadn't she noticed them before she entered the bridge?

The answer was clear: because whoever it was had been waiting in the bushes and was running after her. She began to feel nervous. Was she being paranoid? She increased her pace. But the runner behind her sped up too, and the footsteps rapidly closed on her. Her heart rate shot up. She turned, saw a dark figure coming toward her. The man was not dressed like a jogger. He wore boots, a heavy coat, a hood over his face.

She immediately pulled her Glock, worked the slide, and said, "One more step, creep, and you die."

The man stopped, then pulled down his hood, revealing his face in the streetlamp.

"Okay, Mary," Michael Delaney said. "You slapped me, fine, I deserved it. But shooting me? Nah, I really have to draw the line."

She lowered her Glock. "For godsake, Michael! I nearly shot you!"

He shrugged.

"How did you find me, anyway?"

"The whole time we dated, you ran this same route every single day of the week except Sunday." He gave her a crooked smile. "Nothing personal, but you're kind of predictable."

"What do you want, Michael?"

"Is anybody guarding your apartment?" he said.

"You want to go there?" She smiled sarcastically. "You're joking, right?"

He shook his head. He still had that same muted intensity that had always attracted her to him. She wanted to deny him, but she just couldn't summon the strength. Well, at least she'd make him work for it. "Follow me," she said. Then she set off running as hard as she could. With his big coat and his hiking boots on, she intended to leave him in the dust.

To her irritation, he kept up with her, jogging along easily, not even appearing to get out of breath.

"I hate you," she muttered halfheartedly.

"I've missed you too," he said. And what really got her goat, the big jerk sounded sincere.

DELANEY KEPT THE hood on as they entered the building and rode the elevator to the floor where Mary's apartment was. As she opened her door, Delaney drew the Glock 19 he'd taken off one of the Unit P operators in Boone, made a quick, efficient pass through her apartment. No one lurked in the closet, waiting to ambush him.

"Make yourself at home," Mary said dryly as he holstered the Glock.

"Why thank you." He sat wearily on the couch. He hadn't realized how exhausted he was until he sat. He hadn't had a real night's sleep in a week. "Did you talk to Fairbank?" he said.

"You want a cup of tea?"

"Sure."

She went in the kitchen, made two cups of some kind of minty-smelling herbal tea, poured two cups, came back in the living room, and set them on the coffee table. "Fairbank confirmed that Pardee and Gonzalez are dirty. But that doesn't take me very far. There could be a million good reasons for a couple of guys like that to slip through the cracks. I mean, you'll admit they're good at what they do."

"So was John Gotti. That doesn't make him federal agent material."

"I just . . ." She looked at him for a moment, her dark eyes searching him. "Michael, there's some stuff going on that doesn't add up. In my heart of hearts, I want to trust you. I *want* to believe you. But how can I? It was your gun! You ran. You fired on federal agents. Why did you do that if you were innocent?"

Delaney sipped the tea, burning his mouth. "Look," he said, "let's get this out on the table before we get to that. I feel like a complete jerk about what happened between us, about what I did. I'm not going to defend myself. All I can say is that my divorce was finalized the day we got in that fight, and I was just feeling all mixed up and miserable. I didn't feel like I could be there for you that day. Then the next day I felt mad. Then the next day I felt like I'd look like a jerk if I called you. And . . . I just let pride and fear and confusion keep me from doing what my heart kept telling me to do. And the more time that went by, the harder it was for me to do what I really wanted to do. Which was to pick up the phone and call."

She shook her head and looked away from him. "It was that hard? Just to call me?"

"Hey, how many times did you call *me*?"

She didn't answer.

"Let's let it pass," he said. "Now's not the time to try sorting out how we feel about each other."

The room was very silent.

Delaney took out the Polaroid of Nolan Ferris Jr. and set it on the table. He'd "borrowed" it from Purvis's desk that afternoon. "I talked to Paul Miller before he got killed by Unit P. The Brotherhood had a mysterious benefactor. That mysterious benefactor paid over three million dollars into the Brotherhood's coffers over the past year. All the money was funneled through a paymaster who went by the name of Robert Rectinwald. Rectinwald's real name, I think, is Nolan Ferris Jr. He has some sort of military record—but the Pentagon is not releasing those records, even to legitimate law enforcement people."

Mary Campos sipped her tea. "And?"

He pushed the Polaroid over to her. "I think you can find out who he is. He kept records on a computer of all the money he sent to the Brotherhood. His office went up in flames less than one hour after Dean Fairbank died. I believe that he took off with the hard drive containing the records of his financial transactions. You know what we always used to say when I was on the investigations side of the Secret Service? Follow the money."

"You think this alleged hard drive contains, what?"

"Records of who the money went to, where it came from, probably where it went. We trace that money, find out whose fingerprints are on it, I suspect we'll find it's traceable back to some obscurely funded part of the federal government. Once we trace it to an actual account, we find out who's got signature authority, and it'll be a snap to figure out who's at the end of the money trail."

"What's your evidence for this alleged missing disk drive?"

"Like I told you on the phone, Martin Gonzalez spent an hour and a half torturing me yesterday. During that entire time he only asked one question. 'Where's the disk drive?'"

"Torture." Mary looked at him with a mix of concern and skepticism. "Like what? Cattle prods?"

"Nothing serious. Nothing that left any marks."

She stared at the Polaroid for a while.

"Look, Mary," he said. "You can find out who this guy Ferris is, this paymaster, maybe help me track him down. But to do that, you're going to have to take some risks. Have you got anybody you trust absolutely to work on this for you?"

She slapped the Polaroid on her thigh a couple of times. "Let's say it plain here, Michael. Before we go any further. What do you think we are looking for?"

"Put succinctly? I believe the president of the United States has staged a coup d'état. I believe Morgan Boyd conspired to kill off Dean Fairbank and take over this country. I believe he funded a terrorist organization in order to create conditions which would allow him to pass this so-called Freedom from Fear Act. I can't put it any plainer than that. I believe that he has found a number of people at various levels of government to collude with him—and they're doing it either out of personal ambition or because they genuinely believe the United States is in danger of being sucked under by terrorism."

Mary put her face in her hands. "This is too big for us, Michael. We need help."

"From who? We don't even know who our enemies are."

She rocked back and forth meditatively. "Tunnington," she said finally. "If what you say is true, and we can get the evidence to Senator Charles Tunnington, and he can make it public on the floor of the Senate, we'll be okay. If not . . ."

"I agree completely. Once this bill passes, it'll give Boyd a free hand. The Freedom from Fear Act amounts to virtual martial law. With him controlling troops in the streets and with all the provisions of that bill, he'll be able to send soldiers into offices of the *Washington Post,* seize whatever evidence I've turned up, and walk out again. With impunity. It's now or never."

"But first you have to dig me up some hard evidence. Right now, you have nothing but hunches and inferences and minor inconsistencies. That's not enough."

"I know a guy," Delaney said. "He served under me when I was in the Special Forces. Blew out his knee on a jump and transferred into another specialty. He's in Information Systems now at the Pentagon. He can get at information for us. But you need to make the call."

Mary stared at him for a long time. "This is crazy," she said.

Delaney met her gaze. There was nothing crazy in his eyes, no sign of blind ambition or mental instability or fanaticism. Just the same calm confidence that had attracted her from the first minute she saw him.

"Okay," she finally whispered. "I'll do it."

Delaney handed her a piece of paper with a name and number on it.

She walked down to the lobby, said to the security guard at the door, "My phone's on the fritz, you mind if I make a quick call?"

The guard nodded. She picked up the phone, called information, got the home number for Master Sergeant Alvin Roundtree, then dialed the number.

"Sergeant Roundtree," she said. "I'm sorry to call you this late. This is Lieutenant Colonel Mary Campos from the National Security Council. A mutual friend of ours is in a fix and I need your help . . ."

AFTER SHE FINISHED calling, she walked back up to her apartment where she and Delaney talked briefly, then she helped him make up the fold-out bed in the living room.

"I could stand a shower," Delaney said. "Would you mind . . ."

"Of course not."

She waited until he was done. When he came out, drying his hair, she went back to her room, took a quick shower of her own, brushed her teeth, and stood in the middle of her room wrapped in a towel. A strange feeling was running through her, as though somebody had hooked her to a small electric current. This was madness. It was crazy, crazy, crazy—every bit of it. Presidents of the United States didn't assassinate their way into office. Delaney was blowing smoke at her, using her as part of some warped plan. He would go down eventually. And when he did, Mary would go down with him. If she had even a lick of sense, she'd call Leonard Smith over at the FBI, and HRT would come busting through that door in about twenty minutes. Delaney was using her. He was taking tiny fragments of truth—the barbiturates in his blood, the shadiness of Pardee and Gonzales, some peculiar fire in Reston—to assemble a giant falsehood. That was the only rational explanation for all of this.

But since when was the heart rational? Sometimes you just went on instinct. And her instinct told her that she could trust Delaney. Her pulse thudded in her veins and she felt a rushing in her ears.

Finally she let the towel fall to the floor, walked into the other room, and slid under the sheet.

"Michael?" she said, letting her naked limbs snake over his warm body. "Michael?"

But he was fast asleep.

"Wouldn't you know it," she whispered.

34

Washington, DC
11:25 PM

DIRK PARDEE WAS NOT in a good mood. He'd finally gotten the Boone mess straightened out, and now he was ready to hit the hay in his own bed for the first time in days, when his phone rang.

"What!" he said.

"Colonel, it's Badger. You were right about Campos. The way the FBI's got it set up, they gave the phone company a list of every phone number Delaney has called in the past two years. If anybody on that list calls any other person on that list, the phone company computer flags it. Plenty of them, they're just Secret Service guys calling other Secret Service guys—perfectly innocent. But guess what just popped up? Campos just called a guy in Information Systems at the Pentagon."

"And?"

"So we have our own computer geek. Our geek has very deep access to the computer and used it to figure out what their geek did. Guess what?"

"Badger, I'm not in the mood to play twenty questions."

"Immediately after talking to Campos? Her geek pulled up Nolan Ferris's service record."

"No no no *no,* don't tell me that."

" 'Fraid so, Colonel."

"I'll call you back," Pardee said.

The head of Unit P hung up and dialed John Rancy's secure phone. "It's Pardee. I got extremely bad news. Looks like Campos is playing for the other team."

Rancy swore.

"She just went back channel to some buddy of Delaney's—a Pentagon computer geek. The geek pulled Nolan Ferris's service record. I don't know how or why, but somehow she's working with Delaney. Which means they're on the trail of the hard drive. You want me to take her out?"

Rancy said, "Colonel, this may come as a shock to you, but once in a blue moon there are solutions to life's little problems which don't involve shooting someone in the head. If we're onto her, but she doesn't know that we know . . ."

"We can use her to get to Delaney."

"And to the hard drive. I want you tapping her phone, intercepting her e-mails, watching her house, following her car, bugging her shower—the whole nine yards. If she is, in fact, working with him, then she'll lead us to Delaney."

"Then we pop them."

"No," Rancy said acidly. "Delaney's a smart guy. Let *him* find that disk drive—since the geniuses on your payroll made such a hash of that particular job—then we'll jump him and sew up every single loose end at one throw."

"Yes, sir."

Pardee hung up the phone, dialed Badger again. "Put a team outside Campos's house. Soon as she heads to work, I want bugs in her house and taps on her phone. I'll see you at oh-six-hundred."

DAY SEVEN

35

Washington, DC
3:45 AM

IN THE MIDST of a deep dreamless black void of sleep, a pair of hands clamped over Delaney's head, and a towel closed over Delaney's mouth and nose. The towel was wet and cold. He tried to struggle but couldn't move, tried to breathe, but his lungs felt like they were encased in iron. He began to flail wildly, panic rising and rising.

The darkness reached out to him, tendrils of night, caressing his face, wrapping themselves around his chest, his lips, his eyeballs. The world began to fade and close in. In the center of the narrowing circle of vision, he saw Gonzalez. "Where is the hard drive, Delaney? Come on, we're old war buddies. You can tell your old pal."

I don't know! he tried to scream. But the words only came out as an inarticulate howl. The dark fingers of unconsciousness began pressing into his flesh, squeezing the life out of him, yanking him gently down into the black pool of death below him.

"MICHAEL! Michael!"

Delaney took a moment to figure out where he was. The beautiful features of Mary Campos hovered over him.

"Michael, what's wrong?"

"What?" Michael said.

"You weren't breathing. You were flailing around and moaning. Are you okay?"

Delaney sucked in air, taking several long deep breaths. "I'm okay," he said finally. "Just a dream."

But he didn't feel okay. He was covered in sweat, and he could feel his hands trembling. He tried to steady himself, but the adrenaline was tearing through his veins like razor blades. He still felt like there was a towel around his face, keeping him from getting enough oxygen. He stood up next to the bed and began pacing up and down the room, still sucking hard at the air.

"Michael? Michael, you're scaring me. Are you okay?"

Delaney was not a man who was easily moved to panic: he had made a profession of being able to steady his nerves under the most trying circumstances. But for some reason he couldn't slow his pulse. He felt like the walls were closing in around him.

"I have to get out of here," he said, pulling on his clothes.

"Michael . . ." Mary was sitting up in the fold-out bed, staring at him, seemingly oblivious to her nakedness. On any other day, her smooth brown skin would have moved him to leap back into the bed. But today all he could think of was getting out of the building, being unconfined, moving freely. His heart was beating so hard that his chest hurt.

"It's okay," he said. "I just have to move around a little."

"Michael!"

"I'll be back in a minute. I promise."

Delaney pulled on his boots and his parka, pulled the hood up, thrust his Glock into the waistband of his pants, and walked out of the apartment.

Delaney took the elevator down, walked out the front door, turned left, and began walking down Connecticut. The broad tree-lined avenue was completely empty at this dark hour. The hoods and windshields of all the cars parked along the street were rimed with frost.

Except for a black Jeep Cherokee, with heavily tinted windows.

Delaney put his head down and walked on.

One of the fascinating things about training in any discipline—martial arts, shooting, basketball . . . or protection, for that matter—is that once the training becomes sufficiently deep, the conscious mind ceases to be involved and the unconscious simply does its job unmolested. So it was that Delaney spotted the first team in the Jeep—spotted them without even trying. Even with the tinted windows, he was able to see the two watchers silhouetted against a streetlamp. And once his antennae went up, he saw the second team parked in a van—the same green van he'd seen abducting Ray the wino in Reston—and the third team slowly cruising by in what appeared to be a DC

Police cruiser but wasn't. How many DC Police cruisers had alloy wheel rims? Precisely zero.

The question was, had they made him? With the hood up, he doubted they could see his face. He continued on down the street, leaving the watchers behind, then ambled into the parking lot of a Kroger, where he had parked the yellow Honda.

He was in the front seat, driving back toward Capitol Hill, when he noticed that the panicky feeling he'd felt after waking from his dream had passed completely. He still felt a tingle of nervousness, but the near-paralyzing fear of confinement and suffocation had passed entirely.

THE PHONE RANG. Mary was up now, making coffee and impatiently waiting for Delaney's return. He had been gone for twenty minutes now. What had just happened? She had never seen Delaney like that—pale, sweating, skin clammy . . . But it was his eyes that had frightened her the most. They had been wide and fearful, like the eyes of a trapped animal. He barely looked like the Delaney she knew at all.

The phone rang again. Maybe that was him.

She picked it up quickly. "Yes?"

"It's Sergeant Roundtree, ma'am. I've finished locating that information you requested. Would you like me to send it to you?"

"Can you send it to me by encrypted e-mail?"

"Yes, ma'am."

"Do it."

"Right away."

"And Sergeant? Thank you."

She hung up, finished making the pot of coffee. By the time she had logged on, an e-mail from Delaney's friend Roundtree was waiting in her mailbox.

She pulled up the attached files, found the complete personnel records of Spec 4 Nolan Ferris Jr. He had served his four years with the army as a bookkeeper in a logistics unit, then left active duty to become a member of the 635th Reserve Logistical battalion, where he had served three years and four months before being discharged on medical grounds. A note from a doctor, dated May 4, 1993, contained this unusually candid comment: *The undersigned medical officer believes Spec 4 Ferris to be a malingerer whose complaints are, at best, largely imaginary. However it is medically impossible to prove or disprove Spec 4 Ferris's claims of chronic migraine with any degree of certainty. It is the judgment of the undersigned that the U.S. Army would be better off without Spec 4 Ferris. Therefore I am recommending medical discharge.*

Nolan Ferris's home address—though surely much out of date—was listed as 2135 Shutterlee Mill Road in Staunton, Virginia. His VA benefit listed him at an address in Tyson's Corner. Mary looked at the papers thoughtfully, then put them in her secure briefcase, closed the lid firmly.

Then she sat down and waited impatiently, growing more agitated by the minute. Agitation soon turned to anger. *He'd done it again!—* gotten her hopes up, then walked out without a word.

At seven she made a call to the White House. Things were slow at the office, so she decided to work from home and go over her files at home and return e-mails until later in the morning.

AROUND TEN-THIRTY, she decided to head on into work. She had just gotten into her car when her cell phone rang. An unfamiliar voice said, "Hello, Mrs. Campos?"

"*Colonel* Campos," she said.

"Of course, I'm sorry. This is Ed at Donovan's Rare Books. I have a note here saying you were interested in buying a first edition of Colonel J. J. Graham's translation of Clausewitz's *On War.* I apologize for calling on a Sunday morning, but this is a rare edition—as you know, it's the first printing of the first English translation, the one with the erratum on page forty-seven—and you said you wanted to know the second we got it. It came in yesterday, but I forgot to call you. Unfortunately, in the meantime I did hear from another client who's very interested. I don't suppose you'd have a moment to drop in and look at it sometime today?"

She frowned. Who was this guy? She hadn't ordered a . . .

Then something struck her. Back when she and Delaney had been going out, they had strolled by a store once and she had seen an old translation of Clausewitz in the window. She had made a passing remark about how she would love to give a copy of it to her father, who was a retired brigadier. Delaney must have been held up somehow, and he was establishing contact.

"I was just heading to the office," she said. "I think I'd like to stop by and take a look right now."

SHE DROVE TO the bookstore, which was just off Dupont Circle, parked, and tried the door. It was locked. A man wearing a tweed jacket and smoking a pipe met her at the door, twisted his key, let her in, then relocked the door.

"I think you'll find this one quite nice, Colonel," the man said, leading her to a mahogany counter in the rear of the store. "As a seasoned collector, you'll know that the first edition is quite distinctive. The original had an erratum on page forty-seven, an entire line omitted, which was restored in the second printing. I'll go into the back, but please see for yourself."

She waited until the bookstore owner disappeared, then turned to page forty-seven. A handwritten note lay folded between pages forty-six and forty-seven. It said:

Mary,

You've been blown. There were three teams of watchers—probably Unit P guys—parked outside your apartment this morning. I don't think they made me. But they might have. Don't let anyone know that you know they're onto you. Assume your phones are tapped and your house is bugged. If you got the info we talked about, please leave it with Ed.

Sorry for getting you into this mess.

Love, Mike

She opened her briefcase, took out the faxes of the Ferris personnel files, set them on the counter. Ed came out from the back room.

"So, did you like it?"

"I did."

"It's four thousand dollars."

"Gosh. That seems a little steep. Can I think about it?"

"Of course. But don't think long." He smiled pleasantly, then put his hands on the faxes she had left on the counter. "I'll dispose of this trash for you if you'd like."

DELANEY WAITED half an hour in a nearby Starbucks, reading the sports pages, eating a cruller, and watching the front door of the store. At around seven-thirty, he called Ed Donovan—a retired CIA agent with whom Delaney had once worked closely—and said, "Do you have that new book by Stephen King, the one with the dead guy and everything?"

"Why as a matter of fact we do." Donovan, of course, had never carried *anybody's* latest book.

Delaney hung up the phone, walked across the street and down an alley just in time to see Donovan throwing a box full of trash into the Dumpster. After Donovan went back inside, Delaney approached the Dumpster and picked through the trash until he found the stack of faxes containing the army personnel records of Nolan Ferris Jr.

36

Georgetown

10:45 AM

FOR THREE DAYS Senator Charles Tunnington had been talk-ing. He had talked to other senators, he had talked to staffers, he had talked to reporters, he had to talked to congressmen and scholars and lawyers, he had talked to the president and to members of the ad-ministration, he had met in committee as the impending Freedom from Fear Act was being framed. But now he was done talking.

Debate for the bill was scheduled to begin the following day. As was his custom on Sundays, he had gotten up, made a single cup of Sanka, which he drank black while reading the *Washington Post,* the *New York Times, The State* from Columbia, South Carolina, and the *Charleston Post and Courier.* Then his driver had taken him to the same modest Presbyterian Church in Chevy Chase which he had attended since arriving in Washington almost fifty years earlier.

He put aside the issues of the day, sang the hymns lustily and with-out the slightest shred of musical ability, looked at the stained-glass windows, ignored the sermon, and thought about his wife, who had passed away three years earlier. He made a point every Sunday of thinking back on events in their lives, some happy, some sad, trying to remember them as vividly as his memory would allow. Today he thought back on the first time they had gone to Washington, taking the Southern Crescent from the whistle-stop in Clemson. He had felt full of importance on that day, not long after his first election to Congress—thinking himself to be a man of great promise and grand future deeds. Then the train had arrived, and it turned out there had been some kind of confusion in the reservations and he was unable to secure a sleeping car. He had gotten the impression that if he had slipped the conductor some money, perhaps something could be arranged. But bribery had seemed the wrong thing to do, and so he and his pregnant wife had been forced to settle for coach. He had felt a huge sense of disappointment—shame even—at his incapacity even to secure a sleeping car for his pregnant wife: here they were a U.S. congressmen and his wife, trying to get some sleep on an uncomfortable seat stuffed with horsehair while traveling salesmen and college kids slept on pressed linen in the next car. His wife—who understood his moods, perhaps better than he did himself—had taken his hand about the time they rolled through Greenville, and said, "Charles, you *are* destined for great things." They had fallen asleep on their pair of hard chairs, holding hands, her head against his shoulder.

Tunnington had done a great many things in the Senate over the years, most of which he was proud of, a few of which he wasn't. But had he ever accomplished *great* things? He suspected not. It seemed strange to think that perhaps here, in the late hours of his career, he was about to do the most important work of his life. The time for ambition was over. All that was left now was doing what was right. For a moment he felt a warmth against his neck, as though his wife's head still rested on his shoulder.

When the service was over, his driver took him to his office. His secretary of many years, Mrs. Graham, was waiting. She was nearing sixty, but—having developed alopecia some years earlier, which caused her to lose her hair—she still wore the same blond wig she'd bought twenty years earlier. She had not been an attractive woman even in her salad days, but now with the blond wig, she was downright odd looking. But she was smart, she was loyal, and she was as dogged as a pit bull.

"You didn't need to come in today, Mrs. Graham," he said.

"Oh yes I did, Senator," she scolded.

"No, Mrs. Graham, I'm not talking to anyone," he said. "Not today, not tomorrow. If anyone calls, tell them I will speak again publicly on the floor of the Senate in two days."

Then he went into his office, closed the door, and began reading the Constitution of the United States, starting with the first word and finishing at the end several hours later, taking notes on a legal pad with a cheap ballpoint pen. After that, he began reading the Federalist Papers, one by one, taking his time.

Late in the afternoon Mrs. Graham knocked timidly on the door. Mrs. Graham was not a timid woman, but when Charles Tunnington said he wasn't talking to anyone, then he wasn't talking to anyone.

"Senator?" she said. "It's the president of the United States of America on the phone." Mrs. Graham always referred to the president by his full title. Never POTUS, never "the president," never "President Boyd."

Tunnington smiled. "Tell the president of the United States of America that Senator Tunnington of South Carolina is completely immersed in the writing of a speech, and humbly begs forgiveness for his rudeness in not taking his call."

"Yes, sir."

"And Mrs. Graham? Would you bring me two more legal pads? I seem to be running out of paper."

The Oval Office
2:21 PM

Morgan Boyd's face was hard, and small red spots had formed on his cheekbones. John Rancy knew from experience this was not a good sign. Boyd set down the receiver.

"He's not taking the call," Boyd said.

"What, he's hiding in the little boys' room or something?"

Boyd shook his head. "That old bat of his didn't even give an excuse. Just told me he's not taking any calls." He slammed his fist on the desk. "I'm the president of the United States of America!"

"Yes, Mr. President, you are."

"Can we get this thing to a vote by tomorrow night?"

"Not even close."

Boyd's face calmed. "All right. All right. I think we have to assume that he's going to filibuster. In which case we're in real trouble."

"Yes."

"We may have to make a bold move here."

"Such as . . ."

"Something to slow him down. Come up with a range of alternatives. From the merely parliamentarian to the, ah . . . to the more aggressive, shall we say."

"How aggressive, Mr. President?"

Boyd didn't answer, just stared at him with his empty black eyes.

37

Tyson's Corner, VA
2:30 PM

USING THE VA RECORDS contained in the personnel files, Delaney was able to find where Nolan Ferris Jr. lived—a small house near Tyson's Corner. Delaney had taken a brief nap at a public library, then got in the yellow Honda and drove by the house.

Weeds were growing in the yard, newspapers had stacked up around the mailbox, and the driveway and carport were empty. Ferris was in the wind. Delaney didn't see anybody staking out the house waiting for him. There might be people in the house, though, but he'd never know until he was inside. He decided there was no percentage in going into Ferris's house. If there was anything useful to be found there, Unit P would already have located it. Besides, the risk was too high.

As he drove slowly by the house, he kicked himself for not ditching the car. It was too conspicuous. The problem was that it was getting harder and harder to make himself steal cars: every time he did it, he felt worse about what he was doing.

But it had to be done.

He pulled the yellow Honda into a nearby municipal park and watched the kids playing on a jungle gym. A young mother parked next to him in a minivan and started unloading her children. She was juggling a baby, two toddlers with drippy noses, a tricycle, a box of Kleenex, a mammoth diaper bag, several sippy cups, and a pair of sunglasses, which her baby kept ripping off her face and dropping on the concrete amid gales of laughter. The woman was round-faced and admirably genial in the face of her van full of chaos. In all the confusion, she lost track of one thing: as she herded her gaggle of kids down toward the monkey bars, she had left her keys dangling in the ignition.

Delaney took a deep breath, walked briskly around to the other side of the minivan, stood next to the driver's-side door. The woman and her kids continued to walk toward the monkey bars, not noticing him at all. Delaney put his hand on the door, then stood there, immobile.

Go! he kept thinking. Go now. Now! What are you waiting for?

Finally he opened the door, reached in, pulled out the keys.

What are you doing?

"Ma'am?" he yelled.

The woman and her kids continued on down the concrete walk.

It was like stealing candy from a baby. Only he couldn't do it. God help him, he couldn't steal another car. Maybe from a drug dealer or a convicted child molester. But not from this nice woman. He could try to console himself by telling himself that what he was doing was so vital to the world that it justified ruining this woman's sense of the benevolence of the universe, that by telling himself that he would make it up to her someday, everything would even out. But it wouldn't. Having her car stolen while she was playing with her kids—it would leave a mark on her that would never be erased.

"Ma'am!" The woman turned around, looking at him quizzically, and he held up the keys. "Ma'am, you forgot your keys."

She smacked herself comically in the forehead and walked toward him. "Thank you so much," she said, taking the big, jangling handful of keys from him.

"Got to be careful these days," Delaney said, smiling.

But strangely, the woman didn't smile back. Instead, she stared at him, eyes widening slightly. Then she took a step back and her face went pale. She had her cell phone in her hand. They both looked at the phone. It was obvious she recognized him. If she dialed 911, he was in the soup up to his neck.

They stood for about five seconds—though it seemed much longer.

"Please," she said, "you can do anything you want with me. Just don't hurt my kids."

"I promise," he said. "If you'll just do one thing for me."

"What?" she said softly.

He gently peeled the cell phone out of her hand. "Just don't leave your keys in the ignition again."

IT WAS A NICE gesture and all—a funny line. But in the real world doing nice things for people doesn't mean they won't call 911 on you. She had probably bummed a phone from another mother at the park and gotten through to the police within thirty seconds of his exit from the park.

There was a chopper in the air overhead within a minute, and the sirens had started closing in.

Delaney had never been a big fan of Japanese cars—but he was amazed by the hopped-up little Honda. The fat tires practically kept the little rice burner glued to the road, and the engine seemed capable of revving right up into the stratosphere. He was shifting at 11,000 rpm, and the engine showed no signs of breathing hard. Delaney suspected the engine had been lifted out of a Lexus and crammed under the sheet metal of the Civic, because the car seemed to have no discernible top end. The steering got a little jittery once he hit a hundred and things got downright spicy at a hundred and forty. But all in all, the car was hanging on like a much more expensive automobile. The kid had done a nice job tricking the car out: it wasn't just a big engine—he'd obviously put money into good brakes, good tires, good suspension.

Delaney flew through a neighborhood, downshifting into the turns, tires shrieking, then out onto Leesburg Pike. There was too much traffic, though, and he couldn't get up to a high enough speed to shake his pursuers. Behind him blue lights flashed wildly. He tried to think of a strategy. If he could get onto the right road, he had the horsepower and the maneuverability to outrun the cruisers, but the chopper could stay with him indefinitely. Unless he could get under some kind of obstruction that would block their view, his goose was cooked.

He cut off the traffic-clogged pike into a residential area, started threading his way toward the interstate. Not that the interstate would do him any good either. He'd be able to go fast, but they'd eventually put up a roadblock and a tire strip, shred his wheels, and he'd be rolling down the highway on his rims. Which was a surefire losing proposition.

Suddenly there were two cop cars in front of him. He floored the Honda and drove straight toward them. "Fellows," he said, smiling to himself, "my advice is, don't play chicken with America's most wanted man." The cops wisely peeled away at the last minute, one of them running into a ditch, and he tore on through the neighborhood, doing eighty in a twenty-five mph zone.

People say war is hell—and of course it's true. But what the best soldiers rarely fess up to is how much pure joy there is in combat. When the stakes have been raised to 100 percent—heads you win, tails you die—pure terror often mixes seamlessly with a near-maniacal excitement. Delaney had felt that excitement a few times. And this was pretty close. The initial sense of fear and numbness that came when he heard the chopper above him had quickly turned to a feeling of heightened awareness. He felt almost as though the game little Honda was an extension of his own body, his brain registering every bump in the road, every howl of the brakes, every hiccup of the engine with complete clarity. They'd probably get him, but not before he'd run them a good chase. His mind was focused, his palms dry, his muscles relaxed.

Two police cars started edging up behind him as he tore down a secondary road, engine whining. He pushed harder, braked into a turn, then accelerated out of the turn, the front-wheel-drive car understeering a little—but predictably enough, it didn't give him trouble. One of the two police cars spun out and ended up backward in somebody's yard, taking out a particularly ugly concrete lawn statue—a horrible, garish copy of Michelangelo's *David*.

Delaney simply left the second police car in the dust within half a mile—the cruiser falling victim to the Honda's superior pickup and handling.

The problem, he reflected, was that he was winning the battle but losing the war. If he didn't figure a way out within another three or four minutes, every cop in Northern Virginia would be swarming around him.

He headed back out toward the Dulles throughway, momentarily considering the odds of escaping somehow by airplane. He had just discarded the idea as an exceptionally stupid one when he crested a rise, and there two hundred meters in front of him was a row of four Bradley Fighting Vehicles, and a swarm of green-clad soldiers.

Ooops. Definitely not the Dulles throughway. The options were narrowing.

He slammed on his brakes, pulled a handbrake turn, tires howling as a .50 cal Browning opened up at him. Fortunately in his excitement, the machine gunner aimed a little high. Only one round hit the car—the 750-grain jacketed bullet thudding like a thrown brick as it blasted through the car—and then he was back over the hill, heading back toward what appeared to be about fifteen police cars.

Suddenly the cell phone on the seat next to him began to ring. How was that possible? Then he remembered: he had forgotten to change chips last time he called, so the phone number for the cell was one he'd used before. They must have traced it back to him. He took a hard right, headed south on an unfamiliar road that passed by a midrise office complex. He picked up the phone. "Yes?"

"Hi," an unfamiliar voice said. "You don't know me, but I'm a friend of Mary's. Do what I say and we'll get you out of this."

Delaney considered the offer. Trap? Maybe, maybe not. "Talk to me."

"You think you can make it another three miles?"

"Sure."

"The key thing is, you've got to have a half-mile lead. Can you string them out that far?"

"Maybe."

"Maybe's not good enough."

"I can do it."

"Remember where you and Mary went car shopping?"

"How in the world did you know about that?" They had looked at Volvos at a dealership in Reston.

"Mary told me, obviously."

"Okay."

"Head in the direction of that Volvo dealership. There's an independent body shop on the same strip of road. It's closed on Sundays. But one of the bays will be open. Drive into the bay."

The phone went dead. Delaney threw it on the seat. Trap or no trap? Trap or no trap? He still wasn't sure. They knew about the Volvo dealership, maybe they were for real. Right now he didn't have many other options. He made a snap decision: might as well try it. He downshifted, leaned into the turn as the car screamed around the next corner.

TWO AND A HALF minutes later, he was doing 140 down a four-lane commercial strip. There were dealerships lining the road—Chevy, Nissan, Kia . . . There! The Volvo dealership was coming up on the left. Next to it, S&S Body Shop.

He braked hard, slammed into the turn, banging up over a speed bump so hard the car bottomed out, then went briefly airborne, trailing sparks. He could see the body shop building in front of him, sixty meters away. But no doors were open.

So it was a trap.

Overhead he could hear the chopper's blades smacking at the air.

Then a crack appeared at the bottom of one bay door. He steered toward the bay door as it rose slowly, driving at a good forty miles an hour across the parking lot. He hit the bay door doing forty, the top of the yellow Honda kissing the bottom of the door with a metallic scream. He slammed on the brakes, skidding to a stop just inches from the far wall of the big, concrete-floored room.

Ten feet from his door stood a tall light-skinned black man with intense green eyes who was wearing a long camel-hair coat.

Delaney piled out of the car.

"I'm Special Agent-in-Charge Leonard Smith, FBI. I'm here to help. Hurry!"

An FBI agent? This didn't seem good. Delaney followed anyway. Smith yanked open the back door of the building. It looked out over a loading dock. A forklift was crawling across the parking lot toward them. On the fork was a pallet with a huge cardboard box.

"Into the box," Smith said. "The chopper won't be able to see us."

The forklift approached the building underneath a large cantilevered overhang apparently designed to keep people dry when they were unloading things onto the dock. Delaney followed Leonard Smith as he leapt off the dock onto the pallet, and crawled into the box.

The forklift crawled back across the tarmac toward a small shed, backed inside. Delaney could hear sirens approaching. As soon as they were inside the shed, Smith jumped off the box. A white Ford Taurus sat next to the forklift.

"Into the trunk!"

"No way," Delaney said.

"It's your only shot. If they stop us and you're in the car, you're done for."

Delaney made a split-second decision: in for a penny, in for a pound. He rolled into the trunk, heard the doors slam, and the Taurus began to move.

The car drove for fewer than ten seconds, then stopped. Delaney's heart was thumping. The sirens had gotten closer. He heard yelling, then the Taurus slid to a stop. Then someone was saying something he couldn't make out. Smith replied: "A white guy? Yeah. Ran into the trees back there."

More talking.

"Nah, nah, no problem. Well, good luck."

Then the Taurus drove slowly away. The drive seemed interminable. Finally the car slid to a stop, a door opened, and then the trunk lid popped up.

Smith was standing there with his hand extended. Delaney grabbed Smith's hand, and Smith hoisted him up, helping him out of the trunk. They were in the parking lot of some sort of park, nothing around them but trees.

"What's this all about?" Delaney said. "You're FBI?"

"We can't talk for long. I have to get back to the office extremely soon. But anyway, I talked to Mary Campos. She spent almost an hour trying to convince me that you're not guilty of the crimes we're investigating you for. She tells me there's a missing hard drive which will probably have evidence about a wide-ranging conspiracy, and she says you have a better chance of getting it than anyone else. Obviously I don't like doing what I'm doing right now. It runs totally against my grain. But as things stand, I simply can't pursue this lead outright. If she's right, then the FBI may well be penetrated by whoever is behind this conspiracy. If they find out I know, they'll either knock me off or divert me so I don't find anything useful."

Delaney nodded. "Most likely, yes, that's right."

"I'm taking a heck of a chance here, Agent Delaney."

"I appreciate that."

"There are roadblocks on every major road coming in and out of the area. Right now we're in Maryland in the C&O Canal National Park. As you probably know, it runs for miles out into the country. Hike out a few miles, you'll reach the Whites Ferry Road entrance. In the parking lot you'll find a blue Bronco. The keys are in the left rear wheel well."

"That's a long hike from here."

"Best I can do. I'm cutting it close taking off for this long." The FBI man pointed at a green nylon day pack on the ground next to the car. "There's food, water, and a sleeping bag." He handed a phone to Delaney. "This is a secure encrypted cell phone. Hit any key, it dials me directly. Keep it with you at all times. You may need me to run interference for you. Call me, I'll do what I can."

Delaney nodded. "Thanks for doing this."

The FBI agent studied Delaney's face for a long moment with his odd green eyes. "Delaney, this isn't me doing you a favor. In fact, I can't even begin tell you how much it perturbs me having to operate like this. You want to thank me? Find that hard drive."

"I will."

Smith continued to eyeball him. "You'd better."

38

Richard B. Russell Senate Office Building
5:08 PM

S ENATOR, there's someone here." It was Mrs. Graham again, peeking tentatively into the room and straightening her blond wig. Charles Tunnington looked up from Hamilton's Federalist Paper Number 78. He had read it dozens of times, but he never failed to be impressed with Hamilton's wisdom.

"I told you I'm occupied."

"It's Lieutenant Colonel Campos, the new terrorism czar or whatever she is."

"Tell her to come back next week."

"She's very insistent."

The door opened, and a lovely and very determined-looking woman in an army uniform stepped through. Mrs. Graham's face darkened.

"This is important, Senator," the colonel said.

"Ma'am, the senator—"

"It's all right, Mrs. Graham," Tunnington said.

Mrs. Graham pursed her lips, touched her wig, and retreated from the room. The colonel closed the door but remained standing.

Tunnington said, "Colonel, you may tell the president—"

The colonel interrupted him. "Senator, I'm not here as a representative of the president."

Charles Tunnington blinked. In Washington disloyalty to one's boss was hardly unheard of. But generally, if one were intending to express that disloyalty, one did so through the use of a great deal of code and double-talk. "Is this a personal matter, then?" Tunnington said.

"Not at all."

"What then?"

"Senator," she said, "I have a suspicion you're in a great deal of danger."

The senator gave her a wry smile. "I have a suspicion we all are."

"You're talking metaphorically," she said. "I'm not."

For a moment he thought perhaps she was joking. But then the reality of what she was saying began to sink in. There was nothing on this woman's face that seemed even vaguely humorous. And then something started coalescing in his mind, some half-formed and vague suspicions that had been hiding in the nether reaches of his brain but that he had been unwilling to articulate.

Emotion surged in him—fear and excitement both—of a character that he hadn't felt in years and years. He should have known. If this was truly his moment of greatness, it would not come cheap. Greatness never did. If he was to take a stand, it would be a stand that exposed him to dangers greater than simply being lampooned on late-night television or cut out of the power loop in the Senate. He had been thinking that he could just stand up and make a speech, slow Morgan Boyd's crazy parade until the anger and passion of the moment passed and people started to see straight again. All along he had been thinking that time was on his side. But this young officer's face told him he had underestimated the depth of the water here. To think that he, Charles Tunnington, had been naive about what was really at stake! For a moment he began to feel very old and very afraid. Most of his peers—if they were still alive—were down in Florida playing golf now. Maybe this wasn't his moment after all. Maybe he no longer had the strength. Maybe his wife had been wrong all those years ago. Maybe he was nothing but a bit-part player in the historical pageant, a decent enough fellow who folded when the crunch came.

"Colonel," he said softly. "I think you'd best tell me exactly what you mean."

Staunton, Virginia
8:40 PM

It had taken Delaney half the day to make the hike out along the old C&O Canal, where he eventually located the blue Bronco that Special Agent-in-Charge Leonard Smith had left for him. But once he found it, he knew where he had to go.

The first address in Nolan Ferris's personnel file—the one he'd put down as his home when he joined the army as an eighteen-year-old—led Delaney to a small farmhouse on the outskirts of Staunton. Before driving out to the farmhouse, he had checked a crisscross directory at the public library in town, found the address listed to someone named C. L. Ferris. Probably Ferris's mother. So he was in the right place. The house looked to be close to a hundred years old—though it was well tended, freshly painted. He did a couple of passes in the Bronco, finally parking on the side of a road about half a mile away and hiking through the fields behind the house, pausing in the darkness for up to five minutes at a time.

There was no indication that the place was staked out. Delaney had one thing running in his favor. Since the FBI didn't know about Ferris's connection to the affair, Unit P was the only outfit which might be waiting for him here—and they were probably stretched so thin by their many current responsibilities that they couldn't cover every single base. Particularly if that base was not in Washington, DC.

He crept closer. There was a light on in the house. He moved to the front porch, knocked several times, but no one answered. That was when he noticed the smell. It was a smell any combat veteran knew. He pulled his Glock, kicked down the door, and charged into the house.

Inside it stank like a slaughterhouse in July.

"Ferris!" he yelled.

There was no answer. He scanned the living room. It looked to have been decorated in 1920 and not touched since. There was a black stain in the middle of the threadbare Oriental rug, blood drops moving down the hallway.

"Ferris!" He moved from room to room, checking the bedrooms, his eyes glued to the front sight of his Glock. The blood trail led to the house's single bathroom. The medicine cabinet was open and bandages and medicines were spilled out on the floor. Bloody fingerprints were smeared on the mirror.

Whatever had happened here, it had been gruesome, and it had happened a good while back. He moved slowly back through the house. "Ferris! It's okay! I'm a friend!"

When he reached the kitchen, he realized there was no need to keep shouting. Ferris was surely gone.

An old woman lay on the kitchen table, her throat cut, a week's worth of exposure to the excessively warm house having caused her to bloat and turn a variety of unpleasant colors. Ferris's mother, he presumed. Most likely Unit P had gotten to her, tortured her to try and find out where Ferris was. He looked at the floor, trying to figure out from the blood what had happened here.

There was no blood trail connecting the old woman to the blood in the living room. Which indicated that someone else had been injured or killed in the other room.

Puzzling.

Maybe they had found Ferris. But if they had, Martin Gonzalez would surely have pried the location of the hard drive out of him.

Delaney went back to the bathroom, scrutinizing the blood trail. There was a lot of blood coming into the bathroom. But then the trail coming out was much smaller—the blood drops so small as to be barely noticeable. Delaney followed them—a drop here, a drop there, out through the back door and onto the back porch. The blood drops continued into the yard. And there Delaney lost them.

Suddenly something struck him. The house stood at least five feet above grade, and there were windows in the foundation, as though the house had a basement. But he had seen no entrance to a basement from inside the house. He surveyed the yard.

There: a sloping storm-cellar door, painted gray to match the shutters. He walked to the door—yes!—there was a black smear on the rusting steel handle. He yanked on the door. It opened, revealing a flight of stone steps. He walked slowly down the steps, Glock at the ready. At the bottom of the stairs he found a small, dark room. Like the house above, it stank of decaying flesh. As his eyes adjusted to the light he saw the room was cement floored, with some woodworking tools along one wall, a work bench against the other. And there in the corner was a feeble orange light. He realized, after a moment, that it was a space heater.

And lit by the heater was a single folding chair, and a cot on which a huddled figure lay. It was Ferris. Surrounding him were a litter of empty cans and water bottles. Ferris wasn't moving.

And judging by the smell, he had come down here and died.

Delaney felt the wall, flipped on the light. In the harsh light of the bare bulb mounted in the ceiling, he could see that Ferris's head was wrapped in a bandage through which a great deal of blood had seeped and then dried—probably some while ago. His face was a swollen, mottled mess of green and purple.

Delaney sat down on the folding chair and stared at Ferris glumly.

Was this it, the end of the line? They must have shot Ferris and left him for dead. He'd then managed to get up, bandage himself, and crawl down here to recover.

Only he'd never recovered.

Delaney was about to go when he was surprised to see Ferris's eyelids flutter. Ferris's eyes widened, then he stared. His lips moved, and a tiny, scratchy, inarticulate noise came out.

"What?" Delaney said.

Ferris made the noise again.

Delaney came closer, straining to hear. "What?" he said again, putting his ear up to Ferris's lips.

"Please," Ferris whispered. "Don't. Kill. Me."

"I'm not here to kill you," Delaney said. "I'm here to help. I need to get you to a doctor."

The ailing man shook his head slightly. "No doctor. They'll find me. And kill me."

"Stay here, you'll die anyway."

Ferris's hand snaked out of the blankets, and he grabbed Delaney's arm in a feeble grip. "I'm getting better."

"No, you're not. Your wound has gone necrotic. Can't you smell it? You'll die soon if you don't get antibiotics."

Ferris shook his head.

"Maybe I can get you some antibiotics," Delaney said.

Ferris's eyes closed.

"Ferris."

No answer.

"Ferris!"

He shook the injured man. Ferris grimaced. He pulled back the covers, found a second, ugly wound just below Ferris's left floating rib. It was a grazing shot that had nicked a rib. Ordinarily not life threatening—but without antibiotics, it was infected and oozing. Delaney touched the margin of the wound. His skin was hot under Delaney's hand. Ferris had gone septic, his entire body one big raging infection. He wouldn't last much longer

"I was wearing. A vest," Ferris whispered. "One round. Came. Through the armhole. I guess they thought. I was. Dead."

"Where's the disk drive?"

Long silence. Ferris's eyes closed.

Delaney shook him again. "Stick with me!"

Ferris moaned.

"Ferris! Come on! Where's the hard drive?"

Ferris's eyes opened. "Why. Should I. Tell you?"

Delaney crossed his arms. Guys like Ferris didn't respond to the milk of human kindness. "You're going to die here," Delaney said. "If you want me to get antibiotics, you tell me where that disk drive is."

No answer.

"Your life, for the disk drive."

Ferris's eyes looked slowly around the room as though he had suddenly forgotten where he was.

"Ma?" he said. "Ma, I need some water. I'm scared."

"Stick with me, Ferris!" Delaney shouted.

"Ma? Ma?"

"Ferris!"

Ferris looked at him curiously. "Huh?"

"Where's the hard drive?"

Ferris suddenly grinned broadly, like someone had told a funny joke. "Morgan Boyd," he said, "is a great. Man."

"Do you want the antibiotics, Ferris? Or do you want to die?"

"I never. Believed. In anything. Before."

"The hard drive."

"Before I met. Morgan Boyd."

"Ferris—"

"Morgan Boyd. Has a vision. For the future. I was just trying. To protect myself. That's why I kept it. I would never. Hurt him."

"Where is the drive?"

"He just didn't. Understand. I would never. Hurt. Him."

"Ferris."

Ferris grabbed Delaney's arm. "America got. Weak."

"Please, Ferris."

"Morgan showed me. Time to be . . ." His lips worked, but no sound came out.

"Ferris, do you want the antibiotics or not?"

". . . strong."

The room was silent. Ferris's eyes were closed. His breath was so shallow that Delaney could barely discern the movement of his sallow chest.

Finally Delaney decided it was hopeless. Ferris probably wouldn't make it. But the least he could do was call an ambulance. There was a phone upstairs. He stood and headed for the door.

"Wait." The sound of Ferris's voice so low he almost didn't hear it.

He turned. "What?"

"Don't leave me."

Delaney looked at him.

"I was always. Weak." Tears began slipping out of Ferris's eyes, running down into the bloody ruin which was the left side of his face.

Delaney crossed his arms and waited.

"Okay," Ferris whispered. "Okay. I'll tell."

DAY EIGHT

39

Shenandoah National Park
6:08 AM

THE CELL PHONE rang twice, waking Delaney from a fitful sleep. He grabbed the secure phone that Smith had given him the previous day.

"Smith?"

"Where are you?" SAC Leonard Smith sounded strained, nervous. "What's going on? I expected to hear from you by now."

Delaney sat up in the back of the Bronco, ran his hand through his hair. He'd left Ferris's place around midnight, eventually stopping to park at a campground off the Skyline Drive so he could get some rest. The weather had warmed up during the week, melting the unseasonable snows that had blanketed the area the previous weekend.

"I'm on my way to Washington," Delaney said.

"Did you find the hard drive?"

"Not yet. I found Ferris, though, so I know where it is."

There was a long pause. "Ferris is alive?"

"He got shot by Unit P. They thought he was dead, but he didn't die. He hid out, hoping to recover, but he was septic by the time I found him. He didn't make it through the night."

"Where's the drive?"

"I can't exactly say. I mean, I'll be able to locate it, but I don't exactly have a map."

"What did he tell you? You're not going to be safe in Washington. I've got assets here. Tell me what you know, I'll find it—and then we'll bring you in."

"It won't work like that. But trust me, I'll have it within twenty-four hours."

"Well, keep me in the loop, for Pete's sake! I can't help you if you don't let me know what's going on. We've got some serious time constraints. They're starting debate on the Freedom from Fear Act this morning. There's speculation that Senator Tunnington will filibuster tomorrow. But if anything happens to him before then, this act will go to a vote tomorrow and we're dead in the water."

"You think something will happen to him?"

"For godsake, Delaney. If you're right about this, Boyd has already executed the president of the United States. You think he'd feel any qualms about taking out a senator?"

"All right, all right. I'll keep you posted, I promise."

Delaney hung up, then drove around to the entrance to the campsite, where he used a pay phone to call Donovan's Rare Books. He left a message for Donovan to pass along to Mary Campos. He made Donovan read the message back to him twice before hanging up.

White House Situation Room
7:45 AM

Morgan Boyd was seated at the table with Attorney General John Rancy and General William Fairbank when the director of the FBI, Albert Brown, and the head of the assassination investigation, Special Agent-in-Charge Leonard Smith, entered the room and sat.

Boyd listened closely without speaking as Smith and the director briefed him on the progress of the Delaney dragnet.

Finally Boyd interrupted. "I'm getting sick of excuses, Al. There was a chopper on top of this guy, he runs into a building, next thing you know, he's gone. How the hell could that have happened?"

"We believe he had assistance. If you'd care to watch the tape, there's a forklift that approaches the—"

"No, I would not care to watch the tape," Boyd snapped. "I'm not interested in the reasons for your failure. Let me put this to you as clearly as I can, Al. I'm looking to restaff here with my own people. In chosen positions, of course. But if you fail to find this guy in the next twenty-four hours, you will be out on your ear. Clear?"

"Yes, sir."

"Then get out of here and get back to work."

The shaken director of the FBI rose, as did SAC Smith.

"Agent Smith," Boyd said. "Would you mind staying for about two more minutes? Al, Agent Smith will be joining you shortly. General Fairbank, I think you could safely get back to your post as well."

"Yes, sir."

The room was silent as Fairbank and Director Brown left the room.

"Okay, Agent Smith," the president said, "Attorney General Rancy tells me that you're a man of discretion, that you've agreed to do some very sensitive work for us in this matter."

"I'm doing my best, Mr. President."

"So what's the real story?"

"Good news. As I told Mr. Rancy yesterday, Delaney was on the verge of being picked up by state troopers and police from various Fairfax County jurisdictions. Attorney General Rancy has instructed me that we don't want him being picked up by local law enforcement people. So I rendezvoused with him and told him I was working with Colonel Campos, then I cut him loose. I've got a homing device on him right now. Delaney claims he has been framed and that he's found out the location of some kind of disk drive that's going to clear him."

"What do you mean he's got the location?" Boyd's black eyes bored into Smith's face. "Does he have the disk or not?"

"He's playing it close to the vest. He claims he doesn't know the actual location yet. But he got some sort of information from somebody named Ferris that will lead him there shortly."

Boyd exchanged looks with John Rancy.

"Mr. President, I told him to call as soon as he locates the drive so I can extract him."

"You've definitely got a lock on this guy?"

"I gave him a secure cell phone. It's got a homing device in it. The second he tells me he's got this alleged disk drive, we'll scramble HRT and we'll scoop him up."

"Not HRT," Rancy said. "When the time comes, we'll use Colonel Pardee's unit."

Smith frowned. "Mr. President, I have to tell you I'm a little uncomfortable concealing all this skullduggery from the director. I'd feel a lot better if I had some context—"

"Context?" Boyd pointed his finger at Smith. "Here's the context. Pull this off, you get to be the first black man in history to sit in J. Edgar Hoover's chair. Screw it up, you'll wish you'd never been born. Is that the sort of context you're looking for?"

Smith frowned for a moment, then finally said, "Actually, Mr. President, that puts it in a whole new light."

Northern Virginia
Early morning

Delaney bought a pair of reading glasses, a toothbrush, platinum hair dye, and a tweed driving cap at a Target in Leesburg, then went into the bathroom, where he used the toothbrush to delicately apply the dye to his beard and temples. When he was done fifteen minutes later, the driving cap, the reading glasses, and the grizzled beard had aged him a decade. He looked very Sean Connery-esque, he thought, admiring his handiwork in the mirror.

Then he drove into Washington, DC, slowing at the military checkpoint on the Key Bridge. In front of him two dark-haired men in their late thirties were taken from their cars, frisked, their IDs scrutinized. The young Airborne private who looked into Delaney's car, however, just waved him on, and Delaney headed into George-town.

The Andover Bank was located in an unobtrusive building several blocks off of Q Street, a Federal-style brick structure whose aging front had been modified slightly to conceal a number of cameras and sensors. The Andover Bank was a small but exceedingly exclusive private bank that catered exclusively to a wealthy international clientele.

At precisely 9:00 AM, Delaney climbed the weathered marble steps to the front door, pulled a brass bell handle, and waited for the heavy door to open from the inside. A porter wearing a vaguely military blue jacket with brass buttons smiled and said, "Hello, sir. May I help you?"

"Yes, my name is Jay Fiedler. I'm here to see Mr. Gordon."

"Please, come in."

Delaney stepped inside, finding himself in a mahogany-paneled room furnished with antiques including two gilt-framed mirrors. The mirrors had the slightly opaque look of two-way mirrors: undoubtedly he was being watched by well-armed security guards.

"Please have a seat. Is Mr. Gordon expecting you?"

"No, he's not. I was sent by Mr. Robert Rectinwald regarding his account. I've got all the paperwork right here."

During the previous evening he had drawn up a power-of-attorney form which Nolan Ferris Jr. had signed before he died. Delaney handed the porter some of the fake identification that had been made for him earlier in the week.

"Thank you, sir," the porter said. "May I bring you something to drink?"

"That won't be necessary, thank you."

The porter bowed slightly, then withdrew through a door that slid back into the wall without his even touching it. He was gone for what seemed an unnecessarily long time. When he returned, he said, "Mr. Gordon will see you."

Delaney was led back through the door, past two beefy men whose generously cut suits obviously concealed weapons, then up a curving flight of stairs. "Mr. Gordon is in the second room on the left," the porter said.

Delaney walked down the carpeted hallway and turned into the indicated office. It was furnished, like the lobby, with very nice antiques. The man behind the desk, round faced and balding, wore a bespoke suit of bankers-striped gray serge, a paisley vest, and matching bow tie. He rose and extended his hand without smiling. "Please sit, Mr. Fiedler. I have a few questions for you if you don't mind."

"Of course."

"The signature on this power of attorney," he said. "It doesn't look kosher, to be quite honest with you."

"Mr. Rectinwald is critically ill. He is unable to use his arm properly."

"What's the nature of his illness, if you don't mind my asking?"

"He was shot three times with a large-caliber handgun."

Gordon's eyes widened, but only slightly. "My, my. I hope he's all right."

"To be honest with you, it's looking a bit dicey for him right now. As a result, my presence here is fairly urgent. He has some family matters to settle in the event he doesn't survive."

Gordon studied Delaney's face for a moment. "I'd like to speak to him."

"That's not possible," Delaney said. "He slipped into a coma last night."

Gordon didn't speak.

"I've been Mr. Rectinwald's attorney for fifteen years," Delaney said. "That's a matter of record. If you need further documentation, I'd be happy to supply it."

"I think that would be best."

"I'm afraid I'll have to have it faxed to you later this morning." Delaney would have to get back over to the house of his forger, Winston Rogers, to get the appropriate documentation. He would have done it earlier, but he was pressed for time.

Gordon smiled coolly. "Well, then I'm sure you'll understand that we'll have to wait until we receive it."

"Mr. Gordon, I've examined the trust and account agreement quite carefully. It states that upon presentation of adequate credentials and the password for the account, you are obliged to honor any requests by the bearer of the password." Delaney had not read anything of the sort. But he thought it was worth a try. Ferris had told him that he would have to present a power of attorney, so that's what he had done.

Gordon's eyebrows went up. "You have the password?"

"Certainly."

Gordon smiled. "Well, why didn't you say so? If you would, please repeat if to me for verification." He tapped at his computer keyboard.

"The account is 23-1-12-20-5-18 slash 19-15-18-18-5-12-12-19. And the password is 9 slash 23-18-15-20-5 slash 20-8-9-19."

Gordon consulted his computer screen then said, "Good. If you'd please verify that into the microphone." Gordon pointed to a small condenser mic half-concealed by a brass paperweight on the desk.

He leaned forward and repeated the account and code into the microphone.

Gordon gave Delaney his cool smile and said, "And what may we do for you today, Mr. Fiedler?"

"Mr. Rectinwald wants me to retrieve an item from his safe-deposit box."

"Excellent." Gordon pushed a button on his phone. "Mrs. Garrett, would you come to my office and escort my friend Mr. Fiedler to the vault."

40

Washington, DC
Early Morning

MARY CAMPOS HAD stopped by Donovan's rare books again on her way to work. This time Donovan told her that he would take $3,500 for the Clausewitz. He was very insistent that she take it.

"Would a credit card be all right?"

"I only take cash, I'm afraid," Donovan said, handing her a wrapped volume in a brown wrapper. "But those insignia on your shoulder give me a certain amount of confidence in your character. I'll trust you to drop off the balance next time you're in the neighborhood."

She had then driven on to her office, closed the door, and un-wrapped the volume of Clausewitz. Only it turned out not to be *On War* at all, but a handsomely bound—but undoubtedly valueless—book called *An Encomium of Podiatry*. It had been written by one Dr. Winward Trueblood back in 1907. She leafed through it but found no messages. There was a book mark on page 211, but that was all.

Then her secretary came in and said, "Colonel, I just received a fax for you. It's some sort of medical report."

She looked at the fax. It was from the Northern Virginia Podiatry Clinic. The letter said,

Dear Colonel Campos,
    The results of your exam are in. I'm afraid minor corrective surgery on your left foot is going to be necessary at some point in the near future. The right foot looks all right, though the dysplasia in the left big toe is somewhat worrisome. As you requested, I've sent you the numbers on your Caxton Bone Differential Analysis.
    Winward Trueblood, MD

Attached was a page full, which said CBDA REPORT—SUB-JECT #211. Beneath that was a long list of paired numbers. It took her a moment to see it: the numbers on the supposed medical report were a book code: they referred to words and letters which could be found in the volume Donovan had given her.

She flipped to page 211 of the old medical textbook and quickly decoded the message. It was simple enough. When she was done, she tore off the little piece of paper on which she had decoded the message, chewed it, and swallowed it. Ever since she was a little girl, she had wanted to get a secret message and then swallow it. After swallowing the nasty-tasting paper, however, she decided that once was enough. Been there, done that.

She smiled to herself. Delaney might be a pain in the neck—but give the guy credit, he kept things interesting.

Chevy Chase, MD

9:25 AM

Whatever a geek was supposed to look like, Devi Bannerjee was not it: she was tall, with long wavy black hair, large brown eyes, the mocha skin of a Bengali, and the build of a Hindu temple goddess. Delaney had not seen her in years, but they had gone to high school together, and periodically he had heard things through the grapevine about her. She held a Ph.D. from MIT, and last he had heard, she consulted regularly with the Treasury Department on matters involving forensic computing.

She opened the door and looked at Delaney curiously. For a moment it was clear she didn't recognize him. And then—just like that—she did. Her eyes widened slightly.

"Are you *nuts*, Mike?" she said finally. Though her family background was Indian, she had grown up in South Carolina—her father was a mathematician who taught at Clemson—and she sounded like any other well-educated southerner.

"Look," he said, "as soon as I'm done here, feel free to call the FBI, whatever. But I didn't do what they're saying I did."

Devi opened the door wordlessly, ushered him into a large, well-decorated house.

"Pardon the mess," she said. "The kids have been rampaging all day." He could hear children screaming and laughing somewhere in the house.

Delaney smiled. "Look," he said, "I need a favor."

"What, didn't come to catch up on old times?"

"Not really. We weren't exactly in the same crowd anyway, were we?"

She looked at him with a blank expression, arms folded. "Well?"

"I need some help. A guy stole a hard disk drive with some information on it. I need to verify that the information is still there, figure out how I can access it."

"You know, Mike, to do that, I'd need to see the drive."

He took Ferris's disk drive out of his coat pocket, handed it to her.

"Well then . . ." She peered at the drive. "Standard Western Digital 80 gig IDE hard drive." She kept studying the disk then finally walked down the hallway to a room full of computers. "So how many federal laws am I breaking?" she said as she cleared some space on a workbench topped by a computer that sprouted a variety of wires and cables and connectors.

"I would say mainly harboring a felon."

"I'll tell them you held me at gunpoint." She smirked maliciously. "Maybe I'll say you ravished me too."

"If this works out, that won't be an issue," Delaney said.

"What, the ravishing or the harboring a felon?"

Delaney didn't reply. Devi had always seemed intimidating and exotic to him when he knew her in high school. She still made him a little nervous.

"I had a huge crush on you when I was in high school," she said. "The big silent country boy jock. You were totally not my type."

"Huh," Delaney said. "Who'd of thunk it."

"Any security mechanisms on here I should know about?"

"That's why I brought it to you," Delaney said. "If I knew anything about it, I'd have taken care of this myself."

"Ah. Of course."

She plugged the disk drive into some connectors hanging out of the computer in front of her and then started pecking away at the keyboard. For about twenty minutes, she didn't speak. Finally she said, "Yeah, okay. He's got password protection, some off-the-shelf security measures. But it's pretty wimpy stuff."

"How long to crack it?"

"Depends. Twenty minutes?"

She pecked away some more. Nine minutes later the screen blinked, and a standard Windows desktop appeared in front of her. "Am I good or what?" she said.

"I wouldn't know," he said. "What are we looking at?"

She pointed at a window in the middle of the screen. "That's it. That's the directory of your hard drive. What are you looking for?"

He scanned the list of files. They were simply labeled by year and month.

He pointed at one file labeled January of the previous year. "Can you pull that up?"

"We'll see. It looks like a standard Microsoft Excel file." She clicked on one of the icons. It brought up a spreadsheet with several rows of numbers on it. One column of numbers was labeled SOURCE and another labeled DISPOSITION. Transaction dates ran down the left side of the spreadsheet. The "source" cells each contained a word with an account number. On the first line was an amount, $9,000. The first source cell said NatBank 10239392. The disposition cell on the first line said, Brotherhood Cash. If Delaney was reading it right, Ferris had withdrawn $9,000 in cash from a NationsBank account on January 3 of the previous year and passed it on to the Brotherhood.

He scanned the list. There was not a single transfer greater than $10,000.

"Smurfing," she said.

"What?"

"Anytime anybody deposits more than ten grand in cash into a federally insured bank, they have to fill out a form and file it with the FDIC. As a result drug dealers always move cash around in increments less than ten grand," she said. "It's called smurfing. After those little blue cartoon dwarves on TV."

Delaney nodded.

"Who is this?" she said. "A drug dealer?"

"Not even hardly. You don't want to know who this is."

"Ah."

"What else is on the disk drive? Anything besides these accounting files?"

She closed the window, opened another, tapped the screen with her fingernail. "These aren't accounting files. These are wave files."

"What's that mean?"

"Audio data. Music, speech, whatever."

"Can you play some of them back?"

"Sure."

She brought up another program, played one of the files. It appeared to be a recording of a brief phone call.

You get the deposit?

Yep.

Big Daddy wants you to buy a LAW antitank weapon. Somebody will be in touch.

Okeydoke. Have a nice day.

Dial tone. Delaney didn't recognize the first voice. Mostly likely it was Ferris. But he recognized the second voice as Paul Miller.

"Who's Big Daddy?" Devi Bannerjee said.

"I don't know."

She leaned forward. "Look. Each one of these wave files has a name attached to it. That one was called BROTHER46.WAV. Brother 46, Brother 47, Brother 48. Like all the conversations with that one guy would be called Brother. Then here are a bunch that say UNCLE." She was scanning down a long list of files. "Wait. Here's BIGDADDY1.WAV. If I'm right, and if Big Daddy is the guy in charge, then this phone call would have his voice on it. Want to try that one?"

"Sure."

She brought up the file, hit Play on her audio program. Out of the speakers came another voice.

Sir? Is that you?

What is it? You know we can't speak directly.

This is a secure phone, I promise.

Make it quick then.

I'm just nervous is all. Are we backing the right horse here? I don't think this Miller guy amounts to much. He seems a little . . . I don't think he's real serious.

We went over this when you and I met. I've told you I'm behind this operation one hundred percent. As is my boss. And that I have reasons for what we're doing which may not be apparent to you. Trust me, this is the most important single thing that has happened in this country since World War II. You cannot waffle here. Okay? I am counting on you.

Yes, sir.

Son, you're an American hero.

Thank you, sir.

But deniability on my part—and on the part of my boss—is critical. You and I cannot talk again. Not ever. That's why your, ah . . . your uncle is involved.

I understand. It's just that sometimes I worry about President Fairbank—

President Fairbank will not be a problem. Trust me on that.

But sometimes—

Sometimes nothing. Let me put this in simple terms. If you call me again directly, some kind of terrible accident will very likely befall you. And then someone else will get to be a hero in your place. Are you with me?

Yes, sir.

Then keep up the good work.

And that was the end of the file. Delaney smiled triumphantly. He couldn't believe his luck. That sneaky little Ferris had recorded all his calls as insurance. And this was the smoking gun.

"Big Daddy sounds like somebody," Devi Bannerjee said. Then she shook her head. "Oh, no, never mind. Sounds kind of like that new attorney general guy. What's his name? Clancy?"

"Rancy."

"He's got that same high voice, that same sort of hitch in his vowels. But I don't guess it's him, huh?" She laughed.

"My recommendation," Delaney said. "Don't call the FBI after I leave. Now that you've heard that voice, this has become one of those I-can-tell-you-but-then-I'd-have-to-kill-you sort of things."

"You'd kill me?" she said flirtatiously. "After I bared my heart to you and showed you my disk drive?"

"No." He looked at her grimly. "*I* wouldn't."

"Then . . ." Her eyes widened. "You're not serious! You're not saying . . ."

The room was silent. Finally Delaney broke the silence. "Yeah, Devi, I *am* saying. I'm saying somebody very high up in the White House would have you killed. I am saying exactly that."

She looked at him for a long time, her smile slowly fading. "You're really serious, aren't you?"

"Before I go," he said, "there's just one more thing I'd like you to do . . ."

The White House
11:30 AM

Mary Campos looked at her watch and said to her secretary, "I can't stand sitting here anymore. I'm going to run out for a quick bite."

"Is, ah, everything okay?"

"Hm?"

"The medical report. I didn't mean to snoop but . . ."

Mary smiled. "Bunions," she said. "All the women in my family have bunions. It's just outpatient surgery, nothing to worry about."

MARY CAMPOS STOPPED at a Starbucks, bought a latte and two muffins, then walked down to the Mall carrying the Starbucks bag in her hand. Near the Washington Monument she sat on a bench next to a grizzled, twitchy character in an army overcoat, watch cap, and stained blue jeans. He wore a gray beard and the sort of huge temporary sunglasses given by ophthalmologists and was muttering to himself as he tossed peanuts to a motley crowd of pigeons at his feet.

She sat, waiting for something to happen. This was where the message she'd decoded had told her to sit, though she didn't much relish hanging around by this homeless nut for too long.

After about five minutes she looked at her watch. The pigeon man continued to twitch and mutter angrily.

Suddenly the pigeon man spoke in a voice that was quiet but discernible. She was shocked to recognize the voice: the pigeon man was Delaney.

"Finish eating your muffin," he said softly. "Then go throw the second muffin in the trash over there. There's a bag that looks exactly like yours on top of the trash. Switch it, then head back to work."

She nodded.

"There's a watcher over by the tree—the beefy guy—and probably a support team parked in that blue van. Don't let them see you make the switch."

"Okay."

"Later today I want you to call Smith at FBI to tell him you've got the disk drive. Tell him it implicates all the major players. But don't tell him quite yet. I've got one more thing I need to do first."

They sat silently for a while.

"I'm crazy about you, Mary," Delaney said. "I never stopped thinking about you."

Then he rose and shuffled slowly away—limping and twitching and muttering—as he headed off in the direction of the Jefferson Memorial.

Mary finished her first muffin, then went over to the trash can Delaney had indicated. Shielding the trash from the Unit P watchers, she switched the bag containing the muffin with an identical Starbucks bag sitting on top of the heap of trash. She didn't know for certain what was in it, but she could guess. It was square—about the size of a ham sandwich—but much heavier.

Washington, DC
12:19 PM

Delaney was walking along the desolate railroad yards near Fort McNair over on the south side of the Mall. The yards contained several long freight trains. About fifty yards away a train composed mostly of flatcars began inching forward. Delaney took out the secure phone Smith had given him as he began crossing track after track, moving toward the train.

Smith answered: "Well?"

"I have the drive. I passed it on to somebody for safekeeping."

"Who?"

"I'll tell you shortly. Meantime I have something I need to do. Just to avoid the danger of going through any more checkpoints, I'm going to hop a freight car, take it across the bridge into Virginia. I'll call you later this afternoon."

"So, ah, what's on the disk drive?"

"It's the mother lode. Better even than I'd hoped. Every single money transaction involved in funding the Brotherhood. It includes account numbers and everything. They firewalled the transactions by using cash. But this will allow you to trace the money from the Brotherhood right back to specific accounts. No doubt it will correspond to accounts that Miller controlled."

"Excellent."

"Not only that, he's got audio files."

There was a brief pause. "Of what?"

"Everybody he talked to."

"And who did he talk to?"

"You'll see when you get it. Suffice it to say, there's a conspiracy that reaches quite high in the government."

"You mean . . ."

"You'll see when you get it."

"Delaney, you need to get me that hard drive *now*. I can't protect you much longer."

"I know that. I'll be in touch, I promise. I just have one more thing to do first."

Delaney cut the connection just as he reached the train. It was now moving at six or seven miles an hour—just fast enough that he had to jog hard to catch the train. He grabbed a steel railing on the side of one of the flatcars, hoisted himself up.

The only problem was that he was exposed. He needed cover, a place where choppers couldn't see. He moved slowly from car to car, the train swaying and clattering under him until he reached a car with a huge marine diesel engine chained underneath a tarp. Perfect.

J. Edgar Hoover Building
12:25 PM

Special Agent-in-Charge Leonard Smith set down the phone and thought for a moment. The tricky thing here was that he knew things that no one around him knew. He had to figure out a way to get the FBI doing the work he needed done without anyone knowing that he had an information pipeline direct from the White House. Or that, for that matter, he had helped Delaney escape yesterday and then planted a homing beacon on him. That was one of those little facts that just couldn't be conveniently explained.

"Roberts," he snapped to his second in command. "Get a chopper airborne. Put some of those Unit P guys on it. Some ELINT from NSA has just drifted our way—they think they've got a fix on Delaney's cell phone. NSA's going to give Unit P some kind of black box that'll help them track him from the chopper."

"You don't want to send HRT, sir?" Roberts said.

"These Unit P guys have some back channels going to our great and good friends at CIA and NSA that we can't use. Personally, I'd rather this be an FBI party, of course, but . . ." He shrugged broadly. "You never know what'll happen when this is over. If somebody has to get in front of a Senate committee and say they unlawfully used CIA intelligence assets within the borders of the United States, I'd rather it be those knuckleheads in Unit P."

Roberts grinned. "I see your point, sir."

"Put the chopper up there, let Unit P track the signal. If and when we verify that it's really him they locked on to, we'll let Unit P take him down." Leonard Smith picked up the phone and dialed the director. "Smith here, sir. I've got some news we may want to pass on to the White House."

41

White House Situation Room
1:00 PM

DIRK PARDEE SAT across the table from John Rancy. Morgan Boyd was standing.

"Where are we?" the president said.

"We believe that Delaney has been using a retired CIA operator named Donovan as a dead drop," Pardee said. "At any rate, one way or another, we're ninety percent sure that Delaney got hold of the hard drive this morning and that he put it in Mary Campos's hands."

"You're sure she has the drive?"

"A hundred percent? No. But we're pretty certain. She went to Tunnington's office this morning. Then she went down to the Mall for no apparent reason. My watchers think she was using another dead drop."

"Then do what needs to be done."

"Okay, good. We'll take her down. If she's got the drive, we seize and destroy it, then we hit Delaney. Once he's out of the picture, the Eight-second Airborne will place Tunnington under arrest. He's obviously part of the assassination plot himself. Any fool can see it. Why, he met with this traitor Mary Campos this very morning, did he not?"

"Yes, Mr. President, you're right."

"Delaney to Campos, Campos to Tunnington. My God, will it never end?"

Pardee and Rancy laughed obligingly.

"John," the president said, "we need to get Tunnington out of the way."

"My staff has come up with some parliamentary options. But all they'll do is put off the inevitable. We could obtain a secret warrant, put him under house arrest or pack him off to a Federal Camp."

"Hm."

"Alternatively, we could even trump up some story about a threat on his life requiring us to detain him."

"Or . . ."

"Or we can go full bore."

"Give me a scenario."

Pardee said, "Accidents happen. Especially to old guys."

Boyd shook his head. "No. That's way too aggressive. I'll tell you what I like. Fairbank is our designated fall guy, right? Let's get a warrant, send him in, and detain the senator. I don't like the word *arrest*. I want all the mechanics, even the legal end, the warrants, everything, handled by the Pentagon. Give verbal orders to General Slade, tell him to prepare all the paperwork so it ends up with Fairbank's signature on it. Make sure the paper trail ends inside the Pentagon. Then let Fairbank detain Tunnington. That way it'll be that awful overzealous soldier who's trampling on the Constitution, not the White House. After it's over we can sacrifice Fairbank and come out looking temperate and judicious. Poor man, he's so distraught over his brother's death you can hardly blame him for going a little overboard." He paused. "Eventually we'll need to arrange some kind of bona fide atrocity, I suppose. But that can wait."

"What if some of his men shot Tunnington on the steps of the Capitol?" Rancy said. "Confusion, jostling, a nervous young private's gun goes off by accident, that sort of thing. We could probably arrange to have it go live on CNN. It would kill two birds with one stone."

"I'm shocked that you would suggest that the president of the United States sanction the execution of a senator." Morgan Boyd was deadpan.

"I apologize, Mr. President," Rancy said.

"Send Fairbank to detain him," Morgan Boyd said. "Meantime, Pardee, arrest this Campos woman and get the disk drive."

Front Gate, the White House
1:12 PM

The two black Lincoln Navigators pulled through the gate, and eight men piled out. The Secret Service had placed their names on the authorized list. But authorized to enter was different from authorized to enter with drawn MP5s. The Secret Service isn't fond of anyone wandering into the White House with drawn machine guns—authorized list or no.

Agent Douglas Reed supervised the gate crew. As soon as he saw the Unit P men piling out of the cars with submachine guns hanging from tactical slings, he spoke into a microphone, "Code Red. Secure the front."

Then he stepped from the guard post and said, "Hey! Mr. Gonzalez. You and your men are not authorized to enter with those weapons."

The dark-skinned Unit P team leader turned and smiled. "Oh, but we are, Agent—what is it?—Agent Reed?"

"Reed, yes." Reed turned to his men. "Take cover and acquire targets moving left to right."

The uniformed agents at the gate quickly took cover behind hardened barriers, leveling their M4 carbines at the Unit P men. Plainclothes agents emerged from the White House and moved briskly to positions which would keep them from hitting their compatriots at the gate if they were forced to open fire.

The Unit P men, without instruction, began acquiring targets of their own, defilading behind the armored Lincolns.

"Gentlemen, gentlemen," Martin Gonzalez said, still smiling as pleasantly as a minister on his way out of church on Sunday. "Let's not get itchy fingers here. Place a call to Attorney General Rancy upstairs. He'll verify that our presence, fully armed, is authorized."

Agent Reed spoke urgently but calmly into the microphone. "I need instructions here. Now."

The White House, Second Floor
1:14 PM

Mary Campos looked out the window of her new office on the second floor of the White House. Everyone in the building was rushing to the windows to see what was going on. Three or four staffers had come into her office and were staring out curiously.

"Hey! Guys!" Mary said sharply. "It's just some kind of misunderstanding. Get back to work. Out! Now!"

But she knew why the Unit P men were there. There could only be one reason. They knew about the disk drive. As the staffers started to leave, she grabbed the Starbucks bag, pulled out the disk drive, and thrust it into a brown paper lunch bag in which she had packed a sandwich that morning. Then she scrawled RANCY on the bag in black pen, walked down to the break room at the end of the hall, and stuck the bag in the door of the refrigerator.

She had just settled back into her office when several fit-looking young men with MP5s in their hands plowed into the room, grabbed her, and threw her on the floor.

"Colonel Mary Campos," a man with a soft Latin accent said above her, "you are under arrest for treason, sedition, and harboring a felon. You have the right to remain silent and so on. They gave me a little card to read to you, all your various rights, but I seem to have mislaid it."

The two young men hoisted her to her feet.

"Where is it?" The man was all smiles, but his smile was the kind that never reached his eyes.

"Where is what?" she said.

He snapped his fingers. "Find it. Meantime, let's get her out of here."

Central Detention Facility, Washington, DC
3:20 PM

Mary Campos paced up and down in the holding cell at the Central Detention Facility on D Street. She had been left there for quite some while—though she wasn't sure how long. The Bureau of Prisons guards had removed her watch along with her belt and shoelaces.

Eventually a door opened at the end of the hallway, and she heard footsteps. The door of the cell opened and the slim Latin man from Unit P entered. His face was almost pretty, except for a long hook of a nose, which gave his features the look of a predatory bird. Standing behind him in the hallway were the two big young men who had cuffed her at the White House.

He held a paper lunch bag in his hand that said RANCY on it in black Magic Marker.

"Rancy!" the man said. "That was a terrific touch. Like it was his sandwich in there and nobody better touch it. You're more fun than a barrel of monkeys, Colonel. Very resourceful. Too bad Mr. Rancy doesn't work on that floor or we might have never figured it out."

"Where's my lawyer?" Mary said.

"Oh, that's a sad story, isn't it? Your lawyer. You see, under the temporary executive order, sedition and treason are charges we can hold you on indefinitely without your having access to a lawyer. My name is Mr. Gonzalez. Right now I'm about the only person you're going to have access to."

Mary felt sick. How could this be happening? This was the United States!

"I know how you feel, believe me," the man said. "I grew up in South America and was myself held without a lawyer several times. Once I was even tortured quite severely. Electricity, beatings—oh, my, it was quite unpleasant. Ever since that time I wanted to become an American citizen."

"Well isn't that ironic."

Gonzalez continued to smile. "Does Tunnington know about the disk?"

Mary didn't answer.

"Is there a copy?"

Mary sat on the bed and crossed her arms. "You're wasting your time," she said.

The slim, dark man sighed. "Well, one has to ask politely. Before one turns to cruder measures, I mean."

"Cruder measures?"

"Are you feeling well?" the man said. "You look pale, a little over-heated perhaps."

Mary said nothing.

The slim man turned to one of his henchmen. "Badger, the colonel looks a bit peckish. Would you be so kind as to go get her a large glass of water? Oh and maybe a nice fluffy towel as well?"

Alexandria, Virginia
3:27 PM

The disk drive, of course, was not in the paper bag Martin Gonzalez carried. While Gonzalez was showing the bag to Mary Campos, Dirk Pardee had taken the hard drive itself to the home of a computer expert affiliated with—but not employed by—the CIA, a man with a reputation for not only being skilled at the computer but also for keeping his mouth shut. His name was Gluckman and he was forty-five or so—too old, in Pardee's opinion, for the long rat's nest of hair he wore.

Pardee stood behind Gluckman for about ten minutes.

"You mind?" the computer geek said finally.

Pardee said, "For what I'm paying you, I'll stand wherever I please."

Gluckman snorted. "My industry rate is three times what I charge Uncle Sam. I do government work because I'm a patriot."

"Right."

The geek turned around. "You think I'm joking, Colonel Peckerwood? Find another hacker if you don't want my help."

Pardee had an urge to pistol-whip the computer geek, but he restrained himself. All that mattered right now was results. This kind of character didn't respond to the same sort of motivation that made a Spec 4 leap off his hindquarters and get busy.

"No offense," Pardee said mildly. Then he went and sat down.

Five minutes later the hacker said, "Okay, we got something. Come here."

Pardee walked over, stood next to the hacker. "What we've got here is a bunch of Excel files and then another directory with a bunch of wave files."

"Meaning . . ."

"Accounting data and audio data."

"Pull up the accounting."

The hacker tapped a few keys. Pardee looked at the lattice of numbers on the screen. It was pretty obvious this was the right information. He opened his secure cell, dialed Rancy at the White House.

"It's all there, Mr. Rancy."

"Good. Get one of your men to bring the disk to the White House. I want to personally watch it get destroyed. Meantime, FBI has choppers waiting for you. Smith has a homing device on Delaney. He'll vector you in on Delaney."

"Yes, sir."

"And Pardee? Be sure to, ah, take all reasonable precautions for the safety of your men. If you know what I mean."

"I understand, sir."

Pardee hung up then dialed another number. "Gonzalez, I need you to get your team in motion."

"I'm just getting started with the woman."

"Doesn't matter. It's definite, this is the drive. At this point it's not important what Tunnington does or does not know."

Gonzalez sighed. "What a shame. I was just going to give Colonel Campos a little tending to. She's not looking well."

"Leave her."

"Of course, sir."

Pardee hung up the phone and said to the computer man, "If you'd be so kind as to give me the disk drive."

Gluckman leaned over his equipment, unplugging things, his long gray hair falling in his face. When he'd finally gotten the drive freed, he handed it to Pardee.

Pardee hit him in the side of the head with the disk drive, knocking Gluckman on the floor. Pardee then stood on the man's long hair so that he couldn't sit up.

"My advice?" Pardee said. "Next time we meet, don't call me Colonel Peckerwood."

"There's not going to be a next time," Gluckman grunted.

"You got that right." Pardee kicked him hard in the ribs.

Pardee walked out the front door of the computer guy's condo, tossing the disk drive in the air and whistling. Four of his team members lolled against their black Navigator, their weapons in plain sight. It was a scene that gave him a warm feeling in his chest. Pardee smiled paternally at them.

He was going to enjoy living in Morgan Boyd's America.

42

The White House Situation Room
3:35 PM

"YOU WANT ME TO *WHAT?*" General Bill Fairbank said.

"Look, General, we have evidence that Senator Charles Tunnington is deeply involved with the plot against your brother," John Rancy said. "Campos went to his office this morning. As you probably know we arrested Campos just hours ago. And you're going to love this. Turns out Campos is Delaney's girlfriend."

Morgan Boyd had not spoken since Fairbank entered the room. He just sat, watching Rancy and Fairbank talk, his black eyes absorbing everything.

"You didn't answer my question, Mr. Attorney General," Fairbank said. "You want United States Army troops serving an arrest warrant against a sitting United States senator. Is that correct?"

"That's right, General."

"That's a police matter."

Rancy spread his hands a little. "Come on, General. Aren't we splitting hairs here? For four days you've been in command of troops who've been conducting searches and seizures, running checkpoints, patrolling neighborhoods and airports, and making arrests . . . In short, you've been commanding police units for nearly a week. This is no different."

Fairbank exploded. "It sure as hell is! I know Charles Tunnington. He's a fine man. Where's the evidence?"

Rancy smiled mildly. "General, a small mountain of sealed evidence was presented by an assistant U.S. attorney to a tribunal of Circuit Court judges as specified under the terms of the executive order signed by President Boyd last week. The judges reviewed the available evidence and determined that probable cause existed for the arrest of Senator Tunnington on charges of sedition and conspiracy to commit murder. A legal warrant was issued based on that evidence. Frankly, General, it is not your job to second-guess federal judges. A warrant needs to be served. We have reason to believe that Senator Tunnington may be backed by paramilitary forces capable of outgunning the FBI. President Boyd will not sit by while another HRT unit gets wiped out. This is a job for the army."

"I want to see the evidence myself."

Rancy continued to give the general his mild little smile. "Are you refusing an order, General?"

"I've known Colonel Campos for years. I knew her father. General Campos was a superlative officer. I know Charles Tunnington. His record speaks for itself. For that matter, I know Delaney. What you're saying about these people is inconsistent with everything I know about any of them. This whole business stinks."

"I take that to mean that you are refusing a direct order from your commander in chief."

Fairbank rose to his full six feet three inches, straightened his jacket. "You're goddamn right I am."

"I suspect you'll be sorry."

"The only thing I'm sorry about is that I let myself be used as a tool of this disgusting, unconstitutional power grab."

"General, Michael Delaney has been located," Morgan Boyd said, speaking for the first time since Fairbank entered the room. "We'll be arresting him within the hour. The Brotherhood has been rolled up. This entire episode is about to come to a close. Our ultimate challenge—as I have been preaching to anybody who will listen—lies with terrorists overseas. All we're doing right now is clearing the decks so that we can join that fight in an unreserved manner. This is your last chance to stand on the right side of history."

Fairbank stared at his commander in chief for a long time. Finally he said, "Mr. President, with all due respect, you wouldn't know the right side of history if it fell on your head."

Morgan Boyd's black eyes didn't waver as he met the angry soldier's glare. "You're relieved of command, General. I'll send written orders to the Pentagon in the next ten minutes. But don't worry, we'll see if we can't find, oh, say, a training barracks in Alaska for you to command until your retirement later this year."

AFTER FAIRBANK LEFT the room, Boyd said, "In the press conference at four I want you to announce that Fairbank requested to be relieved of command so he could have some time to grieve his brother's loss. Say all the usual things about him—competence, valor, honor, all the usual tinsel. Then leak a story to the *Washington Times* that there have been allegations of irregularities in his command, sloppy command authority, atrocities committed under his direction, whatever. As soon as the Freedom from Fear Act passes we'll convene a board of inquiry and they'll find that a number of very nasty things were done under his watch."

"Sir, in the Senate right now we've got thirty-six votes solid for the Freedom from Fear bill, and we've got fifteen or so solid against. Everybody's sitting on the fence, waiting to see what everybody *else* is going to do. They're like a bunch of junior high school girls. A stiff wind could blow the whole crowd in the wrong direction. I'm afraid any bad news about the military right now could be that wind."

"Use your head, John. He's leaving one way or another. And my guess is he won't do it quietly. We have to get out in front of him."

"How? What are we going to say he's done? The army has been very restrained so far."

"I don't know, John. Think something up. That's your job. Maybe some Arabs could die in Detroit. Show a little ingenuity here."

Rancy looked cowed. "Yes, Mr. President."

"Start with the thirteen-year-old kid that got shot in Alabama, the deer hunter. Fairbank gave them bad rules of engagement or something. Then work from there."

Northern Virginia

4:17 PM

The two FBI UH-53Bs heading west over Manassas at 140 knots were supported by an Apache gunship. Between the three choppers and the men on board them, Unit P would bring to bear not only a pair of light machine guns, a sniper rifle and the usual complement of small arms, but also a nice GE 30 mm cannon and a couple of 20 mm chain guns. If Delaney resisted, they could throw a thousand rounds at him in a matter of seconds. Even Delaney—who, Pardee had to admit, was a hell of a soldier—couldn't win this fight.

According to the intel from Smith at FBI, Delaney was moving west on a freight train at about thirty miles an hour and was scheduled to reach Culpeper, in central Virginia, around 1800 hours. The train had picked up speed, now that it was out of the immediate vicinity of DC, and Delaney would be unable to jump off. There would be plenty of time to nab him before the train halted again.

The railroad control room had been alerted to clear the rails so that the train wouldn't stop under any circumstances.

"How accurate is the tracking device?" Badger said to Pardee. They were only about two minutes out from the target now.

"It's a satellite transponder," Pardee said. "Uses MilSpec GPS coordinates so it's accurate to within inches."

"Good."

"Okay, boys," Pardee said. "Let me recap. The Apache is going to approach his location and fly close support. If he pops up with a weapon, the Apache is under orders to take him out with the chain guns. If that doesn't do the trick, we put the UH-53s in line formation, one over the car in front of him, one over the car behind. On my order, we fast-rope onto Delaney's location. Gonzalez will be in front. His unit are the stoppers. They'll take cover and fire only if Delaney charges them. And only surgically at that point. We've got a field-of-fire issue here. I don't want you morons shooting each other. My unit will be the assaulters. We'll move forward and we'll pop him. If he flees toward Gonzalez, we take cover and let Gonzalez take him out. Clear?"

There was a hearty cheer from the unit.

"Once again, let me stress, Delaney has already killed three of us down in Boone and evaded a national dragnet. He's a fanatical, disciplined, resourceful soldier. If he comes out with his hands up, I guarantee you it's a ruse. Okay? No matter what he may indicate, this man will go down fighting. Does everybody get my drift? This man is not coming home as our prisoner."

Another chorus of assent.

"Sir?" It was the pilot. The tracking data was being fed through his nav computer. "We're thirty seconds out."

Pardee looked out the window. He could see the train in the distance snaking through the pretty northern Virginia countryside. The train was composed mostly of flatcars. Good. They would be ideal fighting platforms, and there were very few places for Delaney to take cover. They closed slowly on the train.

"I think he's under there," the pilot said, pointing to a flatcar covered by a huge yellow tarp that said CAT DIESEL across the top.

"Handyman Three, take position," Pardee said into his radio. "Your target is on the flatcar covered by the tarp. If he shows hostile intent, chain-gun his ass."

"Roger, Handyman One."

The faster Apache swooped down into position. But nothing stirred on the flatcar as his prop wash thundered against the tarp. Delaney had obviously decided not to show himself.

"All right, boys," Pardee said. "Once again, it's up to the foot soldiers to do the manly work."

He signaled to the two UH-53s to ease into line formation. The big choppers slowly took their positions, dropping to within twenty meters of the flatcars. The two-inch-thick black ropes on which they were about to descend trailed and whipped in the wind. This was an exceedingly dangerous maneuver, one that could only be successfully prosecuted by highly skilled men. Pardee felt a pleasant sense of expectation. There was nothing better than doing the job you had been cut out for all your life, both by blood and by training. He smiled briefly then grabbed his rope.

"Go!"

Then he was falling.

Richard B. Russell Senate Office Building
3:45 PM

Senator Charles Tunnington hummed to himself. He had spent his entire life in public, but in truth he was a private man. He was never happier than when he was writing or studying. The past two days had been like a refresher course in American democracy. He had studied the Constitution, the Declaration of Independence, commentaries and cases, history—and once again the more he read, the more he found himself astonished at the wisdom of the American project. He was practically tingling with excitement. He felt an odd kinship with the men who had molded the nation, almost as though he were having a conversation with Madison, Jefferson, Adams—later figures like Learned Hand or Oliver Wendell Holmes or Lincoln.

But as the afternoon wore on, he had begun to feel a wistful sadness. Soon he would be back out in the hurly-burly again. Tunnington had always had a gift for recitation, and today he had committed huge swaths of text to memory. There were many filibusters in the past where senators quickly moved to tedious tactics like reading newspapers aloud or telling stories about how they courted their wives or how they won the state football championship back in whenever. But Tunnington had decided that before he sank to that level, he would first make a long and closely reasoned speech, buttressed by the thinking of two hundred years of America's greatest minds. Win or lose, it was his intention to put every one of his beliefs into the record before he started talking about his grandchildren or his flower garden, before he started reading the newspaper or reciting lyric poetry.

He had been getting feelers from all quarters before he went into seclusion—from journalists, scholars, and politicians on both sides of the aisle—who were uncomfortable with what Boyd was up to but who were afraid of looking like friends of terrorism if they fought him. Tunnington knew his speech would be running live on C-Span. He hoped it would plant a seed, that people would turn it on and that his passion for the beauty of restrained government would shine through, that as he slowed the juggernaut of Boyd's machine, opposition would begin to take root. If he could just convince one more senator to spell him on the filibuster, they could filibuster indefinitely. And then Boyd would be sunk.

He was interrupted in midsentence by a tap on the door.

"Senator," Mrs. Graham said, "I thought you might want to know. That colonel you sent packing this morning?"

"Yes?"

"She's just been arrested in the White House."

"What for?"

"Treason, sedition, and harboring a fugitive."

"What fugitive?"

"Delaney, presumably."

He tried to square treasonous and seditious behavior with the things that the attractive colonel had said to him that morning. She had told him that he needed to seclude himself somewhere, that he needed to put himself under guard of someone he trusted, that he was in danger of being—well, she had never actually said "assassinated," though that was what she had implied. When she had told him that Morgan Boyd was, in effect, conducting a coup d'état, he had told her that she was delusional and sent her on her way.

But if she was delusional and crazy and part of the plot against Dean Fairbank, then why did she want Tunnington safe? Why did she want him—Boyd's most conspicuous opponent on the Freedom from Fear Act—to be speaking against the act on the floor of the Senate? And why had she just been arrested?

It didn't make sense. But it did indicate that perhaps a few precautions might be wise. "Mrs. Graham," he called, "would you make a phone call for me?"

Northern Virginia
4:28 PM

Pardee hit the flatcar with a bang, went into a crouch, and sprinted to the four-foot-high steel barrier at the front end of the flatcar.

The men in his unit all fell into a neat stack behind the steel barrier, Pardee at the rear, Badger on point.

"Team Two, everybody in position?" Pardee said into his throat mic.

Gonzalez's voice came back. "Roger."

Pardee yelled over the steel barrier: "Delaney! We've got you. There's a sniper and an Apache in the air. You're surrounded. Give up now, President Boyd offers you his personal protection!"

No answer. He poked a mirror gingerly over the top of the barrier, scanned the next flatcar. He could see part of a huge yellow marine engine and some tarp. But Delaney was not visible. If he couldn't see Delaney, Delaney couldn't see him.

"Unit Two," Pardee whispered into his throat mic. "Everybody under cover?"

"Affirmative," Gonzalez said.

"All right, on my command, Badger, Eddie, Dutch, Nick, lay down suppressing fire. Crandall and Agee, lay a frag down on each side of the tarp."

Nods.

"Now!"

Four men rose above the steel barrier and began firing three-round bursts into the tarp. Then the other two operators tossed grenades over the barrier. The grenades skittered along the deck of the next car.

"Down!" Pardee shouted.

The four shooters dropped below the steel barrier, and the two grenades went off almost simultaneously, shrapnel pinging off the half-inch steel plate next to their ears.

"Flashbangs!" Pardee called.

Two more grenades skittered across the next flatcar and exploded, this time with a brilliant flash of white.

Pardee signaled with his hands for the stack to split in half, each half moving around the barrier and up onto the flatcar.

There were two quick bursts of suppressing fire, then the operators began to move, MP5s at the ready. Pardee was the last man around the barrier, heart racing as he clambered over the lip of the next car, rolled under the tarp, and looked for targets. Nothing. Delaney had to be taking cover on the other side of the mammoth diesel engine. The engine was almost fifteen feet long and five feet wide. Plenty big to hide behind. Five more seconds and they'd have him.

"Come out, Delaney!"

No answer.

He signaled for the men to roll out around each side of the engine. They charged down both sides of the flatcar and around the far side of the engine.

"Aw, son of a *bitch!*" Pardee screamed.

A cell phone lay on the scarred wooden decking. But otherwise there was nothing there. Delaney was gone.

"Handyman Three, did he jump?" Pardee shouted into the mic. "Did anyone see him bail?"

Gonzalez leapt across from the other flatcar. He looked at the phone on the deck, then laughed uproariously. "He didn't jump, Colonel. Delaney hasn't been on this train since it left DC. He knew the phone had a beacon, and he left it here as a ruse. I love to watch this guy work!"

"I'm glad you can maintain such a cheerful attitude." Pardee kicked the phone, watched it fly off the flatcar and smash against a concrete bridge abutment in a cloud of plastic parts.

Central Washington, DC
4:45 PM

General Bill Fairbank had intended to conduct a spot inspection of some of the Eighty-second Airborne patrols around the city—soldiers always did their jobs better when they felt like the brass actually paid attention to what they were doing—but now that he had been relieved of command, the inspection tour was obviously terminated.

The question was, what *should* he do just now? Bill Fairbank was not a man to sit on his thumbs cogitating when there was work to be done. His mantra was "no paralysis through analysis." But this was one of those rare times when the thing that needed to be done was not plainly obvious to him.

"Take me back to the Pentagon, Sergeant," he said to his driver. The general's right-hand man, Sergeant Major Tom McCarthy, sat next to the driver.

They headed down Pennsylvania Avenue, stopping at a check-point, then moving on toward the Potomac. Only about a block later, a soldier with an Eighty-second Airborne patch on his shoulder walked out into the street and stopped traffic.

He waved several cars on, then stood in front of the vehicle in front of Fairbank's, signaling to the driver to roll down his window. The vehicle in front of them was a Jeep Cherokee containing the general's security detail.

"I don't like this, sir," McCarthy said. "Where is the rest of that soldier's unit?" McCarthy had an M-16 on his lap. Most Airborne units had gone to the M4, but McCarthy claimed its shorter barrel and lower bullet velocities impeded its stopping power. He raised the M-16 slightly in the direction of the lone soldier.

The soldier who had stopped them was saying something to the driver of the security vehicle. They seemed to be having a disagreement.

"We need to go, sir," McCarthy said sharply.

"Let's not overreact," Fairbank said. "A general in the United States Army does not need to be acting like a scared old woman in the middle of the capital city of our nation."

"Yes, sir," McCarthy said. But his front sight was now resting on the soldier's chest. The soldier moved away from the Jeep, back toward the general's car.

Two men from the security detail piled out of the Jeep, leveled their M4s at the man, and started yelling something at him.

"Sir. Sir!" McCarthy said urgently.

"Look, he's not even armed," Fairbank said.

"Exactly," McCarthy said. "Why *isn't* he?"

The soldier knocked on the back window. He seemed uncon-cerned by the weapons leveled at him. Fairbank could hear his voice through the window. "I need to talk to the general. It's urgent."

Fairbank's eyes narrowed. McCarthy was right. Something was wrong with this picture.

"Sir. General." The soldier outside met Fairbank's eyes. "General, I need a word with you."

Suddenly Fairbank's eyes widened. Then he said, "Let him in."

Sergeant Major McCarthy spoke into his commo unit to the security detail. "Stand down. The general says he's okay." In front of them the two security detail members lowered their weapons, jumped back in the Jeep.

Fairbank's driver hesitated, then hit the lock release. The soldier pulled on the door handle and slid into the seat next to Fairbank.

"Hello, General," he said, saluting crisply. "It's been a while."

"Where the hell did you get that uniform, Sergeant Delaney?" Fairbank growled.

Richard B. Russell Senate Building
4:47 PM

The Secret Service is not an organization that can be easily bullied. A senator's secretary can't just pick up the phone, ask for a four-member security detail, and expect them to show up on her boss's doorstep in fifteen minutes. So Mrs. Graham had not remained as the senator's secretary for twenty-five years just because she typed ninety-five words a minute; she knew how to make things happen in Washington. She had been forced to call on her deepest reserves of bureaucratic jujitsu to honor Senator Tunnington's request for a protection detail. But she succeeded. It took almost an hour, but the security detail had eventually arrived.

"Mrs. Graham," the team leader, Agent David Lim, said, "if there's a specific threat here, I need to know what it is."

"There is no specific threat."

He frowned. "Where is the senator?" Lim was an unusually tall Asian man with a square face and a buzz cut.

Mrs. Graham pointed to the office door next to her. "In there. But he doesn't want to be disturbed."

The Secret Service agents exchanged glances.

"All I can say is he's going to be making an important speech to the Senate tomorrow and he's concerned that someone may try to stop him."

"Like who? Brotherhood operatives?"

"I don't know the answer to that question, Agent Lim."

Lim, obviously stifling his irritation and discomfort at this nebulous and unclear assignment, started issuing orders to his men.

Just as they had taken up their positions someone entered the outer door of the office. Mrs. Graham recognized him as Lieutenant General William Fairbank. He was accompanied by several armed soldiers.

Agent Lim put his hand on his Beretta. "Gentlemen," he said, "this is a Senate office building. No weapons are permitted in here."

The soldiers around General Fairbank were hard-eyed men who didn't show any inclination to take instructions from a civilian.

"It's all right, Agent Lim," said a voice from behind them. Mrs. Graham turned and saw Senator Tunnington standing in the doorway of his office. "They're friends of mine."

Lim didn't look persuaded.

"We're on the senator's side, David," one of the soldiers said. He wore the chevrons of a staff sergeant. But Mrs. Graham had spent enough time in Washington to know what a staff sergeant was supposed to look like. And this man was no staff sergeant. He was too old, for one thing—late thirties probably. But there was an aura of assurance and command in his blue eyes that didn't quite fit the way a noncommissioned officer would act in the presence of a three-star general and a senator. "Besides, you're pretty well outgunned."

At which point Lim's eyes widened. "Delaney!" he said.

Mrs. Graham, to her shock, recognized the "sergeant's" face.

"Agent Lim," Tunnington said. "Take your hand off your weapon. There's not a problem here. I'm instructing you to make no communications with your office, not till I'm done with this conference. Do you understand me?"

"Senator, that man is a federal fugitive. I'm obliged to report him."

"I'll instruct you on your obligations when the time comes," Tunnington snapped. "Right now your job is to protect *me*. Mrs. Graham, I trust you'll make sure Agent Lim honors my request?"

"Of course, Senator."

DELANEY WAS USHERED into Senator Tunnington's office by the aging secretary with the peculiar blond wig. He was followed by General Fairbank. McCarthy and the two other troopers stayed in the outer room. Tunnington closed the door. "May I offer you gentlemen a drink?"

There was a brief pause. "By God, yes, I think you can," Bill Fairbank said. "Given what you're about to hear . . . well, we all could probably stand one."

Tunnington took out three heavy cut-glass tumblers, moistened their bottoms with twelve-year-old MacCallan, and handed them to his guests. "So, General," he said. "What was so urgent that you needed me to interrupt my preparations for this speech I'm giving tomorrow?"

Fairbank took a sip of his scotch, then said, "I'll let Agent Delaney do the talking."

Delaney took his time, giving Tunnington a full description of everything that had happened to him over the course of the past week. He explained about the assassination, and about what he had learned of Morgan Boyd's grab for power.

"The bottom line here," Delaney said, "is that the Brotherhood, for all intents and purposes, is an invention of Morgan Boyd. I believe that the main crimes which were supposedly perpetrated by the organization—the White Sands attack, the truck of chlorine gas in Houston, the bomb at the Federal Building in Atlanta—these attacks were actually coordinated by members of a small paramilitary unit called the Protocols and Procedures Section or Unit P, which was assembled using black-budget funds Boyd pried out of his budget for the Continuity of Government reorg he oversaw."

"The HRT massacre in Alabama?"

"Another Unit P op."

"And the assassination itself?"

"Strictly speaking, no. The shooter, Doyle Pilgrim, was an actual member of the Brotherhood. Unit P probably trained him and equipped him. But he was not a Unit P member, of course not, because that would bring attention precisely where Boyd doesn't want it."

"You have evidence for this?"

"I had a very frank conversation with Paul Miller. He claimed to have no knowledge whatsoever of any of these operations. He knew he was being hunted down, that he would likely be dead within days. So he had no reason to lie to me."

Tunnington's canny old eyes looked into Delaney's own for a long moment. Then he drained his scotch, grimaced. "I'm no fan of Boyd's," the senator said finally. "I think everything that he's doing right now is dead wrong for this country. But this story of yours—it's completely outlandish. Where's the proof?"

"As I said, Senator, the paymaster—this fellow Ferris—stored all of the information on a computer hard drive. He kept that drive after he burned down the office where he had been working. I retrieved that disk drive. It contained a list of every account name and number used to fund the Brotherhood's operations. And some of Unit P's. It may take a few hours to trace those accounts, but somebody from the Office of Management and Budget could do it fairly easily, I expect."

"Yes, you already explained that."

"Then there's the proof, Senator. It's not just my word."

"Earlier in the conversation," Tunnington said, "you told me that you had passed a hard disk drive to Colonel Mary Campos."

Delaney nodded. "Yes, that's correct."

The senator and the general looked at each other.

"You didn't tell him?" the senator said.

"I didn't have time," Fairbank said. "We were in a little bit of a rush."

"What, sir?" Delaney said.

Senator Tunnington cleared his throat. "Son, Colonel Campos was arrested by Unit P this afternoon at two o'clock."

Delaney felt a stab of self-recrimination. He shouldn't have put Mary in the line of fire. It had been stupid of him. "Is she all right?" he said.

The senator ignored his question. "Mrs. Graham tells me that the Unit P agents seized an unusual lunch bag out of the refrigerator. If the disk drive in the bag is your only evidence . . ."

He let the words hang in the air.

After a moment, Delaney felt a ghost of a smile on his face. "You think I would have let that drive out of my sight?" He reached into his pocket, pulled out a Zip-Loc bag, set it gently on the senator's desk. Inside the bag was a small rectangular metal object. A hard drive. "The disk drive I gave to Colonel Campos was a decoy. I felt fairly sure that this guy Leonard Smith was one of Boyd's people. But I wasn't sure. I had to know."

He set a CD-ROM on top of the hard drive.

"This CD-ROM contains copies of every file on the drive. You'll need to get them over to the Senate and read them into the record."

Tunnington looked thoughtful. "But first we have to get there."

"Yes, sir," Delaney said. "And my guess is, they won't make it easy."

The Oval Office
5:21 PM

John Rancy burst into the room. Morgan Boyd was entertaining three senators, fence-sitters on the Freedom from Fear Act, telling them the story about his wife's death at the hands of the Hindu extremists in India.

". . . and in that moment, as she lay there in my arms, the life ebbing from her eyes, I knew that it was my destiny to fight terror and extremism wherever on the globe it is. I'm asking you to—"

"Mr. President," Rancy said.

Boyd looked up. "John, please, I'm busy."

"This can't wait."

Boyd smiled at his former colleagues from the Senate. "Gentlemen, if you don't mind . . ."

They trooped out of the room. "What!" Boyd demanded. "I was just giving them the man-of-destiny speech for godsake. That's three votes, John! Three!"

"I just got a call from a Senate staffer. He said Fairbank has been behind closed doors with Tunnington for the past forty-five minutes."

"Son of a—"

"It gets worse. There's a rumor going around the Senate offices that Delaney's in there with them. And just as I was hanging up the phone, I got a call from our guy at NSA. He says Tunnington's office just put in a call to OMB. They've sent some bean counter over to Tunnington's office."

"Delaney must have made a copy of everything on that disk. He knew Smith was on our side all along, suckered Unit P out into Virginia, meanwhile he's moving in on Tunnington with that hard drive."

"I think so."

"The bean counter's going to trace the money flow back to accounts attached to my COG working group. Then that old goat Tunnington will hit the floor of the Senate, waving the hard drive in the air, and saying I assassinated Dean Fairbank."

"Unless we stop them."

Boyd stared out the window for a while.

"You're sure he's got the drive?" he said finally.

"I don't see any alternative but to assume that."

"Then we've got no choice, do we?"

"Sir?"

Boyd looked hard at Rancy for a long time.

"We could revisit the accidental shooting scenario," Rancy said. "Pardee has worked out a tactical plan. He'll put shooters out all around the Capitol Building. We apprehend Tunnington with army troops; Tunnington's Secret Service protection gets edgy or whatever, there's some confusion and jostling, oops, a nervous young soldier pulls the trigger by mistake."

Boyd sighed heavily. "I really hate this, John."

"So, what, we just detain him until after the vote?"

Boyd was silent for a moment. "No. That's no good. Eventually we'd have to let him out and then he'd start blabbing about whatever's on that disk. We've got to cauterize this thing while we still have a chance."

"So you're saying . . ."

Boyd nodded curtly.

43

Richard B. Russell Senate Office Building
5:28 PM

THE ACCOUNTANT THEY'D sent over from OMB was a short stocky woman who wore thick glasses and a wine-colored wool dress that looked like it had started life as a saddle blanket. Her name was Claire Bishop.

She sat down and looked at the printouts. "These are all the account numbers?"

"That we know of, yes," Delaney said. General Fairbank stood beside him. Senator Tunnington was sitting on the other side of the table in Mrs. Graham's office. Mrs. Graham stood at his elbow.

"So you believe they are connected somehow to black-budget accounts."

"Right."

"CIA?"

"No. The COG project."

The accountant looked up, blinked. "The *Morgan Boyd* continuity of government project? The COG working group?"

Tunnington nodded.

"That's not possible," she said.

"Why not?"

"I'm responsible for COG. There's no off-budget stuff there, no black-budget stuff. It's all in the clear."

"How is Unit P funded?"

"Unit P?"

"Protocols and Procedures Section."

"I've never heard of that. Let me log on remote to the OMB system, I'll see if I can search it out." She spent several minutes messing around with the computer, then finally looked up and shook her head.

"What?"

"There's no such thing."

"What do you mean?"

"There's no such thing as Protocols and Procedures Section. It doesn't exist."

"It's black budget. It's hidden in something else."

She looked impatient. "No, see I have access to all the black-budget items here. Ordinarily all the black-budget numbers are compartmentalized. Only three people in OMB have superuser access, meaning they can search all black-budget line items. I'm one of those three people. It's not there."

Delaney frowned. This was very strange. "Okay, then work backward. Can you search for these account numbers? I'm sure they're governmental accounts. Find out where the accounts are, then trace it back to the budget lines."

She nodded. "Okay." She pecked the keys for a while.

"Ah! Bingo. This account here . . ." She tapped the printout that Mrs. Graham had made, showing fifty thousand dollars' worth of transfers to the Brotherhood. "This account here is the vice presidential protocol budget. Flowers, entertainment, that sort of thing."

"Protocol. Protocols and Procedures," General Fairbank growled. "You'd think you might have caught that first time around."

The accountant looked at the general with an expression that mixed irritation and condescension in equal measure. "Protocol is protocol. Protocol and procedures is protocol and procedures. They are not the same."

"Oh. Thank you for that."

"Boys, girls," Tunnington said. "Let's not get off track. Who has signature authority for that budget?"

More tapping on the keys. "Here we go," she said, pointing at the screen with a thick finger.

"'John Rancy,'" Delaney read.

"That's close enough for me," Tunnington said. "Rancy doesn't pick his nose without asking Boyd's permission. Let's get a couple more. Meantime, General, you might get your boys ready to roll. I had been intending to wait until tomorrow to speak, but it's becoming obvious that I'll have to move the schedule up just a trifle."

Fairbank turned to Sergeant Major McCarthy: "You remember I told you to keep that TRQ ready with the Turkey-43 encryption. I think the time has come to use it."

"Yes, sir!"

"If I may," Delaney said, "could I offer a suggestion?"

"By all means."

Delaney outlined a brief plan.

Senator Tunnington immediately said, "Absolutely not. I wouldn't consider such a dishonorable idea."

The phone rang, and Mrs. Graham picked it up, listened briefly, set it down. "Senator, I just got word from Senator Dane's people. He's got a source inside the judge advocate general's office who says that one of these secret warrants has just been issued. You've been charged with sedition. The source's understanding is that an Airborne detachment intends to intercept you when you attempt to enter the Capitol."

Tunnington exploded. "Sedition! That little weasel wouldn't dare!"

"I think he would, sir," Delaney said.

Bill Fairbank leaned toward the senator and said, "Sun Tzu, the great Chinese military strategist, once said, 'If the enemy is strong and I am weak, I temporarily withdraw and do not engage.' I think you need to consider doing it Delaney's way."

Tunnington, still red in the face, paced up and down for a moment.

"All right," he said finally.

44

The Oval Office
6:12 PM

SAY WHAT YOU WILL about the many fine qualities of the United States Army, but it doesn't turn on a dime. Not easily anyway.

To get members of the Eighty-second Airborne standing in front of the Capitol Building, ready to serve a warrant against a United States senator, sounds simple enough. But it wasn't. It required official notification to the Joint Chiefs that Lieutenant General William Fairbank had been relieved of command both of DOPCOM (Temporary) and of the XVIII Airborne Corps. Lieutenant General Davis Sheffield, CINCUSSOC (Commander in Chief, US Special Operations Command) in MacDill AFB Florida, then had to be elevated to CINCDOPCOM (Temporary), commander in chief of Domestic Operations Command (Temporary). Lieutenant General Sheffield then had to consult his legal affairs officer about the serving of civilian arrest warrants by U.S. Army personnel. The legal affairs officer for USSOC, after being peeled off the ceiling, punted to JAG in the Pentagon. After various senior JAG officers were also peeled off the ceiling, calls were made to DOJ, where John Rancy read them the riot act. The JAG officers called Sheffield's legal affairs officer, who showed Sheffield a faxed copy of a spit-and-bubble-gum arrest procedure advisory, which still bore the logo of the Justice Department, where it had been drafted. Sheffield then drafted an Emergency Order with the arrest procedure advisory appended, forwarded the order to Major General Adam Seigenthaller, commander of the Eighty-second Airborne, who was in temporary quarters in Washington, DC.

Major General Seigenthaller refused the order and had to be relieved of command. His XO, Brigadier General "Jumpin Jerry" Ratliff III, was at Fort Bragg and had to forward an order to Lieutenant Colonel James Dyer, commander of the battalion tasked with guarding the Mall. Colonel Dyer then refused the order and was relieved of command. And so it went.

There was, in short, a great deal of hyperventilation, righteous anger, and confusion going on within the United States Army. And at nearly every step of the way the White House had to step in and whip everyone back into line.

But at the end of the day, the U.S. Army did, in fact, turn on a dime—though a mutiny was avoided only by the most dire threats from the White House.

By the time that Senator Charles Tunnington stepped into Bill Fairbank's armored Crown Victoria, a company of paratroopers had materialized in front of the Capitol under the command of a thirty-six-year-old major named Clyde Batson. Batson—who had received his maple leaf just three days earlier—was an exceedingly ambitious, aggressive, and unself-reflective officer who was looking for any opportunity to distinguish himself. He drew up the first and second platoons at the edge of the concrete parking barriers, which had gone up in the lot by the north entrance after 9/11, then stationed the remainder of his troops at each of the several other entrances and in the basement subway that led over from the congressional offices. He pulled two Hummers up onto the actual steps of the Capitol, their recoilless rifles staring down at the spot where he expected the senator would arrive.

Major Batson had watched the movie *Patton* over forty times and memorized the entire speech that George C. Scott made in front of the huge American flag. Inspired by his hero, he had long ago purchased an outrageously nonreg Smith & Wesson wheelgun with ivory grips, which he had never worked up the nerve to wear while on duty. Nevertheless he had carried it with him for years, waiting for the right opportunity to drag it out and strap it to his leg.

This, he decided, was the moment. *His* moment.

He finished buckling the holster, then stood at the top of the Capitol steps at parade rest with a cigar in his mouth, the salty expression on his face one that he'd been practicing in the mirror since his freshman year at the academy. All he was missing was a pair of jodhpurs and a riding crop.

"Bring 'im on, by God!" he said. "Bring that traitor on!"

PARDEE WAS AT his best under pressure. He'd had to stop the train, fly back to DC, get his boys out of their black assault gear and into civvies, infiltrate them into the Mall, rearm four shooter/spotter teams with .223 Bushmasters (whose ballistics would match those of the M4s carried by the troopers of the Airborne on the scene) at various hides around the Capitol—all without attracting undue attention to himself or his men.

But he had done it.

Shooter Teams One and Two were on the roof of the Capitol, while Team Three stood about sixty meters from the Capitol steps, playing like homeless winos. Team Three—Badger and his spotter, a guy named Bennett—had simply chased some bum off from the shopping cart in which he kept his earthly belongings, and now they had their tricked-out and suppressed Bushmaster lying there under a greasy trash bag. When the time came for the shot, the shopping cart would make a nice bench rest. It was point-blank shooting. Pardee had been amazed to see that—despite being under what, for all intents and purposes, was martial law—bums and crackheads seemed to wander with impunity all over the Hill. Once they got this act passed, he wondered if maybe he could con Boyd into tasking him with rounding them up and shooting them.

Pardee himself stood on the edge of the parking lot, holding an encrypted Motorola commo unit, a press pass hanging around his neck saying that he was a reporter for National Public Radio. As he stood there, a rotund, civilian-looking JAG lawyer went huffing up the steps toward the moron major with the ivory-gripped pistol. He was waving a blue piece of paper.

Good. Everything was set.

The senator would roll up with a bunch of Secret Service guys and maybe a couple of Fairbank's troopers, there'd be a brief standoff, then Team Three would pop the senator. After the senator's head exploded, the Secret Service guys would start shooting at the Airborne troopers, and Unit P would melt away while the ding-a-ling major with the ivory-gripped pistol ordered a rain of fire into the senator and his crew. Delaney would most likely go down in the melee. Probably Fairbank too. After it was over, Pardee would stroll into the wreckage, find the hard drive, and carry it away. It was too perfect, really.

There was a chance, of course, that the senator would try to sneak in some other entrance. But it wasn't likely. There were camera crews stationed here already, tipped off by the White House that Something Big was about to happen. The senator was out to make a point. He wouldn't skulk in the back door. He was one of those dignity-honor-and-principle types, totally predictable: he'd use the front door, try to get his face on TV showing what a big hero of democracy he was.

Pardee smiled, feeling like the luckiest SOB on the planet. There was no happier man, he reflected, than a man who loved his work.

45

SERGEANT MAJOR MCCARTHY raised Captain Phillipe Grundy on the back-channel TRQ as per General Fairbank's instructions, then passed the handset to Fairbank. The general had chosen carefully on this call. Grundy had served on his personal staff in an earlier posting and knew that Grundy was both deeply patriotic and loyal.

The general said, "Phil, this Bill Fairbank. I need to talk to you for a moment, not as a general to a major, but man to man, patriot to patriot."

"I understand, sir."

"You know that I have been removed from command."

"Yes, sir."

"I have access to information indicating that President Fairbank— my brother—was murdered on authorization of command elements very high in the United States government. Do you understand what I'm saying?"

"I'm not sure I do."

"What I'm saying is that, in effect, we are in the middle of a coup d'état. I need your help. But if you help me, you will have to break chain of command, ignore your current orders, and take actions which, if unsuccessful, will result in extremely grave consequences for you and the men who follow you."

There was a long pause.

"If successful, however, we will save our nation."

"We're talking man to man? Okay, sir, I don't like this." There was another long pause. "But if you say it's something that needs to be done, I trust you, sir."

"Good. Here's what I need . . ."

CAPTAIN PHILLIPE GRUNDY climbed out of his Hummer in front of the entrance to the subterranean parking lot of the Richard B.

Russell Senate Office Building and scanned the area. The tall, muscular black man, with close-cropped hair and ebony skin, perceived no immediate threats. Six additional Hummers pulled in around him, creating a defensive perimeter around the door. Grundy issued orders to his platoon sergeant, who made sure that the machine gunners on all the Hummers were ready for action.

He then reached for his TRQ, raised General Fairbank. "We're good to go, sir."

THIRTY SECONDS LATER a black Jeep Cherokee appeared at the top of the ramp. Behind it was a black Crown Vic with the blazon of a three-star general marked unobtrusively on the grille.

Captain Grundy made a circle in the air with his hands, jumped into the lead Hummer. The convoy filed out onto the street, then re-formed in echelon formation, one chevron in front, then the Secret Service Crown Vic, then the Cherokee, then Grundy's vehicle, then a second chevron of Hummers.

At the corner of Constitution, they were halted at a roadblock manned by two squads of Airborne troopers.

Grundy got out of his Hummer and yelled to the second lieutenant who commanded the roadblock. It was obvious from his reaction that he had been told the general's convoy was on the way. "Why are we being stopped, Lieutenant?"

"You're not cleared to enter this sector, sir."

"I'm escorting a United States senator, Lieutenant. Are you saying that you are preventing an elected member of Congress from entering the Capitol grounds?"

The lieutenant made a quick radio call to his superiors and then waved the convoy through.

They reached the parking lot at the east entrance of the Capitol in about a minute. Captain Grundy sized up the situation. It was not good. Two Hummers with roof-mounted recoilless rifles had been posted on the very steps of the building, and at least a company of troopers were defiladed behind concrete barriers. The commander of the unit was standing at the top of the step with a ridiculous wheel-gun strapped to his leg and a cigar in his mouth. Grundy recognized him: it was that horse's ass Batson.

Unfortunately, Grundy's charges were completely outgunned. He drew up his convoy, stepped out of the Hummer. "Major Batson!" he called up to the top of the Capitol steps. "What are your orders?"

"You're not authorized to be here, Major," the major shouted back.

At this point General Fairbank climbed out of the big Lincoln and walked toward the barrier. A young private stepped in front of him, an apprehensive expression. "Sir, I need you to—"

"Step aside, son," Fairbank growled. "My business is with the major." He pushed past the soldier and mounted the stairs. The major at the top of the stairs looked down at him, chewing on a cigar.

"What the hell is that, Major?" General Fairbank snapped at the major, pointing at the nonregulation Smith on his hip.

"A pistol, sir."

"Take it off."

The young major, who was busy trying to look like George C. Scott, swallowed. "General, I'm under orders. You've been relieved of command and are not to be permitted to enter this facility."

"This *facility,* as you call it, is the property of the citizenry of this country. If I choose to enter, I'll be damned if some snot-nosed major wearing a cowboy pistol on his hip is gonna stop me."

The major drew his pistol and pointed it at Fairbank's chest. "Sir, who is in that vehicle? Is Senator Tunnington in there?"

"Put that pistol down, Major." Fairbank seethed with anger.

"No, sir," the major said. "I'll ask you again, who's in that vehicle?"

"That's not your concern, Major."

"Yes, sir, it is my concern."

A second figure approached them—a sloppy, slightly overweight young man wearing the emblem of the judge advocate general's office on his shoulder. He said, "With all due respect, General Fairbank, the major is correct. I have in my hands a warrant for the arrest of Senator Tunnington. If he is in that vehicle, I demand that you release him in Major Batson's custody."

"Over my dead body," Fairbank said.

"I take that as an admission that the senator is, indeed, in the car?"

"Take it as anything you please."

FROM THE CORNER of the parking lot Dirk Pardee watched the confrontation between Fairbank and the ding-a-ling major.

The commo receiver in his ear crackled briefly. "Sir, Goldenrod

Two here." It was the spotter from sniper Team Two. "I'm looking down from the southwest corner and there's something odd happening."

"What?"

"I'm seeing a couple of people walking across the Mall here toward the Capitol. There's a guy wearing sunglasses, a baseball cap, a big coat with the collar pulled up over his face. I think he's got a weapon under the coat. The way he moves? I'm sure he's a soldier."

"And who's the second person?"

"Well, it looks like a lady in a dress. Only . . . if it's a lady, it's the ugliest hag I've ever seen in my life. She's six foot two and walks like she's about eighty years old."

"What's your point?"

"I think it's a man, sir."

Pardee had to reconsider for a minute. Here was this big convoy, Fairbank, big confrontation. But what if that sneaky SOB Delaney was trying to pull a fast one, slipping the Senator in some back door posing as a woman. It seemed crazy—but if that's what it really was, boy, would he look like a moron if it happened on his watch.

"Would you recognize Tunnington's face?"

"I guess. I mean this old broad's got an awful lot of makeup on though."

"Keep watching them. How far out are they?"

"Four hundred meters. The speed they're moving, I'd give them three minutes before they reach the building."

"Keep watching." Pardee switched channels on his radio, went direct to John Rancy. "Sir, it's Goldenrod One. We've got a heavily armed convoy drawn up in front of the Capitol steps. Fairbank's out talking to the commander of the guard detachment and the JAG lawyer."

"Is Tunnington in the convoy?"

"I don't know."

"How heavily armed are they? Could they fight their way in?"

"No, sir. They're outnumbered and outgunned."

"Then we've got no problem."

"Well, maybe so, maybe not. One of my spotters on the roof sees two people walking across the Mall. It's an old lady in a blond wig and a man who could possibly be Delaney."

"Tunnington's secretary has a blond wig."

"Is she six foot two?"

"No." There was a long pause. "You really think Tunnington would try to sneak into the Senate in drag?"

"I don't know the answer to that, sir. We could take this guy out just to make sure. If you want to—"

"If it turns out just to be some weird-looking old lady, that would be bad. We don't want that. Keep watch and keep me posted."

"Affirmative."

GENERAL BILL FAIRBANK eventually decided he was running out of things to say to the major and the JAG lawyer. "I'm going back to my vehicle," he said. "I'll confer with, ah, whomever is in the car with me."

The JAG lawyer exchanged a glance with Major Batson.

While their eyes were off him, Fairbank took a quick step forward and yanked the ridiculous pistol out of Batson's hand, palmed the cylinder release, and dropped the cartridges into his hand.

"Next time you point a gun at a general officer, son," he said to the stunned major, "I'll have you court-martialed." He threw the Smith & Wesson down the stairs. As it wheeled and bounced down the marble steps, he turned sharply and began making his way back down toward the waiting Hummers.

No one stopped him as he opened the door of the Crown Vic.

"GOLDENROD ONE to Goldenrod Four, what do you see?" Pardee said.

The spotter replied, "Two hundred and fifty meters, still closing. The broad in the dress is definitely an old guy."

"What about the second man? Is it Delaney?"

"With the baseball cap and the collar and everything, I just can't make out his face. He's definitely got a weapon under his coat though."

"You got a shot?"

"Sure. Easy."

"Keep locked on the man in the dress."

"Yes, sir."

Pardee had moved away from the other journalists. The knot of cameramen and their handlers had gotten larger. Apparently the checkpoints were not keeping out journalists. He'd have to tell Rancy to make sure the Airborne came down and snagged everybody's tapes, everybody's film, everybody's cameras. The last thing they needed was fifteen Zapruders, everybody spending the next forty years dissecting these tapes for suspicious flashes and puffs of smoke from the grassy knoll.

Pardee watched as Fairbank yanked the pistol out of the major's hand, threw it down the steps. George C. Scott looked like he'd been poleaxed, the poor fool staring as his wheel gun went bouncing down toward the concrete barricade. Pardee knew guys like that, and he'd probably spent two months' pay getting the sharp edges smoothed, fancy sights installed, ivory grips, action reworked—and there it was bouncing down the steps getting the crap beat out of it.

Pardee laughed then changed to the White House freq again as Fairbank got back in the big black Crown Vic. "Goldenrod One here. I think we've got trouble. To me this looks like Fairbank is stalling. I think Tunnington really is trying to sneak in the back door with Delaney. You want me to pop them?"

"Negative, Goldenrod," came Rancy's voice. "I'll handle it. I still want him stopped by an army unit first. Ideally Delaney will come out with a gun, the troopers will respond appropriately, and your boys won't even have to get involved."

"Affirmative."

Pardee ended the transmission then moved around so he could get a better look inside the Crown Vic. He turned and caught the eye of Team Three—Badger and his spotter, still crouched near their shopping cart.

"Goldenrod Three, you still got a shot?" he said.

They didn't answer on the air: Badger just gave him a surreptitious thumbs-up.

At about that point the major must have received a communication from the White House because he yelled something and pointed to the south side of the Capitol. An entire platoon stood and began trotting toward the far end of the Capitol.

Pardee felt uneasy. That left about one platoon at the steps. They were now facing six Hummers with an undetermined number of occupants, and six machine guns. They still had Fairbank's little mobile unit outgunned, but it was no longer a lay-down. You could rest assured that whoever was commanding Fairbank's unit was as good as they came. Whereas George C. Scott up on the steps was probably not the absolute finest officer who had ever worn an Airborne patch on his arm.

"Goldenrod One to Goldenrod Four," Pardee said, calling to the second sniper team, on the Capitol roof. "I want you to reposition. Find yourself a good shot on the convoy by the steps."

"Roger."

Pardee felt like he was playing chess. But who was he playing against? Fairbank? Or Delaney? Fairbank was a charge-the-hill type. But Delaney wasn't.

Fairbank still hadn't come out of the Hummer. What was the holdup? Fairbank was not a shilly-shallier. If he was planning on coming in, he'd have done it.

"Goldenrod Two, how close are they?"

"A hundred meters. It's definitely a man. Got to be the senator, sir. Got to be. Okay, I've got a whole platoon charging around the corner here. They're heading over toward them."

"Keep talking to me."

Suddenly General Fairbank's convoy went into motion, wheeling around in a circle and heading back toward Constitution.

Pardee punched his fist into his other hand. Yes! Fairbank's arrival had been a ruse. They *were* trying to sneak the old man in. So he'd been playing chess with Delaney all this time.

"Ready yourself for the shot, Goldenrod Two."

The major and the JAG lawyer suddenly ran down the steps and headed toward one of the Hummers. They hopped in, and it bumped down the stairs and sped off across the grass toward the south end of the Capitol.

"Here comes a Hummer," said the spotter's voice in Pardee's ear. "Two officers are getting out. They're walking toward Delaney and the senator."

"Hold for my signal," Pardee said. "Hold for my signal."

"They're approaching, they're approaching. The Airborne guys have their guns out . . ."

"Hold for my signal."

Checkmate, Delaney. Checkmate.

Suddenly Pardee noticed that Fairbank's convoy had wheeled around a second time and was now racing back toward the Capitol at breakneck speed.

The rear echelon, three Hummers, broke off and headed toward the south side of the Capitol while everyone else headed around the north side of the parking lot, flying across the grass. Son of a bitch, they were flanking the steps, heading toward the west entrance.

Pardee didn't even have to say anything. Team Three—Badger

and Bennett, the fake homeless pair—started pushing their shopping cart toward the west entrance, trying to keep in position for a shot. Son of a bitch, son of a bitch! There was barely more than a squad at that entrance.

The spotter from the roof said, "The major is shouting something. He just jerked the wig off the old man's head. He's looking really pissed, sir. I think . . . I think . . . Now the little fat officer just threw a piece of blue paper on the ground. I don't think it's the senator after all."

The senator was in the damn convoy! He was going to try heading in the north entrance. The crowd of camera crews was moving around toward the north entrance. Pardee started running. There was still time for a shot, but it was going to be dicey.

He reached the north entrance just in time to see the Crown Vic pull up with a screech. The squad of Airborne soldiers guarding the entrance took cover behind their barricades and their lieutenant stepped out and yelled, "Halt! I need to see IDs *right* now!"

The M2 Brownings on top of the four Hummers were trained on the squad guarding the door.

The door of the Crown Vic opened. General Bill Fairbank climbed out.

"Have you got a shot?" Pardee said urgently into his mic.

"If the senator comes out of the Crown Vic? Affirmative."

Fairbank was yelling something at the lieutenant, who was yelling something back.

"Wait!" the spotter said. "I see a white-haired guy inside the Navigator. Okay, yeah, the senator's definitely in there."

Pardee was being jostled by journalists now. He could see the Washington Monument thrusting up at the sky, the reflection wiggling in the long Reflection Pool.

"Wait till he comes out," Pardee whispered, camera crews banging into him as they fought for position.. "Wait on my signal! Wait on my signal! Wait . . ."

The Oval Office
6:59 PM

Rancy and the president sat hunched over the radio, alone except for a Unit P commo expert, monitoring the frequencies of all the players in the standoff at the Capitol.

"Come on, come on, come on," Morgan Boyd said. He sounded like someone with a bet on the Super Bowl. Only the stakes were just slightly higher.

Rancy grabbed the handset.

"Goldenrod One," he screamed, "tell your shooter to take the shot! Take the shot! Take the shot!"

South Side of the Capitol
6:59 PM

Major Clyde Batson screamed at the old man in front of him. "Who are you? Who sent you?"

The old man grinned. "My name's Horace Dellinger. I've been Senator Tunnington's driver for almost forty years. Never have worn a dress before, though."

"What about you?"

"My name's Sergeant Major Thomas McCarthy." Batson recognized him then as General Fairbank's senior noncom, always two paces behind him everywhere the general went.

The JAG lawyer was picking up the warrant, dusting off the blue cover. "All right, Major, it's irrelevant. Tunnington must be getting in through the other entrance. Let's go."

Batson realized the lawyer was right, but still . . . Trying to arrest a man in a dress. Could it possibly get more inglorious than this?

He unleashed a stream of curses at the two men grinning at him and then hopped back in the Hummer. First his beloved wheel gun getting smashed all over the steps. And now this. The entire mission was turning into a disaster.

North Entrance, the Capitol
6:59 PM

A mane of white hair appeared at the door of the Crown Vic. It was definitely Tunnington. Pardee decided the roof shot would be best.

"Goldenrod Four, do you have a shot?"

"No shot. Secret Service is in front of him."

Pardee turned to the two men standing by the shopping cart. One of them was hunched over the cart. If you hadn't known, you'd have never guessed he was aiming a high-powered rifle from under the greasy-looking plastic bag on top of the pile of trash in the cart. "Goldenrod Three?"

"We have the shot." It was the shooter's voice this time, Badger, his very best man.

"Take the shot," Pardee said.

He heard two sharp cracks.

For a moment he was sure of victory. But then he saw the senator getting out and waving toward the cameras, then moving forward in the middle of a cluster of Airborne troopers and Secret Service agents, their weapons sticking out in all directions so that the little knot of men looked like a human hedgehog.

"Shoot!" Pardee hissed into his radio. "Shoot!"

But then he saw that Badger was lying on his face, blood gushing from one ear. His spotter Bennett was dying too, a hole opened up in his throat and weakly spurting blood.

Who had fired the shot? Well, it didn't matter. He was going to have to take matters into his own hands.

Pardee had drawn his silenced 1911, started to raise it, when he heard a voice beside him. "Don't even think about it, Pardee."

He turned, and there was Delaney standing next to him wearing a backward baseball cap and a blue jacket that said CNN on the front in huge red letters. Delaney had an M4 leveled at him. The bastard had been standing right next to him all this time and he hadn't even noticed!

Pardee felt a flash of emotion—not anger, not fear but . . . what? Envy, maybe? But not just that. Admiration—that's what it was. He and Delaney, different though they were in so many ways, when you broke it all down, they were fighters, both of them. This was what they did. Maybe Delaney had understood something that Pardee hadn't. Maybe the son of a bitch had been right all along, that it was better to stay clean. Maybe the fighting stayed cleaner too when you were unencumbered by ambition and eagerness for profit and all the other crazy compulsions that had pressed so hard on Pardee over the years. All this time, he'd thought Delaney was a sap, a loser, a jerk. But maybe he'd been wrong all along. You kept things clean, it kept your mind on the mission—the mission and only the mission. It kept your mind in the fight.

And in the end, the fight was the only thing that mattered.

For that brief moment, when Pardee met Delaney's cold blue

eyes, he felt wistful for a life that could have been. But what could you do? You fought the fight you were in, then you moved on.

Pardee raised the 1911, pointed it toward the white hair floating in the sea of camouflage and weapons, sure that Delaney would tag him before he had the shot, but going for it anyway. And then—before he had a chance to squeeze the trigger—the white hair was gone. There was no shot.

He immediately dropped his weapon on the ground, raised his hands in the air, and looked over at Delaney, as though daring him to shoot an unarmed man. Delaney hesitated.

"Disengage," Pardee said into his throat mic. "Target is inside the Capitol. There is no shot. Disengage. Disengage."

Then, hands still raised, he began backing away from Delaney's weapon.

"You better go protect your principal, Delaney!" Pardee smirked. "Who knows, there might be somebody inside, lying in wait like a snake in the grass."

Delaney glared at him, then lowered his weapon and ran toward the knot of people at the door of the Capitol. Pardee turned and began jogging briskly away.

46

The United States Senate
7:01 PM

A S CHARLES TUNNINGTON walked into the Senate, the room stirred. At eighty years of age Tunnington moved slower than he once had, but he was still a vital man, a man you'd notice coming into a room, even if you didn't know who he was or what he represented.

But of course here they knew exactly who he was and what he represented. Everything had been prepared for his arrival. His closest friend and ally in the Senate, Senator Abe Dane of New Hampshire, was speaking. He paused while Tunnington approached one of the other podiums.

"Would the gentleman from New Hampshire yield?" Senator Tunnington said.

"I gladly yield to my friend Senator Tunnington."

The sense of relief in the room was palpable. There had been only modest enthusiasm for the so-called Freedom from Fear Act—but most senators had felt that they would be crucified by the outraged public if they didn't support the president's proposals. They looked at Tunnington as a savior. Sometimes leadership is simply a matter of saying what everyone knows but is afraid to say, of having the courage to speak what is true, no matter the consequence.

Charles Tunnington cleared his throat then held up a small rectangular metallic object and said, "Ladies and gentlemen of the Senate, I come to you with strange and horrible news. Here in my hand, I hold irrefutable proof that the president of the United States, Morgan James Boyd, has engaged in a vast and murderous conspiracy . . ."

DELANEY WAS STANDING in the gallery, still wearing the CNN outfit he had put on in the senator's office. As Tunnington began to speak, he stepped out into the hallway, dialed a number on his cell phone. Thirty seconds later, he was talking to John Rancy.

"It's over, Mr. Rancy," he said. "Tunnington's on the floor of the Senate. He's got the hard drive, he's got the accounts. The trail will lead straight to you."

"What do you want, Delaney?"

"The senator is sending me over to the White House. You and I need to talk."

There was a long silence.

"Agent Delaney, I don't think meeting at the White House is such a fabulous idea. Let's make it the Lincoln Memorial."

"See you in about an hour."

47

Central Detention Facility, Washington, DC
7:37 PM

I GUESS THIS ISN'T MUCH of a place for a romantic reunion, huh?" Delaney said.

He was standing behind a yellow line painted on the concrete floor of the jail, waiting for the Bureau of Prisons clerk to give Mary Campos back her personal effects. She took her purse out of the plastic crate it had been stored in, then walked back to Delaney and said, "Romance? Who said anything about romance?"

Delaney shook his head. "Ungrateful. I could have left you rotting away in jail for weeks, but, no, I pulled in a personal favor with my close friend Senator Tunnington, who called his friends at the Supreme Court, who in turn issued a writ of habeas corpus. That's not something the Supremes do very often. Surely I deserve some kind of modest reward."

Mary Campos looked at him for a long moment, then kissed him hard on the lips. "How's that?"

He shrugged, poker-faced. "It's a start."

He put his arm around her, and they began walking back toward the door of the prison. "So," she said. "Where to now?"

"A nice little stroll through the Mall."

The Lincoln Memorial
8:09 PM

Rancy was waiting behind the statue of Lincoln, looking nervous and wearing sunglasses and a sweatshirt with the hood pulled over his head. A crisp breeze was whipping through the building.

"What's *she* doing here?" Rancy said as Delaney and Mary Campos rounded the corner behind her.

"You're the one who put her in charge of the investigation into President Fairbank's death. Don't you think she ought to be here?" Delaney said.

Rancy looked at her for a moment, then finally said, "I guess it hardly matters. I assume you came here to offer me something."

"Take off your sunglasses," Delaney said.

"Why?"

"Because I want to see your eyes."

Rancy shrugged dismissively then took off the sunglasses. His bright blue eyes reflected the clear sky outside the memorial. "Well?" he said finally.

"Senator Tunnington has sent me as his personal representative," Delaney said. "The Freedom from Fear Act is going down in flames within a matter of hours. And you're going to follow. Because we now know that the FBI and various cabinet offices—including DOJ—have been penetrated by your boss's stooges, the senator intends to empower a special counsel to investigate and prosecute those involved with the assassination."

"*Prosecute?* There's no precedent for that."

"There's no precedent for a vice president murdering a president either."

"You have no proof of that."

"You wouldn't be here if you weren't pretty nervous about what we have."

Rancy looked up at the statue of Lincoln. "Lincoln suspended habeas corpus. He used the U.S. Army to attack American citizens on American soil. He seized property without civil due process. He hung traitors on thin evidence. And look at him. We built him a monument. Why? Because he had the courage to do what had to be done."

"Spare us the whining self-justification," Mary said.

"Self-justification? Please. It's going to happen, you know."

"What is?"

"A nuke, a dirty bomb, a biological attack—something. Unless we are sufficiently vigilant, it's inevitable. Morgan Boyd said that every single day. And guess what? Nobody listened."

"We're not here to listen to that," Delaney said.

"Then tell me what you're putting on the table."

"The senator will give you limited immunity in return for your testimony," Delaney said.

Rancy laughed. *"Limited* immunity? What does that mean? And in return for what?"

"Don't play dumb, Rancy. We've got evidence that ties you directly to the murder of Dean Fairbank. But you're Boyd's boy. We know you wouldn't have done it without Boyd's approval. If you hand Boyd to the special prosecutor, Tunnington will guarantee you twenty years in a minimum security facility."

"Twenty years! Gee, don't do me any favors."

Mary Campos interrupted. "Does the name Big Daddy mean anything to you?"

Rancy blanched.

"Mr. Rancy," Delaney said, "we have your voice on tape talking to the paymaster in Reston, about giving money to the Brotherhood to buy missiles. On the same tape you later go on to imply that President Fairbank is about to be murdered. We have your signature on a total of twenty-eight checks that correspond directly both in time and amount to a series of cash deposits made into the accounts of the Brotherhood. You think we won't find more evidence implicating you? I mean, what planet are you from that you think some rat like Gonzalez or Pardee won't flip on you? Either you give Boyd to the special counsel or the special counsel will go for death. In which case you'll spend a few years with all the homicidal creeps at Leavenworth while your appeals run out and then you'll get a needle in your arm. Is that what you want?"

Rancy's blue eyes locked with Delaney's. "I want a written guarantee, ten years at a federal prison camp that has a good library, tennis courts, conjugal visits for good behavior—"

Delaney laughed. "This offer is nonnegotiable. And it's on the table for the next thirty seconds."

Rancy's jaw worked, then finally he sagged. "All right. Twenty years."

"Contingent," Mary said, "on your giving us chapter and verse on this entire business. Verifiable, credible testimony implicating Boyd. When did it start? What did Boyd say, when did he say it, the whole bit."

Rancy looked off across the Mall to the Capitol Building. "I want protection."

"We'll get you to the Capitol. You'll be safe there. On the way over, you tell us what you've got. Call it a good-faith offering. If we're persuaded by the time we get to the other end of the Mall, the deal is done. And you'll get whatever protection is required."

"Let's go," he said. Then he pulled the hood farther over his face, put on his sunglasses again. They started down the steps. Rancy was looking around suspiciously. Because of the remaining troop presence on the Mall, the area was mostly deserted.

"Colonel Campos and I are both armed," Delaney said. "You'll be fine. Now start talking."

Rancy's head was still swiveling from side to side. His long legs moved quickly. "You want to know who caused this whole thing? Dean Fairbank. Why? Because he was weak. He was weak and he had no sense of history, no convictions, no courage. All of the progress we'd made against the terrorists immediately after 9/11? The minute he got elected he threw it all away. All he could talk about was the budget and the farm bill and all this trivial domestic ephemera. What use would a balanced budget be if somebody set off a nuke in the middle of Midtown Manhattan? Well, anyway, after Morgan's wife was killed, Morgan started pushing hard inside the administration to get us back on track against terrorism. And what did Fairbank do? Nothing. He droned on and on about civil rights and constitutional freedoms till you felt like puking, and then changed the subject and started talking about marginal taxation rates or something. Morgan pushed harder. So finally Fairbank cut his legs out. Cut his budget, stopped giving him access to important meetings, stopped returning his calls. And then he handed him this Continuity of Government program in hopes of distracting him and shutting him up."

As they walked swiftly toward the Capitol, Delaney instinctively scanned the terrain for potential threats. So far, nothing. Rancy was right to be paranoid. If Boyd thought his attorney general was about to rat him out, he'd hardly hesitate to have Rancy killed.

"So Morgan decided to use the COG program as a means of building an organization within the administration, a sort of shadow government you might say, so that there would be a number of true believers positioned to step in when the next election came around. But then Fairbank just kept screwing things up. Setting known terrorists free because we didn't have evidence we could use in open court, defunding various CIA special ops people, you name it—he was gutting our whole effort. Then we found out that the CIA had been given some fairly explicit warnings about the attack by those Kashmiri extremists who killed Morgan's wife, and the CIA had failed to act on them because of budget cuts mandated by President Fairbank. I think Morgan came to believe that Fairbank was personally responsible for Joan Boyd's death. Finally one day Morgan just turned to me and said, 'John, America can't afford to wait for the next election.' He didn't say anything more specific, but I knew what he meant."

They were moving across a long, broad stretch of grass now. Completely exposed. Suddenly Delaney saw a point of light flash briefly on top of one of the Smithsonian buildings. Moonlight reflecting off a scope. Probably just a military sniper, part of the battalion from the Eighty-second which was still patrolling the area. But better safe than sorry. He motioned silently for Mary to switch over to Rancy's other flank so that Delaney could stand between the potential shooter and Rancy.

"Crouch down behind me a little, Mr. Rancy," Delaney said. "If I should suddenly, ah, stumble—start running for cover." He pointed in the direction of the Korean War Memorial—a collection of life-size statues of soldiers arrayed like a platoon in combat.

"What!" Rancy said, eyes widening. "Do you see something?"

"I'm sure it's nothing. Let's just keep moving. You were talking about your conversation with the vice president, when he first discussed killing Dean Fairbank. When was this?"

"About six months after his wife was murdered."

"What happened after that?"

Rancy was almost running now, head ducked low. "We moved pretty quickly after that. It was pretty obvious, really, what needed to be done. We needed a terrorist to kill the president. Two birds with one stone."

"That's when you dug up Paul Miller and the Brotherhood."

"Right. We funneled money out of a sort of slush fund we'd set up under the guise of the vice president's protocol budget. Then it was just a matter of putting the pieces together. We hired Pardee to set up the Protocols and Procedures Unit. They were going to be ready as enforcers after we made our move. Initially we thought about making contacts with an Al-Qaeda–related group from Indonesia, but that turned out to be impractical. We couldn't control them. So Morgan said, 'Okay, look, who can we control?' I said, 'Let's find some antiglobalization loonies,' and he said, 'No, they don't speak our language. What about one of these militia groups.' And it just went from there. We recruited Paul Miller, got our hooks in him, and from there it was a pretty simple matter to find the shooter, Doyle Pilgrim. Unit P was tasked with training Pilgrim on the ins and outs of the assassination itself. Unit P also handled the recruitment of Mark Greene."

"What about me?" Delaney said. "What was supposed to happen to me?"

"I guess it's fair to say you were, ah, going to have to fall on the sword."

"Unit P was going to kill me while I was being arrested."

Rancy didn't answer immediately. Finally he said, "They were to take due precaution for their own safety, let's put it that way."

Delaney snorted.

"If I may interrupt," Mary said, "let's be clear. What you're saying is, you coordinated all of this under Morgan Boyd's direct instructions?"

"One hundred percent. He knew and authorized every step I took."

"Have you kept any records to confirm this?"

Rancy smiled thinly. "I'm not an idiot. Of course I kept some insurance."

They were nearing the Korean War Memorial now. A rolling hill and some trees offered them a little temporary protection before heading down the long open stretch around the Washington Monument and the reflecting pool.

"Where did you keep it?"

Rancy smiled.

Then one of the figures in the bronze platoon at the Korean War Memorial began to do something strange. A machine gunner carrying a BAR, standing motionless in the middle of the group, suddenly seemed to move, as though he was splitting in half. And in an instant he became two men: one the eternally motionless man of bronze, the other a flesh-and-blood man wearing cammo and shouldering an M-16.

"Shooter, shooter, shooter!" Delaney screamed. There was nowhere to hide. He automatically drew his weapon, then reached out to throw Rancy to the ground. "Down! Down!"

But Rancy panicked. Apparently he didn't see the shooter among the sculptures because he ran straight toward the Korean War Memorial. Delaney started to chase, but it was too late.

The man with the M-16 fired two three-round bursts, and Rancy's head exploded; he was lifeless before he even hit the ground.

Delaney gestured to Mary to run left while he sprinted to the right. She already had her 1911 in her hand. The shooter swiveled toward her, then—presumably judging her to be the lesser of the threats—changed his mind and pointed his rifle toward Delaney. They were about forty yards apart—a simple shot with a rifle under range conditions, not quite so easy with a running target.

The first three-round burst missed him. He could feel one round kiss his coat, but he was unscathed.

Behind Delaney, Mary stopped, took a determined shooter's stance, fired two quick rounds at the shooter. The shooter ducked behind the bronze statue. She began sprinting again. The shooter turned toward her, fired a three-round burst. Mary kept running, but Delaney could see from the way she was hobbling that she'd been hit—probably in the leg.

It was Delaney's turn to stop and level his pistol at the rifleman. He had been cutting off the angle as he ran. Now he was about thirty-five yards out. A difficult combat shot. But it was what he'd trained for all his life, this one fleeting moment. The checklist had been burned so deep in his brain that it required no conscious thought: eye on the front sight; acquire target; squeeze. His vision had started to narrow, and it was as though he was looking down a tunnel toward the man with the rifle. It was Dirk Pardee. He should have dropped him when he had the chance.

He fired three times.

Pardee lifted his rifle.

Delaney began walking slowly toward Pardee, firing as fast as he could get a sight picture. Pardee was certainly wearing body armor, so he had to go for a head shot. Pardee was behind the statue, nothing visible but two inches on the left side of his face. Delaney kept squeezing and squeezing. He saw two bullets smack off Pardee's Kevlar helmet, another shredding Pardee's left ear, several more digging jagged holes in the bronze face of the BAR gunner. But there was no killshot.

Pardee's rifle seemed to come around in slow motion, turning, turning, turning.

The world had gone completely silent. Delaney could feel the pistol bucking beneath his hand, but he couldn't hear anything at all. He kept squeezing.

Then the Beretta was empty. He hit the clip release and the clip began to fall slowly through the air. His arm began making the slow motion move toward his belt where the spare clips lay. In training, he could routinely change clips, rack the slide, and begin accurate fire inside of two and a half seconds. A small voice in the back of his brain told him that he had nowhere near two and a half seconds. No cover, no ammo, no nothing.

Then the same small voice told him, This was it. He was going down fighting, for whatever that was worth.

Pardee's face began to come out from behind the cover of the statue, his eyes wide and focused and predatory, the rifle coming around, coming around, coming around.

And then, suddenly, there was nothing in his eyes at all.

Pardee's legs went out from under him and he crashed down in a heap.

Delaney looked over and saw Mary Campos, kneeling on the grass. Blood was coming out of her leg now, but her gun was still pointed at Pardee and she was yelling something that Delaney couldn't hear.

Delaney began running toward her. As he ran, his vision cleared and his hearing started to return.

"I got him!" Mary Campos was yelling. Her gaze was fixed on Pardee's corpse, her pupils dilated. "I got him! I got him! I got him! I got him!"

He took the gun gently out of her hand. "Easy, Mary. You're hit."

She looked toward him for a moment with a confused expression on her face. "What?" she said. "I'm *what?*"

He pointed at her leg.

She looked down, blinked, stared uncomprehendingly at the blood coming out of her thigh. Finally she looked up and said, "You know what? That kind of hurts."

Delaney looked over at the lifeless heap that had once been John Rancy. "Dammit!" he said. "Now we've got nothing."

Mary smiled a little, her teeth gritted against the pain. She pulled a microcassette tape recorder out of her jacket. "I wouldn't say that. I recorded every word he said."

48

Richard B. Russell Senate Office Building
11:26 PM

M ORGAN BOYD is a fighter," Mary Campos said. "He's a
zealot, a believer. He's not going to run."

"The colonel's right," Senator Billings, the senior senator from
West Virginia, said.

Mary was seated next to Michael Delaney in Senator Tunnington's office under the mounted head of a mule deer. The Freedom
from Fear Act had just gone down on a ninety-eight-to-two vote. A
handful of senior members of Congress representing both parties
had gathered in the office. Mary and Delaney had just played the tape
of Rancy's confession, and now the senators were discussing ways of
convincing Boyd to resign.

"It'll be a plague on this country if Morgan hangs on," Tunnington
said. "He could sit up there in the White House and stonewall for
months. For all we know he'll try to establish martial law. Some people will follow his orders, some won't. The military will be divided.
It'll be a horrible mess. We could conceivably be looking at shoot-
outs between American military units in the middle of our nation's
capital. This is heading straight for a constitutional crisis."

They looked around the room silently.

"Something occurs to me," Mary Campos said. She had gotten
her leg sewn up by the congressional doctor while the Senate was
voting. Fortunately the bullet had hit neither bone nor major arteries.
"We're still operating under the seven-day emergency powers order
that he signed last week, right?"

Heads nodded.

"Meaning that we could impanel a military tribunal, and arrest
him for sedition. According to the terms of the order, such an arrest

can be effected on the authority of the secretary of defense. I know Adam Robinson. He'll do what's right for the country. Once the secretary of defense is on board, then he can declare Morgan Boyd an enemy combatant. Once that's done, you can slap him in prison with no contact with the outside world, no lawyer, no nothing. Then he can't issue orders or do anything that would trigger a constitutional crisis. You'd have plenty of time to do a nice fulsome impeachment hearing, bring all the facts of the assassination out into the light. Crisis averted."

Tunnington blinked, looked over at Senator Billings, who was not only a ranking member of the Senate but also a respected constitutional scholar. "I hate the idea of doing something like that. But, yes, I think it would be permissible under the terms of his order."

Tunnington shook his head vigorously. "That's doing it *his* way— the *wrong* way. We've got to figure out a strategy that's in keeping with our democratic traditions."

"Even at the price of a constitutional crisis?" said one of the other senators hotly. "Come on, Charles! Boyd will make us look like a pack of jackasses if we don't move hard and fast against him."

"Maybe there's another way," Delaney said.

The senators looked at him skeptically. The expression on their faces made it clear that in their view Secret Service agents were made to be seen, not heard.

"Well?" Tunnington said.

Delaney took off his watch, set it on the table. Everyone looked at the gold watch that Morgan Boyd had given him two years earlier.

"Here's the idea . . . ," he said.

DAY NINE

49

The White House
1:05 AM

DESPITE THE LATENESS OF THE HOUR, Morgan Boyd was still in the Oval Office, still seated at his desk, still wearing his coat and tie. He glared at Delaney with undisguised malice.

"Did you sweep him for bugs?" Boyd said to the Secret Service agent who ushered him into the room.

"Yes, Mr. President. He has a tape recorder, that's all."

"Weapons?"

"Of course, Mr. President."

"Good. Then leave us." Boyd waited until the door closed. They were now alone. "So, Agent Delaney. I got a call from Mr. Gonzalez in the Protocols and Procedures Section. He tells me you have something that I need to see."

Delaney took out the tape recorder he'd gotten from Mary Campos and played the recording of their entire conversation with John Rancy.

Boyd's face showed nothing. "Who knows you have this, Agent Delaney?"

"Other than Martin Gonzalez? Nobody but you, me, and Mary Campos."

"It's all lies, of course. John Rancy was obviously a lunatic."

"I'm sure you're right, Mr. President."

"To think that I trusted a man like that."

"Mm-hm."

Morgan Boyd sat motionless, waiting.

"This will make great TV," Delaney said. "Under cloud of suspicion, fugitive turns himself in, to the president."

"Get to the point."

"The point. Ah, yes." Delaney held up the tape recorder. "The problem is, this tape. You can deny it all you want, but it'll really pretty much flush your presidency down the toilet. They'll find records in Rancy's house or in a lockbox somewhere and you'll come out on the wrong end of this thing, no matter how blameless you are."

Boyd said nothing. His hands were clasped on the desk, his black eyes unreadable.

"What I think is that Mark Greene is the real inside man," Delaney said. "Framing me? That was a mistake. It was too baroque, too tricky, introduced too many loose ends. The whole story works better if Mark Greene, Dirk Pardee, and John Rancy were responsible for everything. It's neater, cleaner."

"I never thought it was you, Agent Delaney. You're just not the type to assassinate a president."

"It warms the cockles of my heart to hear your confidence in me," Delaney said. "But you have to admit, this whole thing has been very inconvenient for me. Very embarrassing."

"Obviously so."

"What I'm thinking is, let's settle this thing so that the American people aren't burdened by the confusion that this tape would bring. Let's settle it right here and now."

"Is that the only copy of the tape?"

Delaney smiled. "Don't be ridiculous."

"I had to ask."

"So, I think you see where I'm going, Mr. President. In light of my . . . inconvenience, I think it's only fair that I receive some modest compensation."

"How modest?"

"I don't think it would be any great trick to pull, say, ten million out of a black budget line at the NSA, feed it to an offshore account."

Boyd said nothing.

"Of course, I'd also like to be given some sort of presidential commendation and get kicked up to GS-15 again. Have my pension restored to what it would have been if I hadn't been demoted after your wife's death. A few odds and ends like that. It's not really about the money, Mr. President. It's more a matter of pride."

"I could see how you'd feel that way. I take it Mary Campos may feel a little . . . underappreciated too?"

"She's thinking national security advisor might be a good fit for a person of her qualifications. After a year or so, Adam Robinson might be ready to leave his position at DOD, and at that point I suspect Colonel Campos wouldn't turn down the office of secretary of defense."

"Is she short of cash too?"

"She agrees with me that ten million is the sort of number that's easy to get your arms around."

Boyd nodded. "There's still the little issue of unframing you. There's a great deal of evidence implicating you."

"You've still got your man Smith doing your bidding over at FBI. I mean, let's face it, I was framed. How hard would he have to work to turn up evidence that cleared me?"

"You're exactly right, Agent Delaney." Boyd sat for a while, then finally clapped his hands. "All right. I want that copy of the tape right now. I understand you've already turned yourself in to the FBI? It'll take a couple of days for Special Agent-in-Charge Smith to turn up unimpeachable proof of your innocence. The details of the financial compensation will be worked out by somebody who will contact you upon your release from custody."

"Good."

"Now, I believe we're done."

Delaney didn't move. "Not quite, Mr. President. Before I give you this tape, I have to know something. Why did you frame me? I saved your life."

"You mean, Rancy. Why did *Rancy* do it?" Boyd shrugged. "I could only speculate."

"Let's skip the BS, Morgan. You want this tape, you tell me why."

Boyd's face stiffened for a moment then settled back into its usual masklike stillness. "You're a good soldier, Mike," he said finally. "Falling in battle is what men like you do. Sometimes you send in a platoon to get slaughtered so the rest of the battalion can survive. It's nothing personal. I admire you a great deal. It was your turn, that's all. For the greater good."

"The greater good."

"Do I have to spell this out? Let's take a fairly conservative scenario. What happens when some angry little maniac from Yemen or Karachi or Chechnya gets his hands on a twenty-pound bag of semi-refined plutonium? He loads it in a backpack full of explosives, goes to the thirtieth floor of the Chrysler Building on a windy day, and pulls the trigger. You've seen the estimates, Mike. Aside from the people killed by the bomb, they'd have to condemn twenty to fifty square blocks of central Manhattan. A trillion dollars of real estate value would suddenly evaporate. The property losses alone might push our entire insurance industry into bankruptcy. Major businesses in New York would fail. The economy would crash. Wall Street would go into a death spiral. Tens of thousands of people would lose their homes. Hundreds if not thousands of people would die of radiation poisoning. And what about the indirect casualties? How many suicides by men who suddenly couldn't support their families, how many wives getting beat up because hubby lost his job and now he's in a really bad mood, how many people's life savings lost, how much pain? How much pain, Mike?"

Delaney didn't say anything.

"And that's the best-case scenario. What if it were a nuclear weapon? What if it were some strain of smallpox we haven't got a vaccine for? We could be talking deaths in the millions."

"And you think you can stop that."

There was nothing on Boyd's face that betrayed fakery or insincerity as he said, "Yes, Mike! That's why I'm here. I saw it written in small letters on my own heart when my wife died in my arms. How much more pain are we prepared to suffer so that we can maintain the luxury of our weakness, the luxury of our so-called freedoms. How much, Mike? You tell me."

Boyd continued to stare at him.

"You think I'm not serious, don't you, Mike? You think this is all just self-serving, don't you?"

Delaney didn't answer for a moment. "No," he said finally. "That's the scary thing. I think you believe every word you say."

"So," the president said. "Now we understand each other. I'm sorry for what happened to you. But if I had it to do over again, I wouldn't hesitate for a moment."

Delaney stood, took off the watch that Morgan Boyd had given him, and turned it around so he could see the inscription. "'That we may be free from fear,'" he read. Then he set the watch on the desk. "I hate to tell you, sir, but there will always be something to fear. That's the human condition. You can't wall it off."

Boyd was not looking at him. The president had picked up a paper on his desk and was reading it furiously.

"Stand up, Mr. President."

Boyd looked up curiously. "Excuse me, Agent Delaney?"

"I said, stand up."

Boyd looked at him curiously.

"Senator Tunnington got a fellow over at the FBI to install a little tiny camera in my watch. I had it turned off when I came in, so the bug detectors wouldn't set it off. As soon as I walked in the room, I just pressed the button, and it started up. We just sent real-time sound and video out to a relay in Colonel Campos's briefcase. Which amplified the signal and sent it to the FBI. Agents are standing out in the hallway. They'll be receiving instructions to come through that door any second now. You might as well stand up and go out with dignity."

Boyd's eyes widened. "You son of a—" Boyd reached out to grab the watch. "Let me see that." He unscrewed the back. A small tangle of electronics fell out.

"The little tube there is the camera, and that black thing is all the electronics. Amazing, huh?"

Boyd picked up the chip, looked at it expressionlessly, then threw it back on the desk.

"I'll give you a minute to collect yourself," Delaney said. "The FBI guys will be in shortly."

He walked out of the Oval Office and stood while the two FBI men who had transported him to the White House secured handcuffs on his arms. "It's just a formality, Agent Delaney," one of them said. "You're still officially under warrant."

"Sure, of course," Delaney said.

Through the thick walls of the Oval Office, the gunshot was muffled.

"No, no, no!" one of the FBI agents yelled.

"Code red! Code red!" shouted the nearest Secret Service agent. FBI and Secret Service agents rushed through door into the Oval Office.

Another agent pushed Delaney roughly out the door into an adjoining room. But not so fast that Delaney couldn't see the body of the president slumped over his desk, a small pistol still gripped in one hand.

EPILOGUE

Richard B. Russell Senate Office Building
Congressional Hearing of the Joint Special Committee
on the Assassination of President Dean Fairbank
9:28 AM, four months later

LIEUTENANT COLONEL MARY CAMPOS took her seat in front of the semicircle of senators and congressmen, and the mob of photographers crawled out in front of her, keeping their heads down so as not to get in the way of prepositioned video cameras, snapped some pictures, then retreated.

"I understand you have a prepared statement, Colonel Campos?" the chairman of the committee said.

"I do," she said. "Having been responsible for the initial investigation into the assassination of President Fairbank, I think it would be beneficial for me to give an overview of precisely what happened."

"Very well, please do."

Mary Campos consulted her notes, then began speaking. "I'll turn to the question of motive later, but first I'll address the question of what actually happened. In sum, Morgan Boyd is directly responsible for the murder of President Dean Fairbank and the so-called terrorist attacks that followed.

"The information I've gathered is based on an exhaustive FBI investigation, a small mountain of documentary evidence, testimony of a number of key witnesses including Martin Gonzalez and other less senior members of Unit P, as well as an interview I conducted with John Rancy before he was killed.

"All right, so what happened, and when did it happen? To begin with, the preparations for the assassination went back well over a year. According to John Rancy, initial attempts had been made to contact an Al-Qaeda–affiliated group in Indonesia, but that effort proved too complicated. With the lack of success there, President Boyd decided instead to turn to domestic extremists. They turned to the Brotherhood, a small militia organization headquartered in Alabama. The Brotherhood did not preach the violent overthrow of the government per se but did generally claim that there would be some sort of violent upheaval in the country, which would result in the downfall of the federal government.

"Rancy began using a slush fund he controlled to fund the Brotherhood. Eventually a shooter was recruited. Pilgrim, as we all know by now, fit a profile that has come to seem all-too-familiar: midthirties, disaffected, spotty employment record, intelligent but directionless, self-educated, washed out of the military for physical reasons, jailed briefly for narcotic possession, toyed with several extreme ideologies including white supremacy. As soon as he was recruited, he went into training, which was operationally directed by Colonel Pardee, a former army officer, who led the small paramilitary unit known as Protocols and Procedures Section or Unit P. Pardee and several of his associates trained Pilgrim intensively for his mission. We now know that Pardee was personally chosen for the role by John Rancy under the direction of then–Vice President Boyd.

"Once Pilgrim was recruited, it was necessary to find one more element—an accomplice within the Secret Service. Unit P was directed to dig into the personal lives of every agent in the president's detail. These men are carefully screened, of course. But sometimes personal problems will develop after becoming team members. Unit P hit the jackpot. They found that Agent Mark Greene, head of the presidential detail, had gotten into some financial trouble related to an investment in a restaurant. They used this as a wedge to force him into helping them.

"Greene's role in the actual assassination was simple. He drugged Agent Michael Delaney and took his duty weapon. (By the way, I might note that a blood sample taken from Michael Delaney's arm only an hour or so after the assassination confirmed Delaney's contention that he had been drugged.) Anyway, Agent Greene then placed the weapon in a plastic bag, which he hid behind a bush near the helicopter landing pad at Camp David. Agent Delaney had experienced some alcohol problems several years ago and had been blamed in the media for the death of Morgan Boyd's wife in the well-known attack in New Delhi. All of which made him an ideal fall guy for the plan. By planting his weapon, suspicion would be diverted from Greene to Delaney. The serial number was filed off his weapon to make it look as though Delaney had attempted to disguise his connection to the crime. According to Mr. Rancy, Unit P had then been tasked to kill Delaney during his "apprehension," thereby further closing off any further investigation into Delaney's presumed connection to the assassination.

"Agent Greene, because of his position with the Secret Service, was able to provide Dirk Pardee with a detailed map of all the security devices positioned around Camp David. Once those were identified to Pardee, he was able to devise a tactical plan for the assassination. This included a specific route and a variety of techniques including camouflage and thermal suppression, which allowed Pilgrim to evade motion detectors, cameras, and various other security devices. A mock-up of the terrain, accurate to the last foot, was built in a remote location in Alabama, where Pardee trained Pilgrim, practicing the insertion repeatedly under a variety of weather and light conditions.

"Once Pilgrim was trained, it was just a matter of keeping him on ice until a suitable moment arrived. That moment came on October twenty-six.

"Pilgrim had been led to believe that an exfiltration plan had been developed. It had not. In fact, Agent Greene had been instructed to shoot Pilgrim as soon as the assassin had done his job. And that is precisely what happened. Pilgrim fired two shots at Dean Fairbank, then fired a third round at Vice President Boyd, a round that was carefully aimed to cause a bloody wound, but not to hit any vital organs. At that point, Greene executed Pilgrim.

"As I mentioned earlier, to deflect attention from Agent Greene, Agent Michael Delaney was framed. Delaney was chosen because, by coincidence, he happened to have a family connection to Paul Miller, the head of the Brotherhood. The fact that Agent Delaney had been given a demotion after questions had been raised about his handling of the attack on Morgan Boyd in New Delhi was simply icing on the cake, giving immediate credibility to allegations that he fit the profile of a 'disgruntled employee.' The mechanics of the frame were fairly simple. Agent Greene placed a number of calls from Agent Delaney's phone terminal at the White House to the Brotherhood's leader, Paul Miller, so that it appeared Delaney had been in contact with Miller; some offshore accounts were established in Delaney's name; some neo-Nazi literature was placed in his computer and on his bookshelves—and the scene was set to make Delaney a fall guy. And then, of course, he was drugged and his gun stolen for use by Pilgrim on the night before the assassination itself.

"Other than the assassination itself, all of the so-called terrorist attacks—the bombing of the Chicago Merc, the missile attack on White Sands, the truck bombing in Houston, and the various other attacks which followed the assassination—were coordinated and carried out by members of Unit P, using weapons purchased and stockpiled by the Brotherhood. The idea was to trump up a domestic terrorist threat in order to allow him to pursue his agenda to pass the Freedom from Fear Act. Brotherhood personnel could have been used for the attacks, but President Boyd and Attorney General Rancy didn't trust their competence, so they delegated the work to handpicked Unit P operatives. Other than Dirk Pardee and Martin Gonzalez, the members of Unit P were generally unaware of the full dimensions of President Boyd's scheme. They were men of action, military men who took orders and didn't ask too many awkward questions. I don't condone their actions—I think it was obvious to all of them that they were committing illegal acts—but they had been assured by their superiors that there were good reasons for these attacks and that their actions had been sanctioned at the highest levels of the government.

"Let's turn to Agent Mark Greene. What happened to Agent Greene? Was he murdered? We simply don't know. All the forensic evidence points to suicide. However, a man in the neighborhood who was returning home late from a party claims to have seen a man who met the description of Lieutenant Colonel Dirk Pardee 'skulking in the bushes' outside Greene's house at the approximate time of his death."

Lieutenant Colonel Campos flipped to the next page of her notes.

"To summarize, all the evidence at this time leads us to believe that the assassination of President Fairbank was personally directed by Morgan Boyd. The details were, as it were, stage-managed by John Rancy and operationally directed by Lieutenant Colonel Pardee. As such there were only a handful of people who had knowledge of the assassination scheme and a slightly larger number from Unit P who were in the loop on the bogus terrorist attacks that followed. But no more than three or four men were aware of the full dimensions of the plan."

Mary Campos looked up at the senators. "Only one major question is left. Why did President Boyd commit these terrible crimes?

Clearly he had been profoundly shaken by the killing of his wife in India. Clearly this led him to conclude that terrorism is the greatest threat to the order and security of the world at this time. But how did he leap to the next step, murdering President Fairbank?

"Based on my conversation with John Rancy, it appears that Boyd believed determination in the country and in the government for continuing a serious fight against terrorism had waned. Boyd felt that only a leader of great resolve and will could keep the United States from eventually falling prey to some truly catastrophic terrorist attack. He felt he was that leader. Moreover—putting aside any personal motives—Boyd believed that President Fairbank had sold us down the river in the fight against terrorism. He was firmly convinced that if our current course were not reversed, a catastrophic attack on the United States in the form of a dirty bomb or a nuclear explosion or a major biological attack was unavoidable. Furthermore John Rancy claimed in a conversation with me that Boyd blamed President Fairbank personally for his wife's death. I don't know. Whatever the combination of factors, he did ultimately decide to remove the president.

"Once President Boyd made that decision, the question was how to do it. According to John Rancy, President Boyd's theory was that hiring a shooter from some sort of existing terrorist network would kill two birds with one stone. First, he would achieve the immediate result of removing President Fairbank from the presidency. Second, by having the shooting done by someone on whom the label "terrorist" could be applied, Boyd would be in a position to use the assassination to ram through Congress a wide range of policies in the form of the Freedom from Fear Act. That was his thinking.

"Morgan Boyd was a passionate man—and passions will lead us astray. He forgot that the great strength of democracy has great vulnerabilities built into it. Those vulnerabilities sometimes cost us in blood. The death of Joan Boyd, the deaths in Oklahoma City, the deaths on 9/11—could they have been avoided? Sure. No doubt. How? By doing what Morgan Boyd wanted to do, by turning this country into a military dictatorship. But you know what else Morgan Boyd also forgot? He forgot that our system and our way of life—however messy and costly it may be—summons the extraordinary from individuals more routinely than any other system yet invented."

Mary Campos paused and looked up from her notes. "Mr. Chairman, I know my job here is solely to present facts . . . but while I'm on the subject of extraordinary individuals, I feel obliged to point out one extraordinary man, without whom Morgan Boyd might well have succeeded in his plan. That man is Michael Delaney. Agent Delaney, would you please stand?"

She smiled and pointed to Delaney, who was sitting in the back of the room. He sat stone-faced, looking like he'd rather be anywhere but there. He lifted one hand in mute acknowledgment of the compliment, but didn't rise from his chair.

It was not customary for members of congressional committees to stand and applaud. But this time they did.

AFTER IT WAS OVER, Mary and Delaney snuck out a back entrance to avoid the crush of reporters. The air was cold, and they put their arms around each other, walking in silence onto the Mall.

"Let's get out of here," Delaney said finally.

"What, you want to get a bite to eat or something?"

"No, I mean out of *here.*" He made a broad sweep with his hand, taking in the Capitol, the Washington Monument, the swath of government offices. "We could just move. Go to Mexico, Jamaica, Thailand, Bali . . ."

She looked at him curiously. "Are you serious?"

He looked around for a moment. "Nah. I guess not. What in the world would we do in Bali? It's all beaches, waves, and warm sun. There's nothing there for people like us."

They both laughed and continued their stroll toward the Capitol.

Singaraja, Indonesia
Four minutes later

Ismail, Mahmood, and the third man walked in single file down the concrete stairwell and into the hot, dimly lit room. Mahmood carried a briefcase. Ismail's hands were empty.

Unlike most of the rest of the predominantly Muslim nation of Indonesia, the island of Bali is populated primarily by Hindus. As a result, its few Muslims feel particularly embattled. Ismail and Mahmood were Balinese Muslims who had gone to an austere religious boarding school on the island of Sumatra run by an imam from Yemen. They had returned home from Sumatra as radicals.

"Well?" Ismail said.

The third man was known to them by the name Zultan, but they assumed that was not his real name. He was a Chechen, with a long black beard, a prominent mole on his forehead, and sharp black eyes.

"I have what you're looking for, thanks be to God," Ivan said. "Do you have the money?"

Ismail nodded to Mahmood, who opened the briefcase he was carrying. It contained small stacks of American currency. Mahmood closed the briefcase.

"Where is it?" Ismail said.

The Chechen handed a smudged pink paper to Ismail. "The sample is at the port in a warehouse. You can claim it there under the name on this manifest. Examine it. When your examination is complete, I'll expect the money in my hotel room. At that point I'll give you a second manifest so you can claim the rest of the material."

"Good."

"But whatever you do, don't open the lead sheathing. The radioactivity will kill you almost immediately."

"We wouldn't think of opening it." Ismail smiled broadly. "Not until it reaches America."